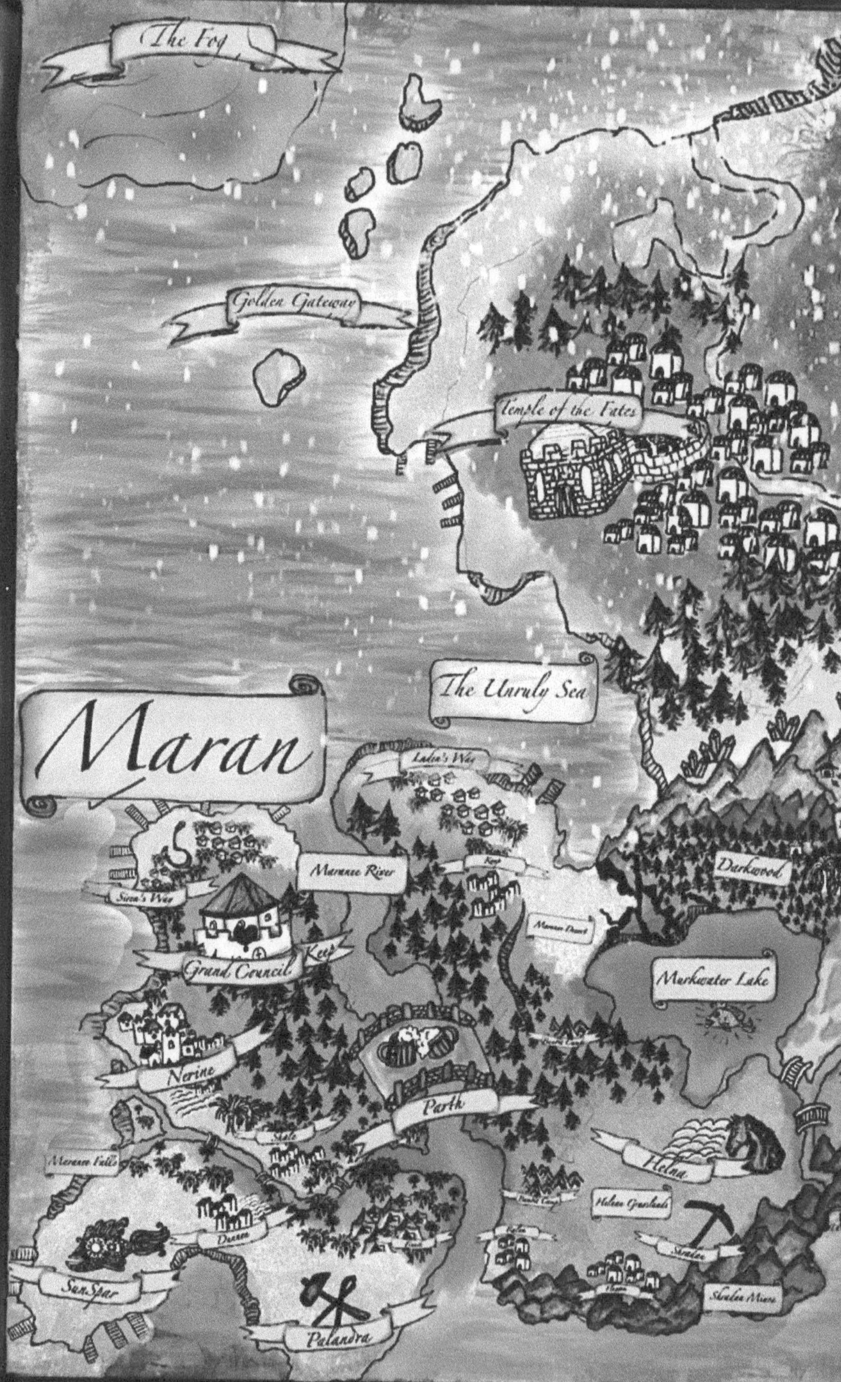

The Fog
Golden Gateway
Temple of the Fates
The Unruly Sea
Maran
Ladia's Way
Marnnee River
Keep
Darkwood
Siren's Way
Marnae Dwarf
Murkwater Lake
Grand Council Keep
Nerine
Parth
Helna
Marnae Falls
Helna Grasslands
Danna
Minder
SunSpar
Palandra
Shadow Miners

Lithe
Whispering Isles
Baskar Mountains
Baskar Desert
Blackwater Swamp
Nolon
N
W
E
S

SEVERED

breyannaevansauthor@gmail.com
breyannaevansauthor.com
@breyannailevans

BREYANNA I.L. EVANS

Also by Breyanna I.L. Evans

YA Fantasy
Azure Light
Azure Light (Written under Breyanna I.L. James)
Crimson Darkness
Emerald Shadow

Bound Trilogy
Bound

YA Fiction
Clairvoyance

Children's Books
What I Do Know
Especially You

Poetry
Accidentally External: A Poetry and Short Story Compilation
(Written under Breyanna I.L. James)

Blog
"Writings" breyannaevansauthor.com

More books are always in the works for this author.
Join her newsletter to stay up to date with new releases!

For my fated other. I choose you.

CONTENT WARNING

Please be aware that this book contains the following: descriptions of wounds, violence, blood, death (including murder), alcoholism and some hallucinogenic material consumption, some sexual content, ghosts, dark creatures and imagery, conspiracy, mentions of miscarriage and trouble conceiving, and mention of injury and poor health of children.

SEVERED

BREYANNA I.L. EVANS

I have a gaping wound in my chest, though no one around me is able to see it, and I've spent the last few weeks struggling to catch my breath.

I stare at my reflection in the mirror, barely recognizing myself. It's strange to see the image of myself when everything I've ever known has changed. Now, I feel like a total stranger. I don't remember the last time I really looked at my reflection; I've been on the road for months. Surely, it was the last time I was here in Helna, though the memory of our time here before is hazy.

As my mamman and I prepare for bed, I brush my long black hair tie it into a braid that trails down my back, and I work to process and organize my thoughts for the hundredth time today.

The first thing I need to wrap my mind around is that magic is real. This concept shouldn't come as such a shock to me: I spent my entire first seventeen years of life feeling like the mysterious injuries I obtained had to be magic related, though everyone I ever spoke to about these notions assured me that magic didn't exist. Still, to learn that these injuries were actually the result of a strange, magical bond I shared with someone I had never met, a mercenary named Alec Montrose, left me feeling more than a little bit surprised. Then to later learn that a witch that lived alone in the Baskan mountains had unintentionally bound us... well, I suppose I'm still processing that.

Second, there's the fact that the aforementioned witch had been holding both mine and Alec's mammans hostage, siphoning their lifeforce in an attempt to restore her youth. Alec and I were able to team up and rescue our mammans, at the expense of the witch's life. All in a matter of moments, we learned that our mammans had been close friends growing up, though Alec and I had never met until I ran across him by chance one day on a business trip to Nerine.

Alec and I had also learned in the same moments that our mammans had made a deal with the same witch years prior in order to ensure the health of their children. My mamman was unaware at the time that I – barely conceived – grew already within her belly. Because Alec and I were present as the witch granted the women's wishes, our bond was formed.

The third thing that has been weighing heavily on my mind is that Alec and I had only just discovered that our bond went so much deeper than merely obtaining each other's injuries, but instead allowed us to sense each other's emotions, passions, and pleasures, and we're even able to heal each other's wounds with a kiss. When our encounter with the witch resulted in her death in exchange for our freedom, the bond Alec and I had only begun exploring together had been severed.

I allow the image of the witch's overgrown black fingernails raking long scratches into Alec's face to resurface in my mind. I relive again the shock I felt when I expected to incur the same marks on my face, only to find my skin there still smooth to the touch.

I recall the frigid wind that blew through the cave we had stood in, and the chill that I haven't been quite able to shake since. I no longer sense the strong tie to Alec resonating deep within me. In the place of that connection now sits a painful emptiness.

But of course, that's not something we can discuss at length with our mammans present. Beyond the fact that we haven't had a private moment together since before we entered the witch Marana's lair, I must admit that I'm worried Alec hasn't noticed the growing distance between us.

I fear that if the bond we had really has been broken, Alec will no longer have any interest in me.

He once told me he'd never felt with anyone the way he feels with me. But that was before.

Before the witch.

Before the broken bond.

Before we spent weeks traveling and making awkward small talk with our mammans. Nobody wants to discuss the complexities of their budding relationship with their parents present.

To add to the whirlpool of chaos that is my thoughts, something doesn't seem right. Although our travels through the Baskan mountains, the forest, and the swamp were fairly uneventful, the very air has felt sinister. Perhaps I'm hyper-focusing on the hole I now feel in my heart, mourning the loss of the connection I have known for my entire life, but the world itself feels much more ominous, and I've found myself suspecting danger lurking around every corner.

I try to reign in my tangled thoughts and focus on something positive.

Alec and I were able to find our mammans and retrieve them from the witch's lair. We were able to make it back down the mountainside, through the Darkwood forest, across Murkwater swamp, and back to Helna without much incident or serious injury. I should be grateful for that, and I am. Better still, I have had the opportunity to bond with my mamman – something I've wished desperately for since my younger sister Lilah was born just before my ninth birthday.

Lastly, after taking a few days in Helna to rest, we're supposed to leave for home in the coming days, and Fates know how excited I am to get back home after so much time away.

My mamman and I are staying in the small room we share across the hall from Alec and his mamman, Julienne, in a little inn toward the center of Helna.

Mamman looks at me with her piercing, crystal blue eyes. She's been shooting me inquisitive glances since she first saw me with Alec, the moment we burst into the witch's lair and found both of our mammans imprisoned, starved, and drained.

"So?" she starts, knowing full well the answer to the question she's about to ask. "Lane, what's going on between you and Julienne's son?" She smiles, implying her question is harmless, but she has no way to know that her words tug at the barbs I feel within me. I brush the loose strands of my dark hair out of my face and sit down on my bed.

"Nothing," I tell her. My tone is harsher than it needs to be, but I don't want to discuss this with her. Not when I'm uncertain where Alec and I stand, anyway.

My mamman and I have never been close enough for me to feel comfortable sharing something so personal with her. After Lilah was born, my mamman had always favored her, so she and I never discussed boys or romance.

Not that there had ever been anything like this to discuss before I met Alec.

"It doesn't look like nothing to me," she presses. "You don't kill a witch for just anyone." My mamman's knowing smile spreads as she grasps the hairbrush from where I've set it on the bedside table and runs it through her silky golden hair.

I've been avoiding this conversation for weeks. At least before we reached Helna, we were all together and focused on surviving the elements. Here, in the privacy of the room we share, I find myself feeling claustrophobic, and although her questions are gentle in nature, she may as well be battering me with them.

"Yeah, well, you don't know Alec," I say snidely. I turn my back on her and busy myself organizing my belongings for the third time today. Organizing and planning and mapping are the only things that have kept me my sanity of late. "He's a sellsword. His job is to kill for other people."

That's not entirely the most accurate definition of his job, but it's the definition that best suits this conversation, so I leave it at that.

From behind me, my mamman's nightgown crinkles as she shrugs. I hear her sigh, and I tell myself to relax. None of this is her fault, and we may not have been close throughout my childhood, but she's been incredibly attentive since we found each other again, and I truly did miss her.

"I suppose that's true," she says. "Still, it seems there's something of a spark between you two."

Tension jitters through my body. How could she say that? Sure, Alec and I shared a kiss when we thought the witch would claim me, but we have barely spoken since we left the caves. I jump to my feet. I need to get out of this room before I say something awful. I know she's trying to be supportive, trying to get to know me, but it all just... hurts.

Although I'm not really dressed for a night on the town, I throw a long, borrowed coat over my long johns, flip my braid so it falls down my back, and pull on my boots.

"Where do you think you're going, young lady?" my mamman asks. She's still smiling, but her hands are planted on her hips. "It's late."

"Well, I'm an adult," I start, looping my bow and quiver of arrows over my shoulder. I never go anywhere without them, especially in Helna. I won't technically be an adult in the eyes of the Women's Council until my eighteenth birthday, just a couple of months away, but after the last several months I've spent on the road, and the things I've faced, I feel I've earned the title. "And I've had countless late nights since I went looking for you. I can't sit here and listen to questions I don't know the answer to all night. I don't know where Alec and I stand with each other. I don't know if we've got anything worth exploring or not, and I certainly don't want to work through all the messy details with my mamman."

My mamman flinches. Her smile fades, and her expression softens.

"I'm sorry, Lane," she says. "I meant no harm. It's just... we've never had anything like this to talk about before. You've never been interested in my Council work, and I feel like we finally have something to bond over. I'm just excited."

I take a deep breath and exhale slowly, letting the air putter out from between my lips. I step forward and give her a kiss on the forehead to let her know I'm not angry with her.

"Sorry, Ma'. I've just... got a lot to process. I can't share it with you yet. I'll be back later. Keep the door locked, okay? I've got my key with me."

I leave the room without waiting for her reply.

The moment I've entered the hallway I begin to feel like I can breathe again. Maybe I just need some time to myself. The tightness in my chest is relieved slightly, and I draw in a deep breath, turn in the direction of the nearest tavern, and get walking.

I don't usually drink. In fact, I hate it.

I hate the taste of spirits on my tongue. Hate the way it makes me feel. Hate exposing myself, letting down my walls, allowing myself to be vulnerable.

In my time with Alec this year, I've watched him use drinking to shield him from his problems, fears, and insecurities. Right now, I understand his thinking. I could use a little help taking my mind off things.

Like nearly every tavern I've been in, this one is loud, crowded, and smells strongly of sweat and alcohol. All the tables are packed, and I want to avoid talking to people as much as possible, so I make my way to the counter.

"Excuse me," I call out to the barkeep over the noise. "I'd like a flagon of wine, please."

My polite request draws raised eyebrows and sideways glances from the people nearest to me, and I ignore them. As the barkeep fetches my drink, I study the dull and dented wooden countertop with an intense stare.

"Do my eyes deceive me, or did I just witness my dear friend Lane ordering alcohol?" a familiar voice says from behind me. My body reacts in two ways, split seconds apart.

First, it warms, begins to relax. Next, I freeze. This is exactly the person I came down here to get my mind off of – precisely why I didn't just go to the tavern on the main floor of the Inn where we're all staying.

"I should have known you'd be here," I say, trying to decipher what expression my face is displaying. Am I smiling? Grimacing? "Probably drank our Inn's tavern dry by now, huh?"

I turn around to see that Alec, of course, is wearing his usual half-smile. He pulls back his shoulder-length, straight blond hair. He seems to have cut it since I saw him this morning, and he's shaved, too. He looks like he might actually be happy to see me, though it feels like it's been years since we've spoken about anything more substantial than the weather.

Fates, we have so much to process.

Alec's amber eyes travel the length of my body, and I soften under his gaze until he speaks. "I love the new look," he says, gesturing at my long johns. My ears and cheeks heat, and I rush to pull my jacket tightly around my torso.

"Don't you like taverns with a little more room to make a fool of yourself in? This place is pretty full up," I say, deflecting my embarrassment. I recall the night we first met, the night I learned through a broken nose and a knife wound to the ribcage that Alec and I were bound.

Alec's grin widens, and I wonder if he's thinking about the same tavern brawl.

Alec eyes the room, then he looks back at me with a dismissive wave of his hand.

"Nah, I can always make room."

I roll my eyes at him. His facial expression shifts, and he puts a hand on my shoulder as he flags down the barkeep. I try to ignore the way the warmth of his touch ignites a fire in my belly that spreads all the way to my toes.

"What are you doing here?" he asks. "You don't drink."

I scoff. The barkeep brings me my drink, and Alec gestures for the man to bring him the same thing I'm drinking. I take a deep swig of the wine I ordered, and the thick red liquid coats my tongue, leaving a bitter taste that trails down my throat as I swallow. My stomach almost immediately feels the burn.

"Tonight, I do." I say, eyeing the scar along his jaw – the only scar that the two of us do not share. I think of everything we've been through together – before we met and in the time I've known him. I think of how deeply connected our lives have been all along.

When we met, I wanted so badly to figure out a way to break our bond as I traveled across Maran with Alec, certain that doing so would allow me my freedom. I thought that was what I wanted. Then we got to know each other as we traveled to find our mammans, and the more I learned about our bond – and the more I learned about Alec – the more I wanted to keep the connection intact.

I take another long gulp, scrunching my nose at the tase as I force the liquid down, rolling my shoulders, willing them to relax.

As Alec waits for his drink, I begin to grow restless, and I plant myself on a barstool and run my finger over the edge of my drink, doing everything in my power to avoid eye contact with him. Looking at him only reminds me of the emptiness I feel and the complicated desire I have to reconnect with him, though now that Marana is dead, I'm certain that's impossible. I fear that if I look into those amber eyes for too long, I might blurt out everything.

Alec sits beside me, making it clear that he's not just going to go away.

My body urges me to talk to him with a knot in my stomach and tension in my back. Now is our moment, after all. Our mammans aren't here. We may finally have a chance to have a semi-private conversation, surrounded by all these drunken strangers. But the second I open my mouth I find myself at a loss for words. What am I supposed to say?

If I did ask him the question that has been weighting so heavily on my mind the last several weeks, would I want to know his answer?

Before I know it, the moment has passed, and the small amount of bravery that's built up inside me vanishes. My shoulders slump. I hunch over my drink and bring it to my lips again.

I wish I'd never found Alec. I wish I'd never gone on this wild journey with him. Before, I could deal with my random, inexplicable injuries that I didn't know came from him, miles and miles away. Now, all I want is to get them back.

Alec's gaze bores into the side of my face, and I wonder if he's also struggling to find something to say. Unlikely. This man is always so sure of himself.

I scowl at my cup.

"You may want to ease up," Alec says, his face mere inches from my ear as he leans in. "I think you're beginning to scare away the drunks."

Startled by his comment, I look around. Although the activity in the bar hasn't changed in the slightest, I do feel a little bit better that he wants to jest with me.

"Oh, I apologize," I reply, feigning guilt. "I didn't mean to frighten the guests." I point to a table nearby that has two customers fast asleep atop it. Alec chuckles. His straight white teeth flash in a breathtaking smile.

"I accept your apology," he says sternly, and his grin expands. "Though if anyone files a formal complaint, you'll have to pay a fine."

For the first time in forever, I actually smile.

"Oh yeah?" I ask, finding myself leaning toward him. "What'll it cost me?" I reach for my coin purse, but Alec places his hand on mine to stop my search.

"A kiss," he says, his voice like silk.

His eyes flick to my lips and linger there, and Fates do I want to kiss him, but the barkeep appears with Alec's drink, and I'm suddenly all too aware of myself. Once again, the moment is gone, and in its place the nagging emptiness returns.

Alec orders a loaf of bread, and the two of us share it, talking as we eat.

We don't discuss anything of importance, though it hangs in the air between us. It is nice to banter with him regardless. I feel much more like myself being this close to him, and that empty feeling seems smaller when he's around.

As we mock the customers around us in hushed tones, it feels as if we're in our own little bubble. We laugh together for some time, and although something is still missing, I feel closer to him than I have since the witch's death severed our bond.

"Well," I say, sobering up just a little bit. I want to stay. I want to lean forward and press my lips against his, melt away in his embrace until every last bit of this void has been filled. I want to continue to explore this relationship we had only just begun. But the warmth and tingling from my wine has made me feel just stupid enough that, if I stay much longer, I might do just that.

I hop down off the barstool, and the tavern spins around me until Alec grasps my elbow to steady me. I do my best to stand up straight as I look at the strong, sharp angles of his face.

"Well?" Alec asks, his smile fading ever so slightly.

"If we're leaving tomorrow, I should go. It's getting late."

I turn to leave.

"Wait," Alec says. Just as I turn back to face him, before I can register what he's doing, Alec draws the breadknife across his palm, creating a straight, thin line across his skin.

The wound immediately begins to bleed, and I instinctively look at my own hand, still expecting to see the same wound appear there. Although I'm shocked by his actions, I feel no pain, experience no wound opening on my hand.

Part of me wants to scan our surroundings, ensure that no one saw what he just did, but I can't pull my eyes off of him.

As dark, glistening crimson drips over the edge of his hand, he places the knife on the bar and reaches forward, pulling my hand toward him.

I try to yank myself free, and I clench my fingers, but the shock of his actions and the effects of the wine make me weak, and he's able to open them easily.

Confirming what I already know, Alec studies my woundless palm. His jaw sets, and his eyes fill with sadness.

"I thought so," he says, his tone flat. He lets my hand go, and it drops lamely to my side. Disappointment is spelled out plainly on his face, and he averts his gaze.

My heart aches as it pounds in my chest. My mouth opens, but I can't get any words to form. I don't know what to do or what to say, so I turn on my heels and flee the tavern.

If Alec follows me, he takes his sweet time. I don't look back. That look on his face told me he may just be finished with me. With each heartbeat, my chest heaves, constricting, filled with a hollow sort of pain, as if someone's shot an arrow straight into my heart. I stomp back to the inn, past the front desk, up the stairs, and to my room.

Perhaps it's the wine in my belly that makes me clumsy, or maybe it's the adrenaline, but it isn't until after I've slammed the door that I remember I'm sharing a room with my mamman. I tiptoe from the door to my bed and lie face down, willing the sting of tears to go away.

The tornado of emotions I feel is heightened and muddied by the wine I drank. I miss Alec. I miss our connection. I miss having the ability to feel what he's feeling.

I can't believe he's just cut himself. I prop myself up on my elbows and stare through the darkness at my clean, woundless palm as the aching in my chest intensifies.

I choke back a sob. I pray to the Fates, whom I've never truly believed in, whispering the words aloud into the quiet room.

"Please don't let this be."

3

In the morning, I'm brushed softly on the shoulder by the warmth of my mamman's gentle hand, and I jerk violently. I've been on the road for months now, and thanks to the things I've faced on my journey, I'm a jumpy sleeper.

"Sorry, Lane," my mamman says quietly.

I rub the sleep from my eyes and sit up, trying to ignore the whooshing sound in my ears and the pounding ache in my head. And Alec wonders why I detest drinking. At the thought of him, every moment of our conversation last night comes rushing back to me. In my memory, every detail of his disappointed expression is magnified.

Thankfully, Mamman brings me back to the present with her crinkled brow and her lips pressed together.

"You were out late last night," she says. Sitting on the bed beside me, she places her hand on my knee. "I didn't hear you come in." Surprising, given how hard I slammed the door as I entered.

A strange realization hits me so fast I feel dizzy.

To my mamman, I'm still the girl that left home on her assigned route to deliver traded goods under Pappan's advisement. I'm still the girl who shares a bedroom with her little sister, the fragile girl that takes medicine for the injuries she can't explain. Except, now I know those injuries were never mine alone, and I haven't been that girl for quite some time.

My mamman couldn't possibly know that, though, and for her little girl to be out all night is good reason to worry. I place my hand on hers.

"I'm sorry, ma'," I tell her. "I didn't realize how late it was when I came back. I've just had a lot on my mind."

Mamman nods, her mouth a straight line.

"That boy?" she asks. It's interesting to hear her call him a boy. He's a trained mercenary who's taken more lives than I care to think about. He's lived on his own for the past five years – since his pappan kicked him out when he was only fifteen years old. He's no boy in my eyes.

"Alec," I whisper.

Mamman nods again.

"Is it him?" she asks, though I'm sure she can tell it is from my sour expression.

"It's complicated," I reply. We're quiet for a moment as I relish in my misery. Then, I realize that Alec is probably just fine. He's probably out drinking and talking to exotic, busty Helnan women as he would have any other time he's visited this city. He may have said he chooses me, but that was before, when our bond was stronger than ever. Now, it's gone. I take a deep breath and straighten my back. "I don't want to talk about him today, if that's alright."

I feel I might have to explain, but my mamman only smiles sadly.

"Of course," she says. "It's still early, and I'm not sure Julienne is awake yet. What would you like to do?"

Over the course of the last few weeks, our party has had one major focus: Get as far away from the witch Marana's lair as possible. Get to civilization, where we can bathe and use the latrine and get some decent rest. Although we've been grateful to be in each other's company, conversation has been sparce.

"Well," I tell her. "I think you have a lot of explaining to do, young lady." At my remark, my mamman chuckles and raises her eyebrows.

Through the dull ache that remains in my chest, something warms. This is the closest I have felt to my mamman in years.

"Where do I begin?" she asks, scoffing.

Letting out a soft laugh, I point to the door.

"You were friends with Alec's mamman?" I ask. "How did you come to know each other? The Council?"

We spend the morning listening to each other's stories.

As a young girl, my mamman grew up in Nerine. I knew this part of the story. No one born in Palandra – other than my sister Lilah – has such golden hair, fair skin, and blue eyes. As a child, my mamman played in the streets of Nerine, and every night at sunset, her own mamman would summon her home. To get back home, my mamman would run atop the small stone walls that line the upper portion of the city's footpaths, and every night her mamman would scold her for doing so, worried that she would be injured.

One night, she was. As she was running home on the tops of those stone walls, my mamman was caught in the path of a Council woman's horse who had gotten away from her carriage. Mamman was not kicked, but she was so startled that she fell backward off the wall and received several scrapes and bruises.

The Council woman showed my mamman such kindness and was mortified by the injuries her horse had caused. She insisted that my mamman come with her and be examined by her family doctor.

Mamman was taken into the Blues, a section of Nerine that is known for its high class, elite citizens who live extravagant lifestyles. The Council woman took my mamman into her beautiful estate, where she was examined and treated by the physician, and where she met the Council woman's daughter, Julienne.

My mamman and Julienne became fast friends, and it wasn't long before the two were inseparable. Months of their friendship stretched into years, and even into adulthood, the two were as close as ever. When the two came of age, Julienne married her sweetheart, my mamman married my pappan, and still the two were close. Then, Julienne and her husband had a baby boy.

For the first time, Julienne and my mamman grew distant, as my mamman was informed that she would not be able to bear children.

Julienne's child was terribly sick, and no physician or healer knew how to cure him. Life went on and time passed, and over the next two and a half years, the two women became estranged as the difficulty of their individual challenges drifted them apart.

It was only when Mamman's work with the Council brought her back to Nerine that she finally reunited with her dear friend. Julienne's son's health had only gotten worse over his short life, and Julienne had grown desperate. In a moment of weakness, she told Mamman that she had learned of a witch in the mountains – someone who could ease their burdens.

Mamman, Julienne, and young Alec made the journey across Maran to the Baskan mountains, where they did, indeed, find the witch.

At first the women were skeptical when the witch Marana told them she could ease their pains. She could heal Alec's ailments, and he would grow to be a strong, healthy man. She could ensure my mamman's fertility – though my mamman was already with child when she embarked on this quest – and ensure that her child would make it to birth. All she asked was that when the time came and she gave her call, the two women would return to pay their debts.

Eternally grateful for even a sliver of a chance to change their fates, the two women agreed, and several weeks later, Mamman and Julienne had returned home, memories already foggy from the long journey.

Julienne's son was cured, and he never grew sick again, though from time to time throughout his childhood, he would appear with injuries he could not explain. And, of course, my mamman gave birth to me just six months after returning home from her trip.

At the end of my mamman's recounting, I sit back on my heels and rest my hands limply in my lap.

"Fates," I remark. "What a tale." Although I know the truth of the story she tells, I find myself having trouble believing it. I'm living proof that her words are true, as is – or rather, was – the impossible bond I shared with Alec.

My mamman nods.

"That's the short of it, anyway," she says, smoothing out the wrinkles in her blouse.

"I can't believe you never told me about any of this…" I murmur.

Mamman shoots me an apologetic glance. "I'm sorry, Lane. We don't talk as much as I'd like, and Julienne and I swore never to speak of the deal we made. Not even your pappan knows what truly happened those months I was away."

"Wow."

I raise my eyebrows, then turn my attention to the blanket I've bunched up in my lap. Mamman puts her hand on mine again and smiles, straightening her back.

"Enough about me and my past. I imagine you've been on quite a wild adventure yourself, since you left home," she says, blue eyes sparkling. "Tell me about that."

And so, over the next couple of hours, I share with my mamman the events of my journey with Alec. I tell my mamman about how I met Alec by chance in Nerine because I thought I recognized him. I recall how we traveled together across Maran, and how Zaid intercepted us to tell me my mamman had been acting strangely, also declaring his feelings for me, and the shock I felt learning of these feelings. I tell her how the three of us encountered savage bandits that were more animal than human.

I also share with her how I learned to fight, and how I learned to play Fates. I share some parts of our time in Darkwood forest, leaving out our experience with what I can only describe as forest spirits, and of course, our night spent together in the abandoned cottage, where Alec and I learned that our bond went so much deeper than simply experiencing each other's hurts. Those memories I prefer to keep to myself.

"That sounds amazing – and terrifying!" My mamman's animated voice pulls me out of my memory of that magical night. "This is precisely why we in the Council travel in highly protected groups." Mamman's tone is scolding, but her expression is full of love. "Tell me more about this 'Fates' you play. I'm surprised I haven't heard of it before. It sounds riveting."

I don't have my own Fates dice set; every time I've played has been with Alec, so we've always used his. Instead, I take a couple of low-burned candles and carve them into makeshift dice, crudely carving in the symbols for each one with the tip of one of my arrows. I carve in symbols for all four dice, using a white candle for the situation, the green candle for the journey, the blue candle for the cost, and I create the fate die from a deep purple candle. I hope the inn keeper doesn't mind us using them this way, but I imagine they have a surplus of candles to be used.

For the remainder of the morning, I sit with my mamman on the floor in our room at the inn and try to teach her how to play Fates. I enjoy every moment spent this way. I've waited years to get this connection back with my mamman. I've missed having this special bond with my mamman, and we find ourselves embroiled in silly games of Fates for quite a while, but a knock on the door eventually pulls us back to reality.

"Ailene?" a quiet voice asks through the door. The high-class, Nerinian accent that's only partially present in Alec's speech tells me it's Julienne. "I haven't heard from you yet today. Are you quite alright?" she asks.

Mamman covers her mouth to stifle a laugh and calls out, "Please, Julienne, come join us." When the door opens Mamman remarks, "I'm failing miserably to play a children's game."

I roll my eyes.

"Perhaps that's why," I mutter. "It's not a children's game. I've earned the very clothes on my back from playing this game throughout our journey to find you two," I tell her, sitting back on my heels. "You should be glad we're not playing for tins, or you'd be fresh out by now."

My comment results in a bout of giggles from my mamman and her friend as she joins us, and I start again instructing them how to play.

It isn't until we notice the sun beginning its afternoon descent in the sky outside our window that we pull away from our now entirely ridiculous game of Fates.

Julienne's stomach grumbles. Ever the lady, just like my mamman, she places a dainty hand on her abdomen and gives us an embarrassed smile.

"Pardon me, ladies," she remarks. "I came in here to ask if you would like to join me. I *was* headed out to get something to eat, and Alec left a while earlier. I would love the company. Would you two care to join me in my quest for... well, I suppose now it would be dinner?"

Mamman and I share a look and nod. As we stand and I reach for my bow, my mamman gives me a glare that tells me I'll be sorry if I bring a weapon into whatever dining establishment we choose, so I begrudgingly leave my bow behind. The three of us stand and leave the inn, wandering the streets in search of something new to eat.

In the streets of Helna, my mamman, Julienne and I giggle and chatter and enjoy our afternoon out on the town. By the time we've reached a restaurant we can all agree on, my own stomach has been grumbling for at least half an hour. My mouth salivates at just the thought of food. Just as we're about to enter a tall, thin looking restaurant called the Stallion, a familiar shape catches my eye. A tall, muscular man with shoulder-length blond hair sways down the street in our direction.

Hoping that my mamman and Julienne don't spot him, I try to usher us in closer to the entrance, but there's a line of people that blocks our path. Great. Now they'll ask him to join us for dinner.

It's then that Julienne notices Alec stumbling our way. She waves her hands frantically in the air.

"Alec, what luck! Join us!" she calls.

I clench my fists and grit my teeth. I look everywhere I possibly can to avoid meeting his gaze. The hurt I felt last night at his reaction to our broken bond manifests itself in anger.

I nod in his direction to satisfy his excited mamman, but I don't speak.

"Goodevening, ladies," Alec slurs. I shouldn't be surprised that he's drunk; he's always like this, though toward the end of our previous trip as we reached the witch's cave, he'd been much more sober. I can't help but feel irked that he's once again drowning himself in ale.

I push my thoughts aside.

"Hello, Alec dear," my mamman says, giving Alec a warm yet wary smile. Her eyes land on me briefly, and then she averts her attention.

"Alec, darling," Julienne pleads. "Say you'll join us for dinner?" She reaches out to rub his arm gently, and I can't help sneaking a glance at him.

Alec gives her a huge, lopsided grin. The smile is purely aesthetic, however. It comes nowhere near reaching his eyes.

"Thanksma'," he says. He nods down the street in the direction we just came from. "I preciate the invitation, but I'vgot a standing appointment and I wouldn'twant to be rude."

"Oh?" Julienne's eyebrows go up.

Alec nods, and this time his grin beams at me. I roll my eyes and turn away, pretending to be interested in a poster on the wall outside the restaurant advertising a new horseradish stew. The line inches forward, and I move so quickly I'm inches from bumping into the group in front of us.

"Oh, could this line move any slower?" I mutter to myself.

"Lane," mamman whispers, bumping me with her elbow.

When I look back at Alec, he's still grinning, and he's staring right at me.

"Well, sweetheart," Alec says to me, his grin mocking. "Have a good time with the parents. I'll be on my way now. The night is young, and theresblenty to be done. You ladies have a wonderful night."

Of course, my mamman thinks he's charming. She and Julienne stare adoringly after him, and I scowl. When we finally get a seat in the restaurant and an older woman with dark coloure on her lips and long dark braided hair brings us some menus, I stare blankly at the pages. It seems that I've lost my appetite.

I try to engage in the conversation that my mamman and Julienne are having – something about a new peace movement and the trouble brewing in some of the villages, I think – but my disobedient mind keeps returning to Alec. I wonder what standing appointment he was talking about. I let a huff of air out of my nose. An appointment with another barkeep, no doubt.

By the end of dinner, I've dug myself into a downward spiral, and I'm beginning to think I just need to restart the entire day. Maybe if I can get some decent sleep, I will wake up and all of this – including my sour disposition – will go away.

Talk surrounding Women's Council dealings has never really interested me, and tonight is no different, especially in my grumpy state. My mamman and Julienne, however, seem to be totally engrossed in their conversation, as if whatever they are discussing holds life or death importance for us all.

I've always thought that the Women's Council, although my mamman takes it seriously, was just an excuse for women to get together, drink tea, and talk about politics in a world where things are fairly peaceful as they are.

After being on my journey, having witnessed for myself just how brutal Maran can be, I find I have a new appreciation for my mamman's career, even if their discussion topics don't particularly hold my interest.

Later that night, after Julienne has gone back to her room and my mamman has fallen asleep, I lie in my bed wide awake listening to her snore softly across the room. My mind whirs, and my thoughts flit so quickly through it that I have a difficult time grasping any of them.

I'll be glad to get moving again tomorrow. I think being here for so long is making me feel trapped; perhaps progress will make me feel better. Fates know I would love to be back home again, getting back into my typical routine. I don't know exactly how long it's been since I left, blowing my baby sister a kiss as I crossed over our village border. It feels like it's been years.

I soon begin to feel so homesick that my stomach aches.

I'm restless, and I need to get out of this room before I suffocate. I hop out of bed and rush quietly to the door.

The moment I enter the hallway I let out a deep, relieved sigh and plop myself down on the stairs that lead to the Inn's bottom floor. I consider going for a walk to get some fresh air, but I remember the last time I took a nighttime stroll through Helnan streets. I'd been ambushed by two men and had to fight with everything I had to escape them before it was too late.

I sigh.

I do feel better being out of that stuffy room, at least.

The light in the stairwell is dim, created by cheap, oil-fueled twinkle lights. I close my eyes and rest my forehead against the stair railing, and after a while, I find myself relaxing, even drifting off into a light sleep. The railing is cool and solid against my skin, grounding me.

"That tired of your ma' already?" Alec's voice asks, startling me awake.

I don't know how long I've been asleep on the stairwell, or how long he's been here. For a moment, I'm too tired to remember how complicated things are between us, and I experience a brief burst of joy when I see him. It feels like coming home.

And then the empty, hollow feeling in my chest reminds me that, whether he's here or not, I'm more alone than I have ever been before.

"Not nearly as much as I am of you," I grumble. I know I'm being petty, but I just can't bring myself to be kind to him right now. In the low light, I can't get a good look at his face. I realize he's probably standing here because I'm blocking the path to his room. "Sorry," I mutter as I scoot over.

Alec takes this movement as an invitation to sit down.

He lets out a huff followed by a dry, humorless laugh, but then silence stretches between us, filling the stairwell until the air is thick and difficult to breathe.

"What are we doing here?" I ask, finding a shred of courage to attempt the conversation I've been avoiding since we left Marana's cave.

I steel myself for the answer, curling my fingers into fists.

Alec turns his head, and I meet his gaze. The lights hanging behind him cast long shadows over his face. He reeks of ale, and I find myself taking shallower breaths.

"What?" he asks. He wobbles a little bit and steadies himself by placing his hand on the steps between us, causing him to lean inward.

"Really," I say, folding my arms across my chest. "What are we doing here? You and me. Why are we here right now?"

Alec takes the time to peer slowly around the confined space of the stairwell.

"We're stopping to get some rest before we bring our mammans home. We'll be back on the road tomorrow," he says.

I scoff. This mercenary is oblivious when he drinks.

"Right. Never mind," I tell him, standing, ready now to go back to my room. I've had just about as much of his company as I can stand right now.

In his rush to stand, Alec tilts a little too far backward. He reaches out at the same moment I catch hold of his hand and pull him forward to keep him from tumbling down the stairs.

"Fates, you big brute," I gasp as I pull his arm. "If you're going to drink like a fool, you may as well get a room on the bottom—" But I'm unable to finish my sentence.

Alec follows where the momentum leads him: right to me. He slams against me, knocking me backward into the wall. I open my mouth to tell him to watch his step, but I can't get a word out. He's knocked the breath out of me.

His chest is warm and heavy against mine, and it makes my heart ache. I give him a little push, and he backs away just enough so that he can look me in the eye. I can barely make out the amber of his irises.

"How did this happen?" he asks. Although I can't see them well, I can tell his eyes are desperately searching my face for some answer to his question. I think he must be talking about how we got to this place on the stairs, and I resist the urge to scold him. He really should be more careful.

Before I can respond, Alec presses his lips to mine. My body tenses.

He's sloppy, borderline aggressive, and he tastes like alcohol. As badly as I yearn to lean in, get lost in his kiss as I have many times before, I can't. This kiss doesn't heal the wound I'm nursing – not like our kisses normally heal me. Instead, it just highlights the pain. I turn our bodies so that his back faces the hallway at the top of the stairs – close enough that he won't fall down them – and give him a hard shove.

Alec stumbles backward and fall on his buttocks, staring up at me blankly. I can't clearly see the expression on his face, but I don't intend to stick around long enough to witness his reaction, anyway.

Without another word, I step over him and scurry back into my room, closing the door and locking it behind me. It's only in the quiet space of my shared room that I notice my heart is pounding and my hands are shaking.

I lie awake most of the night. Once again, I can't seem to get my raging thoughts to quiet.

I can't believe Alec just kissed me like that. Even though I've wanted him to kiss me for weeks, I didn't want it to happen like that. I try to convince myself that the dissatisfaction and disconnect I felt with that kiss was due to his inebriated state and not due to our confirmed lack of connection.

Although I'm not one to believe in the Fates, I find myself praying yet again that the feelings Alec and I had for each other were real... that they weren't due only to the bond Marana created that once tethered us together.

More and more, I find myself praying to the Fates these days. Alec is the only person I've ever been with, the only person I've ever allowed myself to become romantically attached to, and with the absence of that connection I've always felt, I've been seeking guidance even in the most unlikely places.

As the sun begins to rise, I blink away my thoughts for the millionth time and try to squeeze my eyes shut.

My mamman wakes me with the sound of her voice, soft and sweet and familiar.

"Good morning, Lane," she says, brushing strands of messy dark hair from my face. My eyes feel as though they've been filled with sand.

I groan as I finally get them to open.

Mamman smiles. "We've got to leave soon. Today, we're to continue our journey home."

I mumble something incoherent and do my best to wipe the sleep from my eyes. I blink hard several times, and when my vision finally comes into focus, I'm able to see my mamman clearly. She's already dressed in a soft, white cotton blouse and light tan trousers, her hair neatly pulled back into an intricate bun with the bottom half loose, golden curls cascading elegantly down her back.

Although her cheeks are still somewhat gaunt from her time held in the witch's prison cells, her skin is now almost totally back to her normal fair, rosy cheeked complexion, and the last few days in Helna – eating full meals in restaurants and sleeping in an actual bed – have done wonders in filling in some of the weight she lost.

Looking at her now, if I didn't know any better, I never would have guessed that she'd been taken hostage by a witch, starved in a cave, and magically drained of her youth for weeks.

How she can look so good after all of that is beyond me.

I yawn and stretch, dragging myself out of bed.

"Alright," I mutter as I take an eternity pulling myself into a standing position. "Let me find my boots, and I'll be good to go."

My mamman gives me a stern look. She points to the washroom.

"You are not leaving this room until you look at least semi-presentable. Go wash up. I've got clean clothes for you on the sink. When you come out, I will fix your hair," she says.

I want to argue, tell her that I'm perfectly capable of doing my own hair, but it's so nice to have someone fussing over taking care of me that I obey her as a hint of a smile stretches slowly across my face.

I've missed my mamman dearly.

"Yes, ma'," I say. I plant a soft kiss on her forehead as I make my way to the latrine.

When I'm all washed, I get dressed in a new pair of rider's pants, a silky olive blouse that laces up the front with long, fitting sleeves, and a leather vest. I'm not sure how long my mamman has been awake for, but it looks as though she's had plenty of time to shop for supplies. I do feel better when I'm clean and dressed in some nice clothes that haven't been torn or bloodied or dragged through the mud.

Just as promised, when I return from the washroom, my mamman pats the bed beside me, hairbrush in hand.

As my mamman works through my long dark hair, she hums softly, just as she did when she cared for me as a child. I sigh and allow myself to relax, closing my eyes and soaking in the moment, listening to the vague yet familiar song.

"There," she says, placing the brush on the table and picking up a handheld mirror. "Beautiful as ever, but now, you're ready for anything."

I smile at my reflection. I still have some small pink scars from our encounter with the witch that are taking longer to heal now that my bond with Alec has been severed. We've always healed much faster than this, and even healed instantaneously through our shared kisses, but our kiss last night did nothing to speed the final stages of healing for these little scars on my face and arms.

I have some residual dark circles under my eyes, but I look better rested than I have in days despite my lack of sleep last night, and my black hair is done in a loose but neat braid that starts on either side of my face and joins at the back of my neck.

I feel a boost of confidence, and a twinge of guilt shoots through me as I think of how poorly I've taken care of myself these last few months. I'll need to work on that.

We take a few minutes to finish packing everything up. Mamman has been busy this morning, so most of our things have already been stowed away and are ready to go. I lace up my boots and sling my essential belongings – my bow, my quiver of arrows, my bag of provisions, and my satchel over my shoulder. My satchel contains my maps and drawing utensils, as well as the third journal I've read since we stopped to pick them up on our way back through Darkwood forest. Now, I feel ready. Even though there is still quite some time left to our journey, I can almost feel the plushness of my pillow and the warmth of my own bed.

"Ready?" my mamman asks me, and I nod. "Good. I've got some business to attend to at the stables. Go and have some breakfast, and I will meet you at the entrance in half an hour."

At that, my mamman leaves the room with her back straight, totally confident, ready to take on the world.

I'm quick to leave our room, making my way to meet with the woman at the front desk and sign us out of our room, but the woman says my mamman has already taken care of everything, and that breakfast has been paid for as well. She gestures to the dining area with a kind, genuine smile that seems so out of place here in Helna.

I thank the woman and head for the dining area. I get my breakfast at the buffet and take a seat in a small, quiet corner of the room. There are a few guests scattered throughout the dining hall, but for the most part, it's fairly empty.

I'm halfway through my breakfast when I realize I haven't seen Alec this morning. What am I going to say to him after last night? And worse... he was so inebriated last night. Will he even remember?

Fates. I wish things weren't so complicated.

I force myself to take a deep breath and finish my last fresh, homestyle cooked meal I may get for some time. I leave a tip of three tins on the table, brush the crumbs from its surface, and exit the building.

Just as she said she would, my mamman meets me outside with a smile. A man stands behind her, and in his hands he holds the reins to four well maintained horses. If nothing else, the people of Helna care very well for their horses.

"Are these ours?" I ask, tone full of disbelief. How in Maran can she afford four horses? The only reason we have horses back home is because my pappan was able to mark them as a business expense because they help us transport our merchandise, and they were still extremely costly.

My mamman smiles. "They belong to the Council, so we will need to have them returned once we have arrived safely home."

I'm about to mount the large, midnight-black horse when I notice Alec and his mamman across the way. From where I stand, it appears they're having a heated conversation, and Alec's mamman runs her hands over her eyes.

Alec catches me watching him and gives his mamman a big hug before he turns and strides in my direction. Just as I reach up to grab hold of my horse's reins to pull myself up, Alec's hand touches my arm, and the contact makes my stomach flip.

I meet his gaze and see nothing in his amber eyes – no crazed emotions like those they held last night. His expression is guarded.

"Can I speak with you?" he asks, eyebrows raised. He glances at my mamman, then back to me. "Please?"

I take a deep breath and nod at my mamman, who gives me a concerned look. Although she doesn't know our full story or the total complexity of how I've been feeling, she knows enough to understand that being alone with Alec is a bold move for me to make right now.

I let go of the reins I'm holding and pat my horse's flank.

"I'll be right back," I tell it, and the beast snorts softly in response.

I turn to face Alec, pulling my arm from his grip. Although the movement is small, it's not without notice.

Alec's shoulders slump ever so slightly.

We walk just far enough away to be outside earshot of both of our mammans. Then he stops me, and I fold my arms.

"What?" I ask. My intention is to sound strong and annoyed, but I think I sound scared and snappy at least, maybe even whiny.

"I..." he starts, then he trails off as if he's searching for just the right words to say. I'm shocked that Alec – charming and witty and smooth – is coming up short for words. "I wanted to apologize for last night," he says.

I scoff and squeeze my arms tighter around my body. So, he does remember.

"What was that last night?" I ask, raising my voice. The blush that burns my cheeks at the memory extends to my ears and neck, as well.

Alec looks around and gestures for me to keep my voice down. I almost fight him on that, argue that he has no business telling me to be quiet, but I really don't want to worry my mamman, so I relent.

"I am sorry," Alec says. "Last night... I wasn't myself."

"Oh, great," I reply, moving my hands to my hips. "Who was it then?"

Alec shrugs, and I resist the urge to shake him or smack him. Since we met, I've learned to control those urges, because every time he was hurt, I was, too. Although we've now confirmed that is no longer the case, the thought alone is enough to turn the urge into a melancholy empty feeling. Doesn't he know that his actions affect other people?

I sigh and soak in the empty air.

"Well, if that's about all, I'm going to get back. Lovely chatting with you, as always." I don't know why, but I salute him, and I turn to walk back in the direction of our mammans. Alec lets out a frustrated grunt and rushes to step in front of me, blocking my path. My eyebrows raise high onto my forehead.

In this moment, we're so close, almost chest to chest. That's when I catch a good whiff of him.

My lip curls, and my face contorts into what I'm sure is a very judgmental expression. I can't help it.

"You're drunk? Again?" I ask.

"I'm not drunk," he says, putting his hands out in front of him, fingers fanned out as if that's going to stop me.

I stare him down. "No?"

He pushes a breath out through gritted teeth and allows his hands to drop to his sides.

"No. I mean, I was, but I'm not anymore. I just haven't had a chance to sleep and bathe it off. I've been busy. Listen," he says, waving his point away. Now his words are rushed, his tone urgent. "I'm not going with you to Palandra."

"Well of course not," I say. "I figured we would probably split at Parth, then you'd go back to Nerine with your mamman, and I'd go back to Palandra with mine."

Alec rubs his face. He looks as exhausted as I feel.

"No," he tries again. This time his voice is calmer, words slowed, as if he's trying to think of how to say whatever it is he's trying to say succinctly. "I'm splitting with the group now. I've hired some friends of mine to take my place. I've worked with them before, and I trust them. They'll see the three of you safely home. There's something I have to do."

This statement comes as a complete surprise to me.

"We just traveled across the entire country and faced numerous dangers that put both our lives at risk to get your mamman, and you're not going to ensure she gets home safely? What could be so important? Have you *ever* not finished a job before? I imagine this one would be the most crucial." I look around as a group of people pass us on the street. I've never noticed just how many people walk around leading their horses here in Helna. The wind has picked up, carrying the scent of hay and horse manure through the dirt and cobblestone streets. I'm surprised by the grounded feeling this smell fills me with. It reminds me of working with my crew on our delivery routes, taking care of the horses when we camped.

When my gaze meets Alec's again, I find he's gritting his teeth. He sucks in a deep breath, clenching and unclenching his fists.

"This is not a decision I came to lightly," Alec starts, now speaking through his teeth in a low, gruff voice. "You should know I didn't decide to leave her or you without great thought. But I found someone who I think may have some information on what's happening with us. Lane, I *need* to find out what's happening with our bond."

Alec's mention of the bond we've shared squeezes my heart, filling me with an unspeakable hope, and my breath hitches in my chest. If anyone can find someone with answers, it'd be Alec, and if he truly can find someone who knows what's happening to us, I understand why he would decide to break from our party.

I nod slowly, soaking in the implications of his words. "You really trust those men you hired? With your mamman's life?" I ask.

"I do," he says. "They'll keep all of you safe."

I search Alec's face. I think about how lost I've felt since our bond was severed weeks ago.

I remember how when I first met him, all I wanted to do was figure out how to break this bond so I could get my freedom and rid myself of the injuries he's caused my entire life.

I think about how we discovered that our bond was so much more than merely obtaining each other's injuries. How, for as long as we both can remember, Alec and I have been able to feel each other's emotions and sensations, and that when we were together, our bond was stronger than ever, filling us with a closeness I never imagined possible.

Since it's broken, every emotion I've felt has been a hollow echo of what it once was, like someone has ripped away half of me, leaving me cold and exposed and empty.

I want to get home, to wrap Lilah in a tight embrace, to go to sleep in my own bed... but if I could get answers, if I could understand what happened to us, maybe I could find some peace. Maybe I could learn to live just as myself, without Alec's presence within me.

I take a deep, slow breath and let it out even more slowly.

"You swear they'll see my mamman home *all the way to* Palandra, and yours all the way to Nerine?" I ask, narrowing my eyes at him, studying every detail of his face for any sign of uncertainty.

Alec nods. "I swear."

I chew my lip, considering this new information.

"If you're serious that my mamman will be safe, and that they'll take her home, then count me in," I tell him, watching as his eyes widen. "I'm coming with you. I'll go tell my mamman."

Alec has to blink away his shock, and by the time he does, I've already started walking again.

Alec throws his hands out again, reaching for my shoulders to stop me from walking. I reach my hand up toward my bow, threatening to load it.

"You really need to stop doing that," I threaten.

Alec's eyes widen again, but he makes the smart decision to step out of my way.

"I don't think you should come," he says, falling in step beside me. "The people I'm going to meet with... well, chances are they're not the type of people I'd want you hanging around."

I give him a petty smile and push myself to walk faster. "It's a good thing you don't decide who I hang around, then, isn't it? If you won't let me go with you, I'll just stay here alone and see if I can find my own answers."

"Difficult woman!" Alec mutters from behind me. Then, he pipes up with, "Well, if you're coming, then at least let me inform my men. You can talk with your mamman. I'm going to take care of a few things. Be ready to meet me at the fountainhead in the square at dusk."

I savor the irritated tone in his voice – so much like how he spoke when we first met. I do my best to hide the smile the memory paints on my face.

I turn to make some comment about him being so mysterious and question him as to why it must be at dusk rather than at any specific time, but he's already gone.

"That sellsword," I say to no one, then I make my way back to my mamman, who has dismounted her horse and now chats giddily with Julienne. "Ma'," I start. My mamman looks over at me and gives me a curious smile. She excuses herself from her conversation and practically floats over to me. Sometimes I forget how graceful she is.

"Welcome back, dear. Are you ready to leave?" she asks me. "We'd like to make some good progress before it gets too dark out. Julienne was just informing me that Alec found some friends of his to keep us company. Isn't that sweet? Did the two of you make up?"

My shoulders tense and I take a deep breath, reaching out to hold my mamman's hands in mine. I just got her back, and now it feels like I'm losing her all over again. This thought is especially painful when I consider that we've finally started connecting again for the first time in years.

But I need answers. I've had this bond with Alec for my entire life. I don't know how to live with part of me missing, and I have so many questions.

"Mamman, Alec is parting with us," I tell her cautiously. The smile starts to fade from her face, but she nods slowly, pursing her lips. I suppose Julienne already gave her that news. "Ma', I'm going to stay with him."

My mamman's eyebrows crease her forehead with several shallow lines.

"You're not coming home with us?" she asks, peering for just a moment back toward her friend. I lower my gaze, not sure I can handle the look on her face.

"No, I'm sorry Mamman. I want to; I do. There's just something I need to look into, and Alec has the connections to help me. I hope you understand. Alec has assured me the two of you will be safe with his associates, and I'll write as often as I can, so you know I'm okay." I chance a look back at her.

My mamman stares at me for a moment, a deep frown casting shadows over her crystal blue eyes.

"Right..." she says, folding her arms across her chest.

"I'm sorry, Mamman. If I don't get these answers, I'll regret it for the rest of my days," I tell her. Every word of this statement rings with stark truth within me.

I need to know why we were bound.

I need to know how this bond was broken.

I need to know if there's any way to restore that connection we lost.

My mamman steps forward. As she reaches up, the white sleeves of her blouse dangle as she places her hand on my cheek.

She tiptoes to kiss my forehead, then she lifts my chin so that my eyes are level with hers.

"You promise you'll write? As often as you can send a pigeon?" she asks. Her eyes sparkle with unshed tears.

"Or a hawk or a sparrow," I tell her. "I promise. You're really going to let me go?"

Mamman gives me a sad smile. "I haven't been able to stop you from doing what you feel is right before, and you're old enough now that I trust your judgment. If this is so important to you, do what you need to. Just promise me you'll stick with him, and travel safely."

My own eyes fill with tears. I can't remember the last time I cried parting with my mamman. "I'll do my best," I tell her. "Are you sure you'll be alright?"

My mamman waves away my concerns.

"I made this entire journey by myself and came out relatively unscathed; I'm certain I will be okay with the fine company I have this time around. Julienne has told me how wonderfully that boy treats her. I know whomever he chose to escort us home is well trusted."

I'd love to hear what Alec's mamman has to say about him. Imagining him doting over his mamman brings a smile to my lips.

"Please look after Lilah and Pappan... and tell them I'm sorry I'll be away a bit longer," I request. I hope Lilah understands that I miss her every day. I close my eyes and send my love to her.

Mamman and I share a tight, teary embrace. Eventually, she does need to leave town, and just as Lilah did every time I left home with a delivery, I follow my mamman to the gates at the edge of the city.

"Safe travels!" I call after my mamman as she and her party ride away without me.

"And swift return!" she calls back to me.

5

Not sure what to do with myself now, I fix my satchel across my back and decide to roam around Helna for a while. The city isn't huge by any means. It's nothing like the size of Parth or Nerine, but it's sizeable enough to get lost in for a few hours, and so I wander.

The homes and shops here are so different from any other city I've been in before. The whole city is made almost entirely of wood. Wooden framed statues of horses and various crops can be found all throughout the center of town. Animal skin rugs adorn the floors and hang in the windows of every shop. Horsehair jewelry can be found throughout most shops in some quantity, and in the market, I find a shop with everything made entirely of wool: Wool blankets and coats, wool pillows, caps, scarves, and gloves, all intricately dyed and knitted.

When I've wandered the shops and marketplace, I find myself sitting cross-legged on the fountain's edge with an apple, making notes on my maps about the things I've learned about this interesting town. I take slow, distracted bites as I watch the sun set behind the buildings in the center of town.

I try to imagine what Alec and I are about to get ourselves into. I wonder what kind of person we'll get this information from. Will they be kind? Cruel? Will they be honest? And how does a person obtain knowledge about the kinds of things we're trying to find answers for? Surely there isn't some secret school where people can learn about magic and soul-binding deals. For my entire life, I've been convinced – like everyone else – that magic didn't exist.

As promised, Alec meets me at the fountain at dusk.

"Are you sure you're up for this?" he asks.

"I'm up for it, alright," I tell him, folding my arms. "Let's figure this out."

Alec relents, looking displeased about my being here. But our mammans are long gone, and unless he wants me to travel back across the country by myself, he's stuck with me. Alec wears a somber expression as he nods to a man in a dark brown hooded vest, who approaches us from the east. The man nods back as I stand and quickly put away my belongings.

I take a calming breath and force myself to meet the man's gaze as Alec and I approach him. The man has irises of such a light blue that they almost look white, and a deep, long-healed scar down the left side of his face. It splits the prickly surface of his leathery skin from his cheekbone to his neck.

Whatever happened to him must have hurt.

The man doesn't say anything to us for a moment. Instead, he slowly looks me over, his near-white eyes searching my body, and I shift my weight, uncomfortable beneath his gaze. Alec steps in front of me to get the man's attention off me, and I instantly feel better.

"Looking for something?" Alec growls.

The man shrugs, and in a low, raspy voice he says, "This one wasn't mentioned before."

Alec's hand immediately finds the hilt of his sword. Instinctively, I follow his lead, bringing my hand to my bow, the other ready to reach for an arrow should I need it.

"She comes with me," Alec remarks in a tone that says this is non-negotiable. I do my best to hide the tiny smile that creeps onto my lips.

The man sneers at us, revealing two silver teeth among his other rotting ones. He rolls his eyes and gives a hiss of a sigh. The worn, dark material of his hood raises as he shrugs one bony shoulder.

"This way, then," he tells us before turning his back on us and leading us through a slim alleyway. As he moves, I can barely hear him mutter, "It won't be my head if the boss doesn't like the extra guest."

I gulp audibly.

I don't like the sound of whoever this "boss" is.

Although Alec doesn't respond, he keeps his eyes narrowed in the man's direction, and his hand never leaves the pommel of his sword.

The alleyway winds through the city, turning this way and that, and the deeper into the city we travel, the narrower the path becomes until we are forced to walk in a single-file line with the hooded man in the front and me following at the rear.

Finally, when I feel I might suffocate if I have to spend even one more minute inside this ever-narrowing passage, we arrive at what appears to be a dusty dead end. The wall before us is the same as all the other old, warped and weathered wooden walls that we've passed over the last several minutes.

This one, however, gives way as the man knocks.

Two short knocks. A pause. One knock. The same knock is repeated three times, and the wall slides open to reveal a dark passage lit only with small torches.

The man finally turns back to us and grumbles, "Inside. Both of you."

Alec and I exchange wary looks and Alec nods, reaching his hand out for me to take. I don't even hesitate. I'm so worried that they'll close this wall and shut me out, separate me from Alec, that I grasp the hand he's offered and cling to it. To my relief, he squeezes back as we duck through the low-hanging doorway.

"Go straight," the man barks as he closes the wall again and follows behind us.

We follow a system of ropes down a flight of packed-clay stairs and into a tunnel with torches hung far enough apart that most of the tunnel is almost too dark to see in, so I stumble against Alec more than once.

It's damp down here, and the air is thick with the scent of mud and flame. At least that's all it is. In an area like this, it could be much, much worse.

My breathing must be off somehow, because Alec squeezes my hand and looks at me through the darkness with wide, concerned eyes. Even in the dim light provided by the torches, his amber eyes seem to glow – a glow I've melted into many times before.

Butterflies stir deep within my stomach, but I shake them off, turning my gaze to the well-worn path ahead of us.

I'm not sure how long we spend winding through the tunnels, but eventually, we find ourselves at an old waterlogged wooden door.

Our guide grunts as he pushes past us in the tight space, and he bangs loudly on the door with the side of his fist, producing the same knock he used before. The door opens a crack, and someone on the other side mutters something unintelligible.

"We're here to see the boss," the man says before snorting and letting loose a wad of spit onto the clay floor of the tunnel. I can't help but sneer in disgust, and the shock of such a grotesque act has me chancing a peek at Alec. He looks back at me with eyebrows raised, and the two of us stifle a laugh.

I do my best to straighten the expression on my face as the man looks back at us. The feeling of his eyes on me makes my skin crawl and I squirm, which makes him smile. "Got some visitors for her," he says to the person behind the door.

Her?

The door swings open, and a short, heavyset and grimy looking woman lets us into a narrow room that has damp walls with peeling grayish wallpaper that looks to have once been yellow, and old broken furniture. Beside her seat near the door, the woman has an unappetizing loaf of bread and a large drink of ale placed atop a mossy wooden crate.

This woman's gaze feels just as uncomfortable as that of the man leading us, and I wonder where these people come from, but I remember that we're underground, and I wonder if they live down here like this.

The woman frowns deeply at us as we pass her, still following the man. As we pass through the narrow room and step into an even narrower hallway with a slew of doors on either side, I crane my neck to look back at her. A wicked smile is spread widely across her dirty face, sending shivers through me. Why is she smiling? I'm not sure I want to meet whoever these people answer to.

"Is it too late to go back?" I whisper to Alec, who offers me a soft, reassuring smile.

"I'm afraid so, sweetheart," he replies, running this thumb over mine.

Sweetheart. The term of endearment that he used to call me mockingly sends a pang of sorrow through my chest. I hope this visit yields the kind of answers we're looking for.

I pull his fingers more tightly through mine as we follow the man into yet another dusty hallway that smells like mildew. The same grayish-yellow wallpaper peels off all the walls, and the floor is so caked with mud and moss that I'm not sure if it's wooden or carpeted or just dirt.

Somewhere, water drips incessantly into what sounds like a metal bucket, and the sound reverberates throughout the corridor.

Finally, we come to a door at the end of the long hallway. The man knocks again, but this time the knock carries a reverence that wasn't present before. Someone speaks up from the other side of the door, and the man turns the knob and slowly opens it.

"Got your guests, Raider," the man says, tone so respectful it's startling. He bows his head and keeps his eyes low.

"Guests?" a woman's voice asks, putting extra emphasis on the 's' as the three of us enter the room. The hooded man enters after Alec and me, closing the door softly behind him.

This room is much nicer than the hallways we've seen so far, and wider, too. It also has wallpaper covering the walls, but this one is a faded red instead of the grayish-yellow, and it seems to stick much better to the walls' surfaces. The floor – still filthy – has a plush pink carpet, and the furniture – although it's mismatched and still lopsided – all seems to be made of a higher quality wood. In the center of the room stands a round wooden table with a black cloth covering its top.

At the other end of the room stands a woman with her back to us. She's got long legs covered in worn, muddy thigh-high boots and tight trousers that accentuate her wide hips. She wears a faded black corset over a striped gray blouse, and her deep auburn hair cascades in waves down her back below a worn leather hat that comes to a point at the front and the back.

The woman turns to reveal bright, almost silver-blue eyes and full lips painted in deep red coloure that tilt up in the corners. Lips that spell mischief. I find myself sneaking glances at Alec, wondering what he thinks of this stranger.

"Names," the woman says. Her voice has a thick musical quality to it, and her tone is biting. The man nudges my shoulder.

"Lane," I say, frowning. I almost share my family name, Shrayan, but I think I'll hold onto that information until I know I can trust her. There aren't many Shrayans that I'm aware of.

"Alec Montrose," Alec says, giving away everything at once, carefree as ever. "And you are?"

"Alaya Raider," the woman says, gesturing with a black-bladed dagger toward herself. "I distinctly remember only discussing one guest."

In my peripheral vision, the hooded man flinches.

"Take it up with this one," he says, voice defensive. He backs closer to the door as he pushes the blame onto Alec.

In an instant, the woman's face turns cool and collected, and she picks at her long, red painted fingernails with her dagger.

"Very well. Back to your post, then," she says, as though she's grown bored of this entire interaction already. The man rushes to exit, closing the door hastily behind him.

Somewhere in a nearby room, I hear someone cry out. A man, from the sound of it. I turn, wide eyed, in the direction I think the sound came from – to face a curtained doorway on Alaya's left. Alaya steps between me and the doorway, drawing my attention back to the dagger in her grip.

"Nevermind that," she says, jaw set, gaze challenging.

"Does somebody need help?" I ask, fidgeting nervously, trying to see past her.

Alaya raises an eyebrow at me. "No one you need to concern yourself with. Besides, he won't need any help in a minute or two," she purrs.

"But—" I start, but her expression morphs into a poisonous glare that stops my words in my throat. Then her silvery eyes land on Alec, and her lips part to make way for a flirtatious smile that's highlighted by straight, pearly white teeth.

"Well, Alec Montrose. What brings you to my neck of the alley?" she says in a voice like silk, stepping around the wooden table to circle Alec, eyeing him up and down, dagger still in hand.

My gaze flits anxiously from the curtained doorway to Alec's face, which holds his usual half-smile as he soaks in her attention.

"I've got a guy whose informants tell me you're the one to see for answers dealing with... the unordinary," Alec says, keeping his voice steady. Relaxed. Confident. Of course. "I'm here for those answers."

I've seen women react to Alec before. Everywhere we've been together, when women see him, they flock to him. He isn't unattractive by any means, but he oozes charm that draws even the most hesitant women to his side.

"We are here for answers," I butt in, but Alaya barely spares me a sideways glance.

"And what kind of answers are you seeking today, pretty boy?" Alaya asks, stepping close enough to him that they stand mere inches apart. She slides the flat of her dagger's blade against his cheek, but he remains perfectly collected, and his smile holds that familiar confidence.

"Magic. We want to know how it works, and what happens when it breaks," Alec says.

"Ambiguous, but I'll play," Alaya mutters, finally looking at me. "Who's to say magic is even real?"

"You tell us," I say, refusing to back down. "You're supposed to be the expert, aren't you?" Now she steps closer to me, and the two of us stare each other down for a moment before her smile returns.

"I think I like you," she tells me before turning away and walking back to the table. "Well, kid," she says, and I'm not sure if she's addressing me or Alec. "I can't tell you anything with what you've given me. Magic can't just break. That's not how it works. But I can see the topic is sensitive for you both, so I'll tell you what. I'm going to ask a few questions. Answer straight, and I'll tell you if there's anything I can do."

Alec looks to me as if to tell me I need to play by this woman's rules.

"Fine," I say. "Ask your questions."

Alaya's smile widens. She flicks her dagger up into the air, and it plunges into the wooden table with a heavy *thunk*.

"Oh, goody. Let's begin," she says. "What kind of magic are you referring to?"

"There are different kinds?" I ask. The look she shoots me makes me feel stupid for even asking. I suppose there could be good magic and evil magic, but the witch Marana didn't seem purely evil, and our bond seems to have happened incidentally, not by malintent.

"Binding magic," Alec says, swooping in. "Anything that binds people or things together. Ever heard of anything like that?" he asks.

"I'll ask the questions for now, thanks," she says evenly. "Are you looking for a curse? I rarely deal in curses anymore, and you don't seem the type to be able to afford my price."

She eyes me now, and I fight the urge to snarl at her. How does she know what I can or can't afford? I look down at my clean, silky, olive colored blouse. Compared to how I've dressed over the last few months, I feel wealthy.

"No curse, thank you," Alec says. "We just want information. But... curses. If there was a curse that would bind people together, is there something that can fully sever a curse like that?" he asks.

Alaya is quiet for a moment. She narrows her eyes and taps one finger against her red lips, assessing, pondering the information we've shared with her. She brushes her lustrous, wavy auburn hair over one shoulder.

"Alright," she says, tone suddenly much more chipper. "I'll help you. Are you up for a trip?"

I step forward, folding my arms across my chest.

"That easy? Really?" I ask. "A trip where? I thought you were going to give us information."

Alaya turns and rummages through an old, broken chest of drawers and pulls out a large leather bag. She busies herself filling it with various items and articles of clothing.

"I don't have the information you're asking for... if it exists at all. I don't think I've ever heard of magic simply breaking. There's always a catalyst of some sort. But I do know someone who might know better than me," Alaya tells us.

"There may have been a catalyst," Alec says, sticking his hands in his pockets. "But up until a few months ago, we didn't even think magic existed. We'd like to understand it better."

"I thought you were the expert," I mutter, interrupting. Alec shoots me a look, likely hoping I won't offend the person offering to help us, but my comment doesn't deter her in the slightest.

"I *am* an expert, but I typically deal in getting people magic. Simple things. Spells, elixirs, curses, if you can pay for them. The person we're going to see... well, she deals with the outlying situations. The vague ones. The *pure* ones," she says, making a face. "She's the expert of experts, if you will. If anyone has the answer you're looking for, it will be her."

I hear again the man groaning from the other room. I try to sneak a peek, but Alaya keeps her sharp gaze on me, stepping toward us with that dagger in her grip, so all I do is send worried glances to the curtain.

"You're going to take us to her? Why?" Alec asks, confused, goofy smile on his face. Does he not hear the person clearly in pain just feet from us? How does this not bother him?

I nod, doing my best to ignore the poor bastard.

"It seems like an escort would be a lot more expensive than a curse. What's your price?" I try not to get my hopes up, but I can't help it. Could this woman actually lead us to someone who could answer our questions about our bond, how it was created, and how it was broken? Could she help us restore it?

"Oh, honey," she says, pausing in her packing long enough to send me a pitiful glance. "That depends on the curse. And of course there's a price, but I haven't decided that just yet. Besides. I've grown tired of Helna. I've been looking for an excuse to skip town for a while, and this'll give me something to do. You two have piqued my interest."

Alec and I share a look.

Really, we don't have any reason to refuse her, aside from the fact that we've just met her, and I'm unsure if we can trust her. But if she truly can lead us to some answers, I think Alec and I must accept her offer.

"Okay then," I say, reaching out to shake her hand. "We'll go with you."

Alaya regards my outstretched hand with a distained look before crossing the room. She knocks on the door in the same pattern we heard earlier. Within moments, another man opens the door. This one wears a leather vest that's too tight on his large torso and baggy, filthy trousers with patches on both knees.

"Yes, boss?" he asks, avoiding direct eye contact with her. She nods at him anyway.

"Lead these two back to the streets. *Don't* let them wander," Alaya tells the man.

"Yes, boss," he says, sure to keep his gaze downturned. Now, Alaya looks to us.

"Alright, cuties. Get out. I've got some chores to finish up here. You can get whatever affairs you need to in order, then meet me at the northern edge of town in two hours, where the road leads toward the swamp. Two hours, got it? I'm willing to take you, but I don't need to, and I'm not going to wait around. Come on time, or don't come at all."

At that, we're ushered out of the room and back through the same series of alleyways to the streets of Helna.

Once we're back on the main streets of Helna, I find myself relaxing a little bit, though my mind returns to the poor fellow in Alaya's room. Should we really be traveling with someone who doesn't seem to care if another person is hurt? I've got a sneaking suspicion that she was the cause of that man's pain in the first place.

"Well, that was interesting," Alec says, a hint of a smile lingering on his face. I blink at him.

"Interesting? What in Maran are we getting ourselves into?" I ask. But I don't wait for an answer. To be honest, I'm impressed by Alaya. I thought my mamman was intimidating, but

Alaya is on a whole other level. "In any case, I'm going to run some errands. Do you have anything you need to do?"

Alec nods, but he doesn't say anything, and we just stand there awkwardly for a moment.

"Good, well," I say, swinging my arms back and forth. "I'll meet you at the edge of town, where Alaya requested. See you in two hours?"

6

Alec and I go our separate ways, and I head for the nearest postal service.

Once inside, the merchant digs through his stack of letters that no one has claimed.

"You said Shrayan, right? From Palandra?" he asks me, looking over his spectacles at me.

I nod. "That's me."

The man passes me a letter from my sister and two letters addressed to me from Zaid.

Before I found myself entangled in my feelings for Alec, I only had eyes for Zaid, though I was always too much of a coward to do anything about it. He and I worked together, and I didn't see things being anything but complicated between us. When Zaid sought me out to tell me that my mamman had been acting out of sorts – and that he had feelings for me – I began to think differently about things. Zaid had traveled with Alec and me to Helna, making things so much more confusing for me, as I had to grapple with how I was starting to feel about Alec and how I still felt about Zaid. When news came that my little sister Lilah was on her own after my mamman disappeared, Zaid offered to go back to Palandra to look after her until my pappan could return from his delivery. Zaid promised me that he would write to keep me updated.

Seeing that Zaid has kept his promise fills me with hope.

After everything I've been through in the last several weeks, reading Zaid's handwriting – the handwriting I read on all our inventory lists and delivery requests back in Palandra – shoots through me a homesick feeling that brings tears to my eyes.

I think back to the last time I was in the postman's office. I was here with Zaid, reading a letter from Lilah regarding my mamman's disappearance.

I remember how I felt when he offered to go home and look after her while my parents were away. I'd given him a hug, and the two of us had been so close to sharing a kiss, and he *had* kissed my nose.

My cheeks burn a bright red at the memory, and I hold the letters close to my chest before I focus on their content.

Zaid's first letter tells me that he got back to Palandra safely, and that Lilah has been doing a wonderful job taking care of herself. He tells me that she's been putting him to work in keeping the house running smoothly while our parents are away, and he tells me that he's been in contact with my pappan, who should be coming home again soon. He ends his letter with, *I'm thinking of you, Lane.*

The words make my heart flutter in my chest, a feeling that has been buried deeply beneath the anxiety and stress of losing my bond with Alec.

I hurry to open the second letter, eager to read what he has to write next. This one is dated from a week ago. Zaid tells me that my pappan returned home, but that Zaid has continued to check in on my family daily. He tells me that Lilah has been helping him prepare for his meeting with the Council. Then his message shifts, growing more sincere.

> *Lane, I miss you. I hope you've found your mamman. I hope you're safe. While you're out there having your adventure, don't get too comfortable with Alec, alright? I've still got my hat in the ring.*

He ends this letter with the same words: *I'm thinking of you, Lane.*

The sweet sincerity of his letter brings a smile to my lips and fills me with a soft, glowing warmth. I read through this letter once more before moving on to Lilah's. She tells me many of the same things Zaid did about the time they've spent together, but her letter also includes and update regarding her schooling and the letter she's received from the Women's Council. Although she's only nine, she's received a letter from the Council recognizing her potential, and they've offered her a tour of the Grand Council Keep once things settle down and Mamman returns.

I take out some weathered parchment from my bag and write them both back.

I tell each of them that I'm not sure how long I'll be gone, but that I miss them terribly. I tell Lilah how proud I am of her, and that I'll write her again. I tell Zaid that we're headed toward the edge of town, and that I'll write to him again as well, just as soon as I am able.

I thank the postman as he takes my messages, and I pay for his services before I head to the market to purchase some food and other goods for our journey ahead. I don't know where we're going, so I make sure to purchase some extra clothes, as well. After that, I make my way toward the northern edge of town, just as Alaya requested.

At Helna's border, I meet back up with Alec.

"Get all of your letters sent?" Alec asks me, chewing an apple contentedly.

I raise my eyebrows at him.

"How did you know?" I ask. "Did I tell you I was going to the postal service?"

I honestly can't remember. Alec offers me a fresh apple, and I take it as a melancholy smile spreads across his face.

"I've been with you for a while now. You've sent a letter in every town we've been in, checking on your family. Your crew. I knew you couldn't resist checking on them again. I take it Zaid made it back safely?"

Zaid's name sounds strange coming from Alec's lips.

"Yes," I say.

"And Lilah is okay?"

This question gives me pause, and I look at him with wide eyes. His expression is serious, and I'm overwhelmed by the urge to hug him and thank him for caring about her well-being.

"Y-yes, she's great. She immediately put Zaid to work. She's doing well in school, and she's already making connections with the Women's Council."

I reiterate everything she put in her letter, and Alec seems genuinely impressed, which fills me with pride. I take a moment to look at him – really look at him – for the first time in a while.

He seems sober, something I'm sincerely grateful for. I find myself searching his face for answers, trying to memorize every detail. Although his appearance hasn't changed much in the last few weeks, he looks almost foreign to me now.

I take a deep breath, still holding the unbitten apple in my hand. Having something to hold onto gives me strength.

"Alec?" I start, stepping forward. His eyes are wide, expectant.

"Yes?" he asks.

Where do I even start? I clear my throat.

"About our bond..." I struggle to find the words, but this is the first time we've been alone and able to talk about what's been going on between us.

"Yes?" he asks again. His voice is low, and his gaze holds mine for a moment longer before it drops to the ground.

"What do we do?" I ask.

It's a vague question. Truly, I'm not entirely sure what I'm trying to ask. Am I asking him what we should do to move on? Am I asking him what we should do about our relationship, which feels so unfamiliar without our mystical connection? I'm not sure. Perhaps I'm asking what we should do to figure out how to bring the bond back, but we don't even know if that's possible, especially with Marana dead. Her magic seems to be what bound us in the first place, and with our bond severing at the time of her death, it seems impossible for it to be restored. But then... magic in and of itself is supposed to be impossible, too. Maybe there is hope for us yet.

I realize I've been quiet for several seconds as I let my thoughts run rampant, but Alec has as well. I blink away the sting of tears that now wet my eyes and try to get him to meet my gaze.

"Any ideas?" I ask.

Alec shrugs.

This isn't his normal, carefree shrug. His shoulder's barely move, as if they're weighed down by an invisible burden. He's just as clueless as I am.

"We get answers, if we can," he says, though he sounds deflated. He kicks at a loose rock that juts out of the ground at his feet, and I look away for a moment. It's difficult seeing him like this. He's always so sure of himself.

"Well, we've got to do something in the meantime," I say resolutely, squaring my shoulders. "Let's talk. Let's keep talking, until we figure something out, okay? We're doing this together, right? I think that's the first step."

Saying this aloud feels right. It sends a glimmer of hope through me, and I hold on to it tightly. I think Alec feels that same glimmer, because he looks at me and smiles, and the smile finally traces the lines of his eyes.

"I'd like that," he says softly, reaching out his hand and brushing my fingers with his.

"Alright, love birds," Alaya says, coming up behind us. "Let's get moving, huh?"

Alec and I snap to attention, both a little embarrassed to be caught in such a vulnerable moment, though we shouldn't be. Not around this stranger, anyway.

I clear my throat.

"Where are we going, exactly?" I ask Alaya, giving Alec's hand a gentle squeeze before letting his fingers slide through mine, and the cool air is quick to replace the warmth his hand had brought with it.

"North," Alaya says simply.

"Back to the mountains?" I ask, turning my question toward Alec, who's finished his apple.

He chucks the apple core into the field ahead of us, and it disappears among the tall grass.

"Through the mountains," Alaya says, matter-of-factly. "We're going to what most people here in Maran refer to as the Nameless Country."

My jaw drops, and it takes me a moment to regain my composure.

The Nameless Country is where the settlers of Maran, the creators of the Women's Council, originated from. To my knowledge, the journey through the mountains was so arduous and the Nameless Country so vicious that nobody has gone back.

According to Alaya, that may not be the case.

As Alaya moves ahead of us, looking over her shoulder briefly and gesturing for us to follow her through the tall grass, I snap myself out of my shock.

We follow Alaya through the grass for almost an hour before I simply can't contain my curiosity any longer.

"What's in the Nameless Country?" I ask. "I thought there was nothing up there – nothing worth going back to, anyway. The Women's Council moved us southward for a reason, right?"

"You'd be surprised," Alaya says. Although I'm still walking behind her, I can hear the grin in her voice. "There's a whole lot of world up there, and it's a hell of a lot more interesting than this place. You'll see for yourself in a couple of weeks."

As she speaks, we walk quickly through the hip-high grass that surrounds the entire valley where Helna is located. Winter is on its way, and in recent weeks the vivid green of the grass has faded into a soft, greenish yellow. Soon, the fields will be golden. I've never seen the Helnan grasses golden before – I wish we were sticking around long enough to see them turn. As they are now, the light yellow-green is gorgeous.

Now it's Alec's turn to ask the questions.

"A couple of weeks?" he asks. "Getting through Murkwater swamp is going to take us at least a week by itself." He adjusts the bag strapped to his back. Alec's claim is true. We just made that trek twice, and it took us over a week each time.

"Well, it's a good thing we're not going through the swamp," Alaya says, grunting as she bends low to pick something up from the grass, and I watch Alec glance at her rear before averting his gaze. I roll my eyes, doing my best to ignore the pang of jealousy in my chest at witnessing this. Of course, I've seen him look at women this way before, but that was before we became close. Before we deepened our bond sharing an intimate night together. Before he told me I was unlike any woman he'd ever met, and that he wanted to see where this connection between us leads to.

I make an effort to distract myself with the scenery as Alaya wiggles something free from the earth. Right now, we stand before Murkwater Lake.

The lake is just as its name suggests: A murky turquoise color, lighter toward the shores than at its center.

When Alaya stands upright again, she holds in her hands a thick, faded, dirt-covered rope. She gives it a pull, and more rope loosens from its place in the ground, dropping loose dirt and dried grass onto the ground at her feet.

Alaya steps backward to stand beside Alec, whose body relaxes, ready to help her.

"Give this a pull for me, would you, handsome?" Alaya asks, and Alec obliges without a word. He yanks the rope once, then backs up and pulls again, harder this time.

I stumble backward out of the way as a rowboat emerges from the earth when Alec pulls on the rope.

"What?" I ask. "How did you know this was here? There's grass everywhere." I search our surroundings for a landmark of some sort, but I find nothing that might suggest this boat's location was marked.

"I've got a great memory," Alaya replies with a casual smirk on her face. "I know a guy who likes to hide boats here. We're not *technically* supposed to cross the lake this way – too many people have disappeared here, too many boats turn up missing – but the fish you can catch here have a psychedelic effect if you eat them, so some of us might disregard that rule every now and again. People will pay a lot of money for that kind of a good time, especially in Parth. My guy likely won't mind if I 'borrow' his boat for a while."

She winks at me.

Parth. The party city. I didn't know people ate hallucinogenic fish there, or anywhere. Who would want to eat something that poisons their body? It sounds awful.

But I am impressed by Alaya's knowledge, and I can't help but wonder what else this woman might know.

I shoot Alec an unsteady look, but he simply shakes his head, moving to help Alaya with the boat, and she gives him a sly, red-lipped smile.

"Thanks, love," she tells him.

I grind my teeth as Alec grins back at her, and I move to help with the boat as well. It's better than standing here watching the two of them. We drag the rowboat to the lake's edge and hold it steady for Alaya as she throws her bag within and gracefully climbs inside.

Then Alec looks to me.

"Coming?" he asks.

Should I? Probably not.

But of course, I let out a huff of breath and climb into the boat. Alec takes my hand to help steady me as I step inside, and the warmth of his touch makes my stomach flutter. The boat rocks, and my arms dart out, fingers clenching the edge of the boat on either side. While I'm grasping the sides for dear life, Alec steps onto the rocking boat with ease.

I panic, gaze instantly finding the murky water surrounding us. In this shallow water, I can barely make out the shapes of plants and rocks that must be mere inches beneath us. I would hate to fall in.

"Have you never been on a boat before?" Alec asks, trying not to mock my growing unease.

"Never needed to," I tell him as I continue to grasp the edge and slowly take a seat.

Alaya whistles at us before tossing an oar in our direction. Alec and I both reach out to catch it, but as the boat sways again, I close my eyes and try to steady myself while Alec catches the oar and sets it across both our laps. As he catches the next oar that Alaya throws, I open my eyes, and Alec offers for me to take one with a kind smile on his face.

"Think you blokes can talk and row at the same time?" Alaya barks. She gives me one doubtful, judgmental look before reaching over to take the oar back out of my hands. "On second thought, maybe you'd better learn how to *sit* in a boat before you steer it."

Alec chuckles, and I glare at him, but he simply continues questioning me.

"With your love of traveling, you've never needed to be out on the water? I knew your travels were limited to the west when we met, but I thought your pappan would have taken you somewhere on one. You live right next to the sea."

"Why does it matter whether I've been on a boat or not? Have you been on a boat before?" I ask, though judging by the surprise in his tone, I'm certain I already know the answer.

Alec sits up straight and beams with pride before sticking the larger end of his oar into the water.

"Several times," he says. "I stowed away on a ship that went from Siren's Way down to the Shradan Mines when I was seventeen. Dinghies like this are nothing in comparison to the beauty and magnificence of a ship."

Alaya watches the two of us with sharp eyes throughout this exchange, and although I try to keep my focus on Alec as we converse, I can feel her stare on me like an itchy wool. Our little rowboat catches a wave and jumps up a little bit in the water, and I reach out and cling to the wood on either side of me again until my knuckles turn white.

"Are you sure this is safe?" I ask. "This hardly seems natural. How can we possibly stay afloat?"

We hit another series of small waves that jolt the boat this way and that, and Alaya and Alec both seem completely unfazed.

Alaya gives me a wicked grin. "In this water? Well, let's just say that most people prefer to stay ashore. Best not to fall in."

I chew my lip and frown at the water, still clutching the edges of the boat.

Alaya sighs.

"Listen, champ. I've been on this lake many times. You're safe with me, and this fellow seems competent enough to use an oar, so you're in good hands all around. Yeah?" I glance up at her uncertainly, and she winks at me. "Relax, will you? We've got a long ride ahead of us. Try not to suck all the fun out of it."

After that, I keep my worries to myself and just squeeze my eyes shut every time my stomach feels like it's going to come out my mouth with the motion of this unfamiliar territory.

As we continue onward, the waves settle a bit, and I find that despite some nausea, I feel much better, as long as I don't look at the water. Instead, I keep a steady watch on Alaya. I don't know her, and I'm still not sure what could have prompted her to guide us to the answers we seek so easily, especially without first naming her price.

Still, whether I like it or not, at the moment, my life is in her hands.

As the light fades with the setting sun, the green of the lake deepens, turning a dark emerald. If I wasn't so stressed by the words Alaya planted in my head about the contents of this lake, I'd say the water is beautiful. Mesmerizing, even.

Alec sits beside me once we've gotten a little more comfortable, and he smiles easily at me.

"Would it help you to feel a little bit in control?" he asks me, holding out his oar for me to take, but I just stare at him blankly.

"Will I sink us?" I ask. I try to roll my shoulders, which are often tense, but have been extra stiff the last few hours we've been on the lake.

Alaya lights a match and ignites a candle she's retrieved from her bag. She plants the candle on an empty seat in the center of the boat, and I'm grateful for the light.

"Unlikely," Alec replies. He takes my hand and places the oar within my grasp.

My gaze jumps up to check in with Alaya, and she rolls her eyes dramatically before nodding.

"Take the stick. You'd better learn eventually," she says.

I inhale deeply and slowly let the air I breathe – which has a sour, fishy sort of taste – out again.

"Okay," I tell Alec. "What do I do?"

Alec instructs me through the process of rowing, and I recall the time we spent teaching each other on our journey to find our mammans.

I remember fondly the astonishment he had expressed when he witnessed my skill with a bow, and I remember how close we became as he worked to teach me how to fight – with my fists as well as with a sword. My heart aches with longing, and I wish I could bring us back to that time.

Once Alec has taught me how to row, it does wonders to quell my nerves. I feel so much better now that I've got something to do, some semblance of control. And honestly, the repetitive motion, the splash of the oar hitting the water, the swish of it gliding through and pulling back out all soothes me, and I find myself relaxing into the motions.

Alec remains close enough that I can feel his thigh press against mine, and the rowing helps me keep my endless questions, worries, and emotions at bay. For now, it's just Alec and me – and this new acquaintance – on the water. That's not so bad.

A couple of hours after the sun has completely set, Alaya shifts, addressing Alec.

"Okay, big boy, take my oar," she tells him, holding her oar out. He abides without question, moving away and sitting in her place as she stands, and my leg cools where his was pressed against it just moments ago.

I find myself shocked at how the two barely rock the boat now as they move about it.

Alaya sits beside her candle, scooting it over and completely ignoring the burn when hot wax jumps up over the side, spilling onto her fingers.

She digs into her bag and pulls out what looks like a telescope. But as she pulls on it, the rod extends, and she twists the extensions into place.

"What are you doing?" I ask her. I've never seen anything like the contraption she's got in her hands.

"Fishing," she says.

"How can you fish in the dark?" I ask, and both she and Alec look at me as if I've just asked the most ridiculous question anyone has ever asked.

Alaya raises her eyebrows at Alec.

"You said she lives near the sea?" she asks.

"She does," Alec says slowly, chuckling lightly and shaking his head. "She's just spent most of her time... inland."

My cheeks and ears burn as I feel the need to defend myself, but I can't think of a response.

"Never mind then," I grumble. "Fishing."

Alaya lets out a musical laugh and reaches over to place her hand on my knee. "Playing, kid. Lighten up. Your ignorance doesn't really matter here, anyway, because this lake is different. Whether or not you think we can fish in the dark – which we absolutely can – we don't need light to see here."

I shoot her a confused look.

"I don't understand," I say. Alec seems intrigued, as well, and I'm grateful that he's showing signs that he is also not sure what she's talking about.

Alaya rolls her eyes.

"Just watch," she snaps. She reaches back into her bag and pulls her closed fist back out. When she opens it, a wriggling mass writhes about on her palm.

"Worms?" I ask. It's hard to make out just what the shape is in the dim light of the candle, but this woman has definitely had something living in her bag this whole time.

"Yep," Alaya says, smiling. "Care to hold some?"

I curl my upper lip in response and lean back.

"No, thank you."

"Suit yourself," Alaya says. She tosses the entire handful into the water. The worms splash into the water with a quiet *kerplunk*, and Alec and I sit there in silence, staring over the boat's edge into the dark water. Did she just waste her bait? Why bring a handful of worms in your bag only to throw them into the water?

"What?" I start, but I don't have time to add to my question, because within seconds, hundreds of tiny lights swivel about beneath the surface of the water, jutting this way and that around the area Alaya tossed in the worms.

"I'll be damned," Alec marvels. He places his oar at his side and scoots closer to Alaya to get a better look.

"What in Maran..." I allow myself to trail off as the beauty of these lights captivates me. The lights grow in size as they near the surface, and they swim all about, changing color from bright yellow to green and blue as they feed. "Are those...?"

"Fish," Alaya answers. She attaches the last part of her tool to the end: A large net with tiny barbs that reach inward around the top. "May as well catch some while we're out here. I really hate to waste an opportunity. People pay a fortune for the experience these little babies will give you."

As Alaya dips her net into the water and scoops, she captures a whole swarm of the beautiful little creatures. She wrestles with the weight of them, swinging her net around before pulling it up out of the water.

Once she's got the net back over the rowboat, she smashes it hard against the boat's wooden floor once, twice, three times. As she does, the lights fade from the fish, but they do not disappear entirely. Now that I can see the fish clearly, I'm stunned. Each little creature is only about the size of my palm, some ranging a little bit larger to be around the size of my hand – fingers and all. Not only are they still aglow, but they glitter and glisten in the light of the candle. Absolutely gorgeous.

"There," she says. "Easy peasy."

"That's all you'll catch?" Alec asks. How could he be concerned about how many she's going to catch? I can't even form words right now. I've dealt with fish before – trekking loads of them from SunSpar and other places – but I've never seen anything like this.

Alaya doesn't miss a beat. "I can only ever catch one netful. These little buggers are smart, and they're fast. We might have some more luck tomorrow in a different area, but they're all going to be gone in a moment."

Disappointment strikes hard and fast through me. How can they be going already?

I turn quickly and lean over the side of the boat in an attempt to get closer to the water, hoping to catch one last glimpse of the incredible creatures. In an instant, thin, claw-like fingers dart out from behind me to grab hold of my arms, just before I'm about to topple over into the water.

"Watch it!" Alaya shouts as she thrusts me aggressively back into my spot. "Don't you listen? Remember what I said about the water here? People don't come back out. If you value your life, stay put, dumb girl," Alaya growls at me through gritted teeth.

I shake my head, trying to rid myself of the foggy feeling that jumbles my thoughts.

"Sorry," I mutter. "I don't know what came over me." Embarrassed, I look at my feet and try to ignore the pressure of Alaya and Alec's eyes on me.

"I do," Alaya says confidently, clearly trying to let some of her irritation go. "These dumb little pricks are alluring as hell. That's why I bash their brains in first chance I get. Don't want them getting me like they get everyone else."

"You've lost someone to them before, haven't you?" Alec asks softly. I wonder if he's as shocked by this entire experience as I am.

Alaya falls quiet, but she doesn't answer. Instead, her jaw clenches and unclenches, her silence answer enough.

She takes the fish and hooks them by their tailfins onto the edge of the boat so that they hang all around the edge on the inside. She puts her fishing gear away and curls up in one of the spaces between the seats.

"You two seem to have this figured out, now," she says. "Wake me when the sun's up. You two row that way. And handsome, try to keep her from killing herself, yeah?"

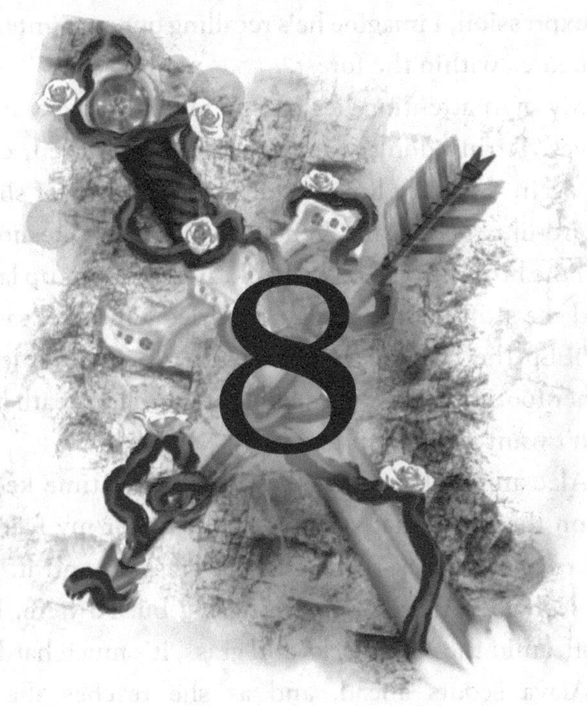

8

Alec, Alaya and I take shifts, rowing and sleeping, throughout the remainder of the night.

When Alaya sleeps, Alec and I discuss our travels, and although it's only small talk, it feels worlds better than the awkward silence that hung between us in the presence of our mammans.

We row throughout the next day as well, and when it's not my turn, I take the time to add information to my maps. I sketch these beautiful fish and write in the information that Alaya shared with us regarding this lake.

It's difficult to write with my charcoal in the ever-rocking boat, but that does little to deter me from improving my maps.

Later in the day, as we approach the shore, Alec peers out at Darkwood forest. I wonder what's on his mind. Judging by his somber expression, I imagine he's recalling our encounter with the ghostly figures within the forest.

My own attention lies on the looming, rocky mountains themselves. I truly don't want to scale their jagged, crumbling surfaces again. My very limbs ache at the thought of slipping on those shard-like rocks again. When we reach the lakeshore, I help Alec pull the boat into the rocky bank. Alaya scoops up last night's haul, and she stuffs all the fish – now dried – into her sack.

"Flip the boat over and cover it up," she orders, easily finding her footing despite the pebbles that roll beneath her boots. "We don't want anyone finding it."

Alec and I obey, and I have a difficult time keeping my balance on the rocks that stumble about under my feet. We flip the boat over and stack rocks and tall grass around it. From up close, it's obvious there's something big buried here, but from farther off, amid the other rocks and grass, it's much harder to tell.

Alaya scouts ahead, and as she reaches the edge of Darkwood forest, I chance another peek at Alec. His face is ghostly pallid, and he swallows audibly.

I recall the conversation we had ages ago when he told me about his grandmamman's ghost following him around until he started training to join the Guard. He had professed to me that his job is often to kill people, and after his experience with his grandmamman, he genuinely believes the spirits of his kills could find him.

I reach a hand out and loop my fingers through his, giving his quivering hand a gentle, encouraging squeeze.

The forest juts out against the lakeshore, so close that Alaya enters its dark depths fifty short paces ahead of us. Every step we take causes Alec's blood to drain further from his face, until I'm certain he's going to be sick.

"Are you alright?" I whisper. Alec looks up at where he can see Alaya through the trees as we enter the forest, and he shakes his head. I nod slowly. I understand not wanting to discuss his fear of ghosts in front of our new "friend."

"Well, let me know if you decide you want to talk," I tell him. I'm torn between the urge to stay at his side to comfort him and the one that tempts me to explore. Last time we were in Darkwood we were on a mission, driven by the need to reach our mammans. Now, our journey is much less urgent, and I'd love to see what I can learn.

Ultimately, I choose to stay at Alec's side, because I know this is a big deal for him. The memory of the ghostly creature we encountered last time we ventured through this forest, paired with the harrowing sounds we heard, is enough to chill me clean through. I slow my pace to match Alec's, certain he's remembering the same experience.

Now that we're within the forest, the light dims as if someone has put a lampshade on the sun, just as it did last time. I know it's late afternoon, and the sun should still be fairly high in the sky, but I can no longer tell its location.

Thick, mossy-trunked trees grow close together, with gray leaves weaving in so tightly together overhead that it's difficult to see where one branch ends, and another begins. Beneath our feet, sparce gray grass speckles the soft, damp, moss-covered earth.

Also like the last time we ventured through Darkwood, I'm startled by the eerie quiet.

It's all too easy to notice the absence of any natural sounds in the silence. We hear no chirping of birds, no swaying of grass or branches in the breeze. The forest around us is totally still, and I catch myself holding my breath.

I can tell Alec feels the same way I do. Although Alaya is still ahead of us and her back is to us, it seems as though the unsettling feeling these woods emit is lost on her.

When the light dims even further, we decide to settle in for the night, and after we've made camp, Alec and I struggle to sit still. Nightfall is the worst time to be in Darkwood forest.

Thankfully, we've not yet reached the white-trunked trees closer to the base of the mountains, though we're taking a path that I'm unfamiliar with. We're closer to the edge of the forest, as if Alaya is trying to skirt us around its depths. Perhaps she does know what lurks within.

Alec gathers firewood and I lay out the blankets from our bags and pull out the supplies I'll need to cook us dinner. I think back to how often Zaid cooked when he traveled with us, and I miss him terribly. I'm not fond of cooking. More than that, though, I just miss his company. I hope he's doing well, and that he's happy. Thoughts of his letters flit through my mind. *I'm thinking of you, Lane,* he'd written.

I chance a quick look in Alec's direction. Thanks to his fear, he hasn't wandered far from where we're making camp, and I can see his silhouette against the darkness. I wonder what Alec would say about my letters from Zaid.

I shake my head, trying to clear away the muddied thoughts as Alaya's rummaging through her bags draws my attention away from Alec.

Before I can ask what she's up to, Alaya opens a jar of some black liquid with a tiny blue light flickering and floating inside of it. She pops the cork, and with a quick motion, she dumps the contents of the bottle into her palm, then thrusts it at the little stack of kindling she's put together. A large orange flame immediately bursts to life, glowing big and bright before dimming to the deep green color that all flames seem to take in this forest.

"What was that?" I ask, sitting up straight and gathering various food items into my hands. I do my best to keep my jaw from dropping straight to the forest floor.

"What?" Alaya asks, raising a thin, perfectly shaped auburn eyebrow. "Never seen a flame draft before?" She asks the question as if I've just inquired if she breathes air.

"Of course not," I tell her. "Where do you come from?"

No one in Maran will even talk about magic. When I was a child and I procured my mysterious injuries without any explanation, I was sure it was magical. I quickly learned not to mention these thoughts, however, because people ignored and chastised me for mentioning such a ridiculous concept. Over time, I joined them in their thinking, convincing myself that my imagination was all the magic our world contained.

Alaya narrows her piercing blue eyes at me across the campfire, which now crackles wildly as she feeds it with some larger sticks. "What's it to you?" she asks.

I stand, carrying the bread and vegetables to my blanket where I can figure out what I'll do with them.

"I'm just curious, is all," I mutter.

I can't figure her out. It seems to me as if her mood shifts as easily as the direction of the wind.

If there was any wind here, anyway.

"Nowhere important," Alaya says easily, shifting yet again. "Everywhere I shouldn't be."

So, her answers are as ambiguous as her moods. Perfect.

Just like that, Alaya changes the subject. She smirks, nodding in the direction Alec wanders. She smiles as he bends to gather more wood. His arms are nearly full, and it seems he'll return to our camp soon.

"So," Alaya prompts, voice like silk. "How long have you two been involved?"

I swallow.

"What do you mean?" I ask. Alec and I have barely spoken. How could she possibly know Alec and I have been romantically involved? Perhaps she's simply asking about how long we've known each other.

"Oh, please," Alaya says, rolling those silver-blue eyes. "Don't play dumb, kid. It doesn't suit you. I've been watching you look at him. Your puppy dog eyes would be visible to a blind man. So, what's the sitch? Have you told him?"

This time, I can't keep my mouth shut. "Excuse me?"

"Come on, Lane. It's just us gals," Alaya prompts. The corner of her mouth tilts up into a mischievous smile.

My shoulders slump.

"It's complicated," I tell her.

Alaya scratches her back with a stick, then waves it about in my direction.

"Isn't it always?"

Alec now makes his way back to our camp, and I straighten my back and press my lips together into a tight line. I send Alaya a sharp look, silently pleading for her not to say a word. She winks and pretends to button her lips closed.

Alec sits beside the fire, and already I can see his body relax in its steady – albeit dim – glow.

It isn't long before darkness has totally fallen, and the only light around us is the dim green flame from our campfire.

That's when the first noises begin.

It starts with a soft whistling, as if wind blows through the thinnest branches of trees just out of our view. Then we hear the giggles. Of course, it's different for each of us. For me, the laughter is that of a little girl, eerily similar to Lilah's late-night giggle. Even though Lilah is miles and miles away from here, across the Maranee River and safe in Palandra, the sound gets to me, and I fight the urge to go out looking for her in the darkness.

"What do you hear?" Alec asks, registering my unease. His voice is soft, but I can hear the hint of fear within it. I recall from our last experience in this forest that what I'm hearing could be totally different from what he's experiencing.

"Lilah," I whisper back. The three of us now sit around the campfire, nibbling quietly away at the remainder of our small meal. Alaya just watches us, and our short conversation from earlier plays in the back of my mind. "What about you?" I ask Alec.

Alec swallows. "My grandmamman," he says. He and I both look to Alaya expectantly.

At first, she straightens and raises an eyebrow at us.

"You're both nuts," she says. "I don't hear a thing." As if the forest can hear her, the sounds intensify, and Alaya looks around us cautiously. "A howl. I hear a cold, lonely, heartbroken howl."

The three of us scoot a little closer to the fire, though Alaya tries to act as if she hasn't moved.

"Let's talk about something good," I suggest, hating every moment we're stuck in this forest. I hope we can pass through quickly. I take a long stick that Alec brought back with him and poke mindlessly at the fire with it, feeling childish for being so afraid. "Perhaps if we talk about good things, happy things, the sounds won't seem so bad."

Alaya chortles, but Alec bumps me with his shoulder. When I meet his gaze, he smiles softly.

"I remember one time, when I was probably eight years old," Alec says. "My pappan and I had a really good day." He smiles, and for the first time since I met him, the thought of his pappan seems to bring a genuine, happy smile to his face. "He'd taken me away from home, so I could start my training to join the Guard. He said he needed to see what I was capable of when my mamman wasn't around to coddle me."

Alaya and I watch Alec's face lights up as he relives the memory, and I find myself startled by the energy with which he recalls the tale. As he speaks, the sounds in the forest seem to quiet, as if the trees themselves and all the spirits within the forest are listening, also.

"My pappan took me on a daytrip to see Grand Council Keep, where he taught me all about the Guard and what it takes to be a member. I was enthralled. Have you ever been within the walls of the Keep?" he asks. I barely have time to nod before he continues, but Alaya's face reveals a scowl, and I'm certain she's never been within. "Well, it's glorious, and there are members of the Guard all over the place. I was mesmerized by their shining armor, and I couldn't stop talking about how these men were trained to serve a purpose: To protect the Council and keep the peace across Maran.

"It was on that trip where my pappan gifted me with Rhetta and Jewels," he says, patting both his sword and his dagger as he sets them on the ground beside him. His expression shifts now, and tears gloss over his eyes. "I was sure that this was my pappan's way of finally accepting me, and for the briefest of moments, I felt happier and more accepted by him than I ever had. When I thanked him on the journey home, however, he told me that he'd had the blades crafted in Palandra when he found out he was going to have a son, but that he had never intended them to be mine when he saw what a sickly child I was.

"It was my mamman's wish that he still gift me with these beauties, though he knew I would never be man enough to deserve such fine blades."

Palandra is known for its skilled blacksmiths, so it comes as no surprise that those beautiful blades were forged in my village, though I am surprised to find yet another thing that tied us together before we were even born. I stare at the sparkling golden pommel and hilt, with round emerald jewels that glimmer even in this dim lighting.

Alaya and I sit quietly, watching the light from the fire dance on his blades. Alaya reaches into her bag and pops something crunchy into her mouth.

Alec sniffles and wipes at his nose.

"Anyway. That was the only day I remember being truly happy with my pappan. That was the first and only time in my life he took me aside to show me something wonderful – to give me a gift – even though he felt I wasn't worthy."

"I'm so sorry, Alec," I say, reaching out to place my hand on his, and he smiles sadly up at me.

Alaya clears her throat as she finishes off whatever she's been eating. "Well, I'm not. We've all got trouble in our past. We've all got pain. And your pappan seems like a real dumbass. You very clearly have earned those blades. I haven't seen you wield them once, and I can tell."

I think Alaya is trying to comfort him, but her tone is harsh, her gaze hardened.

"I guess she's right," I say. "If you hadn't had your pappan treat you so awfully, you never would have worked so hard to get to where you are now. You never would have become the independent, strong-willed man you are today. As horrible as it was, I suppose that has to count for something."

I think back on my own childhood troubles. I was not outright mistreated by my mamman growing up, but I was always last on her mind, always second to my little sister Lilah the moment my mamman found out she was going to carry another child. And now that I'm older and I understand the hardships my mamman went through, how many children she had lost before she could ever have me, I understand why she pulled away from me so much. But as a little girl who only wanted her mamman's affection, that was a truth I could never grasp.

All I knew was that Lilah was the priority.

Still, had I not been through all of that, had my mamman not pulled away and gotten sick, I never would have started traveling with my pappan on his business trips. I never would have learned the trade, honed my negotiating skills. I never would have picked up archery to protect myself and my team on the road, and I never would have found my love of cartography or history.

"It's interesting the way life plays out, isn't it?" I mutter, more to myself than to anyone else, though both Alec and Alaya nod in response. I hear a cold, lonesome howling sound far off in the woods, and I shake my head. "I guess it's my turn, then. Something happy... I recently reconciled with my mamman. Alec, when we were staying in Helna before we had to leave, I bonded with her more than I have since I was very little. I taught her how to play Fates, and she even styled my hair."

Alec sits back in disbelief. "That's amazing," he says genuinely.

"It was probably simply because that's the first time the two of us have spent any time alone since Lilah was born. Still, having that moment with her, staying in our room all day telling stories... That's a memory I'll always cherish."

Recalling the moment brings a smile to my lips.

Alaya speaks up now, ready to describe her own happy childhood memory.

"I grew up a street rat. Never had a real home. Never needed one. No family to pin me down, either. I wandered where I pleased whenever I pleased, and I often got myself into trouble stealing food and other odds and ends," Alaya says with a mischievous glint in her eyes.

"Wow," I whisper, eyes wide. I figured she'd had a rough upbringing, but I can't imagine what it must have been like for her. It's amazing she survived. Alaya doesn't bear my sympathy any mind; she just plows ahead with her story, and as she tells it, her smile is as genuine as I've seen it yet.

"I remember one day I was working to snag a whole cooked pheasant from a deli stand in the market of Nodon when I was caught by the shopkeeper. He was a big man, probably twice my height at the time, and at least three times as wide.

"He'd grabbed the dagger he was using to slice a sandwich and caught me by the wrist with his free hand. I was certain I was going to lose my hand. My blood was boiling I was so afraid, and I thought my heart would explode.

"No matter how I wriggled about, I couldn't escape the big man's grasp. Just as he brought the knife down to remove my hand for stealing, I was able to swing beneath him, using his momentum against him, lifting my legs up over his head and knocking him to the ground. He lost his breath, and he was so shocked that he dropped the knife and let me go. I scooped up the dagger and sliced off his pinky, then made off with both the dagger and the bird."

Alec and I are rendered completely speechless.

"This is a happy memory for you?" I squeak. Just imagining her experience has my heart thumping wildly in my chest.

Alaya grins, and she pulls the black-bladed dagger she was playing with the night we met out of her boot.

"You bet," she replies. "Never been so proud of myself as I was that day."

The three of us fall asleep reminiscing about our happiest memories and doing our best to ignore the sounds of the forest around us.

Sometime in the night, I'm awoken with a jolt when I feel something frigid and wet touch my arm. At first, I'm sure it's Alaya playing some trick on me. Perhaps she's rubbed my arm with one of her hallucinogenic fish. But when I open my eyes and peer around the darkened camp around us, I find Alaya fast asleep and snoring a couple of yards away from me. There's no way she would have had enough time to cross the campsite and lie down in the time it took me to wake up.

The realization sends an icy panic shooting through my limbs. My body freezes as I sit up straight and look around for whatever it was that's just touched me. Our campfire has mostly died out by now, and the already dim, greenish flame is now sputtering out, sending dark smoke fluttering up into the blackened sky.

Something chitters behind me, and I whip around to see what's made the sound.

Immediately, I see the body of a little girl crouching on my side of the fire. She's dressed in a long white nightgown, and the flesh on her astral body hangs loosely off thin bones. In the place where her head should be is the large skull of some animal, though I can't make out what it is.

The girl – thing – looks at me with glowing blue eyes that float amid large, otherwise empty eye sockets. Her head tilts one way, then the other, and all the time she stares at me, I'm paralyzed. The girl chitters again, the sound akin to that a squirrel would make when chasing a friend, except it's a softer, much slower sound.

The creature looks slowly from me to where Alec lies sleeping and back to me again, sighing heavily. She makes a low, deep moaning sound that feels as if it contains all the sadness in the world.

I force myself to take in a deep, shuttering breath as the girl tilts her head yet again, as if she's waiting for me to say or do something. I reach out my hand, though I'm not sure why I feel the need to touch her to be sure she's here and not just a figure out of some awful dream.

The moment I touch her long arm, the girl giggles, and it's the same laugh I heard earlier in the day. The sound echoes in the air beside my ears, and the girl turns and wanders to the edge of the campsite. There she stops and turns back to me, inviting me to join her. My blood runs cold with fear, but I still feel this impossible urge to follow her into the woods. Although she's said nothing, I know she's telling me that there's something she wants to show me, and I'm certain it's unlike anything I've seen before.

I stumble to my feet, and in doing so, I accidentally kick Alec in the ribs, but I hardly notice him as he stirs and then finally wakes. The moment his eyes open he reacts, leaping up beside me, clutching my wrist with his hand. He gives my arm a hard pull, eyeing the girl as he shouts, "What are you doing, Lane? Stop!"

His hollering brings me mostly back to my senses, though I still want to see where this little girl will lead me. Alec seems to have woken Alaya up as well, as she sits up and stares at the girl with the skull of an animal.

"What in Fates' name..." she starts. She rubs her eyes and gasps when the girl doesn't disappear. I find myself feeling shocked by her reaction. The stories she told earlier in the night, even her general demeanor, made me think she's seen everything.

Alaya doesn't waste any time. She scoops up a nearby rock and chucks it hard at the girl, smacking her in the skull, and the girls' eyes glow a deep, dark yellow. She growls – a low, guttural sound – before turning on her heels and racing inhumanly fast through the trees and out of sight.

The moment she's disappeared from view, the sounds we heard earlier blare at us from all sides. Horrible laughter fills the air joined by low howls, high screeches, drumming sounds, sighs, whistles, and other noises that get lost in the cacophony. They vary in intensity and range, but the message is clear: The forest isn't happy with us.

Alec draws his blades, Alaya scoops up her dagger, and I ready my bow, but the three of us just turn in circles, trying to figure out what noise – and what direction – to focus on.

"You had to attack it?" Alec asks Alaya, his tone biting.

Alaya scoffs. "Anyone in their right mind would do the same thing. It was in our camp!"

"We're in its forest!" I holler back.

"I don't understand," Alec says, his voice thick through his gritted teeth. "We're nowhere near those white trees, are we? It took us days to get there last time."

"What are you talking about?" Alaya asks, spinning around when a loud barking noise emerges from the trees, but nothing appears with the sound.

"I don't think so," I tell him, ignoring Alaya's question. "I haven't seen any. Maybe they're angry with us for coming back?"

Anything is possible.

Alec doesn't get a chance to respond or offer any other possibilities, because the sounds suddenly stop. For the briefest of moments, the three of us stand, weapons still drawn, holding our breath. The moment I start to relax again, I hear loud footsteps running through the tree line surrounding us.

My eyes widen in horror, and the three of us adjust, turning this way and that, trying to catch a glimpse of what's racing around our little campsite.

And then we see it.

A large, mostly naked body with the same long, thin arms and legs that we saw on the ghostly creature the last time Alec and I passed through this forest heading for the mountain. Except the one we saw last time was calm and had a curious aura about it. This one seems angry, and it rushes at us on all four limbs like an animal chasing prey, the floating lamp-like eyes within the two large sockets of a deer's skull glowing a deep, dark orange as it barrels toward us in long strides.

I don't want to hurt this creature. I'm not certain I *could* hurt it, and I really don't want to find out, but in the moment I panic. I close my eyes and let my arrow loose as the creature advances ever nearer. My arrow flies, and when I don't hear the sound of the weapon hitting its mark – or hitting anything, for that matter – I open one eye and peek out just in time to see the arrow go straight through the creature then disappear altogether. The creature turns its eyes to me and lets out an ear-piercing screech before it, too, disintegrates into a cloud of mist that then fades to thin air.

I stare at the area the creature was just standing. I don't notice that I'm shaking until Alaya puts her hand on my shoulder.

"Atta girl, Lane," she says. "Thanks for having the guts to do that."

It's only now that I realize the unbearably loud noises have quieted, though they haven't totally faded.

"You shouldn't have done that," Alec says, staring into the forest. When I turn to see what he's looking at, I see nothing but trees and darkness. He turns to me, and his face has drained of most of its color. "You don't know what that was."

"Well, it's gone now," Alaya says, looping her dagger swiftly into her belt.

"I'm just saying," Alec says. He strides to where I stand and grabs me by the shoulders. "I wish you wouldn't have shot it. If it can disappear that easily, there's no telling where it is or when it might come back. And now, it's seen you. Fates, I wish you hadn't done that."

Alec shakes his head and releases my shoulders before moving to sit down on his makeshift bed. His words leave me cold and afraid. He's right. That thing did see me, and who knows what it's capable of?

The remainder of the night passes slowly, with each of us eyeing the woods in every direction we can, as the ominous sounds continue to wail around us.

Finally, however, the blunted sunlight begins to lighten the campsite. We all agree that we're probably safe to get moving again now that we have greater visibility of our surroundings.

When we continue onward, we're exhausted and frightened out of our wits. The sun has not yet fully returned, and what dim light we see by is hardly enough to watch our surroundings well as we trek through the woods, staying as close to the forest's edge as we can.

Throughout the day, we struggle to keep our eyes open, and we're all seeing things: glimpses of other white, bony creatures wandering the forest that disappear without a moment's notice, and we're left wondering if the images are thanks to sleep deprivation or if we're really seeing apparitions. After everything we've been through, the latter comes as no surprise, though it does leave us all the more terrified.

Later in the day, when things have died down a bit and the three of us haven't seen or heard anything unusual in the last couple of hours, I turn to Alaya.

"You seemed really shocked by that thing last night," I tell her, doing my best to watch my footing as I walk.

"Damn right I was shocked. You saw that thing. We were all scared," she says, folding her arms across her chest.

"You've never seen anything like that before?" I ask Alaya, expecting her to chide me for asking yet another stupid question. Of course, she's seen these things before. She's been through these forests numerous times.

She simply shakes her head. "Never. I've been through this forest several times, and I've heard my fair share of strange noises from the depths of the forest before, but I have never seen anything like that. Not here, anyway."

So, why did we see it tonight, and why did Alec and I experience the same thing last time?

"Whatever these things are," Alec says, his tone shaken. "Let's hope that your arrow scared them off and they stay far away, or at least that we get out of their territory quickly. I'd rather not see anything else."

10

As the forest begins to darken again, we're all on edge, each of us worried about what tonight will bring; but we're exhausted from our heightened senses and prolonged fear throughout the day, so we decide to settle in for the night.

This time, Alaya works on cutting open the bellies of the fish she caught the other day while I make a fire. Alec volunteers once again to gather firewood.

"What are you doing?" I ask Alaya as I work at my flint. I'm getting sparks, but my kindling doesn't want to light.

"What does it look like?" Alaya responds, digging her dagger straight into the belly of a fish and slicing it as easily as if it were a piece of bread.

"It looks like you're gutting that fish. Why now? Being out as long as they have been, aren't they going to spoil?"

Alaya chuckles dryly. "These foul things are better spoiled, for the purposes people eat them. It increases the potency of their effect. I give them a couple of days to sit, then I gut 'em and let 'em finish drying out. It's a pretty efficient system. I can just hook them to my bag here and take them along with me as I travel without worrying they won't be good to eat anymore. They were never good to eat in the first place."

I frown as the fish's tacky innards stumble out onto the ground at her feet. The rancid stench fills our campsite, and I scrunch up my nose.

"Do you have to do that where we're going to be sleeping?" I ask. "They smell awful."

Alaya scoffs. "Are you expecting to get your beauty sleep tonight?"

"Fair point," I mumble. Finally, I'm able to get the fire started, and the green flame grows slightly brighter as it engulfs the kindling. I have a small stack of firewood beside me, but we're going to need more soon or else this fire will die out.

I hope Alec is okay. My thoughts of Alec quickly lead me to thinking about Zaíd again, and I chew at my cheek. It would help tremendously to work through my jumbled thoughts aloud with someone. Although I don't trust Alaya yet, I consider that discussing things with her will likely be more comfortable for me than talking them through with Alec.

"Careful, kid," Alaya tells me as she hangs the fish she's been working on over a low hanging branch nearby before grabbing a new fish. "Keep frowning like that and you'll wrinkle prematurely."

"That's about the least of my problems," I mumble to myself. This comment seems to capture her attention and she approaches, fish in hand. The stench is so much worse up close, and I stifle a gag. Has she completely lost her sense of smell?

"What's up?" she asks me. Although I don't catch any genuine concern in her expression, I do see that she's curious, and right now, that's enough for me.

"Remember when I said things between Alec and me are complicated?" I ask, not sure where to start or exactly what to say, but I have to say something. I've got to work through this out loud.

"You mean the conversation we had literally yesterday? Yes, I seem to recall that well enough. What is it? Afraid to tell him how you really feel? Worried he'll reject you?"

Her jests are spot on, and it's too much. Our broken bond. Our emotional distance since. This uncertainty I have that's contradicted when he's around. The fact that I'm constantly fighting the urge to tell him how deeply I feel for him, because I fear now that he doesn't care for me in the same way.

I don't tell Alaya much of this, but I do tell her that I have come to care for Alec, and that he and I have a history that can't just be forgotten, that our lives have been connected magically since before we met. I also tell her about my letters from Zaid, and that although I haven't responded in kind, just reading them feels a bit like a betrayal of Alec's trust. Tears threaten to fall as I share these vague details with my new acquaintance.

When I've finished, she just sits there for a moment, studying me with those sharp, silvery blue eyes.

"Are you going to stare at me like that forever?" I ask.

"Maybe," Alaya says, but she looks away then, leaning back on her heels and then standing up and making her way back to her bag. "You were right. It is complicated."

I'm shocked. After all of this, that's all she has to say? I *know* it's complicated. With all her experience and confidence, all her knowledge of the magic of this world, all she has to say is that I'm right?

"Wait a second," I tell her, scrambling to my feet. "Maybe you have a draft or potion I could take? Something that would allow me to let some of this go?"

Alaya rummages through her bag. "Trust me, you don't want anything I can give you. None of the wares I have with me currently, anyway. I don't think you're built for the kinds of magic I typically deal in. Still, I do have one thing that I think just might help," Alaya tells me.

"What's that?" I ask, trying to peer over her shoulder.

Alaya finds what she's looking for and turns back to me, holding up a small golden ring between her fingertips. It's twisted bronze and gold with a little dent on one end.

"This," she replies with a mischievous smile.

"And that is..." I prompt, not sure what a ring is going to do for me. It's not small enough to fit on a finger or large enough to decorate someone's wrist.

"A whistle."

"Oh, right, of course," I say sarcastically. "I forgot that a whistle is all it takes to solve one's woes." I start to turn away, but Alaya taps my shoulder before blowing into the little dented space. A high, musical tone fills the air around us, and we stand together in silence as she smiles at me and places the ring in my hand. "Listen, Alaya. No offense. That was a pretty sound, but I really don't think that's going to do much..."

But then I hear a fluttering sound, and my argument fades. The sound is faint at first, but it grows louder by the second, and soon the fluttering is joined by a set of wings and a little hawklike body.

"Hold out your arm," Alaya tells me.

"What in Maran?" I ask as I put my arm up.

The bird flies in a tight circle and lands delicately on my arm. It shakes out its blue and brown feathers and turns to preen one of its wings.

"Lane, meet Audy. Audy, Lane," Alaya says. "Audy here is my messenger bird. I rescued him from a bandit camp back when I was eleven, and he's been with me ever since. He's been through the ringer as far as magic is concerned. The group that had him was using him to test their potions and elixirs. Now he's faster than any bird I've ever seen, and he's practically invincible."

Alaya looks at Audy with such adoration it's startling. I didn't think she would be capable of looking at another living creature that way, like she deeply, truly cares for the bird.

"He's beautiful," I say, stroking a patch of silver feathers on his little chest. He makes a soft cooing sound and pecks my finger gently.

"He sure is," she replies.

"Wait, why did you call him here?" I ask. "What good will this do?"

"Well," she starts, reaching over to ruffle some feathers on Audy's head. "You said you're not sure if the way you and Alec were feeling was real. I think you owe it to yourself to explore all your avenues. If you and Alec work out, great. But I think you owe it to yourself to check things out with this other fellow of yours, since the feelings that you had in that department had nothing to do with magic. Take it from me, kid. Magic isn't something to mess around with."

I chew the inside of my lip and stare at the bird. I hadn't thought about it that way.

"And you'd let me use Audy to do that?" I ask. "Why?"

Alaya shrugs.

"I'm bored. I like you. I'm interested in seeing what you discover. Do you really need a reason?" she asks, rolling her eyes at me. "Just take the bloody offer and write the boy. I expect a full report when he replies." Alaya reaches out and pats the whistle in my hand. "This whistle will allow Audy to find you wherever you are, and it never takes him long to get there."

"You're trusting me with this? Just like that?" I ask.

Alaya smirks. "We're traveling together. I sleep five feet away from you every night. If I'm worried you're going to steal him, I can just kill you and get my whistle back. Easy peasy."

I try to assure myself that she's only joking, but then I recall how she looks with that black dagger in her hands, and the screaming from another room when we first met her. I swallow past a lump in my throat.

So, I write to Zaid. I'm not certain what I should say, so I start by letting him know that I'm following up from my last letter to check in with him. I ask how he's doing, how his studies are coming along, how things are going with Lilah. I ask if he's heard from my mamman yet, and I apologize for finding yet another reason to stay away from home. But I tell him that what I'm doing now is important. I tell him that the bond Alec and I shared is now broken, and that we're trying to understand what's happened to it.

I also tell him that I have a friend – though I'm not sure I should call her that yet – who is letting me use her bird, and that the whistle she's trusting me with is supposed to get his letters to me no matter where I am.

It's only once I've finished my third and final draft of the letter and send it off with Audy that I realize something awful: Alec still hasn't returned.

"Alaya," I start cautiously.

"Hmm?" she responds. She's finished gutting and hanging all of her fish, and now she cleans beneath her fingernails with her dagger. I didn't see her clean the thing, but I hope she sterilized it somehow.

"How long has it been since Alec left?"

The both of us straighten and listen carefully to the forest around us. Yesterday when he gathered firewood, he stayed close enough to camp that I could see him through the trees. Now, as I scan our surroundings, he's nowhere in sight. Normally, I wouldn't worry. But here, in Darkwood forest after the events of the last twenty-four hours and Alec's serious fear of ghosts, I'm panicked.

I jump to my feet and start pacing. I'm not sure which direction I should go in, but I have to go somewhere. I stuff Audy's whistle ring into my pocket and scoop up my bow and quiver of arrows from their place beside the fire.

"I'm going to look for him." I throw the words over my shoulder as I walk away from our campsite. I'm not sure if Alaya responds, because all of my attention is focused on finding Alec. I call out his name through the near full darkness. I do my best to watch my footing, though I still stumble about more than I'd like. Part of me worries that I shouldn't be shouting. I still don't know what this forest has in store for us. I don't know who – or what – could be listening. But right now, that doesn't matter. All that matters is that I find Alec and make sure he's okay. I wish we still had our bond. I wish I could tell if he's in pain or afraid.

As I venture through the woods, I keep one hand ready to draw my bow.

I hear quiet sounds as I go – a giggle here, a whisper there – but I do my best to ignore them. I suppose my instinct that there was something watching us as we traveled throughout the day was accurate.

"Alec!" I call again, and this time, my voice is filled with much more urgency. Where has he gone? I squint against the darkness, hoping to catch a glimpse of his golden pommeled blades.

Finally I find him standing perfectly still, staring straight ahead of him to my right.

"There you are!" I shout. "Why didn't you answer? I've been calling you for ages." When he doesn't move, doesn't even look in my direction, my frustration fizzles out instantly. I freeze. I've been through this with him before, the first time we caught sight of a ghostly figure in these woods.

I turn my head slowly in the direction he's looking, terrified of what I'll find there. And when I do, I see... nothing. I step forward and place a hand on Alec's shoulder.

"I'm sorry," he whispers so quietly that the statement is merely a breath in the wind. His bottom lip trembles, and his brown eyes are dark, brimming with tears. His blond hair is slicked to his face with sweat.

"What's going on?" I ask him, worry making my throat tight. "Alec, what is it? What do you see?"

11

A single tear cascades down Alec's face, and I reach up instinctively to wipe it away. This seems to pull him from his trance, and he looks at me, eyes widening.

"What?" he asks. "What happened? Lane, what are you doing here?"

My eyebrows crease in the center of my forehead.

"You were crying, Alec. You were standing right there, and you said you're sorry. Why are you sorry? Who were you talking to?"

But Alec seems genuinely confused. He opens his mouth to ask me something else, and his eyes catch sight of something behind me.

Once again, he gets this faraway look on his face – one that makes him seem equal parts terrified and deeply, truly sad.

"Wait!" he calls, and he pushes past me to chase something I can't see. I turn and take off running after him.

"Alec!" I scream, but it's no use. Alec pays me no mind as he sprints through the woods.

"What's going on?" Alaya asks me as she races up beside me to join me as I chase after Alec. I barely spare her a glance.

"I don't know. I... something's wrong with Alec. He's talking to no one, chasing after something I couldn't even see," I tell her. Whether I'm winded from running or my chest is tight with worry for Alec, my voice comes out thick and low.

"Ghosts?" Alaya asks, easily keeping pace with me, barely breathless at all.

"I don't know," I say, almost tripping over a thick root as I propel myself forward. "If what we saw last night were ghosts, then no, I don't think so. Are there more than one kind of ghost?"

"How should I know?" Alaya shouts as we weave through the trees. Alec is still blasting full speed ahead, going straight for what appears to be a large, hollow tree.

"You're the one who deals with this kind of thing!" I burst, exasperated. "Don't you know about ghosts? Aren't they some type of magic? I certainly never learned about them in school!"

Alaya grunts.

"Fates, Lane. I don't know everything! If they are, they're certainly not any type of magic I've dealt with before."

As quickly as he started running, Alec stops directly in front of this large, hollowed out tree. He stares into it. As Alaya and I catch up with him, a small ghostly child – another one with a deer's head with little antlers on it – reaches out of the hollow and beckons for Alec to join him. Alec reaches his hand out to take hold of the child's, and I somehow know that if he does this, if he goes into that tree, there will be no getting him back.

Every nerve in my body fires as my muscles lurch. I lunge at Alec with everything I have, knocking him off his feet and onto the forest floor. I tumble down with him, and as I do, the ghostly figure disappears within the tree. Now he's really out of his trance, and I hope this time his clarity will last.

"What is wrong with you?" I ask, struggling to catch my breath. The moment I'm able to sit up straight, I pound on his chest with my open palms. My chest doesn't ache from the impact – another reminder of the bond lost between us – but I'm sure he's going to bruise. "What were you thinking? What were you doing?"

I'm not sure at this point if he recalls his actions, but I'm so angry with him for running off, for getting himself lost, for scaring me. I can't lose him. Not more than I already have.

At the thought of losing him to wherever that ghostly creature was beckoning him, I bury my face in his chest, and he wraps his arms around me, pulling me close. For a moment, the two of us just lay there, soaking up each other's embrace.

"If you wanted to cuddle," Alec says, sounding so much more like himself that it brings a hint of a smile to my face despite the turmoil in my gut. "You could have just asked."

I look up at him to find his usual half-grin lighting up his face, though he's still far paler than he typically is.

My first instinct is to respond with some snarky comment, but honestly, I'm just so grateful to have him here that I let my genuine thought leave my lips. "I'm glad you're safe."

My words startle him, and we gaze at one another as the longing in my chest grows stronger than ever.

"Finished?" Alaya asks, turning our attention to her. I'd totally forgotten she followed me to find him.

She's got her hands on her hips and both eyebrows raised.

I sit up and scoot away from Alec, suddenly all too aware of her critical eyes.

"Sure," I mutter, tucking some loose strands of dark hair behind my ears.

"Good. Let's get back to camp before more of those things come out," she snaps.

I spare one last glance at the hollowed tree before us. The darkness within is so deep it looks as if it could swallow somebody whole.

Back at our campsite, things have settled down a bit. We've finished our meal, but after the events of the last few days, I think we're all a little shocked and in our own heads, so for most of the evening, we're quiet.

I make my way to Alec and sit beside him.

"Alec?" I start, voice soft, tone equally curious and cautious.

"Yes?"

"What did you see earlier?" I ask. "The things you saw... it seemed as if you knew them. What was that about?"

Alec is silent for a moment, twirling a broken twig between his fingers as he considers his response. His eyes stare ahead at the green flames that dance lazily before us, and he seems as if he's sorting through a memory.

"I did," he says. He clenches his jaw and shakes his head before running his hand through his dirty blond hair. Then his hand drops to massage his forehead.

"Is it like you said before?" I ask, adjusting so I can see his face more clearly. "You said last time we were here that you worried about seeing those you've killed before. Is it like that?"

Alec swallows and nods, grinding his teeth.

"That... that child?" I ask, barely able to get the words out.

If that child was someone Alec recognized, then I wonder if all the creatures we've seen here in the forest were once real people, taking these strange forms in their afterlives.

Alec nods again.

"I've done a lot of things, Lane. A lot of things I regret. I love my job for many reasons, but I've found myself tangled in some sticky webs. And although I've cut my way out of them, I'll always have a few strings still attached."

"You…" I start, but I can't bring myself to speak the words that sit on my tongue like acid.

Alec turns to hide his face.

"I've not always known I could choose my work. My first jobs, I worked for a man at a bandit camp just outside of Parth. One time he said he'd had some precious items stolen from him, and that he wanted them back. He hired me and two other men – boys, really; we were all about fifteen at the time – to get his items back. We were just supposed to sneak in. That was the plan the three of us set. We would sneak in and retrieve the items, and no one would get hurt.

"But when we got there, the other two boys – who wanted to prove themselves as true members of the camp – killed the couple that slept in the house. A young boy turned the corner as we were preparing to leave. He saw the whole thing, and I… I chased after him."

Alec is quiet for a moment, and I find myself frozen in place. Alaya has heard the story so far, and she now sits across the fire from us, listening intently.

"What happened?" I ask when he doesn't continue.

He takes a deep, shaky breath.

"I still don't know if it was because I wanted to tell him how sorry I was for what we'd done to his family, or if it was that I wanted to scare him away, make him run so that the other boys couldn't catch him... or if I had some other, darker intentions. But I chased him too far, and he fell down the hillside behind his home. He stumbled in the darkness, and he bashed his head on a rock." Alec pauses, letting the pain of the memory wash over him. I reach out to comfort him, but he recoils from my touch. "I buried three bodies the next morning. That wasn't my last shady job, or my last poor decision, but it was the last job I worked for someone from a bandit camp."

"That's awful," I whisper.

"I know," Alec whispers back.

"Wow, Alec," Alaya pipes up. "How surprising. I didn't know you were a kid killer."

I whip around, glaring at her with eyes like daggers.

"Why would you say that?" I ask.

"What?" Alaya asks, throwing her hands up defensively. "I was joking. It's clear that was an accident. As far as I'm concerned, Alec's hands are clean."

But it isn't that simple. It never is. Alec sits up and frowns at Alaya. "That boy lost his parents and his life because of me. We never should have taken that job. We never should have killed that couple, and I never should have chased that boy."

"Maybe so," Alaya says, voice smooth and steady. "But you did, and there's nothing you can do about that. No sense in dwelling on what should have happened when what did happen is set in stone. All that matters is what you do going forward."

I sleep close to Alec that night. He doesn't say anything else after Alaya's comment and he rolls to face the forest away from me, clearly stuck in his memories, but I sleep with my hand on his back, hoping that my touch will offer him some comfort.

The next morning, the three of us set off yet again. This time, we're all quiet, each of us keeping an eye out for the spirits we've encountered over the last few days. Now that I know some of them are people that Alec recognizes, I wonder how they got here, who they are, and who else we might have seen without knowing it. Would I recognize someone I might have known? I think about that giggle that sounded just like Lilah's, and my body shivers. There's no way she's a spirit. Last I heard she was thriving. Perhaps these beings only imitate people we have on our minds.

Or perhaps that little girl's giggle sounding like my sister's was merely a coincidence.

I think about other people I've known who have passed away. Thankfully it hasn't been many. An old woman, a young boy who had gotten very ill... and then of course all the people who have died over the course of my journey with Alec, none of whom I've known personally.

I think about the little girl who tried to lead me into the forest. Was she someone I once knew? I didn't recognize her as someone I met before, and her essence didn't feel familiar to me, though it's difficult to say without being able to see her real face.

By the afternoon, we've made it to the base of the mountains. Here at the edge of the forest, we stand before a gaping black hole in the mountainside. It's surrounded by the thick brown clay that made up the caves that led Alec and me to the witch Marana's chambers at the mountain's peak.

Jutting out from the clay in several places are the large, jagged gray spires that make up the mountain's surface. If we want to go through this entrance, we're going to have to be careful.

"Wait," I tell Alaya as she steps forward into the mouth of the cave. "We can't go in there. People who go into those caves don't come back out again."

Alaya raises an eyebrow at me and narrows her eyes. Her lips make way for a grin that begs me to challenge her. "Oh yeah? Then how did the settlers get to Maran?"

According to the journals I found when Alec and I made our last journey to the mountains, the people who settled in Maran were guided through the mountain's labyrinthian cave systems by Marana herself. I don't feel like relaying the entire tale to Alaya. Honestly, I doubt she'd even listen long enough for me to tell her half of it.

So instead, I just fold my arms across my chest and say, "They had help."

Alec nods.

I'm certain he recalls what I told him of those journal entries when we made our trip up the mountainside, and his face is grim as he agrees with me. After everything we've been through since Alec and I met, we've learned to heed the warnings of others.

Still, Alaya presses. She puts her hands on her hips, looping her long, thin fingers through her belt.

"Yeah, well, so do you," she says confidently. When Alec and I refuse to move and share a wary look, Alaya rolls her eyes. "You've got to be kidding me. Look, do you want answers or not?"

"You know we do," Alec says.

"Then get your asses in there. I've been through these cave systems several times, and I've made it out just fine. I know them well enough to be your guide," Alaya argues. "This is the fastest, safest way through the mountains. Are you in, or are you ending your quest here?"

It's at this moment that Audy comes fluttering in with a high pitched, musical cry. He lands on my shoulder, flapping his silvery wings a few times to steady himself before reaching into a little pouch attached to his talon. He pulls out a tightly wound scroll of parchment, and I stroke his beak gently as I retrieve the message.

Alec frowns at the bird. "Where did this thing come from?" he asks.

"He's Alaya's," I coo, keeping my gaze on the beautiful little creature. "She's letting me use him to send messages back home. Isn't he incredible?"

"He came out of nowhere," Alec says. "How in Maran did he even find us?"

Alaya grins. "That's what he does."

"Thank you," I whisper to Audy. This message must be my reply from Zaid. From home. Holding it in my hands fills me with a deep sense of strength. The sooner we can find answers, the sooner I can return home. I turn to Alaya as I tuck the message into a small pocket in my bag to read later. "Alright," I tell her. "Through the mountains we go."

"Are you sure about this?" Alec asks me as I step closer to the cave's dark entrance.

I take a deep breath and let it out in a huff.

"She's right, Alec. If we want answers, we need to follow her. If she says we can get through the mountains safely, that she's done this before, let's give it a try."

As if confirming what I've just said, Audy flutters over to Alec's shoulder and nuzzles against the stubble that's grown in on his cheek.

At first, Alec's brown eyes are wide with shock at the bird's instant taking to him, but he quickly smiles.

He gingerly lifts a hand to scratch the bird on its head. Finally, Alec lets out an exaggerated sigh.

Just then, Audy perks up as if he hears something strange. His feathers fluff up over his entire little body, and he shakes before squawking loudly and taking flight.

"Should I call him back?" I ask Alaya, confused by the little bird's actions.

Alaya shakes her head. "He'll be alright. He'll come back when you whistle for him. He's found me in these caves before, so I know he'll find you, too. Best let him fly where he wants to before he has to go underground."

Something about the way he took off, though, has my stomach tight with worry.

Behind us, we hear the sound of a thick branch snapping beneath the weight of something heavy, and Alec, Alaya and I quickly turn around to see what's happened, and we're taken completely by surprise.

Surrounding the cave entrance behind where we were just standing, barely within the line of trees, lurk dozens of spirits, all with different animal skulls where their faces should be, staring at us with the same glowing, bright blue eyes. They hang on the trees, perch on rocks and crouch in the grass. All of them stare directly at us, as if anticipating our entrance into the cave.

If this is where they want us to go, I'm not sure I want to, and the confidence that filled me just moments ago has dissipated.

We hear another large branch snap farther off in the distance. This time, the sound is followed by a low, thick growl that makes gooseflesh rise on my skin and every hair on my body stand on end.

"Alec?" I ask, and Alec swallows audibly in response. "Please tell me whatever that is, is someone else from your past..."

"That doesn't sound like anything I've come across," he says quietly, voice shaking.

The low growl turns into an ear-piercing wail, and Alec he puts his hand on the hilt of his sword as every spirit who has gathered to watch us scatters into the forest, eyes turning from that bright blue to a deep yellow.

The creatures all make their own whimpering sounds as if they also fear whatever is headed this way.

"Do you think we can fight it?" I ask doubtfully. I nock an arrow and stand my ground, though everything in me is telling me to run. Whatever's coming our way, if Alec is going to try to fight this thing, then I will, too. From my peripheral vision, I see Alaya shifting her weight anxiously.

The few distant trees that we can see through the gloom bend and crack, making way for something we still can't get a visual of yet.

"For Fates' sake," Alaya mutters. "You both are idiots!" She reaches into her bag and grabs a small vial of dark pink liquid. She shakes it up, and as it starts to glow, she throws it hard at the ground about a yard away from us. The glass vial shatters, immediately sending plumes of maroon smoke into the air. Alaya digs her fingers into my elbow and grabs Alec's wrist, pulling us both toward the mouth of the cave. "Let's go!" she shouts.

We turn to follow her, stumbling over ourselves as we race within the cave. As we do, the creature must come across that smoke, because we hear yet another wail, and this time the creature sounds as if it's in excruciating pain.

"What was that thing?" I ask as we continue running through the darkness of the cave, crashing into one another and running into large spikes of rock that tear at our hair and clothes.

"What's with all the questions?" Alaya shouts, panting hard. We run for another moment through complete darkness before Alaya stops dead in her tracks, sticking her arm up to stop us as well. Her elbow hits me in the chest, knocking the air out of my lungs. I reach out and grope the air, searching for Alec's hand, hoping that he was able to stop, as well. Thankfully, my hand finds his arm in time to halt him.

"Ouch," I grunt, using my free hand to rub the place that Alaya elbowed.

"Wait right there," Alaya orders. She's quiet for a moment, though I can hear her digging through her bag. Then the area around us fills with a bright orange, flickering light. Alaya holds up her hand, gripping a small glass orb filled with a dancing, unnatural looking flame within. The flame bounces against the glass and settles down at the bottom, flickering gently.

"What else do you have in there?" Alec asks, trying to peek into her bag with an impressed smile on his face.

"Ask again later, handsome, and I might just show you," Alaya says flirtatiously. She's almost caught her breath again, though her face is just as flushed as mine. The light from her orb swims within the silvery blue of her eyes. The two stare intensely at each other for a moment, and I clear my throat.

"Um, guys. We're being chased, remember? We probably shouldn't stop. Shouldn't we keep going before the smoke clears and whatever that thing was chases us in here?"

My comment seems to break their staring contest, and they both shift their weight. Alaya nods.

"I stopped us here because I had to. We need light for this next bit, and I knew we were getting close. I think it's around here, anyway."

I put my hands on my hips. "You think?" I ask. I thought she knew these caves.

Alaya rolls her eyes. "Calm down, kid," she says. "I usually don't run as fast as I possibly can into these caves. My measurements might be a little bit off, but..." Alaya ventures forward about fifty feet and stops again, looking down. Then she nods once again.

"But what?" I ask, following her to where she stands.

But I see what she means. Just about ten feet from where we now stand, the cave suddenly drops downward, and several steep drops lead to a whole new section of cave below us.

"Wouldn't want to fall down that by chance, would you?" Alaya asks. She turns and hooks her glowing orb onto her bag.

"Sorry," I mumble, my cheeks burning bright red with embarrassment.

Alec is the first to climb down onto the lower platform, which is almost as deep into the crevasse as he is tall. He reaches his hands out, and Alaya takes them, her light orb swinging this way and that from the motion, casting dancing shadows across every surface within the cave. As Alec reaches up to support her waist, Alaya's hands go around his neck. He sets her gently down before reaching up to do the same for me.

I grab hold of his hands and he helps lower me down. I do my best to ignore the flip of my stomach at the warmth of his hands on my hips. When my feet touch the ground again, I stumble a little bit, but Alec's hands grasp my arms, and he holds me steady. I look up at him through my thick black lashes. Shadows flicker across his face from the light that reaches us from the orb, accenting the little golden flakes in his amber eyes.

"Thanks," I whisper breathlessly. Alec nods.

"No problem," he says. Then he backs away, and the moment vanishes. Alec climbs down to the next platform and helps each of us down, and we repeat the process over and over again until we reach the bottom.

Alaya wastes no time. "This way," she says, striding ahead, waving her hand for us to follow her, hardly waiting for us to catch up, and we scramble after her, neither of us keen on the idea of being lost to the darkness.

We follow Alaya deeper into the cave system. I keep an eye on the path we came from, expecting at any moment to see whatever it was that moved the trees as it barreled toward us. At least for now, I see nothing following us in the darkness, hear no footsteps but ours.

I have no idea what time it is, or how long we spend walking. We trudge through the caves until my feet are blistered and my back and legs are sore.

"What brings you this way normally?" Alec asks Alaya. I've lagged behind a bit, trying to nurse my feet as I continue listening to the caves behind us. The echoes of our footsteps are making me paranoid.

Now that Alec and Alaya are talking, I turn my attention forward to try and hear what they're saying.

Alaya shrugs. "This and that," she says. Typical. But when she looks at him, she smiles before continuing. "I come this way to get my hands on magical items. Potions, elixirs, blessings, sometimes curses, though not as much of those as I used to. The caves seem intimidating, but I've pretty much mapped the mountain out." Alaya taps her forehead to emphasize her point.

"Impressive," Alec says, and his comment makes her smile grow even wider. She reaches up to rub her neck as I glower at them. I actually *could* map these caves.

"Let's stop here for the night," Alaya says. "Lane looks tired back there." She throws a glance back my way. She winks at me, but I scowl in return.

"I'm fine," I say, though my feet are killing me, and I can't wait to take my boots off.

"Are you sure?" Alec says. He looks concerned, which makes me feel just a little bit better.

"Yeah, if you're sure you're good, then we can keep going," Alaya says, and I wave my hands anxiously.

"Wait! Um... well, we could get come rest, if you think it's a good idea," I tell her. If we keep walking without stopping to rest, my feet might fall off. Do these two not feel exhausted from traveling for so long on such hard-packed clay? "That way," I continue. "We can restore our energy for tomorrow. Or today. I'm really not sure what time it is." I look around the cave where we've now stopped.

Alaya nods slowly, knowingly, a smug little smile creeping onto her face.

"No problem," she says, setting her bag down and folding her legs beneath her, already getting comfortable on the hard ground.

Alec and Alaya busy themselves talking quietly together. Although I do my best to keep my attention off of them, I can't help looking at them often. I work to make myself a bed for the night as Alaya pulls out various magical items from her bag, and my curiosity gets the best of me. I have spent my entire life being told that magic wasn't real. If Alaya is willing to share some of the knowledge she's gained, I just have to learn.

I sit beside her on the ground as she sifts through her belongings, pulling out all sorts of trinkets and bottles. I try not to ask too many questions, but the excitement that bubbles up within me makes my queries difficult to contain for long, and Alaya gives me vague, one-word answers as she sorts her goods.

She uses another little bottle of liquid to start a fire like she did before, and the entire cave around us fills with light. I don't think I've ever been so happy to see an orange flame in all my life.

Now that we can see clearly, I'm awestricken by the beauty within this dark, damp cave.

Unlike in the caves that led to Marana's lair, which we lit with makeshift torches, with this bright light, I can see tiny, crystal-clear stalactites hanging from the cave's tall ceiling. The clay with the jagged rocks that make up the cave walls sparkles and glitters as the light twinkles off every surface. Somewhere far off, I hear the quietest dripping sound – a low, lazy drip of thick liquid impacting with a larger body of water somewhere within the cave.

When Alaya begins putting her items back into her bag in a more organized fashion, I take the hint that the show is over, and I make my way to my bed, where I pull out the message that Audy delivered at the cave's entrance.

I unroll the parchment, eager to read what Zaid has to say this time.

Dearest Lane,

I don't want you to take this the wrong way, but reading your last letter, learning that your bond with Alec is broken... I have to tell you... feel relieved.

I'm grateful that you've earned back a layer of safety not having that connection with him, and I'm happy for you to have finally ridden yourself of those pesky mysterious injuries. I feel your travels will be much less risky now.

I'd be lying if I said that a part of my relief isn't due to the fact that I might have a chance with you now. When you were bound to Alec, it felt like the two of you had your own little world... something I couldn't possibly contest with.

Now, I hope you can view me as an option for you.

I understand your need for answers. You're naturally curious, and this bond is something you've dealt with for your entire life, even if you didn't know that it was the cause for all those injuries. Take your time.

I look forward to reading more about what you learn, and about this new friend of yours.

I have to pause in my reading at the mention of my new "friend" and peer up at Alaya, who laughs at something Alec has said and puts her hand on his shoulder. I glare in her direction, but to the two of them, hardly aware of my existence at the moment, so I turn back to my letter.

Lilah is doing some amazing things here. I know she wrote to you before about the letter she received from the Council. We've gotten word from your mamman, and she should be home in another week or so. She told Lilah that when she returns she will accompany her to the Keep to begin her lessons.

Big things are happening! Your pappan is healthy and is doing well. He's very excited to see your mamman again. His new hires are working well, but we all anxiously await your return.

No one leads our team as well as you do.

As for me... I'm doing well. I'm working closely with your pappan on our deliveries, and I've just passed my final examination for my studies.

I've written the Council and requested an audience to discuss how I might be of use to them. I hope they allow me the honor of joining them in some capacity. I feel with the experience I gained watching you work that I could be an excellent trade mediator for them, if they'll have me.

I miss you, Lane. Please keep writing to me. It's incredible that you now have the means to do so anytime. I

I reread the letter several times over, soaking in the words. It's wonderful to hear that everyone is doing so well, and it's incredible to me that his words carry his voice with them, that I can almost hear him say the words as I read them.

I have to read the paragraph where he writes about my bond with Alec extra carefully, and even then, I have a hard time believing I truly understand its meaning.

Zaid wants to be with me. He told me before that he had feelings for me, and of course I had eyes for him since long before I ever met Alec, but to read that he feels like he has a chance to be with me… that's something else entirely.

"What have you got there?" asks Alec, standing behind me and peering over my shoulder.

"Oh!" I exclaim, whipping around and looking up at him as I smash the letter against my chest, crinkling the parchment. Judging by the look on Alec's face, it seems I hid the letter too late. How much did he read?

My face burns, and I wish I could disappear into thin air, still clutching the parchment to my chest.

Despite the bright firelight that illuminates the cave around us, Alec's eyes darken, and his jaw sets.

"What is that?" Alec asks. As I move to put the letter in my pocket, Alec's nimble hands reach down and pluck the letter from my grasp.

"Alec, what are you doing?" I say, jumping to get the letter back. "Give that back!" Alec stands about a foot taller than me, and he simply holds the letter out of my reach. He extends his arm to keep me away from him as he begins to read. His eyes dart back and forth quickly across the page, and he grinds his teeth as he reads.

When he's finished reading, he holds the letter out without a word. Instead, he just stares at me, fuming. I've never seen him look so angry. Honestly, I don't think I've ever seen him look angry at all.

"Lane, what did I just read?" Alec asks, as if somehow my answer will contradict his understanding.

From the corner of my eye, I see Alaya retreat, sneaking away from the campsite and into one of the side tunnels, taking her ball of light with her. Good. She doesn't need to hear any of this. It's none of her business.

"Alec," I start, voice low, hands out, as if he's a frightened animal I'm trying to calm.

"Are you in love with him?" Alec asks. His frown creases the center of his forehead with a sharp line, his movements jagged.

"What?" I ask. "That's absurd. Alec, it's just—"

"Is it?" he snaps. "He seems pretty adamant that you two should be together. I knew he was interested. Anyone with half a brain could see that. But this? Now that our bond is broken, you're just going to Zaid? As if what we have is nothing to you?"

My entire face feels as if it's been set aflame.

"Hold on a minute, Alec. What do you mean? Now that our bond is broken? As if what we have is nothing? We haven't had even a moment to talk. How do we even know what this is?" I gesture between the two of us, flinging my hands about.

I search for the right words, but I'm so overwhelmed with my conflicting emotions that I don't know what more I can say.

Alec rolls his eyes and scoffs. "Right."

He turns to walk away from me, letting the letter fall from his grasp and flutter to the hard packed earth at our feet.

I step forward, reaching out to grab his arm.

"Alec, wait," I plead, but he shakes me off.

"You go ahead and figure out what you think this is. Let me know when you've got it sorted, if I'm still interested."

Alec's words strike me like a punch in the gut, and his tone is callous and cold.

As he walks away, fury bubbles up within me, and I call out, "That's exactly the problem! We're supposed to figure this out together, but we can't even stay in the same area, let alone get a quiet moment to ourselves! I can't figure out what we are on my own, you know. Not when I can hardly speak with you!"

I know my shouting echoes through the caves around us, and that it's very unlikely that Alaya missed any of what I've just said. I'm so upset that my body trembles.

As Alec storms out of view, my legs give way beneath me as I fall to the ground and begin to sob.

13

I want to chase after Alec. I want to scream at him and throw things and get him to sit down with me long enough that we can talk things through. I am completely mortified that Alec read my letter from Zaid, but I'm also furious. I can't believe he's acting as if I've done some horrible thing when I haven't even replied to Zaid about my feelings or said anything romantic in nature. Alec and I haven't had a single moment to decide what this is between us, and he's been flirting up a storm with Alaya since they met! Ridiculous.

Still, I can't get that look on his face out of my mind. Every time I recall the way he looked at me, the anger in his eyes, my heart aches.

I know he and Alaya are probably together right now. I know – thanks to our broken bond – that there's no way for me to tell how he's feeling or what he's doing, but I know from the look in his eyes that Zaid's letter hurt him.

I sigh and wipe the tears from my cheeks.

I will fix this. Somehow. I resolve to talk with Alec and see what we can do to remedy this mess. I'll try to get a moment alone with him soon. The sooner the better.

I want to wait to send my reply to Zaid until after Alec and I have talked, but there's so much I want to say, so much I want to know. I want to tell him about these caves. About the things I've been adding to my maps. I want to ask him about Lilah and the rest of my family. My mamman should be arriving home any day, and I can't wait to hear how her journey was.

In the light of the flickering flame, I write a draft, leaving personal details out. I don't mention Alec, or me, or Alaya. I hold onto the message, deciding that I won't send it until Alec and I have worked this out.

When I've tucked my message into the small pocket sewn into the lining of my satchel, Alec and Alaya are still nowhere to be found.

Part of me worries that they've gotten lost. After all, that's what these caves are known for. I'm sure they're fine; Alec is likely just blowing off some steam, and Alaya... well, she probably wants to steer clear of all this drama, anyway.

I can't say that I blame them.

For a while, I work on my maps, filling in information about these caves.

Thanks to the fact that we traveled the edge of the forest to get here, I have a pretty good idea of our location, and I mark that down, drawing in a cave's entrance. I make note of what I've learned about the caves since I last wrote about them. I write about the clay. The legends. The sparkle, and the multiple layers within.

I also start a separate journal on some loose parchment detailing all of the things I've learned about magic. I start with:

Magic can bind two people, physically and emotionally.

I go on to write about the fish in Murkwater lake, the elixirs and flames and other magical items that Alaya has revealed to us since we met her. If I ever doubted her ability to find us answers, I don't doubt that now, though her motives are still in question.

After a while longer, I lie down to try and get some sleep. I'm not sure when we'll start walking again, but all this emotional turmoil has left me feeling hollow and exhausted.

But I can't sleep.

That little voice that told me Alec and Alaya might have gotten lost is now a nagging thought that won't allow me to turn my attention to anything else. I stand and scoop up one of my arrows, wrapping the end with a bit of torn sock and dipping it into the fire to make a torch. I hate to waste an arrow, but this cave system has no trees or bushes, and without Alaya's magical items, I'm certain I'll get lost in this place if I don't have some good light to see by.

I take the light my torch provides me and exit our campsite in the direction Alec went.

Every step I take brings another nagging thought.

Would Alec abandon this quest if he thought I was no longer interested? He's tried to ditch me before, back when we first met. Who's to say he wouldn't do that again, if he thought there was no longer any benefit to him finding answers?

I hope he's alright. If he and Alaya get lost in the caves, I'm sure to perish in here as well. Alaya says she knows the caves well enough to get us all to the other side, so she wouldn't get lost, likely. At least, not if she's as good as she claims to be, and so far, I can't see any reason for her to lie about knowing this cave system so well.

All these worries subside when I finally find them. I've only wandered a few minutes down the main pathway, listening to my own footsteps echo softly off the cave walls when I hear hushed voices. Alec's is the first voice I hear. He's saying something I can't quite make out, but by the sound of it, he's still upset. As I turn the corner, hope fills me now that I know he's safe, and I'm fueled a new urgency to speak with him. Perhaps I can ask if he'll be willing to step away for a moment, and then—

And then I see them, sitting close together on the floor of the cave, just inside a little pocket area tucked off the main path. Alaya has her arms around Alec's neck, and he leans in, burying his face in her chest.

I nearly drop my torch as my body is filled with a white-hot electricity I've never felt before. I freeze. Half of me wants to shout at them, break them apart, while the other half screams at me to turn and run away as fast as I can before they notice me. How have they not noticed me?

But it's clear they're having their own little moment, and Alec is much too preoccupied with his entire face covered.

It's only when Alaya looks up and meets my gaze with her own, knowing smile stretching across her face, that I find myself able to move again. I shake my head and turn, willing my wobbly legs to carry me back to our campsite.

I don't know if Alec noticed me when I turned around. I don't know if that even matters.

When I get back to our camp, I thrust my arrow into the fire, sending crimson and gold embers pluming up into the air around me, and I half-notice as the embers and smoke flutter up through a small crevasse in the cave's ceiling.

I snatch up my bag, plop myself down on my makeshift bed, and rip up the letter I drafted earlier. Instead, driven by anger and confusion, I write:

The letter isn't outright romantic, but it feels good to get the words on the page, and it feels incredible to spite Alec. From what I saw, he's finding plenty of comfort elsewhere, anyway.

I roll up the message and blow on the whistle Alaya let me borrow. I'm sure that Alec and Alaya hear the sound, but it doesn't matter. They're not going to stop me. Within minutes, Audy comes flapping through the caves and finds his way to me. He lands on my shoulder, but he seems nervous and doesn't sit still for long. I doubt he enjoys being so deep underground, so I attach my letter to his talon as quickly as I can and stroke his belly feathers, trying to give him what little comfort I can.

"Get this to him safely," I plead. "Thank you, little friend."

As I send the beautiful bird on his way, the ground trembles at my feet, sending tiny bits of jagged rock falling into our campsite. My heart pounds as I sit as still as possible, waiting to see what happens next, but when nothing does, I lie down, close my eyes, and fall asleep wondering if these kinds of tremors happen often so deep within the mountains.

I don't know how long I sleep for. I don't know much of anything when I wake, except that Alec and Alaya are back, and the moment I open my eyes, she's laughing at something he's said, and he smiles at her. The same warm smile he's given me countless times.

My insides burn seeing the two of them together.

I grind my teeth and pack up my things without a word. I don't want to spend all day angry about what happened, especially since neither of them has yet acknowledged the fact that I caught them cuddling right after Alec got angry with me for receiving my letter from Zaid.

When I'm all packed, I dig through one of Alec's bags and find myself something to eat.

"Are you two going to flirt all day, or should we actually try to make some progress getting out of these Fates forsaken caves?" I ask through clenched teeth.

Alec and Alaya both raise their eyebrows at me, but they don't respond. Instead, they just pack up their things, stamp out the remainder of our little fire, and they lead the way. I want to walk ahead of them to get some space, but I have no idea where I'm going, so I lag behind just far enough that I can still see them clearly, while also giving myself as much space as I can.

All day, my thoughts consume me. I run through my brief conversation with Alec, how hopeful I felt when I decided I'd finally talk to him, and the complete betrayal I experienced when

I saw them together like that. Perhaps this is how Alec felt reading that letter from Zaid.

I can't seem to get Alaya's little smile out of my head. It's clear she saw me: She looked right at me. Why hasn't she said anything?

When we break for lunch, I sit back against the cave wall, catching Alec's gaze as he stares at me from across the way. I avert my eyes and glare at my boots.

It's only when Alaya sits beside me that I stand up, and it takes far too much effort for me to make eye contact with her. I don't want to look at her. She knows things are complicated between Alec and me. I can't help feeling as if she took advantage of the whole situation.

"What?" I snap at her. "Are you going to stare at me all day, or do you have something you'd like to say?"

Alaya only laughs, though there's little humor in the sound.

"Fates, you're feisty," she says, then she lowers her voice. "Listen, I wanted to talk to you about last night. I wanted to address it yesterday, but you were already asleep by the time we got back. I know you said things are confusing to you right now. I didn't mean to cause any trouble."

"Right," I say bitterly, folding my arms.

Alaya raises her hands, palms up. Alec notices us talking and turns to pack up the rest of his lunch, allowing us some privacy.

"Listen kid," Alaya says. "Alec came to me. He clearly needs some time away from you, and... well, it seems like we have a bit of a spark between us. I'm not saying I want to steal him from you. Fates know I don't want to get tangled up in all your drama. But if you two are going to be fighting, I'd like to be the one to comfort him. If you're exploring your options, it's only fair that he gets to do the same, right?"

My jaw drops. I can't believe any of this, especially not that last comment. This whole thing was her idea to begin with.

I don't know what to say. I want to scream at her for her role in all this, but all that comes out is, "Are you serious?"

Alaya shrugs one shoulder casually. "Well, yeah. I won't chase him down or throw myself at him by any means, but if he comes to me, I'll be there. What do you say?" When I don't say anything, Alaya sighs. I hope that sigh means that she's taken the hint and she'll leave it all alone, but then she speaks again. "Just think on it. I don't want him to be in any unnecessary pain while you're figuring out what you want."

Now my insides are boiling. I whip around to look at her, but she's already walking away with that smooth, confident stride that says she couldn't care less what I have to say about anything she's just mentioned.

But the moment she joins Alec again, I realize one thing she said makes perfect sense to me.

I need to figure out what I want.

14

As we travel onward a later the next day, Alaya says we're getting close to the other side of the mountain, and that we should find our exit soon. The promise fills me with hope. I don't think I could take much more being stuck in such a tight, closed in space with these two. Not after what I saw, and especially not after what Alaya told me.

Things are tense, and by the time we're ready to settle down again and get some rest, the three of us have been so quiet and awkward that I can feel the tension in my muscles. I've just finished my dinner in the awkward silence when Alaya scoots closer to the fire and wipes her mouth on the back of her hand.

"I have an idea," she says, swallowing the rest of her food.

I roll my eyes and mutter, "I think I'll do without any more of your ideas, thanks."

Alaya's silver-blue eyes are piercing as she shares her idea regardless.

"I think we all need to loosen up. You guys are in an awkward situation. You have some drama. So what? I have something that will help you let all that go for tonight," she says, mischievous smile pulling at the corners of her red lips.

I don't think she could do much to help lighten the situation, but I do perk up at the idea that there may be something in her bag that could help me let all of this go. All this drama and fighting has gotten me so wound up that my neck and shoulders are in knots, and resting every night on hard-packed clay isn't helping.

"Lane isn't interested in letting things go," Alec grumbles.

I take a quick peek at Alec, who stares into the fire with an intense focus, his mouth curled into a snarl.

I straighten my back and raise my chin. This mercenary doesn't get to decide what I am or am not interested in.

"Whatever it is," I start. I know this is likely a bad idea. I know that trusting the woman may only hurt me in the end. After all, she's already made a mess of things by encouraging me to respond to Zaid and then expressing her interest in Alec. But that damage is done, and right now, I need to get out of my head. Alec's decision to speak for me gives me all the motivation I need to prove him wrong. "I'm game."

I expect Alaya to offer me a drink of ale or something. Fates know that Alec has his fair share – though now that I think about it, I haven't seen him take a drink since we left Helna with Alaya. But when Alaya reaches into her bag, she doesn't pull out a flask or even a bottled elixir. Instead, she holds in her hands one of the dried fish she caught on Murkwater lake.

The fish is split from mouth to tailfin, and I scrunch my nose at the sight of its dried eyes open wide and staring at me.

"What do you intend to do with that?" I ask.

Alaya's smile curls into a grin.

"Eat it, of course."

I try not to show my surprise. She's already told us that the fish have hallucinogenic properties when consumed, and that people purchase this fish from her for this purpose.

"That's your big plan for letting loose?" I ask.

"It's no big deal, see?" she says. She tears off a small chunk of meat and puts it in her mouth, chewing for a moment before swallowing and opening her mouth for me to see she's swallowed as she holds both her hands out.

Alec's watching us now, silently spinning his dagger between his fingers.

"If you're afraid to try it..." Alaya says, trailing off as she turns to put the fish back into her bag.

I look at Alec, who huffs as if he knew all along that I wouldn't have the guts to try something like this. The firelight casts long shadows under his eyes.

"Give me that," I snap. I reach out before Alaya can put the fish away and snatch it out of her grasp. Fates, the thing smells, but if Alaya can do this, then so can I. Before she can retort or get it back from me, I sink my teeth into the dried flesh on the outside.

Alec and Alaya wear looks of absolute shock on their faces. Their reactions fill me with a sense of deep satisfaction that makes it a little bit easier to chew the fish – scales and all. The meat is sour and tangy on my tongue, but otherwise, it tastes like fish. Once I've chewed well enough that I'm certain I won't choke on anything, I swallow.

Before I can take another bite, Alaya reaches over and snags the fish out of my fingers.

"Easy there, kid," she states, tone wary. "You do *not* want to eat too much of this stuff."

Oops. Did I eat too much? It's just fish, right? I try not to let the worry that I might have made a mistake show on my face.

Alaya tears a small piece of fish off and holds it up for me to see. Of course. Here I am ripping into it with my bare teeth, and she just tore off a little piece. I should have just followed her lead the first time. Alaya holds the piece out to Alec, who for the first time all day, allows himself a little smile.

"Alright," he says, taking the sliver of fish into his fingers. "If Lane is willing to try this thing out, then I guess I will, too."

Alec makes a sour expression when the fish reaches his tongue, but he forces himself to chew and swallow.

"What now?" I ask. I'm not sure how this is supposed to work. I'm not sure what we're waiting for, or what I'm supposed to be feeling. Right now, I feel fine. I feel the same as I always do. Alec and Alaya must be feeling it though, because they're floating, and their skin is changing colors, shimmering and glowing and glittering like the cave walls.

The fire dances in front of us, and as I look into it, the edges of my vision pulse with black and red and yellow.

"Lane?" someone asks, though I'm so mesmerized by the fire that I can't tell whose voice it is, if it's someone I know at all.

"I don't know what I'm waiting for," I say. At least, I think I say it out loud. I'm not entirely sure, because I can feel my lips moving and I can hear the sound of the words, but I have a hard time making a connection between the two phenomena.

The fire burns brighter, and little flecks of various colors come jumping out of it, fluttering slowly through the air. I lean forward. Is that something inside the light? Where did this light even come from? It looks like there are people in there. The light is so warm, so bright, and as I lean forward, I find myself slowly falling through a tunnel of pure white light. I float into a room I can't recognize, and bright colors glare all around me, drawing my attention in a million different directions.

Though all the colors are too bright, too distracting for me to catch any details, I can just make out the white silhouettes of seven tall beings. I can't see their faces, but I can feel their eyes on me, and I'm filled with such awe that I think I begin to cry.

"Who are you?" I ask the beings. Somehow, I know they couldn't possibly be human. They emanate an ancient power. "You're so beautiful," I find myself saying. I almost feel embarrassed saying these words to such incredible beings. Surely, they already know how glorious they are. But I'm filled with such love and acceptance that as soon as I register that embarrassed feeling, it's already gone.

One of the beings reaches toward me, pressing warmth into my chest, right into my heart. At the touch of this being, I see in my mind's eye the silhouette of two people in love, feel the connection they have. I smile at the seven floating around me, but then their light starts to fade, and all those colors blend together, swirling and fading until they finally disappear, leaving me in the darkness.

I must have been dreaming. Though I don't remember falling asleep, when I open my eyes, I find myself lying on my back staring up at the stalactites that cover the cave's ceiling. My body is covered in a cold sweat, and my chest aches.

I start to sit up, but the world turns around me, and I have to lean back on my elbows and squeeze my eyes shut to slow the spinning.

"Woah," I say. When the spinning has subsided, I risk opening my eyes again. I sit up more slowly and bring a clammy hand to my forehead. It takes me a moment for my eyes to focus well enough for me to see anything clearly. When I can finally see, I find Alec and Alaya standing over me, staring with their mouths agape. "Did I fall asleep?" I ask. I must have. Does Alec look worried? When the two don't respond, I add, "You were right, Alaya. When you say this stuff will help you let go, you really mean it. I don't think I thought about anything that whole time. At least... I can't remember thinking about anything."

Alaya swallows loudly and opens her mouth. She closes it, then opens it again.

"I've never seen anyone survive eating that much before. Lane, that was incredible. What was it like?" she asks.

"What do you mean?" I ask. "You were right there. Didn't you experience the same thing? It was only a few minutes..."

Alec puts his hand on my shoulder. My body warms at his touch, and although I know I should still be bothered by everything between us, I lean into him, reveling in the sensation. My brain is still foggy, and any reservations I have about him or Alaya are far from my mind. All I feel is the warmth of Alec's hand on me and the echo of the touch of that being on my heart.

"Lane," Alec says, his tone cautious. "You were unconscious for hours."

I find myself frowning deeply, and my forehead tingles. How could I have been out for hours?

"What?" I stretch and work to stand on wobbly legs. The spinning returns, and Alec steadies me with his strong hands. I allow myself to relax against him and close my eyes. I could stay here all day, but I shake my head and focus again on standing up straight.

"Who did you see?" he asks. If he's still upset about my letters from Zaid, nothing shows in his tone.

"What do you mean?" I reply.

"You kept talking to someone," Alaya says.

"You didn't see them, too?" I ask the two of them. Alec shakes his head.

"We only ate enough to have the color trip," Alaya says, matter-of-factly. "Nobody I know has eaten as much as you ate in one sitting. I honestly have no idea what you experienced."

I raise my eyebrows. My forehead feels strange and stiff. I tell them about the bright colors I saw, and the tunnel of light, and the breathtaking beings. I don't tell them about how the one touched me, though. That bit was so lovely, I'd like to keep it for myself.

Alaya is rendered speechless, and her face is frozen in an expression that spells out genuine surprise.

"Amazing," she whispers. "I can't wait until we get you to Raonni. She's going to have a field day with you, my dear." She reaches over to pinch my cheeks.

I still feel so foggy, as if all of this is a dream.

"I think I need to walk this off," I tell them.

"Here," Alec says, linking his arm through mine and putting it around my waist. "I'll walk with you. I don't think you're steady enough to go by yourself."

Alaya nods at the two of us. "I'm going to write this all down." She looks at me one more time before whispering again, "Amazing."

Alec takes Alaya's little light orb and shakes it up. As it glows brighter, it takes every bit of willpower I have to focus on where I'm stepping instead of looking directly into the light. I want to see those beings again. I want to feel their presence. They felt... magical.

"Thank you for..." I trail off, all of my attention turning to the ground as I stumble a little bit. Alec secures his grip around my waist. "For coming with me. But really, I don't need any help," I tell him.

Clearly a lie.

Alec only nods. If he's still angry with me, he's doing a good job hiding it, or at least he's extra focused on holding me upright as we walk further into the caves. Alec keeps looking back over his shoulder.

"What are you doing?" I ask him.

"Trying to keep an eye on the campfire. I don't want us to wander too far from that light and get stuck down here for all eternity," he replies.

Still feeling fuzzy, I open my mouth and share the first thought that comes to my mind before I can think better of it.

"I wouldn't mind spending eternity down here with you," I say. The idea warms my chest, and I smile up at him. He clenches his jaw and stares straight ahead. Okay... he might still be angry with me after all.

Once we're out of sight of our little camp – but close enough that we can still see the flickering light of the fire bounce off the cave walls in that direction, I pull away from Alec for a moment.

"Are you alright?" he asks, reaching out to help me regain my balance, but I raise my hands to show him I'm steady enough.

"I think I can do this on my own, now," I tell him. I'm still a little wobbly, but standing and walking around has helped me feel much better. I stretch my arms and raise my knees, trying to get my blood flow to chase the numb feeling away.

Alec watches me move my limbs, and when I stop, he reaches out and takes my hand gently in his.

"Lane," he starts. The softness in his tone has me looking up at him, and when I meet his gaze, his eyes are swimming with sincerity.

"Yes?" I ask.

Alec's thumb traces an arch over the top of my hand, sending shivers through my body.

"I wanted to apologize for getting so upset the other night. I promise you that's not how I intended for things to go. That's not how I should have responded."

My brow furrows as I study his face.

"How do you wish you'd have reacted?" I ask warily. I'm not sure I want to know the answer to this question.

Alec's grip on my hand tightens slightly, and he pulls me closer to him, wrapping his arm around my waist again. This time, he holds me close against him because he wants me close, not to hold me steady. His face is so open and genuine, and I lose myself enough in his gaze that it takes a little extra effort to focus on his words.

"Well," he begins, licking his lips. The corners of his mouth turn up into a smile. "I would like to have told you that I'm not afraid of a little competition. I would like to have told you that I'm also in this, and I don't think our bond breaking gives Zaid any more of a shot with you."

He's holding me so close now that I can feel his breath on my face as his words wash over me, setting my stomach wild with butterflies.

I raise my eyebrows at him, refusing to pull away. "Is that right?" I ask.

Alec's smile breaks into a grin. He's got both arms around me now, and my hands rest against the firm muscles of his chest.

"Absolutely," he says.

This is good. It feels right. It feels safe, and familiar, and...

Now I do pull back just a little bit, giving myself enough space to look at him directly. "Alec, there's still so much we haven't talked about. Honestly, I wouldn't even know where to begin..."

But Alec holds my gaze with an intense sincerity.

"I know. I know, and I'm sorry. It's been hard for me too. But what about this? What about we start with this, right here?" Alec gestures to our close proximity. "I promise you we'll talk, and we'll keep talking as you suggested before. But for now, I'd really like to show you that I'm still in this, just as much as I was before."

"What do you mean? Show me—"

Alec bends to close the remaining distance between us as he places his lips against mine, and I instantly relax. Fates, how I've missed him. This kiss is nothing like what I experienced when he kissed me back at the inn in Helna. This is much more like what we've always had, what we experienced with our bond between us.

He dips his head lower to better fit his mouth to mine. The taste of his lips is sweet and makes every part of me sing with how badly I've missed him. My arms stretch up to wrap around his neck, and he pulls me tightly against him.

The two of us are caught up in a whirlwind of emotion and sensation, and all I can think about is how good this is. For a moment, what I feel with him is so similar to what I experienced when we had our bond that I'm not certain it's actually gone. All I can feel is Alec.

I must still be feeling some effects of the fish, though, because each time I close my eyes to deepen our kisses, the same flashes of color from my dream spark across my eyelids, and I can't rid myself of the image of those wondrous beings of light.

15

Alec and I stand in each other's embrace for quite some time, neither of us saying anything. I don't want things to get more complicated than they already are, and I don't want us to go back to being frustrated with each other. So, for now, I just smile up at him, adjusting so I can lean my head against his chest. I wrap my arms around his torso, and he breathes a heavy sigh.

It isn't long, however, before I'm reminded of how things have gotten between the two of us and our escort. I know we can't stay in this blissful silence forever.

I look up at him again, kicking myself for ruining this perfect moment, but I have to ask...

"What about Alaya?"

"What about Alaya?" he repeats, resting his chin on the top of my head.

"Well... do you care for her? If you do, that's something we're going to need to figure out, isn't it?"

"I suppose so," Alec says, crouching down to plant little kisses along my jawline. I'm not sure if he's saying he supposes he has feelings for her or if he supposes we will have to figure things out. "Isn't that something we can discuss later?" he asks.

I want to lean into him and let everything else fade away, but if I do that, we're going to be right back to the trouble we've been in when we come back to reality. So instead of melting against his touch, I pull away.

"No, Alec. This is why things have been so difficult between us. We need to talk. Alaya was the person who told me I should explore all my options if things between you and I were so complicated. She also *just* told me that she intends to be the one to comfort you if you're in need of... company," I tell him. My intention is to sound calm and steady, but most of this comes out in one rushed breath.

Alec's eyebrows shoot up on his forehead, and he taps his chin with his index finger.

"Is that so?" he asks, a smirk playing at his lips.

I roll my eyes. "Easy," I warn him.

Alec smiles and reaches his hand out to caress my face, and I have to fight to keep my eyes open against the warm familiarity of his touch.

"Alright, I get it. Now's not the time," Alec remarks. "Does it look like I'm interested in Alaya right now?"

His thumb runs across my bottom lip before he kisses it. My stomach goes wild.

"Mm," is all I can say.

"Well?" he asks before kissing me again, and all thought flees from my mind.

"No," I say finally. "Not right now."

"Exactly," he whispers. "Now, where were we?"

"But wait," I say, and he sighs. I know I'm bothering him. But I just want us to be clear with each other. "I... um... I kind of responded to Zaid's romantic advances. I... basically said, 'why not?' in my reply."

Now it's Alec's turn to pull back and study me. "Why would you do that?"

An embarrassed blush heats my cheeks at my rash response to Zaid's letter.

"Well, Alaya had told me to explore my options, to see if I really wanted to be with you. Then you got so mad at me, and when I went looking for you, I saw you with Alaya..."

This statement gets his attention, and I watch as shame flashes in his eyes.

"Oh," he says quietly.

"Yeah..." I trail off, rubbing my arms. I take a deep breath and let it out, sending some of the tension I've felt lately with it. "I'm sorry, Alec. I feel like I just keep messing everything up. I'm not good at this."

Alec pulls me into a tight embrace, and when he speaks again, he sounds so sure of himself. "Lane, it's alright. I think maybe you should explore things with Zaid."

"What?" I squeak, my heart squeezing in my chest. How could he tell me he wants me one minute only to encourage me to move on the next? He's not making any sense. "What do you mean? Don't you want—"

Alec presses his fingers to my lips, cutting off what's sure to be a long list of questions, halting my downward spiral before it gets out of control.

"Yes," he says. "Of course I want to be with you. I've told you before – I'm sure. But I want you to be sure with me, too. What better way to discover that yourself than finding out that you can't get what you have with me from someone else?"

I narrow my eyes at him. Sometimes, I truly don't understand this mercenary. "You trust that I won't find it with him?"

Now Alec's confident half-smile is back. He presses his forehead against mine, holding my shoulders in his hands, giving them a gentle squeeze.

"I do. There's no way you'll find what you have with me anywhere else. We were bound, Lane. I know things are complicated right now, but you and I were meant to be together. Everything we've been through, everything we've learned... I can't believe it's all for nothing, and I don't believe it all just goes away, either." He sounds so certain.

"Really?" I ask, the question barely a whisper. Alec gives a single, resolute nod.

"Really."

I frown, chewing my bottom lip.

I know I responded to Zaid in the heat of the moment, and the person I was before I fell for Alec would have jumped at the opportunity to be with Zaid in any capacity. And yet, even with things as jumbled as they have been between Alec and me since our bond was severed, I can't see myself doing this.

Alec must recognize my doubt, because he reaches down and intertwines his fingers with mine, leaning close to my ear.

"If you decide you want me without going to Zaid, that's even better. Trust me, I'd rather have you all to myself," he murmurs, and this statement allows me to relax.

At that, the two of us walk back to camp. The numbness has gone from my body now, and I'm able to walk on my own, but

I still lean against Alec, attempting to hold onto the closeness between us for as long as I can.

When we're just out of sight of our camp, I turn to Alec one last time.

"Would you want to know? How things go with Zaid, I mean. If I did, um, talk to him. Would you want to know?" I ask.

Alec nuzzles my nose with his.

"Whatever you want, sweetheart," he says.

Fates. What in Maran is that supposed to mean?

Alaya barely notices we're back. She's still madly scribbling notes into a diary.

Alec squeezes my hand before letting it go, and the two of us wander off to our individual beds, though an invisible string pulls at my heart from his direction.

As it turns out, I didn't rest well when I saw those seven beings, and after everything, I'm beat. I lie down, my head swimming as I run through everything: My vision, if that's what it was that has Alaya so excited, everything from the other night, my response to Zaid, and of course, the part I replay in my mind the most – my moment with Alec.

I press my fingers to my mouth, where I can still feel the weight and warmth of his lips as if he were still kissing me. Running through the experience in my mind draws up the same emotions and sensations, and I feel as if I might melt right through my blanket into the earth. I wonder if he can feel it, too.

I fall asleep trying to remember a time when my life was simple. My mamman was cold and distant. Lilah was my best friend in the whole world. Zaid was the only person I had eyes for, and I never dared to even talk to him about it. I traveled on my regular delivery routes, and my biggest worries were having to bargain with unhappy vendors, dealing with weather delaying our jobs, and running into bandits or forest cats on the road. When I frequently got injuries that I couldn't explain and pretended to take medicine to cure my ailments so my sister wouldn't worry about me.

All of that seems painfully uncomplicated in comparison to my life today, and I'd kill for the kind of clarity I had then.

16

After a while, Alaya wakes me by kicking my quiver beside my head.

"Wake up, kid," she tells me, munching audibly on an apple. "Time to get moving. Today, we'll see the sun again."

I roll over and sit up as Alaya makes her way to Alec's bed to relay the same message. Her auburn hair has been tied into a thick, intricate braid that looks like it would have taken me hours to do. She's dressed in her usual thigh-high boots, tight leggings, and black corset over a dirty white cotton blouse.

I look down at my own clothes, wrinkled from days of traveling and sleeping in them. I dig through my bag for a change of clothes, finding a soft, pale green blouse and my riding trousers.

When Alec's up and turned away to pack up his things, I change into my fresh clothes and pull on my boots.

I can't wait to breathe fresh air again, feel the sun on my skin. It's only been a few days that we've been in the caves that wind through the mountain, but I've almost forgotten what the outside world is like.

Of course, it's Maran I'm thinking of, not the Nameless Country. I've never spent much time thinking about what the other side of the Baskan mountains would look like. In the history lessons taught in Maran's schools when I was growing up, the Nameless Country was always portrayed to be a wasteland where bad people do horrible things to each other. That's all I know about what we're about to get ourselves into. Oh, and apparently, they have magic.

"Alaya," I start as I stamp out our fire.

"What's up?" she asks, striding ahead with purpose as Alec and I rush to catch up with her.

"What's the Nameless Country like?"

"You mean Lithe?" she asks, barely looking back at me. "It's about the most incredible place you'll ever see. If you thought we had variety in Maran, wait until you see what the world is like with magic woven into everyday life. It didn't used to be that way, but in recent years, magic there is something most people use every single day. Magic to make things beautiful. Magic to enhance experiences. Magic to decorate. It's everywhere. And I make a damn fortune selling it in Maran."

"Sounds like a dream," I say wistfully, picking up the pace. Just the thought of having such a place marked on my maps fills me with childlike glee.

I can tell when we're getting close to the cave's exit, because sunlight – beautiful, soft, and warm – filters in at the end of the tunnel. I can't help myself. The moment I see that light, my feet move faster beneath me, and before I know it, I'm racing toward the exit, toward that pure, magnificent sunlight, toward a part of the world I've never known.

When I burst through the cave's exit, I'm rendered completely speechless.

The mouth of the cave opens to reveal a vast, wide field with dirt so gray it almost looks blue. At the edges of the field stands a tall forest with pine trees that also take on a bluish hue, and large, clear-blue crystals jut out from the ground all throughout the field and sparkle dazzlingly in the sunlight.

"It's..." Alec starts, trailing off, standing beside me and taking my hand in his.

"It's the most beautiful thing I've ever seen!" I finish for him. "Absolutely incredible."

A little giggle bubbles up out of my chest, and I clamp my hand over my mouth. Alaya pauses beside us, looking at us with an amused smile on her face. She actually shrugs at the glorious sight before us.

"It's alright," she says, kicking at a crystal with her boot. The crystal breaks beneath the force of her boot. "Stones are pretty, though, once they've been cut and polished. They don't sell for much, but I'll get a copper or two for 'em." She bends to scoop up some broken shards and tucks them into her bag.

I shake my head.

"Is everything about money with you?" I ask her. "Seriously." I gesture to the land around us. "Just look at this place. Look at this!" I shout, picking up one of the shards from the crystal she's just broken, keeping one hand in Alec's grasp. "You can't tell me this doesn't blow your mind. We don't have rocks like this in Maran. Not anywhere outside the mines, at least, and very few people are allowed to enter the mines in the first place."

Alaya rolls her eyes at me as she stands upright again.

"Seen it all before, remember? Things seem to be less exciting when they're not shiny and new. Isn't that right, handsome?" she asks Alec.

"I don't know about that," Alec responds, giving my hand a little squeeze. "I still manage to get excited about things."

Above us, a flock of large birds with huge red and yellow wings flies by overhead. These birds are similar to the parrots and other tropical birds that live along the southern coasts of Maran, but they're much bigger. Their wingspans must be easily ten feet across, and although they're high above us, I can hear the flapping sounds these giant birds make as they travel.

I can't help it. I'm filled with such joy and wonder I forget my solemn nature and begin skipping and dancing across the field, laughing like a maniac. Alec and Alaya follow slowly behind me, and Alaya yells out something about me being careful not to trip over myself.

I ignore her as I dance my way across the open field and into the forest. The trees here are huge blue spruce trees, and many of them have visible nests within their branches for all kinds of birds. The chirping and whistling of birds high above us fills the air, and it's such a relief, being in a different atmosphere than the caves or Darkwood forest.

I love it.

I love all of it.

We take a break around midday to fill our stomachs and rest our feet for a while, but I'm so excited I can hardly eat. We're still in the thick of this gorgeous forest, and I lie on my stomach on the soft, slightly damp earth with my maps sprawled out before me. I sketch images of the blue crystals, mark an approximate location until I can find myself a map somewhere here to compare borders and landmark locations with. I scribble notes about the things we've seen in the short time we've been on this side of the mountains, hoping I can get it all down without forgetting anything.

I don't even realize that the time for our break is over until Alec crouches down beside me to pat my shoulder.

"Alaya says if we don't get moving, she'll leave us behind. We're still a few hours' walk from the town we'll be staying in, and she says we may be able to reach the temple she wants us to visit before night falls, if we hurry," he says apologetically, glancing at my parchment.

"Oh," I say, trying not to show my disappointment too much. If I wasn't so interested in getting those answers we set out for, I might just stay here for all eternity. I gather up my materials and wipe the charcoal dust from my fingers onto my pants as I stand to join my companions, who are already packed and ready to continue.

Just as we're getting ready to move on, Audy flutters in on tired wings. He lands on my shoulder and rubs his little curved beak against my face before allowing me to remove the message that's secured to his talons.

As I look up at Alec, my face already begins to heat with embarrassment. I responded to Zaid's advances in my last letter. Do I want to open this letter and read what he has to say in return? After everything last night, I'm not sure I do. Especially not with Alec and Alaya just standing there staring at me.

Alec makes a small gesture with his chin and gives me an encouraging smile, reminding me of what he said last night.

"Open it," he mouths to me.

I take a deep breath and unroll the parchment, doing my best to focus on the words written there.

<blockquote>
Dearest Lane,

I'm overjoyed to read this. I was worried you might shy away with my last letter. But I truly care for you, and I want to show you how good I can be for you if you allow me to try.

I wish you were here with me. I think about you every day. I'd love to take you in my arms. I'd love to finally kiss you. Do you remember that moment we had back in Helna at the postal service before I left? I think about that often. I think about what I would have liked to do differently. How I would have kissed you properly, like I wanted to. Perhaps when I see you again, I can show you what I mean.

Your family is doing well. Your mamman is home, and everyone seems healthy and so happy to be together again, though they all miss you terribly. Like me, they worry about you.

I think you've really proven yourself here, though. Both of your parents respect your decision to strike out on your own. They only wish for your safe and swift return.

As do I.

Thinking of you,

Zaid
</blockquote>

I don't know what to say. My eyes flit back and forth over the words again as I read through his letter once more, certain I've misread it. If I thought he was being forward before, this is something else entirely. Did he really write about wanting to kiss me? My stomach turns nervously.

I don't know what to think about any of this.

Thankfully, Alaya clears her throat, saving me from my thoughts. She stomps the heel of her boot into the gray-tinted dirt at our feet.

"Any day now," she snaps. "Unless, of course, you'd like to take an hour to think about and draft your reply. Then we'd certainly be happy to continue to wait around for you all day."

I adjust my bag on my shoulder, which sends Audy flapping his wings to keep his balance. I tuck the message safely into my bag. She's right; I'll need to respond later, of course. Now wouldn't be appropriate.

"Someone's grumpy," I whisper to Audy, who chirps brightly in response.

"I heard that," Alaya calls back. "Get moving, or I'll show you grumpy. I'm not missing the opportunity to sleep in a soft warm bed tonight."

As Alaya rushes ahead, taking the lead as the three of us wander through the forest of giant trees, Alec takes my hand in his. Although we've held hands many times before, I'm all too aware of how his hand feels in mine. I feel every callous, every scar. His hands are larger than mine, and his fingers are sturdy, their heat radiating against my skin.

"Judging by your face as you were reading," Alec starts, bumping me with his shoulder. "Zaid says he's still interested. Probably said something overly romantic, too, didn't he?"

My eyebrows shoot up, and I spare him a shocked glance. "How did you know?" I ask.

"Believe it or not," Alec says, that half-smile creeping back onto his face. "I've spent a lot of time studying your facial expressions. I know how you act when things get romantic or overly personal."

"Oh," I say softly, turning my eyes to the ground as my cheeks and ears redden. I'm not sure how to respond to that.

"Change of subject?" Alec asks.

"Please."

"I really liked watching you dance around earlier," he tells me, his smile growing. "You seemed truly happy. Giddy, even. I've never seen you like that before."

"Sorry... I get excited when I learn new things. See new places. The thought of adding *this* place to my maps, when I've never even seen a map of the Nameless Country... well, I got carried away."

Alec swings our hands backward and forward as we walk. "Don't apologize for being excited. I love seeing how you get with your maps, and I loved seeing you so happy. It's a great look for you. If this is how you get seeing new places you've never mapped before, we should go traveling when all this is over."

"Could we?" I ask. Excitement bubbles up inside me at the thought of finding all new places, especially with Alec at my side. Although I'd love to return home, the urge to see the world has me wanting to dance again.

Just then, Alaya freezes on the pathway ahead of us, holding her arm out as a signal for us to stop.

I open my mouth to question her, but I don't need to. I can see what she's worried about.

Probably two hundred feet in front of us stands a huge black bear with jagged gray stripes on its back, face, and legs.

For now, the creature stands perfectly still, but the hair on its back is standing straight up, and its bright orange eyes have locked onto us. I barely notice its eyes, however, because my gaze lingers on four long, razor-sharp looking fangs, dripping with saliva that glistens in the sunlight that shimmers down through the trees.

"That is one big beast," Alec whispers.

Slowly, I reach for my bow, my years of archery experience on the road kicking in.

"Let's not make any sudden movements, okay? Perhaps if we freeze for long enough, it will lose interest," I say. I've now pulled my bow off my back, inching my fingers toward an arrow.

"It won't matter," says Alaya through gritted teeth, her tone low and gruff. "He's seen us, and once a Lithian Araz Bear locks eyes with its prey, it feasts. Always."

Alaya's words make my stomach drop as cold chills swarm my spine.

"What do we do?" I whisper.

The Araz Bear lets a low, hearty hiss out of its mouth and turns its head to me.

"We run," Alaya answers. Before she finishes her statement, Alaya takes off running, spraying dirt and small pebbles behind her as her boots dig into the ground. She leaps into the low boughs of a spruce tree and begins to climb. Alec reaches over and grabs my hand, pulling me in the opposite direction. The Araz Bear looks between us and Alaya for just a moment before deciding to chase after the bigger meal: Us.

As we reach a giant spruce tree, the creature rears up on its hind legs and lets out a roar that could curdle blood.

"What are we doing?" I shout, throwing my bow back where it belongs, painfully aware of the beast that barrels toward us. "Up! Up!" I leap into the tree's branches, ignoring the stinging pain as tiny pine needles scrape against my exposed skin, and I hope that Alec is following close behind me.

I'm about halfway up the tree when I hear him cry out.

"Alec!" I call as I turn, clinging to the branch I hold for support. Near the tree's lowest branches, Alec fights with the bear, dagger in hand. The bear has Alec's belt clamped in its deadly jaws, and it's doing its best to pull Alec from the tree. Alec swings his dagger this way and that, cutting the beast's snout to ribbons, but the creature holds on.

I don't have much time to waste. I lift myself up and wrap my legs around the tree's trunk to stabilize myself. Then, yanking my bow from my back, I draw an arrow and take aim.

I have trouble keeping my aim steady as the bear pulls Alec's body; and Alec uses one hand to ward it off with his knife, his other arm looped over a branch as he tries desperately to keep himself in the tree.

"Come on, Lane!" I chide myself aloud. "Alec, lean in, toward the tree!"

Alec spares me half a glance, and then he leans against the tree's trunk, closing his eyes tightly. I correct my aim and let my arrow fly straight into the Araz Bear's left eye. The arrow lodges itself deep into the bear's skull, and the creature lets out a sickening whine before its jaw goes slack and its body begins to fall backward, but I don't hesitate. I nock and loose two more arrows, and as they plunge into the same space, the bear plummets to the ground, pulling several low-hanging branches down with it.

The impact of the Araz Bear's body hitting the ground is enough to shake the trees and send flocks of birds flying into the sky in every direction.

With the beast slain, the three of us climb down from our places within the trees. Even as I set my feet upon the ground and withdraw my arrows – with some effort – from the bear's massive skull, my heart beats so quickly I'm certain it'll stop at any moment.

"Thanks," Alec says breathlessly, pressing his hand to my cheek before turning to assess the damage done to his belt. "Looks like the Guard's gear certainly lives up to its name," he says.

"Are you alright?" I ask him. As he turns, I see that his belt is torn partway through in a few places, but it did manage to hold up. Thank the Fates.

"I've never seen you use a weapon before," says Alaya, seemingly out of breath as well. "Color me impressed." She bends to yank out one of the bear's teeth, tucking the tooth into an empty vial and slipping it into her bag. I grunt, unsure how to respond, having some difficulty taking my eyes off the giant bear at our feet.

It takes us a few more hours to get through the forest, and the entire time, guilt gnaws at me for taking that bear's life. After all, it wasn't its fault that we crossed its path. Still, if I had to go back and do it again, I wouldn't change anything. Alec's belt was barely hanging on, and I shudder to think about what could have happened if the bear needed to readjust its grip.

When the trees clear away, we find ourselves on the edge of a beautiful little town. The streets are cobbled with large blue crystals that have been rounded and smoothed. The homes – most of them modest little buildings with smooth, tan walls and dark wooden frames – have intricate crystal windows with gorgeous little designs within them.

Though the sun is starting to set, and people are closing their shops for the day, they all wave and smile at us as if we've known them forever.

This kind treatment fills me with joy. I've done my fair share of traveling across the western half of Maran, and I've never been treated like this, let alone on my first time into town. Many places still treat me like an outcast even after years of trading with them, so the kindness we're shown now is in conflict with everything I've learned about the world.

The Women's Council ran away from the patriarchy that ruled this part of the world, intent upon creating something better, more peaceful. Yet here these people are, greeting us as if we're family.

I make a mental note to do my own digging into the history of this place as soon as I can. I'd like to learn the other side of the Women's Council's story.

Alaya still walks with a brisk pace, passing the shops and homes much faster than I'd like.

"Are we looking for an inn?" Alec asks her, jogging ahead of me to catch up with her.

"No. We're going straight to the temple. Raonni will want to meet the two of you right away, and she'll likely give us shelter for the night," Alaya says. Although I lag behind a bit, taking in every bit of the town as I can, I'm able to stay caught up with them enough to hear her clearly.

I'm excited to meet this Raonni character. If she truly has the answers we're looking for, then I can finally put to rest many of the questions I've been asking my entire life.

The temple is a large, ancient looking building made entirely of enormous gray stones. Despite its apparent age, the temple is clean and well cared for. Large crystal windows reach toward the sky between giant gray stone columns to meet at a pointed dome roof.

Alaya knocks on two large white wooden doors with the side of her fist.

A short woman – just taller than I was at twelve years of age – pulls open the doors and gives Alaya a stern look.

The woman's smooth brown skin is decorated with intricate blue tattoos, and her black hair is pulled back into a tight, modest braid beneath a cotton cap, and even in her braid, her hair flows well past her buttocks.

She has the brightest, clearest blue eyes I've ever seen. They almost seem to glow.

As the woman turns and looks at Alec and me, she gives us a warm smile and steps aside.

"Please, come in," she says as she ushers us inside before closing the heavy doors once again. "Alaya mentioned you might be coming."

Inside the temple is even more breathtaking than its exterior. The golden light from the setting sun sparkles in all directions through the crystal windows, sending glimmering blue and green rays of light dancing across every surface.

The floors and walls are all made from the same large stones that make up the exterior, except that every one of them has been smoothed and carved with intricate depictions of people worshipping magical beings.

Just standing in this building makes me feel somehow closer to the Fates, whom I've never really given much thought or respect to. I've never thought they truly existed. Yet here, standing in their temple, I feel their presence as palpably as I feel Alec and Alaya next to me.

I nudge Alec with my elbow. "Are you seeing this?" I ask him. "Have you ever seen any structure so humbling?"

Alec smiles. He's much more widely traveled than I am, so it's very possible that he has seen something like this before.

"No building," he says, brushing some loose hair from my neck, making my cheeks warm. "That's for sure."

The woman turns toward us, and her smile widens.

"Yes," she says, her voice filled with pride. "This temple is a special one. It is said that this was one of the very first temples built to honor the seven Fates. As its caretaker, I do my best to ensure it remains a beautiful and spiritual place. Come, let me make us some tea. I don't get many visitors from your side of the mountains, and I'd love to get to know you better."

We follow this woman through the temple and watch her make her way throughout the entire kitchen systematically. It's only in this moment that I notice the way she tilts her head to listen and feels around for things, and then I realize...

This woman is blind.

I swear she looked right at us when she opened that door.

As she sets the water boiling, she turns her head in my direction, her smile never faltering.

"I can feel you staring," she says, and I avert my eyes, shame burning my face. Before I can say anything, she raises her hands to dismiss my embarrassment. "It's alright; I'm quite used to it. People who see a highly functioning blind person always act the way you are now. I *can* see things, though. Just not the way you do."

Alaya makes her way to one of the many thick, heavy wooden tables in the center of the kitchen. She pulls out a bench and sits down, gesturing with her head for us to follow.

"I had no idea," I say to her, trying to catch up. "What do you mean? What does that look like for you?"

The woman doesn't miss a beat as she turns and rummages through a short cupboard for some snacks.

"Well, have you ever closed your eyes and seen shapes of things you were just looking at in the sunlight? It's a bit like that. I can sense colors and shapes in my mind still, I just don't get clear images like you see."

"That's incredible," I whisper. "Have you always been blind, miss...?" I ask. When Alec sits beside me, I realize that may not be an appropriate thing to ask.

As if she can tell exactly how I'm feeling, the woman laughs kindly.

"Raonni. No, not always. It's only been since I was fifteen, when I first saw the Fates, that I've been without typical sight," she says. She lays out some pieces of shortbread onto a plate and sets it on our table before sitting on the bench across from me.

At the mention of her name, I perk up even more. *This is the woman we're meant to meet! We've finally made it.*

"You've actually seen the Fates?" Alec asks, raising his blond eyebrows. Alaya reaches over and snatches up a piece of shortbread, taking a bite as Raonni answers.

"Yes, I have. Many times, now. They first came to me one night in what everyone told me was only a dream. At first, I could only hear their voices. When I was fifteen – about six months after they first started speaking to me – they appeared in my bedroom one night. They were so bright and magnificent that I lost my sight entirely. Through that loss, however, the Fates have granted me with many other senses and abilities that I can use for good – much better than I could ever use my eyes."

I'm speechless. Up until a few months ago, I'd been told that magic was only the stuff of a child's foolish imagination. I never even considered that the Fates were actual beings that could be seen and heard before.

"I sense your doubts," Raonni says, reaching across the table to place her hand on mine. That single touch sends shockwaves of sensation through me. I feel the earth beneath my feet, smell the scent of rain and grass on a soft summer breeze. I feel electricity coursing through me.

I pull my hand away and cradle it against my chest as if I've been burned.

"What did you do?" I ask her.

Alec stares at me with his amber eyes open wide. From where he's sitting, I must look crazy. Alaya seems to know better, and her piercing gaze just holds on me.

I look back to Raonni, whose hand still rests on the table where it fell when I moved. Her face is expressionless, and her head is cocked slightly to the side as she's listening to something that the rest of us cannot hear.

Finally, she speaks.

"I apologize, Lane," she starts, her voice quiet but firm. I jump. I don't believe we shared our names with this stranger yet. Perhaps Alaya wrote and let her know we were coming. "I should not have touched you without asking. But you have an energy about you that I've sensed in the world for a long time. I think I'd like to talk with you a bit before we proceed. Can you tell me about yourselves? Where you're from? How you met?" she asks, turning her gaze between Alec and me as if she really can see us.

Alec and I share our basic histories.

I tell Raonni that I come from Palandra, a place far southeast from here. I tell her how I grew up being close to my pappan but barely speaking to my mamman. I share how I traveled all the time with my pappan for his work, and I eventually took over his trade route, and I explain that my work took me to Nerine on the day I first saw Alec and felt something unbelievably familiar about him. Sheepishly, I relay how I followed him through the streets to a tavern and watched as he got into a fight with someone at the bar.

Alec draws in a deep breath, calling my attention to him.

"I didn't know any of that," he says. "I didn't know you were in the tavern that night."

A small part of me feels embarrassed about following him that night, but everything that has come from that decision has changed my life. I find it difficult to believe that, in all the time we've spent traveling together, he and I have never talked about that night.

"I was," I tell him, a small smile creeping onto my lips at the memory, which was certainly nothing to smile about when it happened. "I didn't catch a full glimpse of you when I first saw you, but I knew I needed to see you. You felt so familiar to me."

Alec reaches for my hand under the table. He weaves his fingers through mine.

"Come on," Alaya says. "Let's not waste any more of Raonni's time than we have to. She's a busy woman."

So, Alec shares his story.

He tells Raonni that he grew up in Nerine, that he grew up a disappointment to his pappan because he was a sickly baby, so his pappan always viewed him as weak. He shares with us how loving his mamman was, and how desperately he wanted to gain his pappan's approval, so he trained to join the Grand Council Guard. He tells us how, once he was accepted into the guard, his pappan still couldn't love him, and he sent Alec to live on his own. Alec shares how he earned his living as a mercenary, and that he started out in a dark place before he found his moral compass.

I think back to our time in Darkwood forest with Alaya, and the spirits that Alec recognized as people – children – whose lives he is responsible for taking.

Alec continues to describe that he had caught wind of a job that would pay big, and when he investigated, he found that the Council member he would be retrieving was his very own mamman. He had to take the job.

He went to the tavern to kill some time before he was able to leave, and crossed paths with a man whom he had borrowed horses from on his last job.

He had been ambushed by bandits on that job, and he had lost both of the man's horses in the attack. Alec had promised to pay the man back, but the man refused to wait and had decided to take the payment in flesh.

It's interesting to hear the whole story, and I can't believe after all this time I never thought to ask him what he had owed that man money for.

The world spins around me for a moment as I think about all the little coincidences that had to line up at just the right time for us to run into one another the way we did; for us to discover our bond.

Even the rain leading up to our late arrival in Nerine on that first day had played a role in me catching sight of Alec in the market.

Raonni sits back and listens patiently, absorbing all the information we've given her. From the look on her face, it seems as if she's soaking in a whole lot more than what the two of us have shared with her. It feels as if she's picking up our very thoughts.

When neither of us says anything more, Raonni prompts, "And what about this thing that ties you together? Can you tell me about that?"

Every hair my arms and the nape of my neck stands on end. Neither of us mentioned our bond in the information we provided her. I shoot Alaya an inquisitive look. Perhaps she'd prefaced the reason for our visit in her letter, whenever she might have sent it. Alaya simply smirks and shakes her head.

She just knows.

The tea kettle begins to whistle, and Raonni gets up to remove it from the open flame. The whistle drops in pitch before dying down altogether as Raonni pours hot water into four teacups, then she sets four little bags of herbs to steeping before placing the full teacups onto a large silver tray and moving it gracefully to the table.

She takes her seat again. "Please, tell me," she says.

Now I look to Alec. We haven't told Alaya everything, and I'm still not sure I want her to know everything, but Alec lifts his shoulders in a shrug.

It's possible that I'm being a little overprotective of this special bond I've shared with Alec. But if Raonni can help us, that's what we came for, so I decide to let it go. If Alec isn't worried, perhaps I shouldn't be, either.

I tell Raonni that our mammans were friends growing up, and that Alec was ill as a baby, and my mamman couldn't have children of her own. I tell her of the journey our mammans took together – with Alec – so that they could find the witch who could grant their wishes. I tell her that I was in my mamman's womb at the time, though she wouldn't know that until later.

"I suppose that's what bound us together," I say, rubbing the back of my neck. Relaying all this information, thinking about how many little things had to fall into place at just the right time to make this happen, and how long this has been going on is overwhelming. "Since then, Alec and I have felt everything together. Every cut, every bruise, every big emotion. Even though he and I never met, we felt each other's pains for my entire life."

Now Alec tells Raonni about how we ventured to save our mammans when the witch called them to repay their debts. He tells her about how he had killed Marana so I wouldn't have to stay with her after I made a deal to free them all in exchange for my youth.

The memory is still so vivid. I can still see the tears in his eyes as we shared what we thought would be our last embrace. Remembering it all now brings tears to my eyes.

Raonni sits very still as she listens to the tale.

"The moment I pushed my dagger into the witch's heart," Alec says, his eyes foggy with the memory. "I felt an emptiness that made me wish I'd never unsheathed that blade." Now Alec's eyes are on me, and they glisten with tears that refuse to fall. When I sniffle, Alec runs his thumb over the back of my hand. "I couldn't feel you anymore," he tells me, his voice barely above a whisper. "It was like you'd never been there at all."

So, he had felt it.

Hearing from Alec that I'm not the only one who had gone through the pain of losing that link fills me with relief and the sight of those tears in his eyes and the pain in his voice tells me that loss means as much to Alec as it does to me. This is what I've wanted to talk with him about all along. This is what I've been waiting for.

So many complicated emotions swirl about within me, and all I want to do is crumble into Alec's arms and sob, but I'm all too aware of Alaya's presence as she watches us experience this breakthrough. So instead, I squeeze his hand tightly.

If we get nothing else from this journey, if we get no answers as to how we were bound or what we do now, this will be enough.

Raonni takes a deep breath now, drawing our attention back to her as she delicately lifts one of the teacups from the tray.

"That is a big experience. I'm so sorry to hear of the trouble you've been through, and I'm sorry for your loss. Losing something you've had for your entire life... well, that's no small matter." Raonni's face reflects pain as she touches her cheek just below her eyes. "Now, let's focus on your bond. You said your mammans were together, that unbeknownst to them, you two were also together when the witch granted their wishes."

"The same wish," I add. "The witch – Marana, I mean – she seemed to think that was important. I think that has to be what bound us, though I don't think it was intentional. I don't think Marana knew our bond, even until the end."

Alec nods silently as he recalls our time in the witch's den. "She may not have known," Raonni says, taking a quiet sip from her tea. "But I wouldn't go so far as to say it wasn't intentional."

18

Alec, Alaya, and I all lean forward and listen intently as Raonni explains.

"The witch you describe likely did not know that she bound the two of you together. I would be surprised if she even knew that you were in your mamman's womb at the time. Like all magical beings, Marana was once just a regular woman. While we all have some magic within us – a small thread of what still ties us to the Fates – some are able to channel that magic with time and consistent practice.

"Now, as I said, magic is the bit of our souls that is still connected to the Fates, though over time – and as our belief systems have worn away and altered – that connection has significantly weakened. In many, this link has been diminished to the point that the magic can no longer be accessed without deep prayer and study. Through that small connection, the Fates are still able to influence our lives as they wish."

I raise my eyebrows. "Are you trying to tell us that the *Fates* are behind our bond? *Intentionally?*" Raonni nods as I continue. "Why would they want anything to do with us?"

Alec leans so far forward that I think he might fall out of his chair. His elbow presses against mine on the table. "I have to agree with Lane. That sounds absurd. We're just two regular people. Bond aside, I mean. I've met many people in my travels that are far more deserving and better fit for the Fates' attention."

Raonni smiles as if she was expecting our speculation.

"Aah, yes. *You* think so. But the Fates know your spirits better than you do. They've been waiting a long time for the two of you," Raonni says matter-of-factly.

I busy myself grabbing hold of my tea and taking large gulps of it. The bittersweet berry-mint flavor spreads across my tongue and helps somewhat to ease my nerves.

"I'm not sure I understand," I say doubtfully, my eyebrows furrowing on my forehead.

Raonni nods again.

"I know," she says. "That's why I think it would be best if the two of you follow me. I would like to take you somewhere, where you can see what I mean. Please, finish your tea. That will help."

I look down at my tea, which is now almost empty. Did she put something inside it? I didn't even think to question what herbs she steeped. Alec's tea is now finished as well, but Alaya hasn't touched hers. It still sits on the table completely full, though the exposure to open air has cooled it.

Alaya gives me a smile that says she knew exactly what kind of tea this was.

My stomach twists as my nerves return, and I wring my hands out of habit, but I don't feel any real fear. Although I'm anxious about what I just drank and what's about to happen, I feel a strange sense of purpose settle over me. For some reason, I trust this new stranger. She stands and nods at our tea.

Alec and I exchange a glance, and I raise my shoulders. We're already in this; we may as well see where it goes. I down the rest of my drink and stand to follow Raonni out of the room.

Alaya stays, munching on a piece of shortbread with that mischievous smile plastered on her face.

We follow Raonni back into the temple's chapel, with the large crystal windows and the etched stone flooring and walls. Our footsteps echo across the wide space.

Raonni leads us through a long hallway almost to its end, then she stops in front of us and faces the stone wall. She stares straight at it and lifts her hand to press her fingers against the smooth stone.

I'm just about to speak up, to apologize and tell her that I think she's misled us, when her hand finds just the right place in the wall.

She presses her fingertips further into the stone, and with a quiet grinding sound, the wall retreats from her touch and slides over, revealing a hidden doorway.

"How can she trust us with this secret passageway?" I whisper to Alec, who only shakes his head. "She just met us."

"I know I can trust you with this," Raonni says. "Because I've seen you before. Regardless of the choice you make, I know you. I know you will not endanger the sanctity of this temple, or the secrets of this passage."

Raonni gestures for us to enter through the newfound doorway, and when we do, I stare down at a spiral staircase that curls deep underground.

"After you," she says, waving a graceful hand at the stairs.

Alec steps inside first, then I follow, and Raonni comes in last, closing the passageway behind us. I hope we won't be stuck down here. As we venture further underground, I expect to come across the dank smell we encountered in the alleyways and tunnel systems of Helna. However, as we progress deeper into the earth, cool air brushes against my face, carrying with it the scent of freshwater, mud, and grass.

The lighting down here is dim as small, multicolored lanterns hang every few feet on the stone walls that are now much rougher in texture. The lanterns emit red, yellow, purple, green, and blue lights for us to follow.

The longer we walk down here, the stronger the scent of lavender, sage, mint, and mud grows. The smell is incredibly grounding, and as I close my eyes to breathe it all in, I stumble into Alec's back. He turns and steadies me, his lips parting in a soft smile before he lets me go.

Finally, the staircase takes us all the way to the bottom, and before us opens a room with a similar stone and crystal structure as we saw upstairs, except no sunlight enters this sacred space. In the center of the room sits a large, round blue rug with seven golden roses embroidered into it.

On three of the four walls stand tall bookshelves filled with old leather-bound books. On the fourth wall is a fireplace with a fire already flickering within.

"This is where I come to worship and commune," Raonni says as she passes us into the open space. She crosses effortlessly to one of the bookshelves and pulls out three large, colorful cushions from the bottom shelf. Setting them on the rug, she somehow places them so that each of the seven roses is still perfectly visible. "Come. Join me."

I step forward without hesitation, taking the cushion closest to her, facing the fire. Alec sits beside me, and we wait for Raonni to tell us what comes next.

"This place is remarkable," I tell her, eyeing the bookshelves. I wonder how much history sits within this room. I wonder how many maps and tales are tucked away within those old books.

"Thank you," Raonni tells us. "I enjoy it here. It's much less distracting. Here, sit like this." She sits down with her legs crossed and gestures for us to follow her lead, and we obey without question. "Now, close your eyes and turn your faces toward the warmth of the fire in the hearth. Listen to the world around us. When you feel yourself begin to relax, allow yourself to go into a dreamlike state. Open your mind and your heart to receiving the touch of the Fates. They will guide you. They will share with you the things I have seen, but keep a hold on my voice, so I can tell you when to return to this plane. Do you both understand?"

I nod, keeping my eyes closed, although I'm skeptical at first. I don't believe in any of this, and it's uncomfortable to find myself in a situation where I'm asked to open my mind and my heart to beings that I've never considered to be real.

And yet, as the light from the fire flickers across my closed eyelids, and the warmth of the flame brushes against my face, I do feel myself starting to relax, and I begin to drift off. Soon enough, I feel as if I'm no longer in this room at all, but instead I visualize myself floating on this little cushion across a vast body of water. I imagine that all around me is a bright, colorful fog, with water stretching out in every direction. The water is calm for the most part, with little waves that lap against my seat.

As I float on my cushion farther into the fog, I notice a bright light. I'm drawn to it immediately, with my slow movement through the water accelerating until I sit before the same seven tall, glorious beings that I saw in my previous vision. As before, they seem to be made of pure light. Although I can't make out any distinct features, I can feel them smiling down on me.

I am filled with a deep and sudden sadness, with a knowledge that somehow their light is fading. I see in my mind's eye images of the world slowly crumbling, the land drying up and becoming infertile. I witness people fighting one another and blood spilling. At last, I see two small children that grow up right before my eyes, turning into the silhouettes of two full grown adults. They stand back-to-back, but they hold tightly to each other's hands, and within their clasped hands is a bright light that trails up each of their linked arms and into their chests.

Finally, I am pulled completely out of my dream state as Raonni's voice says, "Now wake, and return to the room in which we sit. Join your bodies in their physical plane, and we will discuss the information you have been given."

When I'm pulled away from my dream state, I feel the same deep sense of sadness that I felt last time I saw those incredible beings, except this time, I take with me a much greater sense of clarity.

I wake just seconds before Alec does, so I'm able to witness the serene look on his face. His eyes are closed, and a slight smile graces his lips. When he opens his eyes, his face flashes with a look of deep loss, but when his gaze falls on me, he smiles so genuinely it makes my whole body warm.

"What was that?" Alec asks Raonni, and it takes some effort to pull my eyes off of him to see Raonni's response.

She nods slowly and takes a grounding breath. The firelight dances across her face as she speaks, and any doubt I had earlier that she has a direct connection with the Fates has completely vanished.

"That, you two, is why you are here. Long ago, when the Fates created this world, everything was right. People got along. They cared for one another. They looked after one another. When the Fates' power was strong, the people were connected and offered prayers and gifts that kept their beliefs alive. As time passed, most people lost their direct connection to the Fates. They stopped praying as they once had, and they began to send silent prayers – *selfish* prayers – to the Fates instead. They stopped bringing gifts, stopped creating altars. When enough people stopped believing, the Fates' light began to dwindle.

"They've known this was coming for a long time. When the Fates saw what the world was coming to, they drafted a backup plan. A failsafe, so to speak – something that would serve as their last hope. When the time was right, and the world was at its tipping point, two heroes would arise to take their burden."

Alec and I sit very still, completely awestricken by Raonni's tale. As she speaks, the images I saw just moments ago replay so vividly in my mind that I can see them.

"That's you," she continues, and her words send shivers racing through me. "The Fates gave Marana her magic, knowing that she would leave the world she once knew, knowing that Marana would ultimately begin making deals with people to support them. In her own way, Marana was playing Fates. She was taking tributes from people in the form of their lives and happiness, but she was also using her power to grant them temporary access what they most desired.

"The Fates laid out a plan. Marana would eventually help two women with the same goal: To have healthy, happy children. When the time came for Marana to act in this way, the Fates were ready. They watched as she used her magic to grant the women's wishes, and when she did, the Fates weaved the destinies of the women's two children together. One child would live on to be healthy and strong, and the other would be born without complications. Furthermore, these children would be bound for all their lives. They would experience each other's pains, feel each other's strongest emotions."

Raonni pauses for a moment and allows the weight of her words to settle over us like a heavy blanket. The only sound in all the room is the crackling and popping of the charring wood within the hearth.

Our bond was magical.

But it wasn't Marana's magic that bound us, after all. It was the oldest kind of magic there was, and if what Raonni tells us is true, then our bond truly was intentional.

"Why us?" I ask. I know I should sit back and listen to the rest of her tale, but as always, my curiosity gets the best of me. "If the Fates wanted us to be bound, why is it that our bond was severed when Alec killed Marana? If they planned this whole thing out, how could they not have foreseen that Alec would take Marana's life and sever the connection they created?"

Raonni weaves her fingers together.

"One of the many differences between Marana and the Fates is choice. When Marana felt that her power was slipping and her life force was fading, she would call upon the people she had helped, and they had no choice but to go to her, and she would use their youth to sustain her immortality until she ultimately drained them of their lives. The Fates do not work that way – they never have. Perhaps they only meant for the bond you shared to draw you together, to draw you to the place where you were initially bound, so that you would give each other a chance."

"I'm not sure I understand," I mutter, frowning.

"Well, we weren't exactly fond of each other when we met," Alec says, smiling fondly at me. It's true. When Alec and I first met, we could hardly stand each other. He thought I was an obnoxious stick in the mud, and I thought he was a careless fool.

"The Fates are dying, now more quickly than ever before," Raonni says, her voice thick with sadness, her eyes filled with tears. "They want you and Alec to take their place. They want you to save this cracking, fading world before it is too far gone, and the timing is perfect. The world is broken enough – people lost enough – that they will likely be ready to accept new Fates. If you show them how, they will accept you as their leaders and protectors. Only you two can restore the balance of the world, and you must do so together. But ultimately, the choice is yours."

"What do you mean, we must do it together?" I ask. Alec spares me a sidelong glance, but I turn my eyes quickly back to Raonni. The room is beginning to spin, and my vision blurs at the edges. This is all too much.

"Lane," Alec starts, but I press on.

"Raonni, why does it have to be both of us together?"

Raonni leans forward.

"Have you noticed that when the two of you are together, things feel right? Balanced? When you share intimate moments – kisses, for example – have you noticed anything changing? An ability you have, perhaps? The Fates chose you because together you have the power to reshape the world. It must be you both together, but in order for you to make real, lasting change – in order for you to have the impact you will need to make – you must make the choice yourself, and it must be genuine."

I scramble to my feet. My heart beats so fast and so hard I fear it might break.

"I..." I start. I'm struggling to get my mouth to form the words I wish to say. I want to tell Alec what I'm thinking. I want to ask Raonni so many questions, but I can't get my tongue to push any of those vital words out of my mouth. "Sorry," I whisper. "I just... I need a minute." Without another word, I turn and race from the room and back to the stairs we descended.

I hear Alec jump up behind me, but I don't look back. When I reach the top of the stairs, I find the stone that Raonni used to close the passageway behind us, and I press my fingers in as she did earlier. The secret door opens with the same grinding sound, and I rush through it, weaving through the hallways until I find myself at a door that will take me outside.

Maybe fresh air will help.

I turn the brass handle and push the door outward, gasping in the scent of fresh, cool air as I enter what looks like the temple's private garden.

It's beautiful out here, and as I step all the way outside, as the cool air enters my lungs through deep, fast breaths, I look around, working to calm myself.

I step into the garden among evenly trimmed rosebushes and soft hedges with bright, wide purple flowers. Different kinds of flowers weave their way in intricate patterns throughout the entire garden, and I find myself plopping down into a patch of red and black dahlias as I work to slow the pounding of my heart.

My mind is swimming.

I can't believe any of this.

I can't believe that Alec and I have come so far, to a whole new part of the world I never knew anything about. I can't believe we've befriended a temple priestess who has proven she has a real connection with the Fates. I can't believe that I saw the Fates' story for myself, witnessing their intentions for us.

I can't believe that Alec and I were *chosen* for this.

On one hand, it's all starting to make sense: The draw I feel for him beyond his familiarity. It appears as though the feelings I have for him do indeed go deeper than our bond, but I worry that they were never *my* feelings to begin with – that the Fates planted them within me so that I would feel inclined to choose Alec and take their place.

What does that even mean? Take their place? If the Fates are dying, does that mean that *everything* will die?

Raonni said that Alec and I have a choice. That's good, and focusing on that for a moment helps me center myself. When I've slowed the panic, it's replaced with anger.

We have a choice, maybe, but at what cost? Do the Fates have another backup plan in case we choose to forge our own paths? Perhaps this isn't the best way to think about our situation, but right now, I feel manipulated.

I just got used to the idea that some of the big feelings and experiences I've had in my life were not mine, but Alec's. Now I'm learning that every moment we've had together, everything I've felt for Alec was predestined on someone else's terms.

That's a lot to process.

It's not that I *don't* want to be with Alec. I love him. As I think the words, I know them to be true. But is it enough to love him if I know that the love I feel may be forced? Is it even mine to begin with? Can I accept love from him – if he chooses me – if I know that it's not wholly his?

It's at this moment that Alec finds me among the dahlias.

He sits beside me, crossing his legs beneath him without a word. He moves to wrap his arms around me, but when I pull away, he sighs and settles for placing his hand over mine.

Now that my heartbeat has slowed, I realize how cold it is out here. I can see our breath escaping our mouths in little puffs of white steam, and I wonder how all these flowers and shrubs are still alive in this cold.

I look up at Alec, who opens his mouth to say something, but he doesn't speak. Instead, he simply closes his mouth, takes a deep breath, and tries again. As he does, the first snowflakes of the year begin to fall.

"I know you're afraid, and if you need some time, I think I could understand that. But I want you to know where I stand and what I think of all this," Alec says, his tone resolute. "A while ago, before we ever reached Marana's cave, you asked me what we would do if the feelings we had for each other were simply a product of our bond. Do you remember what I told you?"

I nod, wiping a stray, freezing tear from my cheek. "You told me you didn't care if it was just our bond, that it didn't matter. You just wanted to enjoy the journey as it happened."

Alec nods, clenching his jaw. He lets go of my hand and reaches over to grab hold of each of my arms, gently turning me to face him head on.

"I meant that then, and the words still hold true now," he says. His amber eyes look dim in the overcast, grayed light, but they plead with me to understand. Snowflakes fall into his hair, rest on his eyebrows and eyelashes, speckle the long stubble that makes up his beard.

"How can you say that?" I ask him. "Don't you want to fall in love with someone on your terms? Doesn't it bother you that all of *this*," I pause to gesture at the two of us with my shivering hands. "Is someone else's design? I've never believed in fate. I've never wanted to, because the thought of not having control over my own life means that there's *nothing* in this world that we can control, nothing in the world that is truly ours. Doesn't that bother you?"

Alec gives me a sad smile. He reaches up and brushes his cool fingers across my cheek.

"Not even in the slightest. If the Fates brought us together, they made the right choice. Of all the women in the world the Fates could have chosen to pair me with, I'm grateful that it's you. I don't care that my feelings may have been prompted. That doesn't mean they're not real, Lane," Alec whispers.

"How do you know? How can you know anything with all we've just learned? It's too much, Alec. It's all just... too much."

Alec grits his teeth, and he gives my cheek one more soft caress with his thumb before he pulls his hand away, heaving a heavy sigh. He leans forward, pressing his lips against the tip of my nose.

"Then I'll give you some time," he says. He stands up and brushes the snowflakes from his shoulders and thighs. "I'll let you think. But don't stay out here too long, okay? It's getting cold."

He turns to leave, and everything in me yearns to call out after him. I want to race up to him, throw myself right into his warm embrace. I want to forget everything I just learned, or at least try to think of our situation the way he does. But I can't seem to get myself to move. I'm frozen in place, and all I can think about is my conflicting desires. I want my own choice. I want my own feelings. But also... I want Alec.

I'm so terrified that this is all someone else's game we're playing, and I don't want to play anymore.

I watch Alec's boots make prints in the thin layer of snow that settles on the ground as he makes his way back inside. He pauses just outside the door and spares me a final glance.

"Lane," he says, so softly I almost don't hear him. "Do what you need to. Think about it, of course. But please also consider this: You should listen to what your heart has to say. If it makes you happy... if *I* make you happy, then what does it matter if someone else is pulling the strings? We deserve happiness, and if everyone else's happiness comes with it, then isn't that a good thing? Think about the difference we could make."

I want to tell him that not everyone is in the business of saving people, that everyone else's wellbeing shouldn't fall on our shoulders, but he's gone before I can say anything, and I'm left sitting in the snow among the freezing flowers.

19

I sit for a while out here in the cold, picking petals off the flowers that surround me and thinking about what Alec said. Eventually, I know I need to go back inside. If I don't, I'll freeze out here, and they won't find me until spring. Here I'll be, lying in the garden, curled up into myself and still processing what my next step should be.

After a while I do get up, and I make my way back inside.

Once inside, I see that Audy has returned. He perches on Alaya's shoulder and coos lovingly. When he sees me, he flutters over and lifts his leg so I can remove the message attached to it. As he does, Alaya leaves me alone in the empty prayer room to read

Zaid's newest letter, an update because he hasn't heard from me since his last message arrived.

I unroll the message with the weight of everything I've learned today heavy on my heart. My chest feels like it's constricting.

I take a deep, calming breath and begin to read.

> Dearest Lane,
>
> I miss you. How are you doing? By now you've got to be somewhere new, right? What is it like where you are now? Your mamman has been back, and she and Lilah are leaving in two days for Grand Council Keep. Little Lilah is a true prodigy, and if she chooses to join the Council when she is of age, she will be an incredible leader. I can't wait to see the changes she will make.
>
> My studies are going well. I've been accepted for an entry position for trade management in the Council! I will be traveling with your sister and her mamman to the Keep. I am so excited, Lane. With everything you have taught me, I feel like I can really make a difference. Thank you for helping me with my best chance.
>
> I think of you every day. I want nothing more than to see you again. See what you're drawing, listen to you think out your next move. I'd love to hold your hand in mine, wrap my arms around you.
>
> Well, I'd better finish packing. Please, tell me what you've been up to.
>
> Write again soon,
> Zaid

His question about my surroundings and his news of his and Lilah's progress make me feel a little bit better. It takes my mind off of everything momentarily, and I sit down on the stone floor to write him back, pulling out my charcoal and some blank parchment.

Zaid,

Things are amazing over here. Alec and I have made it to the other side of the Baskan mountains. Zaid… this is nothing like I have ever imagined. Magic is real, and people use it here freely. The landscape is vast and blue and gorgeous, and the people seem amazing. They welcomed us right away! How strange is that? I think it's pretty clear we're not from around here, and still people smiled at us and waved as we entered town. I can't wait to tell you about all of this in person, where I can show you my new maps.

It's amazing to read that you and Lilah are doing well. Congratulations to both of you, though I can't say I'm surprised. You're both incredible, and each very capable of achieving your best chance on your own.

I pause in my writing for a moment, reading again the sweet words that he wrote, letting them tangle with the rest of the complicated things I can't seem to wiggle out of. I chew on the end of my charcoal pencil for a moment as I try to decide what to write in response. I'm driven to respond in a romantic way, if for no other reason than I know it's not in the Fates' perfect plan. But I don't want to lead Zaid on out of spite again. That wouldn't be fair to any of us, so I decide simply to write what's on my mind instead.

Thank you for your kind words. All the things you mentioned are things I'm sure would be obnoxious to anyone else. It's sweet that you find those things to look forward to. I've got to be honest with you, Zaid. The thought of you wanting to hold me in your arms… it's all a bit of a shock to me. But it does sound nice. It sounds so uncomplicated and pure that I can find myself drawn to the thought. Especially since those are all things I wanted for so long.

I need to tell you, however, that Alec and I have met a priestess who has shown us the path the Fates have laid out for us. The bond that Alec and I had was part of something much larger. I don't want to get into it too much right now, because it's overwhelming and it makes my head hurt. I'm not sure about any of it. But I want to be honest with you in the name of fairness and tell you that everything is complicated right now. I'm sorry if I can't give you more than that. I hope you understand.

Write again soon. I wish you safe travels and swift return, and have a wonderful time at the Keep.

Best of everything,

Lane

Feeling a little bit better about things having written some of it down, I roll up my message and reattach it to Audy's little talons.

"Thank you, friend," I whisper to him as he spreads his wings and takes off, exiting the building through an open window that lets a frigid draft into the temple.

I find Alaya in the kitchen, sipping something that smells like caramel.

"What is that?" I ask, taking a seat beside her. Alaya regards me with a sideways glance.

"The best caramel bourbon you'll ever taste," she replies, taking another sip. She smacks her red lips together, and they part to make way for a smile.

"Bourbon?" I ask.

"Spirits? Alcohol?" she says with a tone that tells me I should already know this.

At that moment, Alec joins us in the kitchen. He brushes against my arm as he walks around the table.

"Don't mind if I do," he says, sitting beside me, reaching across the table to grab a big wooden cup and grasp the decanter of liquid that rests on the table. Alec pours himself a drink and takes a sip. His amber eyes grow wide, and he makes an excited "mm!" sound as he draws his free hand to his lips.

"What?" I ask.

"That's delicious!" he remarks. "Lane, you must try this. It doesn't taste like spirits at all." I look to Alaya, who raises her cup to me but says nothing.

I hesitate for a moment. I'm all too aware of the tension in my shoulders and neck, the exhaustion I feel from all of our traveling. The weight of learning that the entire fate of the world is somehow on my shoulders, and that the feelings I have for Alec may have never been really mine.

I could use a drink.

More than that, I could use a sweet treat.

"You know what?" I say. "I think I will have some." I reach over and grab a cup, filling it up about halfway. This action gets raised eyebrows from Alec and a smirk from Alaya.

"Good girl," Alaya mutters, returning to her own drink.

"I don't know, Alaya," Alec says, his voice full of surprise. "You don't know Lane that well, but she doesn't drink. I've only seen her drink twice in all the time I've known her, and neither time has gone well."

"Oh well," I say. "Life is about change, right? It's about choice. So here I am." I raise my full cup and disregard the liquid that splashes over the brim. "To choices."

Something sad flashes across Alec's face, but he smiles anyway and raises his own cup. "To choices."

Alaya stares at us for a moment, then she rolls her eyes. "You two are ridiculous. Whatever. To choices."

The three of us clink our cups together and take a drink. The taste of smooth, rich caramel with the tiniest bitter aftertaste spreads across my tongue, and I too find myself closing my eyes to enjoy the drink. The flavor is sensational. The drink tastes like caramel, but it also tastes strangely the way that an old book smells. It tastes like history, like knowledge.

"Oh, that is good!" I say, my face burning as the gulp makes its way down, warming my chest and my stomach as it goes. "The caramel is so strong and smooth! There's very little alcohol taste!"

"I told you!" Alec says.

"I told you," Alaya remarks.

I find myself smiling as I take another big drink. I let the taste of sweet, rich caramel wash over my tongue, deciding to let everything go for now. I won't worry about Zaid. I won't worry about Alec, and I *definitely* won't worry about the Fates. For now, I will enjoy this drink. I will explore this rich culture around me, learn what I can, and I'll go from there. Maybe I should write *that* in my next letter to Zaid.

"Oh!" I say, turning to Alaya. "I meant to ask. Does Audy have any favorite treats?"

"Treats?" she asks. "He's a bird."

I sit forward and place my elbows on the table. "I know that, but I just thought it would be nice to reward him. He's done such an incredible job passing my messages back and forth, and I'd love to get him something nice for his hard work."

Alaya scoffs.

"You're so weird. Well... he likes corn. You could get him some of that, I guess."

I smile, and when I turn back to Alec, he's grinning at me, and this time that smile goes all the way to his eyes, making them sparkle.

"What?" I ask him, but he only shakes his head.

When we finish our drinks, Raonni finds us and offers us some dinner. She suggests that we stay here in the temple for a while, claiming that the Fates would be honored to have such guests under their roof. The thought almost makes me want to leave just to spite them, but I seriously love this building, and a temple is an incredible place to learn about the history of a place.

Alec begins to object, to suggest that we will find an inn or something instead, but I interject.

"We'd love to stay. Thank you."

20

The room I've been invited to stay in is lovely. It's just down the hallway from Alec's room, and I'm not sure where Alaya is staying, or if she's made other arrangements, just that she's not located in the same hallway that we are.

Inside my room I find the same carved stone walls and floors that are found elsewhere throughout the temple, and the room is simply decorated.

A soft bed sits in the center with clean white sheets and a deep maroon comforter. A fire crackles steadily in the hearth beside a single, worn velvet chair.

Heavy maroon curtains drape over the same incredible crystal windows found in the rest of the temple. I've got a chest of drawers with fresh linens and some night clothes within. A bathtub and latrine sit over in one corner, with a small shelf beside them with soaps, towels, and candles supplied.

I unpack my bags into the drawers and draw the curtains back, marveling once again at the incredible workmanship of the windows here, and I open my window to let in the chill from outside. In contrast with the heat of the fire, the cool air is refreshing, calming me as it brushes against my bourbon-warmed cheeks.

On the ground floor below my window stands the temple's garden, now covered in snow. Even frosted over, the garden is beautiful, just like everything else in this temple. Raonni and the others who live here take such good care of the place. Tomorrow, I hope to explore. Tomorrow, I hope to ask Raonni if this temple has a library. But the exhaustion I've felt from our travels and the news of the day urges me to get some rest. I close the window, draw myself a bath, quickly get myself clean, and climb into bed.

Throughout the night, I dream I'm walking through the garden below my window. In the center where I sat earlier among the dahlias, Alec stands waiting for me. He gives me a smile, and I return the smile eagerly. I race toward him, and the two of us collide together, wrapping our arms around one another in a perfect embrace.

Snow falls all around us, and as we cling to one another, the snow begins to melt. The world surrounding us seems to shift and bloom, and when we press our lips together, my entire being is filled with a sense of rightness and purpose that I can't ignore. I lean into him, and as we kiss, the entire world seems to heal.

All through the night, I dream this way. In every dream, the two of us are together. In every dream, I see the world as it could be – happy, safe, and whole – and it's difficult to think about anything else.

When I wake in the morning, I feel just as exhausted as I was before bed, as if I was up all night fighting off those dreams, though each time I think about them, excitement bubbles in my chest. Could Alec and I really have that affect?

But then I realize... that's probably just what the Fates want me to feel. I rub the sleep from my eyes.

It's not fair to say they'll give me a choice and then fill my night with dreams like these.

I throw the comforter and sheets back, climbing out of bed and getting dressed.

I wander the hallways of the temple until I find Raonni in the kitchen, cooking breakfast as easily as if she can see everything in front of her. It's strange how often I forget about her blindness.

"Sleep well?" Raonni asks me. I grunt a wordless response, but I brighten up as I remember my resolution from last night. Today is a study day.

"Raonni, do you have a library here? In the temple, I mean?" I ask, eyes wide and hopeful.

"Of course," she replies, turning to smile at me. Her bright blue eyes glitter as if she loves to learn as I do. She gives me directions, and as I turn to take my leave, she stops me. "If you're going to be studying, you may want to take some breakfast with you." She reaches over and slides a porcelain plate with thick toast and jam in my direction, feeling the edge of the table with her fingertips to ensure she doesn't push the plate too far. "I'll bring you some lunch if I don't see you in a few hours."

I nod.

"Thank you Raonni," I tell her, but I hardly wait for her response. Instead, I grab the plate she's passed my way, already turning to exit the kitchen in search of the library.

I follow the directions she's given me, and after only a couple of wrong turns, I find a wide set of double doors with crystal windows. Peering through the windows reveals walls filled from floor to ceiling with books and scrolls within. I can barely contain the excitement that bubbles up in my chest as I pull the doors open and step into the large room.

The architecture of this room looks much the same as the rest of the temple – same walls, same floors, same big crystal windows. The difference, however, is the wide wooden shelves that take up every bit of free space along the walls, each filled entirely with books and scrolls. A large wooden table stands in the center of the room, encircled by simple, redwood chairs. Atop the table is a stack of maps and a collection of inkwells, and I let out a little squeal.

I haven't used ink in so long. Carrying ink with me as I travel is too impractical, too messy, so I've had to settle with being on the road with my charcoal pencils in my satchel, where I keep my typical writing utensils and my maps.

I step forward as the sight takes my breath away. Where should I start? I turn to my left, choosing the shelf closest to the door, and I begin filtering through the books, looking with great care at each one. Each book has its title etched into the leather on the spine and along the front cover, and I run my fingers over the lettering, imagining how Raonni must feel them.

On this shelf, I find the histories of the Nameless Country, officially named Lithe. I find old maps of this country, and I compare them to the sketches I've made, creating my own, more complete version of the map to add to my collection. As it turns out, Lithe is surrounded by quite a few small islands that follow the same rules and belief systems as the Lithians do.

I spend the day reading all about the Patriarchy that the Women's Council fled from before they settled in Maran. The Patriarchy wasn't intended to be all powerful or all consuming, but over the years, with each new Patriarch that rose to power, that power became the only thing on his mind. The people didn't matter. When the Patriarchy's focus shifted to attempting to gain the power of the Fates, the Fates pulled away almost completely, and that pull shifted the focus for many people, leading to a lack of pure faith that spread across the world like a disease.

At the time the Women's Council broke away from the Patriarchy and formed their own community, sneaking away in the night, the continent was ruled by a Patriarch called Romulus Rathe. He was greedy and corrupt as all the others had been, but he was also ruthless, invading other territories in search of anyone who had a connection to the Fates.

After the Women's Council and their followers got away safely, the rest of the people who remained in Lithe decided to make a change of their own, and this decision led to a full-fledged revolution.

Many people discovered magic within themselves when they willed this rebellion into action, and with it they were able to overthrow the Patriarch and redesign the Patriarchy. The government that Lithe has now allows for all sorts of freedom and choice, starting with the widespread use of magic. People here elect their leaders now much like people in Maran elect our Women's Council members, and much like the Women's Council, if a person has made a significant impact, their heirs are likely to have a place within the Patriarchy if they wish to join.

A detail I find refreshing is that the Lithian government does not exclude men.

I'm so engrossed in what I'm learning, eagerly scribbling notes and sketches, that I barely notice when Alec comes and goes from the library throughout the day. He leaves me little snacks, brings me lunch and tea, which I consume little of.

It's only when the sun has begun to set, and the light dims enough that I have a difficult time reading the materials in front of me that I look at the pile of things that Alec has brought me.

Throughout the day, Alec has carried in sandwiches, tea, small portions of delicious looking desserts, as well as a single red rose, now limp in the stem from its lack of water throughout the day. The rose sits over a note that reads, *Meet me in the garden at dusk for a surprise.*

My heart flutters in my chest.

I peer up at the sky through the large crystal windows. The sun hasn't set yet, but it's close. Have I missed him?

I push back my chair, straightening my papers as I brush them into my satchel. I stack the rest of the books I am reading into a neat pile to return to tomorrow, and I scoop up the rose, which has had all its thorns removed, and exit the library.

I'm almost to the prayer chamber that makes up the main section of the temple when I hear two hushed, hurried voices. I lean closer, certain that these two voices are familiar to me. As I peek into the room I stand just outside of, I see Alaya and Raonni across a desk from one another, each leaning with her palms against the table.

"You can't go back on it now," Raonni says, her tone urgent and scolding, her voice low. "There's far too much at stake."

"I know," Alaya says. She jerks a frustrated hand through her auburn hair. "But I can't do this, Raonni. Not if I'm meant to lead him back to her. *I want him.*" Alaya's voice wavers. I've never heard her voice waver before.

"You're meant to convince him that Lane is the right choice, Alaya," Raonni warns. Her voice is cold and serious.

Alaya grunts.

My eyes widen, and I back away. As I do, my boot scrapes against the stone floor of the hallway. I don't wait to see if they've noticed me. I take off toward the doors that lead into the garden, and I burst through them. I almost fall on my face when I trip over the stone pathway that weaves through the garden, and it's then that I crash into Alec. He catches me with strong hands as I collide with his chest. My heart is pounding, and I look up at him desperately.

"Alec, we need to talk," I tell him. "Alaya is—"

Alec reaches up and presses his warm fingers gently against my lips.

"Let's not worry about anything else right now," he tells me, his voice soft and calming.

"No, but the Fates—" I start again, but once again, he interrupts me.

"I don't want to talk about Alaya, or the Fates, or anything else. I just want you to come with me. There's something I want to show you," he says. He backs away, taking my hand in his as he leads me further into the garden.

"Alec, please. I just overheard Alaya and Raonni talking."

"Nothing they could possibly be talking about is of such consequence to us right now. If there's an issue now, I'm certain it will be here when we come back," he says.

"Alec!" I snap, pulling my hand from his grasp, but he keeps walking forward. "Just let me explain what's going on. Stop walking, will you?" As I catch up with him again, I jump in front of him, blocking his path and forcing him to look at me.

"Lane!" he says. His face flushes, and he grits his teeth. "Seriously?"

"What?" I ask. "You need to know."

But I follow Alec's gaze as it jerks down to my feet, gesturing with a flick of his hand. I've stepped on a picnic blanket that's been laid out over the snow. The blanket contains a bottle of wine and a chocolate cake decorated lavishly with raspberries.

In my attempt to get his attention, I've knocked over the wine, spilling it everywhere, and trampled straight through the cake. I lift my boot and shake it out slowly.

"Oh..." I say. "You did this? For me?" Guilt pangs within me. I should have watched where I was stepping. I feel awful.

Alec clenches his fists. "Fates, Lane. I'm trying, okay? I don't want to talk about anything right now but us. Why do you have to make this so hard? Why does this have to be about Alaya, or the Fates, or anything else? Why does *everything* have to be so difficult with you?"

His words sting, and tears blur my vision. All the urgency I felt before has left me, replaced with a guilty cold that sits like a boulder in my chest.

"I'm sorry, Alec... I—"

Alec shakes his head, letting out a gruff sigh, as if he's trying to force every bit of frustration he feels to leave him in a single breath.

"Just... never mind." Alec's tone is steely, and the disappointment on his face makes my heart ache.

"Alec," I whisper past the lump that forms in my throat.

"Enjoy your cake," he says, face so openly angry I'm surprised he's not steaming in the winter air. "I made it."

At that, he turns and walks away from me, leaving me in the snow for the second time in the last twenty-four hours.

21

What is wrong with me?

I look down at the romantic spread Alec has made for me, at the cake that he baked.

I didn't even know he *could* bake.

This all must have taken him hours, and I've just stepped all over it. If there was ever something that represented our relationship, it would be this moment right here. Alec has created something beautiful for me, and I've ruined it.

I sit down, taking off my boots and shaking the rest of the cake off them.

I work to clean up my mess, thinking about ways I could possibly make this up to him.

Maybe I just need to get away for a bit. I stand, scooping up the bottle with what little wine remains within, and I collect the rest of the mess into the picnic blanket, shaking off the snow. I carry the blanket into the temple's kitchen, where I set it near the table. I bring the rest of the wine up to my room, then I leave the temple behind, venturing into town in search of something I can get for Alec to apologize.

What I initially thought was a little town that surrounds the temple is actually a large, ancient city, with buildings made up of large, gray and cerulean colored stones. The rooftops are all made of petrified logs that have been split down the middle and covered with dark, rich, black clay.

As I wander through the streets in search of a bakery, I smell the scent of perfumes, the ashy, metallic smell of a blacksmith's shop that makes me homesick, but mostly, I smell the thick, fresh scent of pine on the breeze that blows through town. It's only when I'm a few buildings down from the bakery that I finally smell the fresh bread and the sweet aroma of newly baked desserts.

When I open the door and ring the little bell that hangs in the doorway, a woman with hair such a bright blonde color that it looks almost white stands up from behind the counter, setting a pan of muffins on the countertop.

"Good day, my dear," she says. "What brings you in today?"

I smile nervously at her. It's not very often that I enter a shop like this as a customer, and it's even more rare for the employees or business owners to treat me with the kindness this woman has just offered.

"Good day," I respond. "I'm not sure, yet. I think I'm just looking for now. Thank you."

The woman nods and turns to work on rolling a thick bread dough out on the countertop, kneading it with her hands and elbows. I can't help but imagine Lilah in a place like this. She's always loved to bake, and I think if she didn't have her heart set on a position in the Council, she'd be so happy working as a baker.

I look around the shop as the woman works. All around me, shelves are filled with incredibly scented breads and gorgeous desserts: cookies and cakes, cinnamon buns, lengths of bread twisted together and dipped in chocolate, and so much more.

I'm trying to think about what Alec might want when I recall a conversation we had ages ago, when he told me of a fond memory he had with his mamman one day traveling with her for some task the Council had given her. He'd wandered off to follow a wonderful scent and came upon a bakery selling fresh sweetbread. When his mamman found him, she was so worried about him. He said she had given him the sweetest embrace, and when he told her why he had wandered away, she had purchased the sweetbread for him.

I smile and turn to the baker.

"Excuse me, ma'am," I say. The woman halts her task to look back at me, but she shows no sign of irritation for me having bothered her after I just told her I didn't need help.

"What can I do for you, dear?" she asks, smiling widely.

"I'm looking for some sweetbread for someone very special. I don't want to get him just any sweetbread. What would you recommend? Which is your favorite?" I eye the selection of sweetbreads on display, and I'm overwhelmed by the variety I find there.

The woman's smile grows. She brushes the flour off her hands onto her old, flour-dusted apron and makes her way around the counter to join me in front of the sweetbread shelf.

"It can be overwhelming, I know. You've come to the right woman, though. Sweetbreads just so happen to be my favorite thing to make. Tell me about this special someone of yours. What are they like?" the woman asks me, her brown eyes twinkling.

"Well, he's very sweet. He's always in a good mood, always trying to make the most of any given situation. He loves to drink, and talk, and dance. He's so confident, always trying to have fun, but there's so much more to him than that. So much depth, sadness, history. He was born to protect others." It's only when I say this last statement that I realize how breathless I am talking about him this way, and I mean every word. My face flushes, and my heart beats rapidly. "Well, that's the short of it, anyway. He's... he's just wonderful."

Tears twinkle in the woman's eyes, and she wipes her cheeks with the back of her hand, smearing flour across her right cheek.

"That's just beautiful. He sounds like a dream," she says, turning her attention to the shelf in front of us. "Let's see..."

"Thank you for your help," I tell her as she searches the shelf. She nods, concentrating, and finally finds the sweetbread she was looking for.

"Here, I think this one will do nicely. Raspberry and orange. A sweet, citrus and tart flavor that will be phenomenal by itself and pair well with any ale out there." The woman beams proudly. She finds her way to the counter again so I can pay for the bread.

"This is perfect. He'll love it. Thank you again," I tell her. When she gives me my total, I pay her and tuck the sweetbread box carefully under my arm.

Just as I'm about to turn and take my leave, the baker puts her hand out, gingerly placing her fingers on mine.

"A man like the one you described doesn't come around often, dear. I'd cherish him if I were you," she says. Her voice is sweet and kind, and her words reflect her tone, but they resonate deep within me.

I know I should cherish him. He's incredible. But the same nagging part of my brain can't help but wonder if this woman's words are yet another attempt by the Fates to push me in the direction that they want me to go.

I thank the woman once more and leave the bakery. I wind my way through town, in no particular hurry to get back to the temple. I would love to get back to the library, and more than that, I should get this sweetbread to Alec while it's still warm, but I have a lot on my mind, and the cool evening air riddled with the scent of pine trees has me slowing my pace.

I stop at another shop closer to the temple, remembering my promise to purchase Audy a treat. I purchase some corn-based bird seed and tuck it away safely into my satchel.

I wander past many other shops just closing up for the evening as the sun sinks low on the horizon. Several children play in the streets, bouncing bright balls of colored light between them, the light changing color each time it hits the ground or lands within another child's grasp, and I marvel at the sight. What a foreign concept. Sure, I played games like this in my childhood, but with the magic that they bat back and forth so casually... everything seems filled with so much more wonder and joy.

Eventually, I tear myself away from the wholesome sight, and as I draw nearer to the temple, I notice people holding hands, sharing something from a bottle that allows their voices to become musical tones that one might hear from rare birds – definitely not sounds that a human being should be able to make. The bright, trilling sounds mix with their laughter and float up visibly into the ever-darkening sky.

I do eventually make it back to the temple. At this point, the sun is a mere sliver on the horizon, its tangerine rays peeking through the trees to the west.

When I enter the temple, I do my best to sneak through the prayer chamber and away from the kitchens without being seen. I don't feel like talking with anyone right now, least of all Raonni or Alaya. I can't face them after everything I heard today. I don't want to think about the Fates, or Zaid, or Alaya having feelings for Alec.

I especially don't want to think about Raonni conspiring with Alaya to get me to follow the Fates' great plan.

All I want is to give Alec this gift and tell him apologize for making such a mess of things.

I climb the stairs to the hallway which contains both my room and Alec's. I've just begun setting the box of sweetbread down outside his door when it swings open, and Alec looks out at me, his expression instantly returning to the frown he wore earlier when he sees me. He's shirtless, clearly just out of the bath. His blond hair is slicked back and wet, sending little droplets of water rolling down his bare chest and onto the top of his trousers.

Although I've seen him without clothing before, this seems like an intrusion of his privacy, and I quickly avert my gaze.

"Sorry, sorry," I say, holding a hand up to block his chest from my sight. "I didn't mean to interrupt. I just – those are for you." I start backing away, gesturing to the box on the floor, but his voice stops me.

"What's this?" he asks as he bends to scoop the gift up off the floor, his frown morphing into his typical half-smile. "Radelle's bakery, huh? What's in here?"

I just stand there as Alec opens the box. I hadn't intended to be here when he saw the sweetbread, and I'm not entirely sure what I should do with myself now. So, I just watch his face as he realizes what I've brought him. His eyes swim with tears. The half-smile is replaced with a soft, sweet smile I don't think I've seen before.

"You remembered?" he asks me, his deep amber eyes searching mine.

"Of course, I remembered," I say. I wonder why he's so shocked. He cocks his head to one side and studies me for a moment. "I just wanted to apologize. I know I've made a mess of things lately. I know I *keep* making a mess of things, and I can't promise I can stop that... the conflict just... ugh, it seems to follow me. But I just wanted to let you know that I do care about you. About us. I just... Um. I'm going to stop talking now."

Alec is silent for several seconds, but it feels like an eternity. My face burns and my palms begin to sweat. I shuffle my feet, preparing to turn and go back to my room, but he speaks up again, once again stopping me in my tracks.

"Thank you, Lane. Really. Would you like to come inside?" he asks.

My eyes immediately drop back to that bare chest. Alec raises the sweetbread box up high and shakes it a little bit to draw my attention back to it.

"I'd love to share with you if you're up for it. Nothing like a bit of a late dessert, right?" he says.

"Oh, well, if you *want* to share..." I find myself muttering, cheeks flushing a deep red. I don't know why I feel so flustered. Alec steps barely to the side to let me into his room, still standing close enough that I have to slide through the doorway against him. I'm close enough to him as I pass that I can smell the soap he bathed with.

Although I keep my eyes on the floor, I can feel the heat of his gaze on me.

22

Inside Alec's room looks much like the inside of mine. Bed, bath, latrine, fire cracking arrhythmically in the hearth. He's got his clothes from the day sprawled out on the end of his bed, and he strides over and scoops them up into his hand before tossing them into the corner of the room.

The firelight splashes against the crystal windows, sending bits of blue-green light sparkling throughout the room to mix cozily with the light and shadow the fire emits. The light dances across his chest and face. I've always noticed how much lighter his skin looks than mine, but in this light, he's radiant.

I watch as Alec moves near the hearth and sits down, crossing his legs beneath him. He pats the stone floor covered with a thick plush maroon rug beside him, inviting me to sit with him. I will my feet to work and sit beside him, trying to get my heartbeat under control. I've been this close with him before, and Fates know I've been alone with him, so why do I feel so nervous right now?

Alec opens the box, which closed most of the way when he sat down. He picks up a piece of the sticky sweet bread in his fingers and offers the box to me.

I reach into the box. The sweetbread is still warm, but the icing on top has cooled, leaving a waxy texture on my fingertips as I grasp the dessert.

"Shall we?" he asks, and I nod, smiling. He lifts the dessert to his lips, parting them to take a bite, and as soon as he does, I can practically see the memory he's reliving on his face.

I take my own bite, and I'm transported to a much warmer, simpler time as well, but I don't have any specific memory associated with this taste.

Over the next few hours, Alec and I share in friendly conversation. We don't discuss the plan the Fates have in store for us, or our bond, or the complicated nature of our relationship. We don't discuss anyone else.

Instead, we share our memories, reminisce about how we first met, share our own perspectives of the journey we took across Maran in search of our mammans when they went missing.

Right now, in the glow of the firelight, with the taste of orange-raspberry sweetbread on our tongues, everything seems funny now, even our encounters with the various bandits we came across along the way. We laugh about the bandits that attacked us with brown burlap flour sacks over their heads.

As we laugh, Alec and I lean into one another, and it feels so wonderful to relax and joke with him. Even in our travels before when we were getting to know each other, we didn't have this much fun. I'm certain that's my fault for being so serious all the time.

But I let myself have fun tonight.

I let myself play and joke and laugh.

Alec laughs so hard he has to hold his sides when I pretend to be Rodrick, Alec's informant from Parth. I take a piece of sweetbread and hold it up to my nose with my bottom lip as a makeshift mustache, and Alec can't control his laughter.

Later still into the night, Alec and I lie together on the carpet before the fireplace, sharing the dreams we had for ourselves growing up. When I was young, before my mamman ever conceived Lilah, I wanted to be an artist. I had visited a few places here and there with my parents when I was a small child, as both of my parents traveled for work. I always loved to admire the art that hung in the galleries, depicting people with high class status: chiefs, priestesses, etc. I thought I would love to create art for people like that, and I dreamed especially of having my art displayed on the walls of Grand Council Keep.

"I think you should do that," Alec says, propping himself up on his elbows to get a better look at my face.

"What? Create art for entitled people?" I ask sarcastically. "I think that dream stopped becoming a possibility a long time ago. Have you met people of high status in Maran? Very few of them are people I would consider creating something for. Not that I've practiced that skill much, anyway."

Alec smirks. "People can surprise you if you let them," he says softly. "I'm serious, though. I've seen your maps. Can you imagine doing a full-scale map to hang in the Keep? The one they have only includes Maran's borders. Knowing what you've learned about this place, can't you see your map of Lithe and Maran – maybe even the whole world – hung up where our leaders can see it? You could remind them of what's truly important. You could share with them the things that have changed. I think that would be worth working toward."

As he speaks these words with such vigor, I can actually imagine it, and hope sparks within me.

"You know, maybe you're right. Maybe I should do something like that..." I trail off, letting my imagination run wild with the fantasy of how good things could be if everyone in Maran knew what was up here. If everyone in Maran used magic like the people in Lithe do. I'm certain our people would enjoy their lives so much more. As I consider this, I see the faces of all the people I've worked with in the past few years, all the people who go to work every day with deep frown lines on their faces. Surely, things could be better than that.

Perhaps I'll work on that. When I get back from all of this, maybe I'll start the project. I think I'll talk to Zaid or my mamman about what I've learned about this place, too, and see if they can speak with someone at the Council about setting a meeting with me. For now, though, I just want to relish in this perfect moment.

"What about you?" I ask Alec, rolling over to get a better look at his face, daring to reach up and caress it with my open palm. "Tell me what you wanted to be when you were young and didn't have the weight of the world on your shoulders. What did you want to be when you were little?"

Alec ponders the question for a moment, pursing his lips and narrowing his eyes.

"To be honest, when I was *really* little, all I can remember wanting is to be healthy. I remember wanting to be strong like my pappan, to be a guard," Alec says. He's got this faraway look in his eyes, as if he's reliving the whole experience of growing up the way he did. "I guess... given my circumstances as a young child, that's all I ever really wanted. Even though I was very young, I knew how my pappan perceived me. I knew he thought I was weak, pathetic. I wanted to prove that I could be strong, too. That I could be someone who could protect my mamman, or anyone, for that matter... That I could do something for the world."

I sit quietly for a moment, thinking about how difficult that must have been. Alec was only three when I was born and he regained his health. This means for his entire youth, he knew his pappan was disappointed in him. I can't imagine living like that. A child so young should have no awareness of anything but the wonders of the world.

"I'm sorry," I whisper to Alec, reaching over to take his hand in mine.

Alec looks at me with a shocked expression on his face. He adjusts to place his other hand atop mine. "Thanks," he says. "It wasn't easy, but it doesn't really matter anymore. I know my pappan will never look at me with pride. It just isn't in my dice."

I give his hand a squeeze. "*I'm* proud of you. I know how strong you are," I tell him, and I mean it.

"Well, I have that, then," he says, smiling softly at me. "Who needs the approval of their pappan when they have it from the girl of their dreams?"

Alec's tone is so soft, so sweet, and I don't realize I'm leaning in until his lips are close enough to mine that I can smell the sweetbread on his breath. He leans in slowly as well, closing the distance between us, brushing his lips so lightly against mine they feel like a butterfly's wings against my skin. I press forward, pushing my lips against his; and he grunts, rolling over to wrap his arms around me as he pulls me tightly against his chest.

I don't know how long we spend together this way, rolling around on the rug in front of the hearth, exchanging hungry kisses and caresses.

Each heated kiss is traded for another eager touch, and all I want is to feel him against me for as long as possible. His chest is already bare, and my fingers rake across his muscles on their way to remove my own shirt. As I do, Alec sucks in a deep breath before he leans back in to kiss me yet again.

"No," Alec grunts against my lips, moving his hands to stop mine from untying the lace of his trousers. The word freezes my actions.

"No?" I ask, pulling back a little bit to get a clearer view of his face. My stomach sinks. "Do you not...?"

Alec is quick to recover, brushing my face with his hand, his fingers tangling in my hair as he pulls me in to place a kiss on my forehead.

"Not here, on the floor," he says. Before I can say anything else, he scoops me up, holding me tightly against him as he carries me to his bed. "You deserve so much better than that."

I squeak. This all feels so unlike me, so carefree, and yet, I feel so comfortable with him that the thought is fleeting.

As Alec lays me down, his amber eyes are light – almost golden – as his gaze travels the mostly exposed skin of my torso before landing once again on my face.

"Fates," he whispers, eyes wide. "You're beautiful."

Normally, I think I would want to curl away and hide myself. Although he's seen me naked before, it's different now. For one thing, we've got the light of the fire with us, whereas our first time was lit only by an old, flickering candle. This time is also different because I've had regular baths since we arrived here at the temple, so I feel much less grimy. Under his gaze, I don't feel the urge to hide away. Instead, I reach up and run my hand gently across his chest, letting it rest for a moment over his heart.

"You're sweet," I tell him as my hand slides up across the back of his neck to pull him down to kiss me again.

Alec pulls away to plant kisses across my collarbones, shoulders, and the base of my neck before returning his attention to my lips.

We spend much of the night this way, exploring each other, and for the first time in quite a while, nothing else is on my mind. For the first time in I don't know how long, I don't worry about anything except the person I'm sharing this moment with.

Our first time, everything was new, every sensation heightened due to the bond that we shared. This time, although I feel close and connected with him, I can't feel everything that Alec feels. I can't tell what *I* am making him feel, so instead, I pay close attention to every sound, every movement, every face he makes, and it makes the experience somehow more intimate, with both of us being so aware of each other in a whole new way.

Afterward, as I lay in the warmth of Alec's bed with his arms wrapped around me, listening to the sound of his heartbeat against my ear, I run through the entire experience in my head.

I fall asleep in his arms feeling so exquisitely happy that I feel just might cry. How long has it been since I let him hold me like this? It feels like it's been forever.

In the morning, I wake to find Alec still holding me close, and I can't help the heat that rushes to my cheeks, or the smile that spreads across my lips as I recall the details of our night together.

"Good morning, sweetheart," Alec says. Already I'm smiling so widely that my cheeks are growing sore. Alec presses his lips to the tip of my nose, then kisses my forehead. The stubble on his chin scratches my forehead, and I giggle, loving this chance to be so close to him. "How did you sleep?" he asks me.

"To be honest," I start, craning my neck to see his face as best I can without pulling away from him. "That's the best night's rest I've had in my entire life."

I lay my head on Alec's chest and, although I'm not looking at him in this moment, I can feel him smiling just as I am.

"I can agree with that," he says. We're quiet for a while, just lying there together as his chest rises and falls with his breath. He breaks the silence as he brushes some of my dark hair from my neck, running his fingertips along my hairline and down my back. "I want this, Lane," he says, voice so full of raw emotion that it takes me by surprise. "I want *you*. I want this every day of my life – waking up with you like this. I don't want you to pull away... or choose someone else. I just... want you to know."

I prop myself up now to get a better look at him.

"Oh, Alec," I sigh. I want to tell him that I want this, too. That I'll choose him. That none of the other complicated things matter. I open my mouth to tell him all of this when there's a loud bang on the window outside his room. "What..." I start, voice so startled that it almost sounds muted. Alec's body tenses, and his grip tightens. "What was that?" I ask.

Alec keeps his eyes on the window as he kisses me once more on the forehead. All the softness is now gone from his expression as he slides out of bed, grabbing a bedsheet to cover himself with as he moves to investigate the sound.

23

"Alec?" I ask, stepping forward, pulling the comforter off the bed to wrap it tightly around my body as I follow Alec to the window to investigate. "What is it?"

Alec cautiously pushes open his window, and as he does an icy breeze bursts into the room, bringing with it large, fluffy flakes of snow that swirl around on the violent wind. Alec's bare shoulders relax and he breathes a sigh of relief when he leans through the window.

As he peers out, I find myself holding my breath in anticipation. It's only when he draws his arms back into the room, carrying a little hawklike bird in his hands that I let out the breath I've been holding and shuffle over to them both.

"Hello, little birdy," I whisper to Audy. Seeing this little bird reminds me that his whistle is still tucked away in my bag from the last time I used it; and my bag now sits on the floor beside the door in Alec's room in the same place I left it last night when he invited me in. "You scared us half to death," I tell him.

At the sound of my voice, Audy perks up and shakes his little head, fluttering over to me and landing gently on my shoulder. His little talons prick into my bare skin with a tickling sensation, but I don't mind.

"This creature is amazing," Alec breathes, and as his eyes take in the sight of Audy and me, his expression softens.

"He is, isn't he?" I respond.

Alec crosses the room to stand by my side as I work to detach the message from Audy's talons. Alec wraps his arms around my waist and nuzzles the back of my neck.

"I like seeing you this way," Alec says as I wave at Audy, who flies back through the window. Alec's fingers trace the length of my collarbone as he presses a kiss onto the base of my neck. "You seem happy."

A quiet moan escapes my lips as I lean into him, letting the memory of last night wash over me. "I *am* happy," I tell him, and he responds by holding me even more tightly against him.

He bends, scooping me up into his arms, and carries me to the armchair in the corner of the room, situating me and my tangle of blanket onto his lap.

As I unroll the message, Alec rubs little circles on my back between my shoulder blades.

"Stop it," I tell him, though my words carry no weight. "You're distracting me. I want to see how Lilah is getting along with the Council. She should be there by now."

I hold the now open message in my hands, and as I read, the smile fades from my lips entirely.

Lane,

I write this letter with a heavy heart. I hope you receive it soon, and that you aren't far from us.

We've made it to Grand Council Keep, but under dire circumstances. We were traveling the road halfway between Palandra and the Keep when we were ambushed by bandits much like the ones that you, Alec and I came across near Helna before. Like those ones, these acted like animals with reflexes faster than I could contest with.

There were so many of them. Several of the guards who traveled with us were killed, and all of us were injured.

Lane, Lilah was hurt, badly. I tried to protect her, but I failed. Words cannot express how sorry I am that I failed. Despite the patchwork job your mamman did on Lilah's wounds, by the time we got to the Keep, she'd lost far too much blood. She's been unconscious now for two days. The medic at the Keeps says... she's unsure if Lilah will recover.

Please, Lane. If you are at all able, get here soon. I don't know how much time Lilah has. It all seems so grim.

I'm so sorry.

Zaid

I stare at the parchment in my trembling hand as my other hand clasps across my mouth. Tears have welled in my eyes, and they now spill out freely onto my cheeks.

"Lane, are you alright?" Alec asks, moving to catch sight of the letter in my hand. "What is it?"

I jump to my feet, not caring when the comforter slides off my body. "Alec, I need to leave. It's Lilah. Oh, I should never have left her for so long!"

"What do you mean?" Alec asks, doing his best to make sense of what little information I've given him. "Lane, what's wrong?"

"Look," I tell him, holding the letter out barely long enough for him to take it before I scramble back into my clothes from yesterday.

"Right," Alec says slowly. He immediately stands and begins digging around in search of his belongings. Within moments, he's got two full bags packed and ready to go. "Lane, go pack your things from your room and write Zaid back. Tell him we're on our way. I'm going to talk with Raonni and Alaya and see if they know the fastest possible way to get us back to the Keep."

"O-okay." It takes everything I have to stay focused on his words, I wipe tears out of my eyes with the back of my sleeve and work to get my boots on. "Oh, you stupid – ugh!" I shout when I struggle to get one of my boots on. I chuck it across the room and cover my face with my hands.

Alec scoops up the boot I've thrown and strides to my side. He takes both of my arms in his hands, gently peeling my hands away from my face before wrapping me into a tight, secure embrace.

"We're going to see your sister," he tells me, rubbing my shoulders as I let out a helpless sob. "Go."

I turn, taking my boot from him and stumbling down the hallway to my room. There, I stop to get my boot on and begin opening drawers and throwing my belongings into my bags. I scribble a frantic note to tell Zaid we'll be there as soon as we can. I use Audy's whistle to call him back to me, and it takes several tries for my trembling fingers to fasten my message in place so I can send Audy on his way.

Then I march straight to the kitchen in hopes that Alaya will be there.

I almost crumple to the floor with the relief I feel when I do find Alaya, Alec and Raonni talking in the kitchen.

"Oh, thank the Fates," I whisper. "Alec, what have you learned? Is there a faster way to get back to Maran than the way we got here?" I ask, turning my attention now to Alaya. She opens her mouth to respond, but for a moment she just shakes her head.

"The tunnels are the only route I've taken. I don't know a faster way, Lane. I'm sorry," she says.

Raonni steps forward, setting her cup of tea gently on the tabletop.

"I know a way. Our boats don't sail your way often – we learned long ago that the Women's Council wishes not to associate with us, and the current between here and your ports are dangerously strong, but with the Fates on your side, you just might make it back safely. If you'd like, I can contact someone to try and have the boat ready for you by the end of today, though it will likely be a week before you see Maran's shores."

I nod. "Thank you so much. Yes, I'll take the chance of rough seas. I need to get back to my sister," I tell her.

Raonni bows her head in response. "I'll send a message now, then," she says, walking briskly past us and out of the room.

I dry my eyes and turn to Alaya.

"Are you coming with us back to Maran?" I ask. "Do you want Audy's whistle back..." I start, turning to find the whistle in my bag, but Alaya puts her hands out to stop me.

"Hang onto it for now. I won't be coming with you, but I can catch up with you later. In the meantime, you keep Audy. You're going to need him to send me messages," she says.

Alec cocks his head to the side. "You're not coming? Alaya, is there anything you might be able to do for Lane's sister?"

Alec's question shocks me. I don't know how it didn't occur to me to ask the woman who deals in magic if there's something she can do to help.

Alaya narrows her eyes and purses her lips. "I'm not certain what's wrong with her... I'd need to see her, I think. I've got some business to attend to here, but I'll catch up with you. Lane, write and keep me up to date."

24

As we wait for the ship to arrive, now dressed in thick fur coats and tall, clunky snow boots that Raonni procured for us, I pace up and down the docks. Like everything else has been over the last few days, the docks are covered in snow and ice.

I keep slipping because I can't seem to stop myself from pacing, but I just can't help it. My stomach is in knots, and I've now wrung my hands red. Alec follows me around with his arms out, attempting catch me before I go tumbling again.

For the last two hours, Alec has tried to get me to sit down. I know he's trying to comfort me, and that none of this is really his fault, but I feel annoyed with him. If I was never bound to him, I wouldn't have traveled so far away from home, and my bond with him would never have broken. If my bond wasn't broken, then I wouldn't have gone even farther from home to find answers. If I wasn't so far away from home, then I could have been traveling with Lilah. Maybe I could have protected her.

I know my anger is misplaced. I know that none of this is Alec's fault. Truly, it's the Fates that bound us. It's the Fates that allowed our bond to be broken. And it's the Fates that allowed Lilah to be hurt.

I also know that it's useless to think this way. I can't do anything to the Fates for what they've done, but I need someone to blame. I need someone to be angry with to keep myself from curling up into a little ball and crying myself to sleep, and so far, being angry with the Fates has done nothing for me.

It's only when a man approaches that I'm able to stand still for a moment, allowing myself to hope for good news. The man is dressed in a fur coat and snow boots akin to those that Raonni provided for us, and on his hands he wears thick, stitched leather gloves.

"Your ship will be ready to go soon. We're just loading the last of the provisions, now," the man says. You're lucky we had so many people available to help us on such short notice. The Fates must have you in their favor."

His words are salt in an open wound, and I scowl. "You have no idea," I mutter, staring out at the dark, gray, angry looking sea. Heavy snow clouds shift slowly overhead, carrying with them a heavy, frozen breeze.

Snow sprinkles onto the man's thin line of a mustache, and the flakes melt quickly under the heat of his breath as he speaks. "With such a rush on our departure, we don't have time to call in our master captain. He's away on another voyage for at least another week. His eldest son is willing come in his stead, if that's alright with you. He's well trained, and I think he'll do a fine job, but he's young. Truly, he's really the only one who has the power to lead our crew right now." Despite the man's words of encouragement, he seems a little bit concerned.

I don't care that we won't have the master captain on board with us. I just need to see my sister.

"That's fine. He'll do," I say hurriedly. "Is he ready now? I'd like to speak with him."

The man gestures with a mitted hand down the docks to a young man who supervises a group of men and women rolling barrels onto a large wooden ship. Other men and women work aboard the ship, and though I don't know just what they're doing, they move about purposefully, clearly getting everything ready in a hurry.

"He's just there," the man says. His brow creases, and I thank him curtly as I make my way to the captain, doing my best not to slip again on the ice. Alec tags along at my heels, still with both arms out behind me, just in case.

"Excuse me," I say to the young man, tapping him firmly on the shoulder.

He turns, and the fur-covered collar of his coat flutters in the icy breeze as he faces me.

"Ah, you must be the one in a hurry," he says, smiling at me with squinted eyes, holding one hand up to shield his face from the wind. He's probably my age, if not a little bit older. He's just starting to get bits of red facial hair growing on his upper lip and along the edges of his chin, and his face still carries the roundness of his youth.

"Lane," I say, stuffing my frigid hands into the pockets of my coat and wiggling my fingers around to try and keep them warm. "Raonni mentioned that this voyage may take a week. Is that true?" I do my best to sound polite. After all, he is leaving in a rush to take us in this weather.

The man nods slowly. "It's hard to say for certain," he says, looking up at Alec. "These things are never exact. The fastest way to Maran is to get to Siren's Way, but their harbors are closed to any ships that are not Maranian. We'll have to work our way down the coast to find a harbor that will be open to us, but I think we can dock near Laden's Way. Additionally, the sea in these parts is unpredictable, and the currents strong. Especially in this time of year, it might take longer."

My expression falls, and the chill in the air causes the tears in my eyes to sting.

"We understand," Alec says, placing his hand on my shoulder. I can just feel his thumb tracing circles through my coat. "We appreciate whatever you can do."

"Listen," the man says, ducking down to meet my lowered gaze. "I'll do my best to get you where you need to be as quickly and safely as possible."

"Thank you," I say, sniffling and nodding my head.

"Of course," he says, sympathetic smile stretching his dry lips. "Now, we're going to be on the water for a while, so we're just getting the rest of our supplies in order. You might want to check the markets and purchase anything you may want to have in that time. We'll meet you back here in about an hour."

The man smiles at me again, and again I nod. Alec's hand pats my back.

"That sounds great. Thank you again," he says, and he leads me carefully away from the docks. I let Alec take my hand in his as we make our way to the markets.

We spend the next hour purchasing various goods: Some food, some warm clothing, some little odds and ends we'd like to bring home with us for our families. I find a lovely crystal necklace with a large, tear-shaped pendant in the center, cut from the same blue crystals that lie about the ground everywhere here in Lithe, polished to perfection. I purchase this item for Lilah, tucking it deep down in my satchel for safekeeping. All through our time at the market, I keep turning back to check the docks, and every time I do, Alec draws my attention to whatever pretty thing he's holding, asking, "Do you think Lilah would like this? I'm certain she'd like this."

I do appreciate his trying to keep me distracted, but I'm crawling out of my skin. All I want to do is get on that ship, despite my fear of being out on the open water.

When we've purchased our goods and packed them away into our bags, Alec and I sit on a little wooden bench together and watch the snow fall. As we do, children run through the large, thick flakes that fall from the sky in a hurry, laughing and playing and splashing bits of color and light from little jars, and I'm startled by the stark contrast of the care-free nature of their hearts and the weight that feels as if it's crushing mine.

Finally, the captain flags us down from the docks and informs us that the crew is ready to set sail.

As we board the ship, I take one final look at Lithe, and I wonder if I'll ever return to this mysterious place, filled with magic and color. But I turn my face toward the setting sun in the west and then turn southward, toward Maran – and home, and Lilah – and as we set off, I grip the thick wooden railing on the ship's edge as the wind carries us out of the harbor and into the open sea.

Our first night on water is beyond rough. The winter weather brings an angry storm that has the entire ship rocking so badly I'm certain it'll tip completely over at any minute.

The entire afternoon was tense and quiet as the storm rolled in, and I had a hard time keeping any food down from the motion of the ship on the water. Now, as the night's storm blows us this way and that, I stumble around our little room in the cockpit as Alec sleeps on his cot like a baby.

When a large wave shoves the ship hard enough that I go flying off my feet and onto Alec's cot, he wakes with a start. He snorts, working to open his eyes as yet another wave sends me reeling. If I can't find my balance, I worry I'm going to be jostled around until every bone in my body is broken. At this point, I'm seriously considering having somebody tie me up to something that won't move.

Alec rubs the sleep from his eyes and reaches out, taking me into his arms.

"Are you alright?" he asks. The only light in our little cabin now is from a magical orb that hangs overhead and glows with a soft, warm yellow light that a candle might emit, except it does not flicker. Instead, it rocks and roils gently within its container, gracefully churning with the motion of the waves that jostle us aggressively. In the dim lighting, Alec's features grow concerned when his eyes focus on my face. "You don't look well..."

I press my hand to my mouth.

"I think I might be sick again..." I admit as the ship rocks again. Just then, a knock on the door demands Alec's attention. He moves me to his side, where I fall back onto his cot. When I steady myself, he reaches over and places my hands on a rail that runs across the cabin just above the cot.

"Hold onto this, okay?" he says, brushing some loose hair out of my face. "I'll be right back."

I clutch the rail as if my life depends on it, and in this storm, perhaps it does.

"Sorry to disturb you at this hour," the man with the mustache that we spoke with earlier says when Alec opens the door. The man peeks nervously through the doorway at me. "Captain wanted me to tell you both to brace yourselves. It looks like the storm's going to get rough."

"*Going to?*" I groan, but I'm interrupted when another churn of the ship sends my stomach roiling. "Oh, Fates," I mutter, closing my eyes against a wave of nausea that overcomes me. Alec thanks the man and closes the door, turning back to me with that same concerned look on his face. With some effort, he's able to stay balanced well enough to make his way back to my side.

"Here," he says, scooting back into the corner at the edge of the cot, pressing his back against the wall behind him. "Come here," he says, holding his hand out. Warily, I take it, and he helps me move over to where he sits. He turns me so my back presses against his chest, and he wraps one arm around me, the other pressing against the wall to help absorb some of the movement of the rocking ship.

I clutch his arm with both of my hands, so tightly that I fear I might bruise him. Although it's now been a while since our bond has broken, I'm still alarmed by the realization that if I bruised him, the same marks would not appear on my arm.

I want to apologize for everything. For our bond being broken, and for causing him so much trouble when all he's doing is trying to help me. But with the motion of the storm, it's all I can do to stay upright. I can't find all the words I wish to share with him. So instead, all I can offer is a desperate, "Alec, I'm sorry."

We remain this way all through the night, sitting up huddled close together in the corner of our cabin, holding each other through the storm.

The next several days pass us by in much the same manner, though I'm grateful that the weather has improved somewhat, and none of the rest of the time so far has been quite so awful as it was on the first night.

I spend most of my time below deck, trying to distract myself from my nagging worries. I try to draw, try to work on my maps, but the motion of the ship makes that task nearly impossible to do well, and my heart's not really in the activity anyway, so I let it be for now. I wander the lower parts of the ship, asking anyone I come across if there's anything I can help with.

I learn a lot of new things in these few days as I try to busy myself. I don't spend much time on deck – I'm terrified that if I spend too much time up there, we'll to hit a big wave and I'll go toppling right over the railings. Instead, I work below deck, helping to cook and clean and fix things down here.

On the sixth day, when the weather clears enough that the smallest rays of sun come shining through the clouds and the wind calms, I receive another letter as I stand on deck looking out at the sea for the first time in days. For the moment, the vast body of water sprawled out before me is calm. Seeing Audy flapping his little wings vigorously in our direction sends my heart racing. I'll finally receive word as to how Lilah is doing.

In his brief letter, Zaid tells me that there has been no improvement to Lilah's condition. Her bleeding has stopped, and her wounds seem to be making slow progress toward healing, but she still has not woken, and the medics at the Keep still don't know that she will.

My heart breaks. I forget how slowly everyone heals in comparison to how quickly my own wounds have always healed.

I feel awful, and all I want to do is lie down and disappear until we reach land again. I'm just headed back below deck when Alec bumps into me, carrying a plate of hot food.

"Oh, good," he says. "I was just going to find you." When he sees my face, he immediately shifts to ask me what's wrong, but I put my hand up to stop him before he can say a word, wiping the tears that stream down my face.

Alec gives a single nod. He places the food on the floor at our feet and pulls me into a warm hug, holding me silently as I sob, letting the fear I feel consume me.

I hate that this is the fastest way I can get to Lilah. Every time I've asked someone how long we'll be, the answer changes. From what I've been able to gather, we still have another two or three days if the weather holds well, and based on my maps, it's seeming as though we'll have another week or so to travel on foot from where we'll dock to the Keep.

All through the next two days, I fight the incessant thoughts that trigger my anxieties during my waking hours. I fight the fear that I refuse to say aloud – the fear that my sister will no longer be alive by the time I reach her.

The idea is so horrible it runs my blood cold, but it comes into my mind so often that I've picked my fingers to bleeding.

Over these few days, Alec doesn't say much... or if he does, I don't hear much of what he says. He smiles at me constantly, though the smiles seem hollow; and he's always close by, always reaching out, putting his arms around me, letting me know that he's here if I need him. I love him for that.

Alec and I are up on deck one day, and Alec is in the middle of telling me for the thousandth time today that we'll be there soon, and that everything will be okay. I've opened my mouth to thank him, pressing my hand against his shoulder, when something on the horizon catches my eye.

"What is that?" I ask, narrowing my eyes against the glaring sun to get a better look. "Is that a cloud?"

"That's no cloud, missy," says one of the crewmates as he walks by, carrying a basket of fish. "That right there is Maran."

My eyes grow wide, and I jump so high in excitement that I nearly lose my balance, and I catch myself on Alec's arms just before I topple over. Alec's hands steady me, and he mutters something about how I should be more careful, but I barely hear him, blood rushing through my ears as I celebrate.

"Land! Oh, Alec, look! We've made it! Look!" I shout, grasping Alec's shirt and pointing like a child at the small sliver of land in the distance.

It still takes several hours for us to get even close to that piece of land, however; and all the while I pace back and forth across the deck, keeping my eyes glued to the slowly growing land mass, afraid that if I look away it'll disappear. The sun is starting to set now, and my anxiety creeps back in.

The moment the ship is docked, Alec races ahead of me to get off the ship before I do. Once he's off, he reaches up for my hand, and when I take it, he helps me down. The moment I stand on dry, still land, my legs give out beneath me. The world seems to tilt, and I lose my balance, falling into Alec with a heavy thud.

Our young captain laughs and says, "Welcome back to land, Lane. Good luck getting rid of those sea legs."

"Sea legs?" I ask.

I remember being on the rowboat crossing Murkwater lake and how my legs felt a bit like jelly for a couple of hours after I got back on land. This, however, is entirely different. I feel as if I've lost complete function in my legs.

Alec smiles as if he can tell exactly what I'm thinking.

"It'll come back to you," he says, holding me upright. "Just give it some time. In the meantime, you're welcome to stay right where you are, or I could always carry you." I look down at Alec's body, pressed firmly against mine for support.

"Right..." I say, working to correct my stance enough that I'm not pressed right up against him.

I've been so tense and so thoroughly consumed by worry over the last week that I've mostly kept to myself, and I realize now that we haven't even talked about the night we shared together before I got Zaid's troubling letter.

Why does this keep happening?

I swear, once I can see Lilah, once I know she's safe, I'll be able to relax enough to talk with Alec about everything. For now, that's my focus. Get to Lilah, then talk with Alec.

25

"Where exactly are we?" I ask, looking around at our surroundings. The soft, white sand beneath our feet sparkles in the sunlight. It's not quite the same as the tan, grainy sands near Palandra, SunSpar, and Nerine; and in all my travels, I'm not sure I've ever seen sand so light in color.

"We're just outside Laden's Way," Alec says, scanning the area, confirming what the captain had predicted was correct.

"Oh!" I say. "I haven't been to Laden's Way before." I remove my arm from around Alec's waist and dig excitedly through my satchel, sorting through my many maps.

I find one map that I made notes on when Alec and I first met his contact in Parth. I think I remember Rodrick mentioning that he hails from Laden's Way. I kneel in the sand to get a better look, grateful for the opportunity to rest my already tired legs. I run my finger over the map before me.

"What are you doing?" Alec asks, crouching down beside me and taking a look over my shoulder at the mess of papers I've spread out.

Sure enough, when my finger lands on the tiny sketch of a village that represents Laden's Way, I find the note I made back in Parth, in a time that now feels so like ages ago. Rodrick, Alec's contact, does live in Laden's Way, and said that if we were ever in Laden's Way, we would be welcome.

"Aha!" I say, snapping my fingers and jabbing the note on my map with my index finger. "I thought I remembered this correctly. Your friend Rodrick lives here. Do you think he'd let us stop in for a meal and advice on the fastest route to take on our way through?"

Alec nods, his lips hinting at a smile.

"Absolutely. Let's go pay him a visit."

Alec and I stand, dust the sand off our bodies, and thank the crew that got us across the sea safely. Then, we part ways with the crew, trampling through the white sand on wobbly legs.

Alec helps me walk the path to the small village that makes up Laden's Way. The village is located very near the sea, with several docks all surrounding it to the north, and the Maranee river rushing in from the sea to the west. To the east, wide beaches with the same beautiful sparkling sand stretch out all the way to the sea, and to the south lies the forest that will eventually take us across the Maranee river by Parth's great bridge to Grand Council Keep.

With Alec guiding me, it only takes a few minutes to reach the village from the docks, and when we do, I'm in awe.

Palandra is protected by large walls on all sides. I've never seen enough of SunSpar without an escort to see how their people who live closest to the sea have built their homes, but from what I have seen, all the buildings there are constructed of stone and sand and seashells.

Here in Laden's Way, all the homes we pass are little wooden huts built up on stilts with tall ramps that lead from the sand to their doorways.

A mixture of old and new palm fronds make-up the majority of the roofs we see as we trek through the village to Rodrick's home. His hut is located immediately behind a fish market, and although it's now late in the afternoon, Alec knocks heartily on the door as if it were midday, apparently not worried in the slightest that we might be disturbing Rodrick's dinner.

Regardless, Rodrick opens the door with a smile on his bearded face. His entire face lights up when he sees us.

"Well, well, well," he says, deep voice booming. "I didn't expect to see you two still together after all this time. No one has heard from you in quite a while. Alec, I'm glad to hear that your mamman is home and doing well. Excellent work, as usual."

"Awe, Roddy," Alec says, fanning his face dramatically and batting his eyelashes. "You flatter me. Listen, we've got a bit of a situation."

Rodrick's smile fades, and he strokes his dark beard as he studies me. At the mention of our "situation," the joy I feel at seeing someone familiar and visiting a new place dissipates, and the knot in my gut instantly returns.

Like flipping a switch, now all I can think about is how far we still are from Lilah.

"Right," Rodrick says. "Come in, you two. Mina and I were just sitting down to dinner. We'll grab you some."

We step inside the home and are immediately hit with the strong scent of freshly cooked fish and citrus fruits.

A bowl of rolls has been placed on the center of the table, and a woman with dark hair just like Rodrick's and a belly that looks as though she's at *least* eight months with child wobbles over to the table with a large wooden plate that holds two large, steaming, salted fish.

My mouth starts to water. We've eaten plenty of fish on our voyage from Lithe, but this looks like it was made with incredible care, and the fish we ate on the ship was always made as quickly as possible in order to feed so many people.

"Hello," I say to the woman. "Would you like some help with that?"

The woman grunts as she sets the fish on the table, then stands back up, holding her lower back. She smiles at me with kind but tired eyes.

"Oh, it's no problem. If I need help with setting the table, I've got a whole mess of trouble ahead of me," Mina responds.

Alec says, "It's nice to see you again, Mina."

At my confused look, Rodrick explains, "Mina minds the fishing boats while I'm away. She's been going out there on the water until about a month ago, and she hauls more fish than most of my crew." Rodrick looks at Mina with eyes that sparkle with adoration, and she shoots him the same look back.

"Wow, that's incredible." I tell her. "When are you due?"

"Three weeks' time," she says, running her hands across the width of her belly.

Three other little children with the same dark hair and olive complexion come running around the corner, chasing each other around the dinner table with fish skulls in hand.

The only little girl looks up and says, "Ma! They're teasing me again!" She looks at me and hides behind her mamman before saying a timid, "Hello."

I smile and wave at her as one of her brothers shouts, "Who is that with Uncle Alec?"

I send an inquisitive glance Alec's way.

"Uncle Alec, huh?"

Alec only shrugs in response, the tips of his ears reddening ever so slightly.

"They're our dinner guests," Mina says sternly. "And we will treat them as such, won't we? Go put your bones away and wash up. Supper is ready."

Dinnertime with Rodrick and his family is filled with laughter and stories, but when things settle down a bit, Rodrick asks, "So what's this situation?"

Alec and I quiet, and a somber feeling settles over the entire room. Mina gets up out of her seat with some effort.

"Why don't I get these children to bed?" she asks. The children all groan in response, but then they say respectful goodnights before leaving the room. When the children have gone, I try to explain what's happened; but I get choked up and my voice fails me altogether.

Alec explains the letter we received from Zaid about their encounter with the bandits, and the poor health condition my sister now faces.

When Alec finishes, I'm able to find my voice well enough to add a quiet, "We just need to get to her."

Rodrick listens intently to our plight, stroking his beard.

Finally, he says, "Alec, you know where the blankets are?"

Alec nods. "I do."

"Right. You two stay here for tonight. I'll send word and see what I can find out, and we'll send you on your way in the morning. If you can go on horseback, you'll have at least a few days before you reach the Keep, and we don't want to waste a second of it." Now, Rodrick addresses me. "The house is smaller than it used to be, so you'll need to sleep on the floor, but Alec will get some warm blankets for you to rest on. Night in these parts can get chilly."

As Rodrick stands, I thank him for his hospitality.

"Please tell your lovely wife that the food was wonderful," I tell him.

He gives me a single nod and smiles. As Alec wanders off into the hallway around the corner, Rodrick approaches me and puts his hand on my shoulder.

"I'm sorry for what you're going through, Lane. Mina and I will pray for the best outcome for your sister. In the meantime, take care of that one, will you? Alec's got a good heart, but his head's a little crooked. Thinks *he's* the one who needs to do all the protecting." Now Rodrick looks in the direction of his wife and children in the other room. "We know different, don't we?" he asks with a subtle wink of his eye.

"Of course," I tell him. Thinking of Alec the way Rodrick sees him fills my heart with joy.

As Alec returns to the room and begins to lay blankets onto the floor, Rodrick grunts.

"Well, I'd better get in there and do my part. Goodnight Lane, Alec," he says. "See you before the sun."

I recognize this saying from my travels. Fishermen must get an early start on each day, often long before the sun rises. I nod and smile.

"Thank you again," I tell him.

When Rodrick leaves the room, Alec and I lay side by side on the floor of this little hut, staring up at the ceiling. After a while, Alec shifts, drawing my attention to him.

"How are you holding up?" he asks.

Tears sting my eyes in response to his question. I wish more than anything I could be at the Keep already, but I know we've got to journey sensibly.

"I'm okay. Or rather, I think I will be. We just need to get back to her as quickly as possible," I tell him. After a moment's pause, I add, "Thank you for asking."

Alec nods. Though it's not quite dark out yet, this family is set on fisherman's time. In this moment, though, I'm grateful to be resting so early. I hope to sleep off the still wobbly feeling in my legs from being aboard that ship for so long, and I'm excited at the chance to wake up early and keep moving.

Alec smiles softly. He reaches out his hand and entwines his fingers with mine. I hold onto his hand tightly, but my grip loosens as I start to drift off.

"We'll be there soon," Alec says. He leans over and kisses me on the cheek before rolling onto his back. He keeps his hand in mine for the entire night, and as I fade into a deeper sleep, I think about all the ways Alec has changed the lives of the people we've come across since I met him.

26

Although we sleep on the floor of Rodrick's small sitting room, I sleep better than I have since we boarded that ship. When I wake, I'm surprised to find that Alec, Rodrick and Mina have been up for quite some time, quietly moving about and doing their morning chores.

"Good morning," Rodrick says, closing the hut's front door behind him. He and Alec stand in the doorway, both dressed as though they've been awake for hours.

"Good morning," I say through a yawn, rubbing the sleep from my eyes.

"Great news," Alec says. "Roddy and I were able to secure some horses. We should get to the Keep in no time."

At this news, my heart sings. All the fogginess left over from my dream state leaves my mind in an instant, and I jump up.

"That's amazing!" I say. The blanket I used last night falls off of me as I wrap my arms around Alec's neck in a big hug.

"Alright, you two, break it up," Rodrick says as his wife reenters the room. "We know what happens when you do that for too long..." Rodrick's eyes jerk toward Mina's big belly, and the four of us laugh, but I do pull away from Alec then, and my cheeks warm with a blush.

Mina hobbles over to us with a large, heavy looking sack in hand. She passes it to Alec with a grunt. "For your journey. Plus a little extra," she says, and Alec beams at her.

"Thank you," I say, awed once again by this family's generosity.

I give Rodrick and his wife a hug. Rodrick whispers in my ear, "Remember what we talked about, Lane. Take care of the bloke. It gets tiring always looking after everyone else. He deserves someone who has his back."

"I will," I promise, and Rodrick pats me on the shoulder.

"Your horses are outside. Don't want to leave them too long, now. Someone might take off with them," Rodrick says, backing away to hold hands with his wife. "Safe travels, you two. We wish you a swift return to the Keep."

Alec and I say our goodbyes and make our way through the door before climbing atop two Brabant horses. Their large hooves and strong legs carry us through the soft beach sand quickly, and it isn't long before we've entered the forest.

We ride throughout the day, as the sun rises up over the trees, lighting all the palm fronds and pine needles with its warm rays. It moves across the sky as we pace ourselves, keeping at a steady canter.

When the sun is high and hot in the sky, we break for lunch to allow our horses to rest, though I don't eat much. I don't feel particularly hungry with so much on my mind, so I pick at the bread in my hands, crumbling it into tiny pieces that I roll between my fingers.

"We will get there soon, Lane," Alec says, tone soft and sympathetic. I meet his gaze, seeing so much kindness in his brown eyes that it startles me.

"I know," I say. "I just wish I could be there already. Or better yet, I wish she'd never been attacked in the first place."

"Yeah..." Alec strokes the dark blond, now short beard on his chin. "Perhaps you could send a letter? Let them know that we will be there soon and ask if there have been any updates?"

"That's a great idea," I say. I grab out my charcoal and parchment, and my map of the area, measuring out the approximate distance we have left to travel. O, horseback, it looks like we could make it to Parth by the end of the day. I blow into Audy's whistle, and in a matter of minutes, the little bird appears, excited as ever to carry my message to its destination. As he appears, I realize that in all the craziness of the last week, I forgot to give him the treat I purchased for him.

I secure the message to Audy and dig around in my bag for his corn. I pull it out and give him some before sending him on his way.

I am sure that the letter will reach the Keep in at least a couple of hours, though I'm still not sure how Audy gets where he's going so quickly. Knowing that we should get to Lilah in the next day or two fills me with a new hope. I brush the crumbs off my clothes as I stand and tuck the rest of my untouched food back into our bags. Alec eyes me worriedly as I do this, but he keeps his concerns to himself.

As I put away my map and my other things, I ask, "Are you ready to keep going?" Alec gives me a solemn nod. I wonder what's on his mind, but for now, I keep my questions to myself. I don't want to prod him about how he's feeling if I'm not in the headspace to really listen and respond.

We ride the rest of the day through the forest in silence, and the closer we get to the Keep, the less tropical our surroundings become. The trees that surround us are no longer palms with large leaves. Instead, the trees here are primarily aspens and pines, and even the smell of the air shifts as we work our way further into the forest.

The scent of the pine needles and fresh running water fills the air around us, further accenting the hope and excitement that I feel being so close.

As the sun begins to set around us and the Maranee River comes into partial view, Alec stops at a wooden post in the road, pulling his horse off our trail. He dismounts, grasping his horse's reins in one hand.

"What are you doing?" I ask him. "Alec, we've already stopped for lunch. We need to keep going." My horse must feel my anxiety, because it shifts its hooves uneasily in the dirt.

"Come here for a minute; I'll show you," Alec replies, and a hint of a smile creeps onto his face as he begins to lead his horse to a patch of tall bushes.

"Fates, Alec. Can we please—"

"Just *trust* me," he tosses over his shoulder, leaving me no choice but to follow him as he disappears through the shrubbery.

I grumble my frustration as I get off my horse and lead it by the reins after him. The moment I break through the bushes, however, I see why he's stopped here.

"Oh," I mutter, feeling foolish for fighting him. Before me, Alec has paused to hand over his horse to a man in a feathered cap, who stands beside a horse of his own. Behind the man is a rowboat anchored to a post that sticks out from the water of the Maranee River.

As I approach, Alec's smug grin makes me roll my eyes.

"We'll cross here," he says to me, dropping a few tins into the man's hand. "Go on, give him your horse. He's one of Roddy's eyes. He was called out here early this morning to wait for our arrival, and he'll get the horses safely back to Laden's Way for us."

"You know, you could have just clued me into the plan," I tell him, turning my horse over to the man, who smiles at me beneath a bushy mustache.

"Where's the fun in that?" Alec asks me, though his attention is already focusing on untying the boat from the post. "Besides, you were fast asleep when we got things started this morning, and after the week you've had on that ship, you needed the rest."

"The water's calm today," the man says to both of us before I can respond to Alec. "You should be able to cross in no time. What luck!"

"Something like that," I mutter under my breath, and I ignore the confused look the man gives me in response. Instead, I say, "Thank you for being here, and for this boat."

The man nods. "I've got another gentleman that will be crossing back over the river this evening, so you're welcome to just dock it on the post across the way."

"Perfect," Alec says.

"Thank you," I say.

Alec gestures to the boat. "After you, my dear," he says, smiling at the hesitant look on my face.

"Oh, great," I say. "Another boat." I've gone from never being on a boat in my life to being on three boats all in the span of a few weeks, and after my experience on that ship, I think I could do without another boat experience for the next decade.

Still, my sister needs me, so into the boat I climb, clinging to its edges as I slowly sit down. My eyes widen and my grip tightens when Alec gets in, rocking the little boat from side to side. I'm not certain I'll ever get used to this.

"Don't worry," he says, shooting me a reassuring smile before turning to pick up a couple of oars from the boat's bottom at our feet. "After that ship, this will be nothing." Then he turns his attention back to the man with the horses. "Thanks again, mate!" he calls. "Tell Roddy I owe him one."

The man waves his hand high in the air above him. "Safe travels!"

The man was right. With the calm, steady water and the both of us rowing, we cross almost the entirety the river's width in just over an hour. When we've nearly made it across, Alec cocks his head to the side.

"What's up?" he asks, running his oar through the water with ease.

I give him a confused look.

"I'm rowing, same as you," I tell him.

"No, I mean, what are you thinking? You've got that look on your face."

High above us, a flock of birds passes us by, squawking loudly. The fluttering of their wings overhead fills the area above the river with the sound.

"What look?" I ask, drawing my attention away from the birds and back to Alec.

"The look you get when you're trying to solve a difficult problem," he says. "Thinking about Lilah?"

His words take me by surprise. I'm not sure I have a look that says all that, and I wouldn't expect him to recognize it if I do.

I nod, staring at the sunlight that sparkles on the water's surface and trying to ignore the presence of even more tears in my eyes. I take a deep breath.

"Yeah. I'm trying to figure out what I can do to help. It's just hard because I won't know how things are really going until I can see them for myself. You can only glean so much information from a letter, you know?"

"Right," Alec says, his face pensive.

"If we can just get there," I start. "If we can just get Alaya there as soon as possible, I'm hoping there's something she can do that the medic hasn't tried. With her magic, there's got to be something."

"We'll be there soon," Alec tells me again.

"I know, but—" but I trail off when Alec points behind me. My gaze follows his finger, and sure enough, we bump softly against the western shore of the Maranee River. Through the dense forest around us, we can't see the Keep, but we've got to be close.

I jump out of the rowboat, sending it rocking, fumbling over my own feet. Alec climbs out carefully behind me and drags the boat to a nearby post while I pull out my maps. A quick look tells me that we are, indeed, *very* close to the Keep.

"Come on, Alec!" I shout, waving my maps through the air before shoving them quickly back into my bag and taking off running. In my peripheral vision, I watch Alec rush to tie the boat to its post as he takes off after me.

"Wait up!" he calls, but I can't help it. We're so close!

After a few minutes like this, a break in the trees reveals the tall stone walls surrounding Grand Council Keep.

We race along the wall's edge until we come to the Keep's front gates. The Keep is positioned so that the gates face the forest to the southeast, and I know from previous visits that somewhere along the tall stone wall that surrounds the Keep on every side, two or more guards are patrolling the perimeters. At the sight of the huge wooden doors, I let out an excited giggle before taking the knocker in my grasp and banging it against the gate loudly several times.

A moment later, a small opening in the door reveals a pair of wrinkled, dark brown eyes as a creaky old voice on the other side says, "State your purpose."

"I've come to see my sister, Lilah Shrayan," I tell the person behind the gate, lifting my chin and doing my best to catch my breath. "She and my mamman Ailene are staying here."

As the doors unlock and slowly open, I take Alec's hand in mine and squeezing it tightly, straightening my back and curling my other hand into a determined fist.

The little old woman those brown eyes belong to hops down from a stool as two large men in full armor stand cautiously behind her.

"And this one?" the woman asks, narrowing her eyes suspiciously at Alec.

"Is with me," I reply, tone steady. "Please, I'd really like to see my sister."

The woman's harsh gaze softens ever so slightly, and she nods. "Follow me."

The two men turn to close the gates as the woman leaves her post to guide us.

Alec and I follow the woman through the Keep's vast, familiar hallways. As we do, I listen to the familiar sound of our footsteps echoing over cold stone. I reminisce about the time I spent here with my mamman as a small child, daydreaming about the paintings and maps that hang on the walls. Knowing that Alec also grew up with ties to this place makes me feel a closeness to him that I've only been able to get minor glimpses of since our bond was broken.

The longer it takes us to walk through the halls on our way to Lilah, the more anxious I feel. But finally, we find the room in which she's staying.

At this point, the sun is setting, and although the window in Lilah's room faces the east toward where the sun would rise, the setting sun sets splashes of orange and pink across what sky we can see through the trees outside.

"I'll leave you here, but don't get any ideas about wandering," the woman says. "Should you need anything, there will be someone around soon."

As we enter the room, I feel as if I might collapse. Zaid and my mamman are both sitting beside Lilah's bed, blocking my view of my sister. At the sound of our entrance, they both look up. Zaid's eyes land on me, and his face brightens, his cheeks making way for an eager grin. Then he catches the sight of Alec holding my hand and registers the closeness between us, and his expression drops. In that split second, I worry he can see all that's happened between Alec and me since we last talked.

"Thank the Fates you're here, Lane," Zaid says, practically jumping out of his chair. He and my mamman rush over and embrace me with tight, warm hugs. I let go of Alec's hand to pat my mamman on the back, and she pulls away, tears brimming in her eyes. From a single look, I can tell that she hasn't been eating, and the puffy bags beneath her eyes indicate she hasn't been sleeping much, either.

"I came as fast as I could," I say, and my voice threatens to break. "I know I didn't get here nearly fast enough..."

"Never mind that," my mamman says, brushing away tears that roll silently down my cheeks. "You're here now. That's all that matters."

"How is she?" I ask as Alec and Zaid exchange stiff, awkward hellos. But I ignore them for now. All that matters is my little sister. "How's Lilah?"

"There's been no change since Zaid last wrote you," my mamman says softly. Her voice wavers as she says, "Oh, Lane. It was awful." Fresh tears spill out across her cheeks. Her golden hair is disheveled and dull, her cheeks gaunt. She looks utterly exhausted, and I wonder exactly how long it's been since the last time she's slept.

"Where's Pa'?" I ask. "He should be here."

I look around the room expectantly, and my mamman puts her hand on my shoulder.

"He was, love. He just left earlier today. He had to get back to train some new crew members and alert Chief Bron of the dangers on the road. They're to make a plan to handle these challenges, then he will meet up with us again soon," she says. Hearing this allows me to relax just a little bit.

"Good," I tell her. I hope he gets back here, soon. We all should be together, though I'm hit with a new worry that the roads may not be safe enough for him to travel to us.

And then I see my sister for the first time. She lies with her eyes closed and her arms resting at her sides. She'd look as if she's sleeping peacefully enough if it weren't for the scrapes and big yellow bruises that cover her exposed forearms and her face, and the bloody bandage that's wrapped around her head like a crown. Her golden hair is pulled back into a beautiful braid – surely my mamman's doing – and it helps somewhat to distract me from the bandages on her head. She's lost much of the baby fat that rounded her plump cheeks since the last time I saw her.

I force myself to look away and address my mamman past the lump that forms in my throat.

"Mamman," I start, moving to Lilah's bedside. "I'd love some time with her, if that's okay. Why don't you go try and get some rest? I'll watch over her for a while."

My mamman looks at me skeptically, but she eventually relents, letting her shoulders sag. "Of course. I... I suppose I could use a bath... I'll be back to check on you both soon." She gives me one more tight hug before gathering up an armful of her things from the floor and leaving the room.

"We'll be here," I tell her, though she's long gone before the words leave my lips.

27

"Lane," Zaid says, stepping forward and gently placing his hand on my elbow.

"Zaid," I croak as I turn to meet his gaze. I can barely see him through the blur of my tears, and I swallow past the knot in my throat. "What happened? Please, tell me what you remember. I need to know."

Zaid pulls up an extra chair as I sit beside my sister's bed, reaching over to put my hand on hers.

Her hand is cold, and although the thought has my mind racing and my stomach churning, I can't help thinking about how lifeless her little hand feels.

"We were almost here, Lane," he says, pulling my attention from Lilah's hand back to his face. His dark eyes are pleading. "We were so close, passing through the woods between Parth and the Keep when we were ambushed. Our travels before this had been rocky – your mamman's guards had to fight off two other bandit attacks before this one – but this... It was different. These were the same bandits we came across near Helna, but they were stronger, and there were at least twice as many of them. Some of your mamman's guards lost their lives in the struggle. The other was critically injured, but the doctor now says he'll be alright. Your mamman actually took down a number of bandits herself. I was working to fight off a couple of them who were trying to get Lilah when another came up from behind her and pulled her off her horse. They... they cut her up pretty badly before I could get to her."

Zaid stops talking.

He swallows audibly, hastily wiping at his eyes.

I reach over with my free hand and pat Zaid's arm. All this time, Alec has been silent, and if he's bothered by this small exchange, he's doing a great job hiding it. He pulls up the last chair in the room and sits at the foot of Lilah's bed.

"Please continue," I urge Zaid as softly as I can. "I need to know what happened."

"I fought them off, and when there were too many of them, and I couldn't move Lilah without them tackling her again, so I just crouched over her. I tried to shield her from as many as I could. It was then that another group of guards traveling south from the Keep heard us and came to our aid. There were enough of them that we were able to get the bandits to retreat, but it wasn't soon enough. The damage had already been done."

"That's awful," I whisper, fighting back a sob as I picture the ordeal. The other bandits we came across earlier in our journey

– before Zaid joined our party – were just your typical folks. People wanting money, or extra food. People looking to rob us. But the ones that attacked us on our way to Helna were ferocious, animalistic, driven by a motivation I still don't understand. I shiver thinking about their wet, grayish skin and the way they jumped about on all four limbs like dogs. I can't imagine having to fight off more of them, and I'm horrified that Lilah had to see them, let alone experience a close encounter with several of them.

Now Zaid finds his composure and keeps going. "It was so awful... There were so many more of them, and they attacked us on the main road in broad daylight. I've never seen anything like it..." Zaid's voice is filled with fear, and he shakes his head sadly.

"Have you?" I ask, turning my attention to Alec. He stares absently at the foot of Lilah's bed with a frown deeply furrowing his brow, but he perks up at my question. "Have you ever seen anything like what Zaid described?"

"Nothing quite like he described..." he starts. "Yes, I've seen those like what we came across near Helna before, but never so many. They have been known to attack in broad daylight, but as far as I know, they've never left the grasslands. I'm not sure what they were doing all the way on this side of the river near the Grand Council." Alec's frown remains, and he strokes the soft, short hair on his chin, puzzling.

"Fates," I say, but my voice is yet again barely above a whisper. "What is happening to the world?"

The three of us sit in silence for a moment when I notice that Zaid's left hand is bandaged and bloody, the bandages going up his arm below his sleeve, and he looks to be missing at least one finger.

"Zaid..." I start, voice wary, shifting in my chair so I can get a better look. "Did that happen when..."

Zaid's eyes fall to his hand, and then he turns and hides it behind his back. "Oh. Yes, that... it happened when I went after the one who pulled Lilah off her horse." Zaid's dark eyes swim with tears, flitting back and forth as he looks down at his feet as he relives the memory.

"Thank you," I whisper to him, and when he looks at me, his face is filled with a deep sorrow that makes me want to pull him close. I can't believe the sacrifice he made to keep Lilah safe. Instead, I just put my hand on his shoulder. "Thank you for what you did for her. For being there."

Zaid only nods, and the three of us go back to sitting in silence.

I look at my two friends, thinking through everything we've been through together.

"You guys?" I ask. My voice is weak, and I clear my throat, hoping to get it to work a little better. "Can I have some time alone with her? I'd like to just be with her right now if that's okay."

Alec and Zaid jump to their feet, muttering their various versions of "of course." Zaid gives me a tight hug, tighter now, I notice, with one arm than with the other.

He smells like the sea. Like the forges back in Palandra. He smells like home, and I cling to him for a moment, wanting nothing more than to be back at home with my family, like we were before all of this happened, waking up late in the morning after some strange dream, reassuring Lilah that I was alright. Having her scold me for wanting to keep my injuries from our parents. Having her ask me if I was sure I'd been taking my medicine.

Fates, how I miss her. I can't believe it's been so long.

I let Zaid go, and he gives me a sweet smile.

"I'll be nearby if you need anything, okay?" he says. I nod and do my best to return his smile, and he makes his way to the door. In the doorway, Zaid stops and turns back as Alec approaches me.

"Are you alright?" Alec asks me with his voice low. I can tell by the look on his face that he knows the words are meaningless, but I appreciate him for asking, nonetheless. I can't find the words to respond as more water works tumble down my face. I shake my head, and Alec's warm, strong hands find my arms, then my face. He cups my face in both hands, wiping away the streaming tears with his thumbs before pulling me into a tight embrace. Through the hair that covers my ears, he whispers. "I'm so sorry for all of this, Lane. If there is anything I can do..." he trails off, and I simply nod.

Of course.

If there was something he could do for her, then of course I would ask. But right now, there's nothing any of us can do. I squeeze Alec with all my might, and then I let him go, too, as he turns to follow Zaid out the door.

As the door clicks quietly closed, all my strength leaves me and I collapse into the chair beside my sister's bed. Now that I'm alone, there's nothing to stop the sobs from racking my entire body. And they do, for quite some time. I lay my head on Lilah's bed and clutch her arm as the fear and pain of everything comes out of me in loud, mournful sobs.

"Lilah," I cry, scooting closer to her, wishing with every fiber of my being that she'll wake up right now and squeeze my hand, tell me everything will be alright. "Lilah, I'm so sorry. I... I can't believe this has happened to you. It should have been me. I should have been there for you. I'm so... so *sorry*."

I'm overcome by another round of horrible sobs, and it takes everything I have not to turn around and break everything I can get my hands on. I stand, clenching my fists so tightly that my short fingernails draw blood. I look up at the ceiling.

"Is this what you wanted?" I ask, addressing the Fates, my tone so bitter that I hardly recognize my own voice. "Why would I do what you want when you let *this* happen? This is *your fault, all of you.*"

If the Fates are powerful enough to foresee that Alec and I would be a good fit, if they are powerful enough to bind us together for our entire lives to ensure we would find one another, then they're certainly capable of protecting my baby sister in her travels. Why would they let this happen?

When the rage doesn't quiet, I force myself to take some deep breaths and sit down again beside Lilah. I look her over as I run my thumbs absently over the new little cuts in my palms, trying to figure out what she needs, what I can do for her.

I should focus on that.

I lean over and adjust her pillow. When Lilah was little, she always flattened out her pillow before bed, telling me that it was better for her neck if her pillow wasn't fluffy. The doctors here have done an excellent job of keeping her pillows fluffed, but they don't know her. They couldn't know that she doesn't like that. I do my best to flatten her pillow as best I can, removing the extras. I pull her blanket higher up onto her chest and brush tiny loose strands of golden hair from her face.

"I'm back, Lilah," I tell her, tone now soft and filled with love as I realize one thing I can do. I can tell her about my travels. She's always loved hearing about the places I've been when I get home. "You'll never believe where I've been. I made it all the way to the other side of the Baskan mountains. And you know what? The world up there is gorgeous. It's *so* different from here. You'd love it. You'd better get all healed up so I can take you there. I know you'll be the one to figure out how we can bridge a connection with them and make things better for everyone."

I sit in silence for a moment, trying to think about what she'd like to hear the best.

"Lilah, you wouldn't believe it, but they've got magic up there, in Lithe. That's what they call the Nameless Country. Lithe. Anyway, they've got all kinds of magic up there, and *everyone* uses it. It's wild!

"I've met so many wonderful people there, too. I met a priestess who is blind, but she moves around like she can see everything. I didn't even know she was blind when I met her. And I met a man. I think you'd really like him. His name is Alec. And guess what! He's the reason for my condition – the reason I've always gotten those injuries. He gets mine, too! Or... well, he did. He doesn't anymore.

"We were bound by magic that came all the way from the Fates, if you'll believe that. *And* I met a real live witch that bound us together. But she had Mamman, and she was going to take me, so Alec had to... um... take her life. That seems to have severed the bond we had."

I tell Lilah all about the journey Alec and I took to find our mammans, focusing extra attention on the happy details, as these have always been Lilah's favorite. She lies perfectly still in her bed, but I tell myself that she's listening, saving up all her millions of questions until she's awake.

I take a moment to write to Alaya and Raonni back in Lithe and inform them that we made it safely, and that I hope Alaya is planning to join us soon.

I fall asleep sharing the tale of my travels with Lilah, reminiscing about how she's always loved to hear about my journeys when I come home.

I wake when a strong, warm hand rests carefully on my shoulder. I jolt upright, and although sleep blurs my vision, I scan the area around me in a panic. When I notice that it's Alec who has woken me, I relax a little bit and release a heavy sigh. My face feels like it's sagging, and judging by how tired my eyes are, I can tell I look awful.

"Sorry," I say, doing my best to rub the sandpaper feeling from my eyes. "I guess I fell asleep."

"Right on the edge of her bed," Alec says. His tone is gentler now than I've ever heard him speak before, and my bottom lip trembles.

"Yeah," I say. My eyes turn to Lilah. I brush back her golden hair, dulled from a lack of washing. I'll need to ask her medic if I can move her enough to unbraid her hair and wash those golden curls of hers. "I didn't realize I was so tired. I guess the journey wore on me more than I thought it had."

When I look back at Alec, his amber eyes are glossy, his mouth in a straight, tight line.

"Lane," he starts, but he takes a deep breath before continuing. I do my best to keep my eyes on him. I feel as if Lilah will disappear at any moment if I look away for too long, so I hold her hand tightly in mine as I meet Alec's gaze.

"Yes?"

"I know this is likely a silly question to ask," he starts, stepping closer to me, pulling up a chair and scooting so close that our knees touch and our eyes are level. "Are you okay?"

My gaze drops to my lap.

"I'm..." I start, but I have to pause to take a shaky breath. There they are again – those tears that fall without permission, sliding steadily down my cheeks. I blink to clear my vision, but that only sends more tears plummeting down my face.

With my free hand, I reach up to wipe them away, but Alec's hand is already there, and his thumb gently caresses my cheeks as he clears the tears away.

"That's what I thought," he says. He leans forward as I do my best to stop myself from crying again. He pulls me into his embrace, lifting me up onto his lap so I can bury my face in his chest, completely soaking his shirt.

"I'm so scared, Alec. I don't think I've ever been so afraid in my life. What if she doesn't wake up? What if she... what if she *does* wake up and she's different now? I keep coming back to the thought that if I had just been here..."

Alec leans back and lifts my chin, looking at me sternly. "Then you *both* would be in this condition. Lane, you heard Zaid. Trained members of the Guard were killed by those bandits. We ran into just a few like them in the grasslands near Helna, and the three of us barely made it out alive. With so many... I'm grateful that you *weren't* there."

"But—" I start again, but he shakes his head.

"If you were there, you would have ended up in the same state, then there really would be nothing you could do to help her," Alec says, his tone softly scolding.

I must not have been asleep for long, because the sun is finally setting, sending the last fading rays of sunlight to filter in through the windows, casting dark golden beams of light onto the stone flooring of the Keep.

I fall silent for quite some time. I'm not sure if it's only a minute or if it's longer, but it feels like forever as I watch the dust particles dance around in those last rays of sunlight, trying to sort through all the conflict in my heart.

"I'm so scared," I say again, leaning back against Alec's chest. His arms adjust, pulling me closer to him, holding me more tightly.

"I know," he whispers, pressing his forehead against mine. "You're here for her now. Focus on that. Whatever you need to do to help her, let me know. We'll do it together, okay? You're not in this alone. You don't have to shoulder *any of this* alone."

These words melt some of the ice around my heart, and I look up, searching Alec's face, wondering what I must have done to deserve someone who cares so much. Maybe it was all the Fates' grand design, but to me, it really feels like luck.

"Alec?" I ask, voice barely above a whisper.

"Yes, Lane?" he responds, whispering back. My eyes dart to his lips, and in that moment, I reach up, wrapping my arms around his neck, pressing my lips to his.

The two of us instantly relax, and that warm familiar feeling spreads throughout my body, scaring away the darkness that has settled like an anvil in my stomach.

Our lips part and our tongues collide, and I lean into the comfort of his kiss. I squeeze him tightly around the neck with my arms, tangling my fingers in the length of his hair, knowing that the moment we part, this wholeness I feel with him will dissipate.

"Wow, Lane. Is... this..." a small feminine voice croaks. It sounds ancient, thin and worn, and it takes me a moment to realize that the only other person in the room with us... the only person who could have said that is...

"Lilah!"

I straighten up and whip around so quickly that I practically fall out of Alec's lap onto the floor. I scramble up and hover over Lilah. My fingers flutter worthlessly, pointlessly over her body and her head, trying to decide what I can do to help her. I want to scoop her up into my arms and never let her go, but she looks so small and fragile that I just stand there, worried that I'll hurt her just by standing so close.

Lilah gives me a weak smile. Now that her eyes are open, I can see that they're dull, tired looking instead of their usual bright, crystal blue. She tries to raise her hand to hold mine, but it drops limply back onto the bed at her side before it even makes it into the air. I take it and weave my fingers with hers very carefully.

"Is this... what... you're..." she trails of for a moment, wincing. She swallows audibly with a pained expression on her face, and I turn to Alec.

"She needs water," I tell him, eyes pleading. "Can you find her some? She needs a drink. And find my mamman, please. She should be here."

Alec nods and leaves the room without another word, already searching the hallways for someone who can help.

"Is this what... you're... up to... these... days?" Lilah asks me. Her dim blue eyes flit to the doorway, in the direction Alec went. Her smile returns.

My cheeks burn, but all I can think about is how wonderful it is that she's awake. I'm thrilled that, despite her clear pain and lack of energy, she's playful with me. Hope fills me with a bright light that shows in the grin that stretches across my face, so wide that my cheeks hurt.

"Oh, Lilah," I say. I'm able to quell the excitement in me long enough to sit down again, though I scoot the chair so close to Lilah's bed that I have to sit with my legs crossed beneath me on the chair. "I'm so grateful you're awake. I was so worried. How are you doing? Are you in pain? Can I get you anything? Can I do anything for you? I'm so sorry you had to go through all of this..."

Lilah lets go of my hand and raises her fingers, slowly shaking her head.

"One... thing..."

"Oh, right," I say as my face begins to burn again. "Sorry. One thing at a time. How do you feel?"

Lilah rolls her eyes at me. Even though she looks gaunt and frail, the expression on her face makes her seem so much older than her nine – almost ten – years.

"Like I... got... attacked... by a... group of... crazy people," she says. She works to sit up, and I rush forward immediately, helping her lift her head, then her shoulders, then her back. I help her scoot back against the headboard of her bed, adjusting the pillow to support her back as she continues. "Like I... was booted... off my horse."

I find myself nodding like a madwoman.

"Of course. You would feel that way, wouldn't you?" I ask. "I'm so sorry."

Lilah gives the tiniest shake of her head. "Is this what... you've felt like... with your... condition?"

My condition, right.

It's been weeks since I obtained any injuries that weren't purely my own fault, my own experience. Oh, there's so much to explain to her, but all I want to do now is make sure that she's comfortable.

Lilah tries to sit up a little bit straighter and does her best to take in a deep, albeit shaking breath. She looks up at me with those big blue eyes of hers and smiles weakly.

For a moment, neither of us says anything. We just smile at each other, allowing the other's presence to fill us with nostalgia. It's been months since we've seen each other, since she chased after my caravan as my crew and I left for our last delivery job, waving goodbye as she always has. How I've missed her.

Suddenly, Lilah's expression grows concerned as a deep frown crinkles her brow.

"How have you been doing?" she asks me, able to string together slightly longer sentences now that she's sitting. "In all your letters... you never mentioned... how your condition was treating you. Surely, you must... have run out of medicine. Unless... you found another doctor on the road?"

Lilah's concern for me as she's been lying in a bed for over a week recovering from her attack fills my heart with such love I could fly. That's Lilah, though, always fussing over everyone else.

"Actually," I tell her, leaning forward, placing my elbows on the bed at her side and resting my chin on my hands. "My condition isn't what the doctor thought it was, after all. Turns out, it was never a medical condition, after all."

Lilah's eyebrows shoot up, and her eyes grow even wider. I do my best not to stare at the dark circles beneath them. "Really?" she asks, tone full of wonder. "What was it, then?"

"I promise I'll tell you when you're feeling better. It's a lot to process," I tell her, but she shakes her head slowly, that frown creasing the center of her forehead again.

"Come on, Lane. I haven't seen you in *ages*, and I just... woke up from the most awful dream... I've ever had. Please? Can't you just distract me for a while? I've missed you terribly."

I sigh. "Are you sure you're up for it?" I ask, brushing her forehead carefully with my fingertips.

"Promise I am!" Lilah replies, eyes lighting ever so slightly. Her cheerful tone widens my smile.

"Well, you know that guy who just left the room?" I ask, my cheeks and chest heating bit at the memory of her waking as we kissed.

"Of course." Lilah rolls her eyes. "I don't have memory loss. I'm not sure I've ever seen you *flirt* with a boy... let alone kiss one like *that*... I didn't even know you were interested in boys."

I think of all the other things that Alec and I have done together, all of the things I never would have dared to do before I met him, and my cheeks redden further. I continue hastily.

"It turns out that all those injuries I couldn't explain actually belonged to him," I tell her. I sit back and allow her a chance to process, but she looks at me blankly.

"What?"

I don't blame her in the slightest for being confused. Fates know I've felt my fair share of uncertainty in the last few months.

"It's true. His name is Alec, and he and I have been bound by magic since before I was born. Every time he got hurt, it caused an injury to appear on my body, as well. And the same happened to him whenever I was injured. Wild, isn't it?"

Lilah works to sit up straighter. With every word we share, she seems a little more herself.

"Lane, you can tell me the truth. I don't know why you're making up stories. I'm not a little kid anymore. I know that *magic* isn't real," she says, trying to sound stern and grown up.

Her tone carries the echo of every adult I spoke with about my condition as a child, everyone who told me that there had to be a medical explanation for what I was experiencing, everyone who dismissed any mention of magic. But I can see that little sparkle in her eyes at the thought, and I know at least some part of her longs to believe me.

"No, I swear it," I insist. "Magic *is* real. I've seen it. I wrote in that last letter I sent before... before all of this happened. But there's a whole world outside Maran waiting to be explored, and it's so different. Lilah, almost *everyone* out there uses magic in one form or another. The woman that bound me to Alec was just one magic user out of many."

I can see Lilah's façade start to wither away at my promises of magic and mystery outside the world we've always known. The idea brings some color back to her cheeks, though she's still too pallid, her features still worn and tired.

"I knew it..." she whispers to herself before looking back up at me. "Can I see how your bond works?"

My heart aches just a little bit at her request.

"Oh, Lilah, I'd love to show you, but I can't. When Alec and I found Mamman to bring her back home, she was being held captive by the witch that bound us together. And... well, in order for all of us to get away safely, Alec had to... um..."

"Kill her?" Lilah offers.

I nod. "Yeah, that. When he did, the magic she had bound us with disappeared, though I feel that some part of it still lingers. I feel it when we're close." I say this last part mostly to myself, and I have to blink away my thoughts and refocus on my sister as I start to relive the feeling I had just now as we shared a kiss. "Do you want to know the coolest part?"

"You haven't even told me the coolest part yet?" Lilah asks, bewildered.

"Nope. The coolest part about all of this is that when we were bound... we could actually *heal* each other's wounds. Like magic."

"Really?" Lilah asks. She tries to lean forward, but she winces and drops back onto her pillow, letting out an exasperated breath, clearly frustrated by her exertion.

Guilt pangs in my gut like a knife. I've gotten so carried away telling her about all the wonderous discoveries I've made recently; I should have known not to get her too excited. She looks utterly exhausted again, and despite her best efforts, her eyes begin to flutter closed.

"You lie back, Lilah," I tell her. "Get some rest. I promise I'll tell you everything when you're feeling stronger." I brush aside the few dirty golden curls that have fallen out from beneath the bandage on her forehead, those that are too short to stay in her braids for long. She must feel as tired as she looks, because she doesn't even fight my request. She just nods quietly and allows her eyes to close the rest of the way.

"You'd better," she murmurs.

It's in this moment that my mamman rushes into the room. "How is she?" my mamman asks. "How is my baby?"

I hold my finger to my lips and mouth the word, "quietly" as my mamman takes a look at Lilah, who now snores lightly, her head tilting to one side. I lean forward and work to lay her down again, and my mamman sits beside me.

"Did she really wake?" my mamman asks, fresh tears trailing down the length of her face.

"She really did. Do you want to sit with her for a bit?" I ask. "I think I'd like to go for a walk and get some fresh air. Maybe figure out where I'm going to stay."

"Of course, love," my mamman replies. "You get all settled, and I'll be right here when you come back. Oh, and Lane. When you do get settled into a room, leave your bow, okay? This is a civilized place, and you're a guest."

It takes every ounce of self-restraint I have not to roll my eyes at my mamman. I know she's serious. Although I've grown so attached to having it within reach at all times since I left Nerine with Alec months ago, I know the greatest thing I have to fear here in the Keep is my mamman's wrath if I don't mind my manners.

So, shooting one more look of adoration at my snoozing siter, I turn and wander through the hallways of Grand Council Keep, feeling as though the weight of the world has been temporarily lifted from my shoulders.

I wander around the fortress that makes up Grand Council Keep until I find an entrance to a beautifully kept garden – though I can't help but think this one is not nearly as vast or as beautiful as the garden at the Fates' temple back in Lithe.

In the garden, I breathe the cool evening air deeply. Snow has just started to fall in this region, though none of it sticks to the ground just yet.

I pace slowly around the garden, paying little attention to where I'm going. Instead, my mind keeps circling back to what I said to Lilah.

The coolest part about all of this is that when we were bound... we could actually heal each other's wounds. Like magic. I was going to continue by telling her that we first discovered this ability through a kiss.

In the moment, that didn't seem like an appropriate detail to share with my little sister, but now the thought sticks in my mind like an arrow in its mark.

When we were bound, Alec and I could heal each other's wounds through a single deep, meaningful kiss. We haven't been injured much recently – at least, we haven't been injured in the same way – and our kissing has been scarce through everything, but maybe... just maybe...

Could our kiss – our closeness – have *woken* my sister?

29

Over the next few days, Lilah continues to wake each day.

She brightens a little bit more with every visitor she gets, but she tires easily, and it's difficult for her to hold a conversation with anyone for more than a few minutes.

Every day, she asks me to tell her about the magic I experienced in my travels, but she doesn't stay awake for long, and the questions she asks aren't what I expect.

She keeps asking me questions like, "What kind of magic did you see? Can you see that magic improving the state of Maran?"

These days, improving the state of Maran is just about all she's interested in.

More than that, she keeps telling me, "I'd give anything to be healed already. I'm so tired of not being able to move my body. I *need* to do what I can to help take care of Maran."

It's strange; although she's only nine, she's matured so much since I left home, and she's lost a good deal of her playfulness. She's always been responsible, getting up early to complete her day's work so she could play. She's always been interested in the Women's Council, and it's always been her goal to help make our country a better place. But now there's a solemness and a determination that wasn't there when I left her running through the streets of Palandra, waving goodbye.

Every day, Lilah gives every possible effort she can to standing. She's getting restless, and it shows in how often she tries to get up, but each attempt is met with failure and results in her feeling frustrated and discouraged.

On the fourth day, she gets so angry that she throws her pillow at the wall and angry tears streak down her reddened face.

"You just need to give it some time, darling," my mamman tells her, voice soft and encouraging. She reaches out to rub Lilah's shoulder, but Lilah bats mamman's hand away.

"I'm *tired* of being stuck in this bed, ma'," Lilah whines, tossing herself back against the bed with a wince. "You saw those bandits. Every moment we waste is another moment they're out running rampant. Fates know what they're up to, now."

Hearing my sister curse and seeing her get so angry, is a little more than I can handle today.

I think I'll see who I can find that might be able to give me some answers that will put Lilah more at ease.

I also wonder what Alec and Zaid have been up to these last few days. I've been so focused on Lilah this week that I haven't even paused to consider that the two of them may have crossed paths, and I've seen little of either of them.

"Ma'," I say, giving my mamman a reassuring pat on the back. "I'll come back a little later. Do you need anything? Lilah, can I get anything for you?"

When neither of them answers me, I turn to exit Lilah's room, and as I turn the corner into the hallway, I bump into Zaid just outside. His face expression is initially grim, but the moment we cross paths, he smiles at me.

"Oh, Lane," he says, waving cheerfully. I've been avoiding him the last few days, spending every free minute I can with my sister, and trying to dodge the conversation we need to have regarding our letters. "I was just coming to get you. We've got some news I think you should know about. Come with me?"

At this point, anything would be better than watching my sister struggle.

"Sure," I reply, sticking both of my hands in my pockets. "Lead the way."

I listen to our footsteps echo off the stone walls, reverberating through the hallways of the Keep like discordant drums. We wind through the rounded hallways and up a flight of stairs before Zaid knocks on a heavy wooden door.

The woman who opens the door looks as though she must have come from Dunnen. Her clothes are plain, various shades of brown and tan. Her dark skin is freckled, and her beautiful, crinkled black hair is pulled up into a tight bun on top of her head. Her face wears the deep-set expression of someone who rarely smiles, with deep frown lines permanently creased into her face.

She moves away from the door without speaking, and Zaid and I enter the room to see a wide, crescent shaped corridor with a long rectangular table in the center. All chairs have been pushed to one side, and several people stand around the table, staring down at what appears to be a map of Maran.

Among the women standing in the Council room, I find Alec, who leans over the table with both palms pressed against the wood to support his weight. He looks up and regards me with a curt nod, but there's a softness in his eyes that warms my belly and reminds me of that last kiss we shared... and the power it may have had to wake my sister from her slumber.

I've been meaning to talk with him, share my theory with him, and see if he thinks we might be able to heal her that way. We haven't been alone long enough for me to speak with him yet, and it doesn't feel right to ask him to kiss me for any other reason than because he wants to.

But Lilah's health is important, and every day we waste only makes her angrier.

I'm pulled from my thoughts as Zaid returns to the table, and I follow him as Alec speaks up.

"I'm telling you, I've been there," Alec says to the group. "They can help us. The people in Lithe have been looking to make contact with us – we've just given them plenty of reason to stay away. But if things are getting this bad here, we're going to need more support than we have right among our ranks."

Alec's comment receives various responses. Some Council members nod solemnly, while others mutter their disagreements.

A woman adorned in golden armor with long white robes speaks up from across the table. She's from SunSpar, for sure, and I perk up, interested to hear what she has to say. SunSpar has always been so secretive and secluded as a community. Whatever she has to say will be news to me.

"You suggest that we contact the descendants of those who pushed our people out of their homes and forced them to settle here, and ask for help? We should not stoop so low. We cut off all contact with them for a reason, and we've got plenty of help here. We have warriors who are trained to handle pests like these," the woman says, holding her chin high in the air.

The way this woman calls the bandits that hurt my sister "pests" has my skin crawling and my blood boiling, but another woman interjects before I can say anything.

"I agree with Salma. You may have travel experience, Mr. Montrose, and you may be standing in for your mamman while she recovers from her travels, but you are not a member of this Council. The decision is not yours to make," the woman says. She's got long, olive green robes decorated with horses embroidered in light brown thread that adorn the neckline, sleeves, and bottom half. Our Helnan representative, certainly. Her light, straight brown hair brushes over her shoulder as she turns to her peers. "We have cause to be concerned about the increasing number of bandits throughout our land, but this is an internal problem. We should take care of it internally, with our own resources."

"If I may," Zaid says from beside me, raising his hands and drawing everyone's attention to him. His movements are stiff, and his bandaged hand is missing his pinky and ring finger. I cringe, bringing my hand to my mouth.

A woman who wears long white robes with the Women's Council sigil embroidered on the breast nods her approval. I recognize her from my childhood visits to the Keep as the Grand Countess, the leader of the Women's Council. Zaid gives a little bow in response to her acknowledgement. The Women's Council has accepted him into the Keep, but offering his opinion in an official Council meeting is a risky thing for him to do.

"Please," the woman says to him.

"Like all of you," he starts cautiously. "I have never been to the Nameless Country, this Lithe that Alec speaks of. But I have personally seen these bandits on more than one occasion. There is something different about them, something dark. To best inform ourselves, I believe we should listen to our friends who have visited this strange land and hear what they have to say."

Hearing Zaid back Alec's suggestion is surprising, to say the least. I lean forward to get a better look at his face, but he remains stoic.

The women around the table seem to listen better to what he suggests, however. It seems as though his training and studies have made a good impression on them.

The women begin to speak all at once, each sharing her idea of what's right.

Alec is in the heat of their debate right alongside them despite others making it clear he does not hold the authority to speak, so I lean over and bump Zaid's elbow with my arm.

"What's going on?" I ask him, feeling as though I've just woken from a long sleep. "I feel like I'm missing something important here."

Zaid gives me a small smile and leans down to talk into my ear so that I can hear him over all the chatter.

"Those bandits that attacked us near Helna, that ambushed us on the road to the Keep... they are growing in numbers, somehow becoming more organized than we thought originally expected. Every day their groups seem to expand and spread, and they're no longer attacking simple travelers on the road. They're getting into villages, breaking into people's homes. Last we heard, the groups are making their way north. It seems as if they're headed here: They're headed for the Keep."

My eyes widen with the horror of it all.

I find it difficult to believe those animalistic bandits we fought off months ago could be so organized as to have an agenda like that, or that they would do anything besides seize the opportunity to prey on unsuspecting travelers that have the misfortune of crossing their paths.

"They've got to have a leader," I say, more to myself than to Zaid. "There's no way they'd be moving in the same direction in such a way without something driving them. Even your... more typical... bandits don't work that way, and they definitely don't work in large groups. Where are they all coming from?"

Zaid shrugs, and several women in the room shuffle heatedly as they continue to argue.

"Nobody knows for sure. Some say they've just appeared as if from nowhere. Others claim they've been in our cities all along, hiding right under our noses in alleyways and sewers. One thing is for sure – we need to stop them."

"Hence Alec's argument for outside reinforcements," I confirm, piecing it all together. Zaid nods.

"Right. I agree with him. At the rate with which these bandit groups are expanding, I'm not sure we have the capacity to handle this internally anymore," Zaid mutters, eyeing the group.

I bite my lip nervously as I wrack my brain for some kind of solution.

"Hold on a second," I tell him, stepping forward. "I've got an idea."

Without waiting for a response, I turn and make my way to the Grand Countess.

"Excuse me," I say politely, though I dare to tap her on the shoulder to get her attention. She looks at me with her eyebrows raised high on her forehead.

"Yes?" she asks. This woman has some of the darkest skin I've ever seen, and she has a sort of glow about her. Her wide lips purse as she regards me, and I give a slight, respectful bow.

"I'm sorry to interrupt your conversation. I'm not sure if you remember me—"" I tell her.

I work to recall the last few lessons my mamman gave me regarding Council etiquette.

"Of course I remember you," the Countess says. "Ailene's daughter, the traveler. I always hoped to see you in this Council chamber, though I hadn't foreseen that it would be under such unfortunate circumstances."

I nod slowly. I'm startled that this woman remembers anything about me, and I'm flattered that after all this time she still held a hope that I would join the Council. I want to apologize for choosing a different path, but now isn't the time for that. I need to get to the point while I've got her attention.

"May I speak freely?" I ask, trying to hold some formality despite the tense situation. I am a guest here, after all.

"You may," she says, though I can tell she's itching to turn her attention back to the group.

"I've come face to face with these bandits, and they are far from anything our crews have encountered in the past. I've also been with Alec to Lithe and seen the way things are over there. It's incredible, and the atmosphere there is nothing like I've ever imagined. They use magic over there, even in their daily lives," I tell her. At the mention of magic, the Grand Countess's eyebrows raise even higher on her brow, her expression incredulous, but I press on quickly. "Here, magic is regarded as nothing more than foolish, childish imaginings. But I know the truth, now, and you all should, too.

"Now, I know you are right to be wary of outside supports, especially given the history of the migration and the patriarchy our ancestors escaped from all those years ago. So, I have a suggestion. A middle ground, so to speak. Something to test the waters."

I clench my fists and steel my nerves.

"Go on," the Countess prompts.

The few women immediately surrounding the Countess have quieted to listen to what most certainly sounds like the ravings of a lunatic.

I take a deep breath and continue.

"I know someone who deals with people from Lithe frequently. She trades in the magical items they use. I am hopeful that she will be back in Maran soon, and with your permission, I'd like to call on her and have her weigh in. Not only could she offer some insight to the likelihood that the Lithians would come to our aide, but she could also offer suggestions for resources we could utilize, and she may even be able to offer more information about what we're up against."

When I finish making my case, I feel out of breath, and my entire face is flushed. My heart feels as if it beats a million times a minute.

The Countess seems to ponder my words for a moment, then she gives a solitary nod.

"Well, only a fool would make a decision without looking at all of her options first. If things are getting as bad as they seem to be, it would indeed be foolish of us not to take every possibility into consideration," she says evenly, startling the Council members around her. The Countess lifts her chin and addresses the entire group with a calm, steady voice that commands their obedience. The crowd immediately hushes.

"Esteemed Council members," the Countess says, holding her hands up, and the sleeves of her robes dangle below her open palms. "I have heard your voices, and I have considered your opinions. Now, I have made a decision. These young people have traveled places we have not been, and they are the only ones among us who have faced these demons we speak of directly. They have made an acquaintance who will demonstrate her knowledge of what the citizens of Lithe may have to offer, and we will reconvene again once we have heard from her. For now, go to your chambers. Eat, try to relax, pray if you are so inclined. Fates know we need the help."

The women around the table seem to accept the Countess's command without argument, though many are clearly unhappy with the announcement. They say their goodbyes quickly and excuse themselves from the room.

Alec looks across the table at me and mouths, "Wow!"

I can't help but blush a little bit as I smile back at him.

"Lane," the Countess says as the last few Council members leave the room. "How quickly can you make contact with your acquaintance?"

"I will do that now," I tell her without hesitation. "One of the incredible things this acquaintance has introduced to me is the power of extremely quick communication."

The Countess nods her approval. "Very well, then. I'm glad to have you here, in any capacity. Though I respect them highly, you have more real-world experience than many of our Council members. I look forward to hearing from you in our future meetings. Come find me when you receive a response."

"Th-thank you," I stutter, awestricken by her kind, unexpected words.

"Until then," she says, patting me gently on the shoulder. "Have a good night."

30

Back in my designated chambers, I pace back and forth anxiously. It's been five hours since I've sent Audy to find Alaya.

The sun is long gone now, and the large, full moon casts long shadows across the stone floors of my otherwise dark room.

I've tried to distract myself until I can receive a response from Alaya, but nothing has done the trick.

I know Audy is a magical bird, but I know that expecting him to track down Alaya and get word back to me in less than five hours is unreasonable.

Still, I can't help but wring my hands as I wait.

After listening to the sound of my footsteps echoing in the silence, I decide to remove my boots. The sound of my bootheels clicking against the stone floor has been a comfort to me, a metronome of sorts against the cacophony of worries that prattle about my brain. Perhaps if I no longer hear those sounds, I might be able to get my body to finally settle.

I plop down on the edge of the large bed the Council has provided me, and the plush white bedding folds in at my sides.

Just then, a soft knock raps at my door.

Frowning, I stand and make my way across the room. No one should be awake at this hour, and there's no reason I can think of why anyone would want to visit me so late in the evening. When I open the door, I find Alec standing on the other side, concerned frown furrowing the center of his brow.

"I figured you were still awake. Thought you might be up worried," he says. I'm not sure if it's the bond we shared, or if some small part of that bond still lingers within us somehow, but Alec knows me well. I step aside and invite him in.

"Not sure what else I'm supposed to do," I mutter. As he enters the room, I close the door behind him.

"Sleep?" he offers, and the two of us turn to face one another. I tap my hands awkwardly on my thighs.

"Right," I say. "I'm not sure that's in the dice for me. Not until I get a response from Alaya, anyway. The entire Council is depending on her for answers, and it's not like those bandits are just going to take a break."

"There's only so much you can do right now," Alec says as he walks slowly around my room.

"I know," I mumble. At this point, I've chewed my nails short with anticipation. I find myself thumbing them as I stand across the room and watch him wander through the moonlight. "What are you doing up this late, anyway? Just figured you'd take a stroll through the hallways in the middle of the night?"

"Actually," he says, stepping now toward the bed. He sits down on its edge and leans back against the plush pillows that rest upright against the large pine headboard. "I was restless myself," he says. "I wanted to come and check on you. I thought the two of us would sleep better if we were together."

He puts his arm out and pats the bed beside him. I raise an eyebrow at him and cross my arms. His tone is innocent enough, and his eyes are wide, totally lacking the flirtation I expect to accompany a statement like this from him.

Both my eyebrows raise even further, and I do my best to keep the smile off my face.

"Is that right?" I ask. I step toward the bed. "I hope you know, with everything going on right now, I'm not so sure I'm in the mood to fool around with you," I tell him, but the soft, half-smile on his face makes my words feel meaningless even as they leave my lips.

"No funny business from me tonight, promise," he says. "Now come here." He reaches across the bed as I sit tentatively beside him. He wraps his arms around my waist and pulls me snug against his body, and I let out a startled yelp and then cover my mouth. These large buildings are well constructed with thick stone walls, but the stone tends to carry an echo, and the last thing I want is to disturb someone here in the middle of the night.

Now that he's got me close, Alec's arms wrap more tightly around me, and sighs, resting his head on my neck.

"Tell me what's on your mind?" he murmurs into my hair before pressing his soft, warm lips against my cheek. I breathe deeply and try to let go of some of the tension I've been accumulating lately.

"Oh, everything," I tell him.

"Everything?"

"Pretty much. Lilah," I start.

"I thought so," Alec says, and I reach my hand up, weaving my fingers into his wavy blond locks.

"I'm worried about her. She's truly unhappy with how slowly she's healing, and at this rate, I myself worry she may never fully heal..." I say.

I've had these words bounding around inside my head for days, and now that I've finally said them out loud, I feel equally relieved and guilty for admitting them.

Alec's hand reaches up to run his fingers through my hair.

"She will, Lane. It just takes time. You know that."

"Yes, I know. Logically, I understand that. But I can't help but wonder..." I trail off, unsure how to talk to him about this.

"You wonder what?" he prompts when I don't continue.

I let out my breath in a slow exhale.

"It feels like... like *we're* the reason she's awake. You heard the doctor. Things were looking grim. The doctor worried Lilah wouldn't wake up at all, and she just happens to wake the moment we kiss in her presence, when we *know* what our kisses have done for our wounds in the past?"

Hearing the words out loud, I realize just how absurd they sound. But I also know that having a magical bond caused by the Fates themselves also sounds crazy, and that statement is irrefutably true.

"Huh," Alec responds.

"I just don't believe that's a coincidence. Not knowing everything I know now," I tell him.

Alec shifts against me, raising his head to get a better look at my face. I roll over and meet his gaze. In the darkness, with only the moonlight to illuminate them, his eyes seem so much darker than usual – a rich chocolate color instead of their typical amber brown. I wish I could fully read the expression on his face.

"I see..." Alec says. "Why don't we test that theory?"

His question takes me by surprise, and I prop myself up on my elbows to get a better look at him.

"What?" I ask.

"If you think our kiss may have healed her, I can believe that. They have healed us," he says.

"But that was when we were bound," I state, chewing my bottom lip.

"Right," he replies. He pauses for a moment, and in the darkness, I watch as he purses his lips, considering his next words. "Who's to say our bond is totally gone? I know that the Fates want us together. I know that when I'm with you, I feel whole. I still feel that connection. Around you, I feel healed. Perhaps that bond isn't completely severed. After all, Marana bound us, but it was the Fates' will that made it so."

Could this really be? I know I've felt the same wholeness around him that he just mentioned... but could it really be that some part of our bond is still here? I don't want to let myself believe it, fearing that it's all too good to be true.

But still, my heart sings at the thought, and I put my hand on Alec's chest, trailing my fingers down over the soft material of his shirt to the puckered scar on his torso, where he was stabbed on the first night we met.

The night I realized we were bound.

"Do you really think so?" I ask. My voice is barely above a whisper, afraid that saying them aloud might take away any chance of them actually being true.

Alec raises his shoulder in response.

"It can't hurt to try and find out, can it?" he asks.

Excitement roils within me, and I give him a tight hug.

"How would it be? If we could heal others the way we heal each other?" I say, my voice muffled against his shirt.

After a moment, Alec speaks again.

"Have you considered asking Alaya for help?" he asks. When I just look at him, confusion spelled across my face, he continues. "In case our theory doesn't test out how we'd like it to. She deals in magic for a living. Surely, she's got to have something that could speed along your sister's recovery. It's worth asking her, I think."

He's absolutely right, and to be honest, I have considered it. Although I wouldn't admit this before the Countess, that is one reason I wanted to invite Alaya to join us here. If she really could somehow find a way to help Lilah, then I have to give it a shot.

Now my mind returns to the other tumultuous thoughts that have kept me awake for the last several hours.

"Alec?" I ask.

He must have started to drift off, because he jumps a little bit as he responds with a "hmmm?"

"It feels like something's coming, doesn't it? Something bad," I say, keeping my voice hushed, staring at the little beams of moonlight that stretch across the room. "I felt it before I stood in on that meeting earlier – I've felt it for a while now, actually – but now I can't get it off my mind. It feels like a storm is brewing. I only wish I knew what was coming."

Alec squeezes my shoulder, rubbing his thumb along the two-inch-long scar on my bicep. I look down at his identical scar. I can barely see the bulge of it beneath his shirt.

"Whatever it is," he says, sleep blurring his words together. "We're in for some turmoil. I don't think the Council even knows what to expect, but in all my experience with bandits, I've never heard of anything like this. It seems that they're motivated by something greater."

"We have to do something," I say.

At this point, with Alec here beside me and my body finally still, I've relaxed enough that I have trouble keeping my eyes open. They keep fluttering closed as I listen closely to the *thump-thump-thump* of Alec's heartbeat.

"Together, Lane," he murmurs. "We'll figure this out. Now let's try to get some rest. We've got a lot of work ahead of us tomorrow."

31

In the morning, I wake just as the sun's first beams of light paint hints of color across the sky, and I wriggle out of Alec's embrace, doing my best not to wake him. As I get dressed into some fresh clothes, I'm startled by a soft tapping on my window. I cross the room to find Audy fluttering about just outside the window. I suppose he hasn't found another way into the building yet. I rub my eyes and rush to open the window and let him in.

Audy drops to the gray stone windowsill to rest his wings while I retrieve the message at his talons.

When I unroll the message, my heart drops into my stomach, and my shoulders sag. The message is blank. Immediately, I dig through my belongings – which I've decided to keep in my satchel the last few days rather than putting them away – and scribble another note onto the little blank scroll.

I can't help the pang of irritation that rushes over me as I write. My first worry should be that Alaya might be in danger if she hasn't responded, but this feels like a game. She wouldn't have attached a blank message if she was seriously hurt. It feels more like she's only playing with me, but I am not in the mood for one of her games.

Just as I start to roll up my response, there's a loud bang on my door followed by a trickling sort of scratching sound. On the bed, Alec stirs and rolls over, and I work to steady my pounding heartbeat.

When I open the door, I'm met with Alaya's auburn hair, crimson lip coloure and stark, silvery blue eyes. For a moment, I just stare, completely dumbfounded. When the shock wears off, I narrow my eyes at her and fold my arms across my chest as she invites herself into my room.

"What are you playing at?" I ask as I close the door as softly. It's still early, and I don't want to wake anyone by slamming things around... if they haven't already woken from Alaya's obnoxious knock.

Alaya's eyes dart to Alec still laying on my bed, and she smirks, but she keeps her remarks to herself.

"Whatever do you mean?" she asks, feigning innocence. "I'm here, aren't I? Why would I write you a note to inform you when I was planning to announce my presence in person? I hate sending messages via letter if I can help it. *If* the message isn't intercepted, the receiver still might misconstrue its meaning – they're *so* impersonal, don't you think?"

Alec rolls again and wakes, looking around groggily as Alaya takes confident steps around my room.

"Hmm," I grunt, frowning at her as she moves.

"Like this one," she says. Her fingers duck quickly into her pockets to retrieve the message I sent last night asking her to come to the Keep. "You ought to be careful what you write in one of these, my dear. One might think you care for the good health of your sister over the wellbeing of your country."

Alaya holds the parchment up with two dainty fingers, and I reach up to snatch them from her grasp.

"Hey—" I start as she darts away carelessly, causing me to stumble forward.

"Ah-ah," she says, shaking a long, pointed finger at me. "I think I'll keep this."

"What does it matter if her family is more important to her than the rest of the country?" Alec asks. His voice is low and gruff with sleep, but he's standing now, and he makes his way to my side, slipping his hand around my waist. "I care a hell of a lot more for my family than I do about those bandits causing trouble out there. That's natural. No one could fault her for that, especially given the condition her sister is in. Besides, Lilah has great standing already with the Council, so looking out for her *is* looking out for everyone else."

I beam up at Alec.

"Thanks," I say softly to him, and he smiles back at me with a quick wink.

Alaya rolls her eyes.

"Whatever," she says. "Still keeping it. So, now that I'm here, shall we go see that precious sister of yours? Where is she, anyway? Certainly, you wouldn't let her out of your sight after all she's been through, would you?"

"Wait a second," Alec remarks suspiciously, turning to Alaya with narrowed eyes. "How did you get in here? The gates don't open until after the sun has risen."

Alaya flits her hand through the air, waving off his question. "Same way I get anywhere. I invited *myself* in."

I roll my eyes and suppress a scoff.

"Alaya, if you're going to show these women that they can trust you, you're going to need to follow their rules *by the book*. You're in their territory, now. You may want to remember that if you want to keep your head," I warn her. "I suggest leaving whatever way you came from and coming in through the gates when they open. Then, you'll report to the *Council* first. Once you have *official* clearance, then we can go take care of Lilah. She's doing better. We can wait that long."

Alaya raises her thin, red eyebrows at me.

"Are you certain you want to wait until after their business has been addressed? You know, these political discussions can take quite some time. I could just slip in there and see what I can do for your sister before I go around the front. In and out, super quick," she says, a smirk playing at the corners of her mouth.

As tempting as her offer sounds, I know we need to play by the rules.

I nod slowly. "Yes, I'm sure. The last thing I want is for someone to catch you trying to help her and cut you off right in the middle. Just be careful, please."

Alaya sways her hips as she adjusts her weight, and her arms fold across her corset.

"Fates, I thought if I was going to be inside the Keep that I'd at least get to have a little bit of fun. But fine. We'll do it your way. I'll follow the damn rules."

"Thank you," Alec and I say simultaneously.

"You want to come with me, handsome?" Alaya offers. "I've got probably an hour to kill before the sun's all the way up. I could use someone to keep me entertained until then."

My jaw drops, but Alec doesn't miss a beat.

"No, thanks. I've got plenty to focus on right here," he says. His hand finds mine, and he weaves our fingers together.

Alaya pouts. "Are you sure? I could get pretty lonely out there, waiting all by myself."

"Something tells me you'll manage," he replies, and I'm shocked by his quick responses. It's been quite some time since I've watched him turn somebody down.

"Ah, well," she says, running her gaze up and down his body. "Can't blame a girl for trying."

At that, Alaya turns and sneaks out through the door to my room and disappears into the hallway, and I can't help but imagine a little fox sneaking through a henhouse. Alaya's always felt a little bit on the dangerous side to me, but sneaking into Grand Council Keep is a whole new level of crossing the line. As she leaves, I find myself letting out the breath I must have been holding, and the tension in the room lessens significantly in her absence.

"Wow," I mutter under my breath.

"Agreed," Alec murmurs. He leans over and plants a kiss on my forehead.

"Thanks for saying all that," I tell him, squeezing him around the waist with both my arms.

"You bet," he says. Then he pulls back to look at me clearly. His eyes sparkle as they search my face. "I meant every word."

"Yeah?"

"Every one of them," he confirms.

A smile creeps onto my face, and I poke Alec in the abdomen with my index finger.

"Then *you* need to have a talk with her. It's clear she thinks she has a chance with you, and watching her try to convince you... well, *I'm* pretty convinced. You're going to need to set her straight."

"What?" Alec jests, adjusting his grip on me. He spins me in a full circle before pulling me back in so that my body presses against his. "Jealous?"

"Of *her*?" My voice squeaks. "Yes. Absolutely. How could I not be? She's wild and beautiful and dangerous. I'm just..." I trail off for a moment, lifting one shoulder in a halfhearted shrug. "Lane."

Alec only laughs.

"What?" I ask, leaning back to look at him, though he keeps his arms locked tightly around me.

"That's ridiculous."

"Ridiculous, is it?" I ask, this time poking him in both sides as he wiggles away. I'm surprised to find that he's ticklish. I've never noticed or thought about it in all our time together. As he backs away, I stare him down, determined to make him laugh some more. "What was it you said about me being ridiculous? Get back here. I'll show you who's ridiculous!"

I chase Alec around my room for a minute, and when I finally catch him, I tackle him and continue to poke him until he begs me to stop. The sound of his laughter is music to my ears. It's never been so clear or so jovial before, and I bask in the sound.

Finally, he turns on me and pulls me into a deep kiss that erases all thought from my mind.

When we part, he asks, "You know what's funny?"

"Hmm?" I say, trying to coax myself out of the daze his kiss has left me in.

"You've fallen right into my trap," he says.

Now his fingers dig into my sides, and as he tickles me back, my laughter rings out against the stone walls of my chambers.

"Stop!" I plead with him. "You're going to wake the whole entire Keep!"

"You're the one laughing so loud!"

"I can't... help it!" I say between exasperated breaths. Finally, he lets me go, and I stand up and straighten my clothing. "There," I say now that I've had a moment to catch my breath. "That's better. Now, I'm going to go check on Lilah. You should probably go get some new clothes. One might think you've spent the night in someone else's room."

Alec grins at me, standing also.

"They wouldn't be wrong," he says, kissing me on the neck as I shoo him away with a grin on my face.

I open the door to my room, and as I do, I'm faced with the image of Zaid, poised to knock. When he sees me with Alec, his expression falls, and he lets his hand drop limply to his side.

"Oops, looks like someone else has an important conversation to have, too," Alec whispers to me. He places a quick kiss on my cheek before sliding past us in the doorway.

Zaid jumps away as if Alec has a plague, but he never takes his eyes off of me. I listen as Alec's footsteps fade down the hallway, and I wish I could go with him.

My cheeks flush, and my heart suddenly feels so heavy.

"Um..." I start. "Hi, Zaid. What are you doing up so early?" I ask, plastering a friendly smile on my face.

"Did you spend the night with him?" he asks, ignoring my question, cutting right to the chase.

Fates. How much of that conversation did he hear?

I wrack my brain for something to tell him.

Nothing... like *that*... happened last night, but I can't exactly tell him that it's not what he thinks, because Alec and I *have been* intimate with each other that way before.

I try my best to evade the question.

"I was just on my way to Lilah. Would you like to join me? I wanted to go down and see about getting her some breakfast first. You could walk with me, if you wanted to."

Zaid's face remains serious, and to my horror, his eyes fill with tears. "Lane, did you?"

My gaze falls to the floor. My next thought is to tell him that it's none of his business, that what happens in my room is private, but that's not fair. Not after all the letters, all the words written and the hope I've given him.

I sigh. "Maybe you should come inside."

Zaid enters my room without another word, though the solemn expression on his face tells me everything I need to know about what he's feeling right now. Once he's inside and I've closed the door again, I notice his eyes turn to my bed, with its still wrinkled blankets. He turns to me expectantly.

"I'm not sure where to start," I tell him honestly, sticking my hands nervously into the pockets of my trousers.

"Start with the truth, Lane," Zaid says, his tone flat. I don't think I've ever heard him speak like this before. He's always been so warm with me. "Don't beat around the bush. Don't lie or try to avoid hurting my feelings. I need to know."

"Well..." I trail off. Fates. It's as if every word I've ever learned has suddenly fled from my brain, but I need to say *something*. "Last night wasn't... we didn't... I think..."

What *do* I think, exactly?

The way he's just standing here looking at me, waiting for me to explain what's going on, I decide it's probably best if I just sort through my thoughts with him right here. After everything I've put him through, that's the least I can do.

I take a deep breath and let it out shakily.

"You think?" he presses.

"Right, sorry," I mumble. I make my way to my bed and sit at the foot of it. Zaid follows, doing his best to keep me from avoiding eye contact with him. "Things have been so complicated, Zaid, and I'm really sorry about that. I want to start there. And start by saying that I never expected things to go this way. I... I wanted to be with you for so long."

I tell Zaid all about the vision I had with the Fates and their fading lifeforce. I tell him about their plan for Alec and me.

I tell him – in as little detail as possible – the intimate moments Alec and I have had together, and that our kiss, our closeness, may have been the thing that healed Lilah so that she could wake. Zaid knows how much that means to me.

I tell him that I can't take something like that lightly, however I feel about everything else that comes with that fact.

Zaid's face droops.

"You're choosing him, then, aren't you?" he asks.

I want to tell him it's not as simple as that, but all I can do is nod, swallowing any arguments I might have made.

"What about all our letters?" he asks, working to blink away the tears in his eyes. "What about all those things we said? All that time we've spent working together. Doesn't that mean anything to you?"

"Of course it does," I tell him, reaching out to take his hand. He has to know that.

"Have you considered all that you might lose if Alec is your choice?" he asks me.

"What?" I squeak. His words make my body grow cold. "What do you mean? Are you telling me you won't be around at all?" My voice breaks, and I too find myself blinking past tears that now roll quietly down my flushed cheeks.

Zaid runs his hand through his dark hair in frustration.

"I can't, Lane. I love you. Don't you see that? If you... if you choose *him* over me, I don't think I could bear watching you together every day, knowing I never got a chance to show you how happy I could make you. I never got a chance to even *try*."

His words are a dagger in my gut.

"Zaid, I—" I start, working to speak past the lump in my throat. I feel as if all of the air has suddenly been sucked out of the room. "I don't know what to say."

Zaid reaches out in desperation, gripping both of my hands in his so tightly that his eight remaining fingers leave little white prints in my skin. His hands are calloused and scarred from all his time apprenticing in various trades. I've always loved that about him – his never-ending efforts to be better, to learn more.

"Say you'll choose *me*," he pleads. "Say you'll give me that chance I've been waiting for. Lane, please. Don't choose him. Not until you've given me a chance."

I'm shaking now, and my entire face burns. "Zaid, it's not as simple as that. I can't just choose you." Zaid moves away, his expression openly telling me how much I'm hurting him. I gasp, pulling one hand away from his to rub the bridge of my nose. "It's not like I wanted any of this! For the longest time I wanted you, Zaid! But I have to consider what I know. The Fates..."

"But you hate that the Fates have chosen your path for you," Zaid argues. "You told me before that you never even *believed* in the Fates. So, spite them. Make your own path."

"Being with Alec saved my sister, Zaid," I tell him, my voice so quiet now I'm not sure he's heard me. "I know it did. I can't just ignore that."

I can tell by the way Zaid's shoulders droop, the way his expression goes cold, that he knows there's no getting past this for me. He pulls his hand slowly from mine.

"So that's it, then," he says numbly.

"I'm sorry, Zaid. I care for you, deeply, and I truly don't want to lose you. But there's so much more going on here, and it's not all black and white. It's more complicated than that, and being with Alec... it's one puzzle piece that fits. I've got to see this through now that I know just what weight this decision carries. I'm... I'm so sorry."

Sniffling, I reach out again to touch Zaid's shoulder, hoping to offer him some kind of comfort, but he shies away from me, keeping his eyes on the floor.

"You've made your decision then," he says. Though tears stream down his face, his tone is expressionless. "So be it."

"Zaid," I start. I have no idea what I could say that would do anything but make things worse, but he interrupts me anyway, holding his hand up to silence me.

"Don't. You've made your decision. This is a mistake, Lane, and you're going to regret it." His words are softly spoken, but they ring within me as if he's shouted them.

My mouth falls open, but I can't find anything more to say. I watch through blurred vision as Zaid exits my room, and I'm left with the distinct feeling that his words are true: Things will never be the same between us again.

32

I sit in my room, watching the sun rise as it casts long shadows through my window. I know I need to get moving. I need to see Lilah, meet with the Council, see what Alaya can do to help.

But I just sit here, staring blankly at the floor, paralyzed by the deep sadness that fills my heart and the fear I feel that I have just lost a wonderful friend. Why must things be this way? Have I really made such a mistake?

Silent tears fall onto my lap and the cold stone floor, and for a brief moment, I wish I'd never made that journey to Nerine. I wish instead that my crew and I had been deterred by the storm that had slowed us down all those months ago, and that we'd left our final deliveries for naught.

If I never met Alec, everything would be so much simpler.

But my gut feeling tells me that things are better having met Alec, and I can't help the way I feel around him.

Finally, somehow, I find the motivation to stand. I cross the room on legs as wobbly as if I'm walking for the first time, and I open my window to watch as flurries of tiny snowflakes flit through the sky, making their way to the ground to join the others that must have fallen in the night. I let the icy breeze carry the snow into my room and brush against the tears on my face. I allow the cold to fill me to my core.

I curse the Fates for choosing this life for me.

I curse them for making things so difficult, and for hurting someone I care so deeply about.

More than that, though, I curse myself for ruining things.

The bitterness I feel helps to dull the ache of my sadness. Using it to fuel me, I pick up my satchel and carry myself to the door. I will check on Lilah first. I will meet with the Council, and I will see what Alaya can do with all the magic at her disposal. I will mourn the loss of my dear friend and the potential romance that never blossomed, but for now, I will do what I've always done. I will push forward.

I move numbly through the hallways of Grand Council Keep, and as I cross the long hallway that has large windows overlooking the garden, I marvel that – despite the snow we've been getting – the fountain in the center has water that still has not frozen.

I barely remember going down to the kitchens. People talk to me, and I must respond to them, but I don't recall saying anything specifically.

When I reach Lilah, I hand off a tray of food to my mamman and sit down at Lilah's side. She's asleep right now – she's been sleeping a lot since Alec and I woke her – and I reach out to take her hand in mine. Her hands are small, smooth to the touch, and cold.

I stare at her for a long time, lost in thought, ignoring my mamman's concerned glances, and doing my best to keep from crying again. I need to do something that will get me away from my thoughts for a while, but it's all I can do to keep from crumbling as the memory of my conversation with Zaid plays over and over in my head.

Soon, Alaya is at the door, guided by the doctor.

"Got official directions here, Lane," she says smoothly, her tone cool and callous. "You proud?"

My mamman takes one look at Alaya with her dark auburn hair, her bright red lips, silver-blue eyes. She notes the daggers slung on either side of Alaya's wide hips and the blouse beneath her corset that's open far enough to show plenty of cleavage. Mamman raises her eyebrows at me.

"Introduce me to your friend, Lane?" she asks.

Right.

"Ma'," I start, gesturing to Alaya, though my heart isn't in it. My hand flops loosely at the end of my arm. "This is Alaya. She deals in... well, magic. She's here to see what she can do to help. Alaya, this is my mamman."

"Good to meet you," my mamman states, ever aware of her manners. Alaya clicks her tongue and nods at my mamman.

"Heard a lot about you," Alaya says to my mamman, but she doesn't follow up with anything else.

This short comment leaves my mamman confused, of course, but Alaya ignores her as she makes her way to my sister's bedside. As she does, I notice the bag she's got slung across her shoulder, and I wonder where she stashed that when she came to see me this morning. The bag bulges on the sides even more than usual, and various objects clatter around inside as she slides it off her shoulder and sets it on the bed. Although I didn't explicitly ask her to help Lilah in my letter, and she was already on her way to the Keep when she received it, it looks like she packed a few extra things that might help, anyway.

"What are you going to do?" I ask her, picking nervously at the nubs of my chewed fingernails before gesturing at the bag. I'm nervous about Alaya using magic to heal my sister, but I'm sure that the effects of strong, intentional magic from someone who knows what she's doing will be better for her than whatever uncertain effects may come from my untested theory with Alec. Maybe with the two paired together we'll be able to heal her completely.

"I'm going to help. Isn't that why you wanted me here?" she asks. She's usually not this short with me. I wonder if Alec has had the chance to talk with her already. She pulls out a bright green vial and looks it over before setting it down on the bed.

She mutters little incomprehensible comments to herself as she moves from bottle to bottle. When she's pulled out a handful of containers of various shapes, sizes and colors, she lays them all out on the bed side by side and frowns at them for a moment, pursing her lips.

Her eyes dart back and forth over the labels as if she's contemplating something important, and it takes everything I have to keep myself from asking what she's waiting for, or what she's thinking about, or what any of these elixirs will do.

As she digs, Alaya places one of her light orbs on the ground beside her among the other bottles she deems unworthy for the task at hand. I don't know why, but I reach over while she isn't looking and scoop up the light orb, which is warm to the touch, and set it gently within my satchel.

Finally, when I think I've all but died of old age, Alaya nods once, reaches decidedly over to grasp two bottles: One is large and round and filled with what looks to be a bluish smoke, and the other is a small triangular vial with a deep purple liquid and a bright red label.

"I'm going to need total darkness in here if this is going to work," Alaya says without looking up from the bottles in her hands.

My mamman moves to my side and shoots me an uncertain look. "Do you trust her?" she asks under her breath.

"I think so," I tell her. "At least with this. If anyone can accelerate Lilah's healing, it's going to be someone who deals in magic. Alaya is an expert."

Alaya smirks, and as my mamman begins to draw the shades over the windows, Alaya speaks up.

"You sure you don't want a curse?" she asks, barely looking up at me. "There's a lot less that can go wrong if you're *looking* for a bad outcome."

From across the room, my mamman sucks in a hiss of breath.

"Alaya!" I snap. "Seriously."

"Alright, alright," Alaya relents. "Still, you know with magic there isn't an absolute guarantee. I'll do my best to help her, but magic can be unpredictable. You should know that."

I nod. "Please, just do what you can to help her. She'd give anything to be healed."

I feel as if, now that I've made my decision to follow the plan the Fates have in store for me, the least they could do is help ensure my sister is healed, and I send a silent prayer to them with this message.

Alaya turns back to her bottles. "Right, then. I'll need to focus, so if you two can't be quiet, you'll have to leave. Yeah? I'm looking at *you* with your endless questions, Lane."

My mamman, still standing at the window, turns to me.

"We'll be quiet," I confirm.

"Good," Alaya says. "Now, one of you guard the door. If anyone interrupts while I'm working, there's no telling what could go wrong."

I look to my mamman, and she gives me a slow blink. She makes her way from the window to the door, opens it, and peeks outside. When nobody walks by, she closes the door and presses her back against it.

"Oh, and one more thing," Alaya says as she twists the cork out of the bottle with the bluish smoke. "I don't do anything for free. You and I will need to discuss the terms of your repayment."

"Later," I promise her. "Please, just help her."

Alaya closes her eyes and takes a breath that seems to draw into her all the light that remains within the room. She begins to whisper something unintelligible over the bottle with the blue-gray smoke inside, and as she does, the smoke starts to glow. The grayish hue remains the same, but now the swirling smoke carries a light within it. Alaya continues to whisper as she finishes pulling the cork from the bottle and places her palm over the opening.

Holding the bottle with both hands, Alaya lowers it toward Lilah's face. Then, slowly, she pulls her hand away from the top, tilting the bottle and allowing the smoke to slither out of its container. As Lilah inhales in her sleep, she breathes in the bright smoke, and it disappears in a moment.

Lilah's body obtains a soft glow, first in her face, then her throat, then her chest as the smoke works its way into her lungs, and I can't believe my eyes. In my peripheral vision, I see my mamman raise her hand to cover her mouth.

A moment later, Lilah's hands begin to glow softly as well. Alaya turns Lilah's hands over so that her palms face the sky as she reaches for the other vial.

Alaya carefully twists the top off the smaller vial. In the darkness, the deep purple liquid looks almost black, and as Alaya tilts the bottle to empty its contents into her hands, the room is filled with the scent of lilacs, a summer breeze, ripened fruit, and snow. She rubs her hands together and presses them against Lilah's palms. I swear I hear a low sizzling sound as the glow within my sister's body turns from that light grayish blue to a bright, warm pink before the glow disappears altogether.

My mamman and I perk up, but we're careful not to say anything or make any noise.

Alaya continues her soft whispering. In the last moment, Alaya reaches into her pocket, pulling out a handful of what looks to be some kind of dust. She sprinkles it onto Lilah's face and chest, then hovers her hands over the area as the dust brightens and then fades completely.

When Alaya stops whispering, Lilah opens her eyes, and the scents that just filled the room dissipate immediately. Lilah looks up at me through the darkness in the room and grins.

I look to Alaya to make sure I'm allowed to speak now. Alaya lets out a sigh, and after a moment of studying my sister, she nods her approval as a slow smile creeps onto her red lips.

I rush to Lilah, and my mamman does the same. Alaya barely has enough time to back out of the way as the two of us embrace my baby sister with a force we haven't dared to use since she awoke.

"How are you doing?" I ask Lilah. "How do you feel?"

My mamman runs her hand over Lilah's forehead to check her temperature as Lilah's grin widens.

"I feel tremendous. Scoot, scoot. I need to get up!" she says with a toothy grin.

Mamman and I stumble over each other as we move to get out of Lilah's way. She hardly waits for clearance before she's on her feet, dropping her blankets in a crumpled mess on the floor.

The joy that fills me at seeing my sister stand with such ease momentarily overshadows the hefty burden of my earlier conversation with Zaid, and we celebrate her healing together, hugging and laughing and crying.

It's only when I notice that Alaya has turned to duck out of the room that I break from the embrace and scoop up my bag as I hurry to follow her. Just outside the doorway, I call out to her.

"Alaya," I start. As she turns around, something seems off about her. She looks almost sad, but she still wears that subtle smile on her lips. "Where are you going?" I ask.

Alaya gestures with in the direction she was just walking.

"To meet with the Council. They're not just going to let me wander this place now that they know I'm here. You should be there, too. You are, after all, the reason I'm here. They'll probably want you there to answer to them if I'm not what you promised."

Right. The Council.

Zaid is likely to be there. My stomach drops.

"That's right. Let me say goodbye really quickly, and I'll walk with you," I tell her.

I peek back into the doorway and say goodbye to my mamman and my sister for now, and I walk with Alaya to the Council room we met in last night. As we're about to enter, I stop her, gently catching her forearm with my fingertips.

"Alaya," I start. I reach my free hand into my satchel, silently scolding myself for taking something that belongs to her, but something stops me, and I pull my hand out empty.

One of Alaya's eyebrows makes an arch on her forehead at my touch, and I immediately let go.

"Sorry. I... I wanted to thank you. If you'd like to discuss payment now, I'd be happy to—"

Alaya raises her hand. "One thing at a time, kid. We'll take care of this first, and when I've thought of my price, I'll let you know."

I'm startled by her words, but I mutter a quick, "of course," and we enter the Council room.

33

"She may be one of our citizens by technicality, but she is *not* someone we can trust!" Salma exclaims as Alaya and I enter the Council room. "If what miss Shrayan and Mr. Montrose say is true, then she has *frequented* the Nameless Country, bringing back with her Fates know what, and smuggling illicit goods through the mountains!"

"We are not equipped to handle these so called 'shades'," replies another woman, one I hadn't noticed yesterday. Her tone is heated, matching the red and orange gown she wears, beaded heavily with various, warm-colored jewels. If I had to guess by her clothing, I'd say she likely hails from Nodon, far to the east of us.

I scan the room, hoping and dreading to find Zaid.

He's nowhere to be found.

All the Council members around the table are so focused on their conversation that Alaya and I sneak right up to the table unnoticed.

"Well, it's a good thing your lovely little ally here summoned me, then, isn't it?" Alaya asks, taking a place at the table as if she's been a part of the Council all along.

Everyone's eyes turn to her as she folds her arms across her chest. I stare at her, stricken with awe that she'd be so bold as to speak out of turn at a Council meeting her first time visiting the Keep. From across the table, I spot Alec's amused expression, as well. The rest of the Council does not find her rude behavior so amusing, however. Several Council Women are so red in the face I'm surprised they're not steaming.

"One does not simply waltz into the Council chamber and speak without first being addressed by someone on the Council," someone mutters from across the table, but I don't look in time to catch who has spoken.

The Countess holds her hand up to silence the others, and she regards the two of us as we stand side by side at the table.

"Lane, Alaya. Welcome to our Council meeting. I'm afraid our situation has only worsened since we met late yesterday. New scouts bring reports of increasingly violent and more frequent bandit activity, as well as accounts of what are only being described as shadow people cropping up all across Maran. Nobody knows where these shades are coming from, but their message is clear: They mean us harm."

If Alaya is frightened by this new information, she doesn't show it. I, however, am filled with a cold that makes the icy weather outside seem like a pleasant dream. I didn't think anything could be worse than those animal-like bandits.

I clear my throat.

I speak, hoping that my voice will not betray the fear I feel.

"Do these reports carry any specific descriptions of these shadow people?" I ask. "Anything we might be able to use to prepare ourselves?"

The Countess's expression is grim: Her sharp jaw is set, her mouth stretches out in a tight, worried line. "We know they appear to blend in with the shadows, even in direct daylight. Our reports state that they carry with them blades so sharp they can slice through wood, and that they seem to be able to... separate... when struck with physical weapons."

My eyes flit to Alec, who's already looking directly at me. I search his face, and I mouth, "Do you know about these?"

Alec shakes his head. He clenches his jaw, and from across the table, I see him ball his hands into fists.

"Right," I say, my mind already running the information through my mind, searching my memory for anything I've read before that might help. "Alaya?"

She doesn't miss a beat.

"We'll need a research team. I assume you have some big, fancy library here somewhere?" she asks the Countess, who shoots Alaya a warning look, but she nods, and Alaya continues without a care. "Lane and Alec, you two should get to the library. See what you can find that might have any mention of shades or shadow people. Women of the Council, allow me to demonstrate some goods I think will definitely support your cause."

"And what," says the woman in the jeweled robes, raising her chin and looking down her long, straight nose at Alaya. "May I ask, are these goods going to cost us?"

Alaya smirks, eyeing the woman's garb. "Nothing you can't afford," she replies instantly. "Nothing you won't be willing to pay, I assure you." Alaya sets her heavy bag down on the table.

I resist the urge to snap at her for her appalling behavior.

I thought she would at least show some restraint in the presence of the Countess, but she doesn't seem to care about anything more than making a tin.

"However crass she may come across," I tell the Council, giving Alaya a reproachful look. "Alaya is right. I've witnessed what she's able to do with the magic she's about to show you." Several of the Council members cringe at my use of the word "magic," but I keep going. "Just this morning she helped to *heal* Lilah. I saw it with my very eyes. Lilah is up and walking around as we speak."

At this new information, the entire Council erupts with murmurs of surprise and doubt, including Alec, whom I haven't spoken to since he left me in my room this morning. He and I have a lot of catching up to do.

"Very well," says the Countess, who seems strangely open to everything I've suggested so far. "Alaya, please. Show us what you can do. We've no time to waste. Lane, Mr. Montrose, please make your way to the library at once and gather as much information as you can. Lane, I will meet with your mamman when we're finished here and catch her up. I'd like to see how Lilah is fairing, anyway. Fellow Council members, once this demonstration is finished, I would like you each to send your fastest birds to your respective communities for any information that might be helpful to our cause."

Alec and I leave right away, following the Countess's orders as we make our way to the library.

In the library, Alec and I get right to work. Within the first couple of hours, we've read through several scrolls, but our bodies are already beginning to ache being hunched over like this. With each minute that has passed, I've found myself growing all the more restless. There's a lot on my mind. I feel an urgent need to tell Alec that I've made my decision and let him know to be on the lookout for Zaid. I don't think that Zaid will cause any trouble, but these days, I'm finding I can't be sure of anything.

"Well," Alec says, standing up to stretch his back. "I think it's high time we get some lunch, don't you? I'm going to see what I can dig up for us to eat. Do you want to check that section over there?" Alec gestures at yet another tall, dusty shelf filled with thick books and old scrolls.

I mutter some in acknowledgement as I chew my bottom lip, trying to decide what to do. As he prepares to leave, I take my chance. It's got to be now. Zaid is still somewhere in this Keep, and I don't want Alec to find out about my decision from him. I take a quick breath and rush to stand, worried that Alec will walk out the door and I'll miss my chance to tell him.

"Alec, wait," I blurt. He pauses, turning to look at me. I hesitate for only a moment, but I push myself through it. "I... I need to tell you something."

Alec cocks his head to the side curiously. I'm not certain what he expects me to say, and I swallow loudly as he asks, "Yes?"

"It's... it's you," I say, stumbling over my words.

Alec frowns.

"What?" he asks.

I move my seat aside and step forward, reaching my hand out in his direction.

"It's you that I choose. You're the one."

Alec takes several seconds just staring at me with a strange look on his face. "Are you serious?" he asks me cautiously.

"Yes."

I want to tell him *why* I'm choosing him.

I want to tell him that I don't want to resist this pull between us anymore. I want to tell him that I think we can do so much good for the world if we're together, and I want to tell him that, bond or no bond, when I'm with him, I feel whole. But of course, I can't get any of these words to come out.

In the end, it doesn't matter. In the briefest of moments, Alec strides toward me, crossing the distance between us, face so open and filled with emotion that I can't seem to read them all in the time it takes for him to reach me.

He scoops me into his arms and spins me around in the warmest, tightest embrace I've ever experienced, and I can't help the giggle that escapes my lips.

"Oh, Lane," he whispers against my neck, pressing kiss after kiss against my neck, my shoulder, my jaw. Although I can no longer see his face as he holds me close, I can feel the grin he's wearing. "Fates, it took you so long I was beginning to worry you'd never decide. Or at the very least, that you wouldn't choose me."

His words fill me with guilt, and I squeeze him tightly.

"I'm sorry I took so long… I don't know why I have to think everything through so thoroughly. Especially this, when what we have has been special from the start. Am I too late?"

Hearing from him how long he's been waiting gives me pause. I suppose it's possible that in all this time, he might have lost interest, especially with how preoccupied I've been since I learned of Lilah's injury.

I pull away so I can get a better view of Alec's face, and it's so serious that my heart drops.

"This is what I've wanted all along," he says. His eyes are sparkling, and a sweet, sincere smile plays at his lips. "It could have taken you all the time in the world. You and I belong together, Lane. Even the Fates agree. Yes, of course I still want you. A thousand times, yes."

I'm so relieved and touched I feel as if I might float.

I choke back a sob as the two of us return to our tight embrace, and as we do, I press my lips to his. The world around us seems to pause in its turning and fill with light. Is this what I've been putting off? I don't know what I was thinking. This is wonderful. This is magical. This...

This is what the Fates had in mind all along.

The thought is stark in my mind, and the single sentence is enough to remind me of the urgency of our situation.

I pull back again and hold Alec's gaze.

"Alec?" I ask, voice quiet.

"Yes?"

I clear my throat. "The Fates are dying. We're running out of time. If they go, who's to say if we'll have a chance at stopping these bandits? Things are getting worse, and if there's anything we can do to help the Council against these new enemies, we need to do it, but we must work quickly."

Alec's shoulders tense and he gives me a solemn look as the two of us consider our options.

"Raonni," we say simultaneously.

"Exactly," I tell him. "I'm going to write her right now. I've still got Audy's whistle; he'll reach her quickly. If anyone knows what to do, it ought to be Raonni," I say, already turning to dig through the stacks of books and scrolls in search of my satchel.

"Perfect," Alec replies. "I'll go find some lunch." When I give him a confused look, he raises his arms defensively. "What? This is big stuff we're doing. We shouldn't work so hard on an empty stomach. We'll be able to think so much more clearly after we've had something to eat."

I roll my eyes at him, turning back to my task as I do finally find my satchel.

I reach into my bag and grab hold of the cool metal of Audy's whistle.

"Lane?" Alec asks.

When I look back up, Alec stands right beside me. He leans down and grasps my hand, turning me to face him fully as he kisses me so deeply, I think I might melt into the stone floor at my feet. I lean into him and let out a soft moan as my entire being fills with warmth. His arms move to wrap around the flat of my back, and my hands run up his solid chest and curl into the hair at the nape of his neck.

"I choose you, too," he says against my lips. My eyes open wide and fill once again with tears, and when I open my mouth to respond to these precious words, I hear a grunt from the doorway. Alec and I turn to see Zaid standing just outside the open door.

Zaid's features look much darker than usual as the deep frown he wears casts shadows over his face.

"Zaid," Alec says, nodding respectfully in Zaid's direction. Alec's eyes turn back to me, and I can tell he's wondering if I've broken the news to Zaid yet. I let go of Alec and take his hand in mine.

Zaid ignores Alec's greeting and glowers at me.

"I should have known," he says.

"What?" I ask. My first instinct is to hide from the tension in the room, but I stand my ground.

"I should have known this is what would happen. That the moment you rejected me, you'd be crawling right back to him. Of course, you'd give him everything." Zaid's tone is filled with resentment as he takes an angry step forward. "It doesn't matter. You're going to regret your decision. I swear it."

Zaid turns on his heels and stomps away, leaving Alec with his mouth agape and me with a painful knot in my gut. Suddenly, I feel exhausted.

I release Alec's hand and pinch the bridge of my nose, moving my fingers outward to rub my eyes.

Alec pats me on the shoulder.

"You're doing the right thing, Lane. Don't let him bully you for choosing what you want just because it wasn't him."

My eyebrows shoot up.

"No? You're telling me you wouldn't have been angry if I chose him instead?" I ask. As horrible as I feel to see Zaid so unhappy, my heart still tells me I've made the right decision.

"Oh, no," Alec says, shaking his head and folding his arms. "I'd be furious. But I wouldn't take it out on you, or him, for that matter. I can't fault you for your choices, and I understand why he was an option. He's a good guy."

"I never thought I'd see him like this, though..." I mutter, allowing my sentence to trail off as I stare at the floor as if it has the power to somehow solve all my problems.

"It's pretty surprising," Alec agrees. He squeezes my shoulders. "How about that lunch? Do you need anything else? Want me to stay in here with you for a while longer?" Just then, Alec's stomach growls loudly, and I let out a dry laugh.

"No, I'm okay. I just need some time to think," I tell him. "I'm going to get writing this letter to Raonni. You go ahead and get some food. When I'm finished, I'll get back to these books. I'll see you when you get back."

"Alright," Alec says, planting a quick kiss on my cheek. "I won't be long."

Despite the heavy atmosphere that Zaid's presence left lingering in the room, Alec bounces away, and I get to writing.

In my letter, I explain as much as I possibly can to Raonni. I inform her that Alec and I have decided to follow the path that the Fates have set for us. I describe the urgency of the situation here in Maran and explain that Alec and I feel we can do something more to help if we had the Fates' support. I ask if she knows what we should do next, and if by simply choosing one another we have saved the Fates, or if there is something more we need to do.

I also ask if she knows anything about these shadow people or the strange, animal-like bandits that are causing such trouble here. If anyone has knowledge of these kinds of things happening, I hope it will be Raonni. After all, her ties to the Fates have allowed her to see things that normal people cannot.

When I finish the letter, I send Audy off with it, already waiting anxiously for a response. I try to focus on getting back to work. Having told Alec that he's the one I want to be with has made me feel so much lighter, and I can't believe it took me such a long time to tell him what I should have known all along.

Looking back on the journey Alec and I have taken together, the choice seems so simple, though I recall how much I've struggled since I learned of the Fates' involvement.

Still, something feels different. I feel a sort of warmth that I hadn't felt before, and I wonder if this is the Fates' favor shining down on me.

Alec and I spend the rest of the day digging through old books and scrolls, and I do my best to stay focused on finding anything that will help us.

We find a few mentions of the Fates, some old works that mention dark creatures that appear in legends, but nothing seems concrete, and none of what we read seems like it will be much help to us. In our search, I find a strange looking scroll tucked away in the back of a bookshelf, written in red ink on dark, stained parchment.

As I read, my brow furrows.

"What's that?" Alec asks, setting down a new stack of books he's just collected from another shelf.

"Listen to this," I say, making my way to the table with the scroll in my hands.

"Well, that's heavy," Alec says. His words are meant to be lighthearted, but I can see in his eyes that he feels the same weight in his chest that I do.

"I'm not sure I like the sound of that," I say, setting the scroll on the table. "I don't think I like that at all."

We don't hear from Raonni until late in the evening. When her message arrives, it's scrawled in surprisingly neat handwriting, and I have to remind myself yet again that this woman is blind.

Raonni's letter inspires the historian in me, and I find myself thrilled about the possibility of exploring a new area – one not many people have likely gone. Still, the serious nature of our situation weighs on me.

Right away, Alec and I track down the Countess to speak with her about what we've learned. Due to our limited time, we don't tell her all the complexities of our bond and the Fates' involvement, just that we've asked a priestess of the Fates how to get their help. We ask her permission to travel below the Keep, informing her that the water we may find down there could help us in our fight against the enemies headed our way.

I expect her to look at us as though we've gone completely mad, but she simply looks exhausted.

"Lane, my priority is to protect the Keep and the whole of Maran. Whatever you need to do to protect our people, do it," the Countess says, her voice like a sigh.

I work to blink away my shock. "Oh, of course. Um... Thank you. We'll get going, then." Alec and I link hands and begin to turn away.

"Just one piece of advice," the Countess starts, holding her hand up, and we turn back to her. "Be careful; and move as secretly as you can. Even with my leadership, there are some within the Keep that do not think you belong. They are respectful in my presence, but they may wish you harm, or at least stop you from exploring areas they feel you're not meant to be, even with my blessing. Avoid running into them if you can."

With that, we leave the Countess to prepare, and Alec and I each go back to our own chambers to change our clothes.

It has been one of the longest days. I can't believe that this is the same day that Alec and I woke up together, the same day that I had that painful conversation with Zaid, the same day that Lilah was fully healed, and I made my choice. In the last eighteen hours, everything has changed.

The sun has now set, leaving only a tiny sliver of red light on the horizon when Alec knocks on the door to my chambers.

"Are you ready?" he whispers, and I nod.

Alec and I stand dressed all in black, hoping we will blend into the shadows well enough should anyone cross our paths.

I arm myself with my bow.

I've been so uncomfortable without having it on me every day within the Keep, so although I hope I won't have to use it on our way below, I welcome its familiar weight across my back.

Holding a map of what I hope is the correct blueprints for the Grand Council Keep from the stack of scrolls and books we looked at earlier, I tiptoe with Alec as quickly and quietly as possible through the hallways and stairwells down to the ground floor. The sooner we get that water, the sooner we can fulfill the Fates' wishes and help restore peace to Maran.

As we traverse one of the winding stairwells, Alec and I see someone coming, the light from the lamp they carry giving them away before they come into full view.

This particular stairwell is a spiral with vast glass windows that contain large potted plants on the outer side of the stairs as the well curves further down toward the ground floor.

In an instant, I step back, pulling Alec with me as I tuck myself behind one of the large plants. Alec and I crouch down, doing our best to blend into the darkness as I press a finger to my lips. We must stay quiet. With the state of things these days, we're not sure who might cause us trouble.

Alec and I were able to hide just in time, and it's a good thing, too: The person who saunters past us is none other than Zaid himself. The words he said earlier still echo in my mind, and I'm grateful that he's unable to see us from where we hide. He doesn't even look around him as he walks. Instead, he keeps his dark eyes straight ahead, his face grim.

I can't help but wonder what he's up to, where he's going, but the knot in my gut tells me I shouldn't ask. So I let him pass us by, working to stay hidden.

Once he's passed and we can no longer hear his footsteps echoing down the hallway, I let out a deep breath. Through the darkness between us, Alec whispers, "Are you okay?"

I nod, doing my best to shake off the tension that creeps up my spine and settles into my shoulders.

"Let's keep going," I suggest. We both stand as quietly as possible and work to get out from behind the potted plants without making too much noise.

When we're free again, we continue down the stairs, and it isn't long before the stairwell brings us to the ground floor of the Keep where the oversized entry doors allow people supervised access to the Keep throughout the day.

At the bottom, I use the dim light from the still-lit main foyer to read our map.

"Okay," I whisper. "It looks like if we stick to this wall here, it should lead us to the door we need." I tuck the map back into my bag as quietly as I can as we crouch down and creep along the wall closest to the stairwell, doing everything we can to remain within the shadows.

A few times we have to pause as the guards on the main level pass us making their rounds. Fortunately for us, they pass by without a glance in our direction, and we're able to make it to the door I mentioned without being caught, though I swear each time they pass that they'll hear my heart pounding in my chest and call us out.

I reach up and grasp the doorhandle, giving it a turn to no avail. The door is locked.

"Fates, what now?" I ask, trying to keep my growing frustration in check.

"Here, let me," Alec says, pushing me gently aside as he crouches before the door. He reaches into the lining of his belt and pulls out a pair of long, thin pins. At my inquisitive look, Alec shrugs. "I once told you I had a troubling start when I began living on my own. I fell in with the wrong people. Although I did many things I regret in that era of my life, I did gain a handful of skills that still come in handy from time to time."

My jaw drops as he works with the lock, but after only a minute or so fiddling quietly with the door, Alec manages to pick the lock, swinging the door open to reveal what looks to be an old, unused closet. The closet is dark inside, but we're still able to see well enough to get by.

Toward the back of the small space, however, is another little door, barely visible behind a few hanging robes.

We enter the closet quickly, and Alec closes the door behind us. When we open the smaller door – which is thankfully unlocked – we come to yet another spiral staircase.

On we go until we reach the bottom of our final set of stairs. Once we've reached the bottom, the darkness is almost impossible to see through, but I can feel soft dirt beneath my boots and hear the sound of water dripping from somewhere in the area.

"What now?" Alec asks, bumping into my back as I halt and dig through my bag. Thanks to my strange behavior earlier in the day, I now have in my possession one of Alaya's magical light orbs. I shake it as I've seen her do, sloshing around the liquid inside until the orb begins to glow a soft, warm orange.

"Did Alaya give you that?" Alec asks, a look of obvious surprise on his face. "I don't imagine you'd feel comfortable telling her where we're going. I didn't know you were so close."

I give him a wry smile. "You're not the only one with a few tricks up your sleeve," I tell him, though the confusion I still feel regarding my actions bothers me. I don't think I've *ever* stolen anything before today.

Alec's face lights with a smile.

"Sexy," he says, and my ears and cheeks begin to burn.

"Let's go get that water, shall we?" I ask.

"Let's do it," Alec replies.

The area we stand in now does have a dirt floor. In fact, aside from the stone walls and the stairs behind us, this place looks like no one has been down here since the Keep was constructed.

We follow the sound of dripping water through several open cavernous areas beneath the Keep as we wander further and further into the darkness deep in the earth. Finally, we see a bit of soft light up ahead. It's a gentle white light that shimmers over all the walls that are no longer manmade from stone but instead carved from clay.

"Well, I'll be damned," Alec mutters, and although he says the comment softly, his voice echoes loudly throughout the space, and I feel as if we've disturbed a peaceful silence that has been here for ages. "If there ever was a magical water that the Fates were tied to, it'd be here."

He's absolutely right. As we approach the white light, we find that it comes from within the water itself. The water is in a small natural pool that shimmers and glistens and seems to move about on its own, but now that we're up close to it, the dripping sound seems to materialize from nowhere. There's nothing dripping into this body of water, though the sound comes from this exact spot.

The water itself glows in much the same way as the orb I carry in my hand.

"Wow," I whisper as I bend to set the orb on the ground at my feet.

"You brought something to put it in, right?" Alec asks me for the second time since we left my chambers.

"Yes," I reply, reaching into my satchel and pulling out an empty perfume bottle that I found near the bath in my chambers. The bottle is a little bigger than the size of my palm at the base, and thinner toward the top. "I just hope this will work," I tell him. "Raonni didn't exactly mention how much of this water we would need."

At the mention of Raonni's name, the water begins to bubble, the light within it growing brighter.

It rises up out of the pool and takes Raonni's form, startling me so thoroughly that I stumble backward into Alec's chest. He shifts to catch me before we both go tumbling, and we take a moment to regain our wits and stand upright again.

"Sorry to have startled you," Raonni's likeness says. "I didn't have time enough to travel to you given the urgent state of things in your continent. Matters in Lithe have also grown increasingly hectic in the time you've been away, so I'm afraid I wouldn't be able to leave Lithe at the moment, anyway."

I straighten my clothing and blink away my surprise.

"How are you doing this?" I ask her. This is probably the last thing I should be asking, especially since I have no idea how long she can be present like this for, but as someone who has barely been introduced to magic, it all baffles me.

Raonni's likeness smiles. "It's a water communication spell," she says as if this is the simplest thing in all the world. "Using this spell, I keep my physical body where I am, but I can transfer my consciousness to any body of water I can visualize. It won't last long, I'm afraid, so allow me to give you your instructions."

Alec and I nod in unison, listening intently.

"What do we need to do?" I ask.

Raonni nods. "Right. Take the bottle you've brought and dip it into the pool at my feet. You're going to need to fill it up all the way."

"It's not a large container. I could only find a perfume bottle," I tell her apologetically. "Is that okay?"

"Yes, that should do. Fill that," she says.

I do as she commands. I twist the top off the empty perfume bottle and dip it into the water, which is cool and refreshing and seems to hug my fingers, the light drawing toward me and softly caressing my fingertips.

Once I've filled the bottle and pull it back out of the water, the liquid within seems to writhe and glow as if it is alive. It glows with the same soft white that the pool does.

I stand and twist the cap back onto the bottle as Raonni tells us what to do next.

"You are going to need a sunrise. That's the most powerful part of the day, when the sun breaks over the horizon to shed its first beams of light onto the land. This is when the Fates' connection to our world is strongest. At sunrise, you will need to stand within a body of water that can be touched by that light. Do you have a place in mind that will work?" Raonni asks.

I look to Alec.

"It will be cold, but I think the fountain in the Keep's garden should work well enough. When I passed it earlier today, I noticed that it hasn't yet frozen over," I tell him.

"I'm in if you are," Alec says, reaching out to hold my hand. At this sign of affection, Raonni smiles, and I wonder yet again if she can somehow see us.

"Wonderful. In order for the ceremony to be binding, you both need to be standing within that body of water just as the light from the sun falls upon it. When those rays of light touch the water, spill the contents of that bottle at your feet and recite the following:

'I choose you, my Fated other.
Let the dawn bring us a new day.'"

Alec and I share a look.

"Got it," I tell her. "Is that all?"

"When you both have said these words, share in the power of a kiss. Once you have done these things, the Fates will know your true will has been sealed, and they will relinquish their burden unto you."

"Doesn't that sound lovely," Alec asks facetiously. "We get to take their burden!"

I roll my eyes.

"Is this what you wish?" Raonni asks. "It will only work if this is truly your heart's desire." Raonni's words strike a cord in me, but I know now that the choice I've made is the right one.

"Yes, this is what I want," I tell her, squeezing Alec's hand tightly in mine.

"Absolutely," he returns, his eyes twinkling as he smiles at me. "*You* are what I want, Lane."

"Then go," Raonni says. "You have until sunrise to prepare. I will be with you in spirit."

Then, without another word, the shape of Raonni's body shifts back into a column of water that slowly shimmers back down into the pool at our feet.

"Alright, then," Alec says. "Just when I thought I was getting used to this whole magic thing... Shall we get going?"

"Soon," I tell him. I crouch down and dig out a scrap of parchment and some charcoal from my bag. Laying it out as flat as possible on the ground, I scribble down the words that Raonni told us to recite.

"What are you doing?" Alec asks as I scoop up the orb at my feet and stand back up to dust myself off.

I hold up the piece of paper, feeling proud of myself for thinking ahead.

"I don't want to forget these words and mess things up. Do you?" I ask. This brings a smile to Alec's lips, and he leans over to kiss me.

"You're something else," he says with his soft lips still pressed to mine.

Just then, we hear a loud sound, as if a landslide has occurred. The ground around us begins to shake, and when the shaking subsides and we're able to get our bearings again, Alec and I look at each other in horror.

"That can't be good," I say uneasily, stuffing the perfume bottle full of magical water into my satchel. "Let's get out of here."

# 35

Alec and I race back the way we came, through the tunnels and caverns beneath Grand Council Keep.

As we run, several more earsplitting crashing sounds shake the earth, and each time these noises arise, Alec and I are almost knocked off our feet.

We scramble up the stairs we came down, working to help each other up as we go. We pass through the little robe closet, and I stop briefly at the door that will take us back into the foyer.

"What are you doing?" Alec asks me, his blond hair whipping him in the face as he turns to look at me.

"Shouldn't we look out there first? Make sure the coast is clear?" I ask.

Alec opens the door and sticks his head out, then he turns back to me with eyes so wide they just might eject from his skull.

"I don't think it's going to matter," he says. "Let's go."

Before I can protest or question him, he grabs my hand and pulls me through the doorway.

Although there are now many people in our area, nobody spares us a single glance – they're all too busy running about the place. The grand double doors have been completely obliterated, and large splintered pieces of them are scattered all throughout the foyer. Several of the same kinds of bandits that attacked us near Helna in our previous journey jolt about the Keep on their hands and feet, leaping wildly, working deftly to cut and slash at anyone they can get their blades to contact. A handful of bodies litter the floor, and a fire rages outside the Keep's doors.

I'm frozen with a horror that fills my entire being and runs my blood frigid at the sight before me, and it's only when Alec pulls at my arm again that I'm able to break my trance.

"Lane, we need to go," he says urgently, yanking at my arm with one hand as the other pulls his sword from his belt. "Find your sister and your mamman. Try to get them to safety, somewhere the bandits won't find them. If anyone comes into your path, shoot them."

I shake my head in an attempt to clear away my shock, pulling my bow from its place on my back, grateful now that I had the sense to bring it with me.

"What are you going to do?" I ask him, suddenly terrified at the thought of being separated from him. We step back into the shadows and watch as a man from the Guard to my left cuts the head clean off one of the bandits.

"I'm going to follow you and make sure no one else does," he says. He leans over, kissing me desperately. I relish in every split second of that kiss, and it's over too soon. "If we're separated for too long and dawn approaches, meet me at the fountain in the garden. And Lane?" he says as I nod and begin to turn away. "Take this." Alec reaches to his belt and unsheathes his beautiful golden hilted dagger, pressing it into the hand that isn't busy grasping my bow. "Just in case."

My eyes widen, but I don't have time to ask him if he's sure about this. I know how he gets about other people touching his beloved blades. I tuck the dagger carefully into the side of my belt and nock an arrow.

"Thanks," I tell him before trailing toward the stairway that will take me to where my sister has been resting. Alec follows close behind me.

At the bottom of the stairwell, Alec is attacked by a bandit that's caught sight of us. Using its arms and legs to propel itself forward, the bandit manages to tackle Alec with enough force to topple him to the ground.

"Go!" Alec shouts when I stop to help him. "I've got this. You find your family."

Alec elbows the bandit in the face and rolls to climb on top of it, driving his sword deep into the bandit's chest.

The moment I see that Alec is safe again – at least for now – I push myself forward, taking the stairs two at a time until I reach the top, working to steady my breath as I go.

When I reach the floor where my mamman and my sister should be, I'm startled to find that the entire floor seems extremely quiet. There are almost no lamps lit within the hallway, and only the soft light that creeps out from under various doors – and the flickering light coming in through the windows – illuminate the path before me. While I can hear faint screams from the floors below me, I'm grateful that the danger doesn't seem to have reached this level yet. Still, each step I take is guarded, deliberate. My bow is drawn, arrow set to fly at any moment.

When I reach my chambers, I open the door and peek inside in case my mamman or Lilah has heard the commotion downstairs and come to check on me. The room is empty and dark. When I reach my mamman's chambers, I find that they are also empty and devoid of light. Surely with everything going on downstairs, nobody is sleeping.

Then an icy chill curls down my spine as a sickening thought creeps into my mind: Did Lilah and Mamman join the fight? I peer over my shoulder in the direction I've come from, but I see no sign of Alec, and I hope he's alright.

I still have Lilah's room to check, and I pray to the Fates that I will find my family in there. I grasp the handle, holding my bow and arrow with my other hand. As I open the door, I hear a muffled whimper from inside, and I push the door the rest of the way open and draw my arrow again, preparing myself for whatever I might find inside.

In the dim lighting of the room, my mamman and my sister stand huddled together near the window. When I see them, my body is flooded with such an overwhelming sense of relief that I fear I might collapse right here. I allow my shoulders to relax as I lower my arrow, though I don't put it away.

"Fates, you two," I mumble breathlessly, kicking the door shut behind me. "I thought I might have to go searching for you in all the mess downstairs. Thank goodness you're both in here. Are you alright?" I ask.

"Lane, what's going on down there?" my mamman asks, ignoring my question and holding Lilah close. She gestures out the window at the fires that litter the streets outside the Keep. "What in Maran is happening?"

"If I had to guess," I start, crossing the room to check on my mamman and sister, trying to focus on the relief I feel that they're okay and not the worry eats away at my gut that Alec hasn't gotten here yet. I hope he's close enough that he knows where I went. "I would say our fears that the bandits were headed our way were spot on, and that we've spent all our time squabbling instead of strategizing."

"What do we do?" Lilah asks. Her young face is determined as she tries to appear strong and in control. I admire her for that. "We've got to do something."

I ponder her statement for a moment. I hate the thought of leaving them here in this little room, but I also know that neither of them is trained or equipped to fight, and the thought of having my baby sister face the bandits that nearly killed her sends me reeling.

"You two are going to stay right here in this room, unless you know of somewhere you can go that would be safer than here," I reply.

My mamman considers, and her eyes dart to the door as a shrieking howl sounds down the hallway in the direction of the stairwell. The noise cuts off abruptly, and I hope Alec has finally caught up with us.

"There's an old passageway," my mamman states. "On the first floor. I'm not sure if anybody has been there – I studied the structure of this building when I was a girl, and even I thought it was a myth until I chanced upon it when Lilah and I arrived here. Still, I think that would be a good place to go. It's all stone – no carpets or wood of any kind, so if fire is a concern, then that may be the best place to go. At least then we wouldn't be out in the open for just anyone to attack."

I nod, and my gaze flits once again to the fires outside.

"Old passageway it is. Both of you, grab whatever you need, quickly. Mamman, do you think you can lead us there?"

"I do," my mamman says resolutely.

My mamman and Lilah gather a few things and prepare to leave the room. To my surprise, my mamman pulls a straight edged, eight-inch dagger out of her purse. As my mouth hangs open, my mamman holds it up.

"What?" she asks defensively. "Those bastards got my baby girl once. They *won't* get her again." Her words are just as heartwarming as they are shocking.

We don't waste another second. I open the door and peek through, hoping to catch sight of Alec, but I see no trace of him.

I take a deep breath and hope he will find us soon. I need to get these two to safety, and there's no time to waste. I turn to head back to the stairwell, but my mamman taps me on the shoulder and shakes her head.

"What?" I whisper, and she points in the opposite direction.

"This way," she says. "It's faster."

We creep down the hallway, praying we won't be caught by anyone we don't want to run into. I think if there are Council members up here, they're too afraid to unlock their doors, let alone go wandering about the hallways, especially after that last shriek so close by.

My mamman leads us to a much smaller stairway, likely used by Guard members and other hired staff in patrolling the hallways and serving the Council members. This smaller stairway is much narrower and has no decorations for us to hide behind, but it also doesn't show any signs of being occupied. My mamman moves to enter the stairwell first, but I stop her with a brush of my hand.

"I'm armed," I tell her, holding up my bow. "Let me go first, just in case." Before she can argue, I step in front of her, and we keep moving.

We work our way down the stairs with me in the front with my bow at the ready, and my mamman in the back, armed with her dagger. When we get to the bottom of the stairs and open the door that leads out onto the main floor, Lilah gasps, and my mamman rushes to cover her mouth.

Just outside the door, mayhem ensues.

A swarm of ten or more bandits lies dead on the floor, their unnaturally dark blood spilled out across the stone and their limbs sprawled about them, blades still tied to their palms.

More shocking, though, is the horrific scene of those of our people who have been killed. The bandits show clear signs of slit throats and stab wounds, but those on the Guard and unwitting staff members of the Keep have been torn to shreds. Their mangled bodies are almost too gruesome to recognize.

"Look away, Lilah," I tell my sister with my voice low. "Close your eyes. Here grab onto the strap of my bag, and just keep walking with me, okay?"

Lilah whimpers in response, but she does what I ask. She clutches onto the back strap of my satchel and allows me to lead her through the mess.

"This way?" I ask my mamman, keeping my voice down, taking my eyes off the path for just a moment to confirm we're headed in the right direction. My mamman nods, but then her face distorts to make way for a look of complete terror.

"Lane, look out!" she shouts, pulling on Lilah – the only one of us that she can reach – as a bandit comes bounding into view. I whip around to face it just in time for it to tackle me, and memories of fighting these things off in the Helnan grasslands come flooding back to me. This time, however, I'm prepared. This time, I knew they were coming.

Like all the others, this bandit is entirely clothed in black and gray terrycloth, and only its hands, feet, and mouth are exposed. I can see a faint outline of the bandit's eyes from behind the cloth, but not well enough to make out any details. Its breath is hot on my face, and it smells of rotting flesh.

The bandit knocks my bow from my hands as it wrestles with me on the blood-soaked floor, but I still have Alec's dagger. If I can just get my hands on it...

I cry out as the blades strapped onto each of the bandit's palms dig into my hands, sending deep, stinging pain up through my arms. I think I hear Lilah call out to me and my mamman pull her back again, but my hearing is fuzzy with my blood rushing through them as I focus on the bandit before me.

I struggle to get my hands free as the bandit yips and drools all over me.

"Fates," I grunt beneath the bandit's weight. "*Let me go!*"

In that moment, I'm able to get my knee up between the bandit's legs, and I press my foot hard against its torso. It pulls back just enough to loosen its grip on my hands, and I reach for the dagger on my belt.

Sliding the dagger free, I raise it as high up as I can as the bandit struggles to get a hold of me again, covering my arms in shallow little slices. Finally, I bring the dagger down hard into the bandit's neck. The bandit lets out a strange squeal and its jaw goes slack; and it's only in the all new absence of growling that I realize the thing was even growling in the first place.

Panting, covered in drool and soaked by the bandit's dark, hot blood, I shove it off of me and struggle to my feet, scooping up my bow and the arrows that spilled from the quiver on my back. My chest heaves. My lungs are on fire as I work to catch my breath, and when I look to my mamman and little sister, they stare at me in disbelief.

Somehow, I'm filled with an even greater sense of urgency than I was before. I need to get them to safety. Now.

"Where do we go?" I ask my mamman, barely recognizing my own strangled voice.

We get back on track, weaving through the mess of bodies at our feet as my mamman gives me hushed directions as to where we should find the secret passageway.

We have another close call as a couple of Guard members fight off a handful of bandits to our right as we cross the hallway. As I draw my bow to help them, my mamman clears her throat.

I look back at her, and she shakes her head, mouthing the word, "don't."

Leaving the Guard members to fend off those bandits on their own fills me with guilt, but my mamman is right. I'll need these arrows to protect my family.

It's a good thing I saved my arrows, too, because the moment we turn our next corner, another bandit creature leaps up at us, nearly knocking me to the ground. It immediately rushes around me, its flailing limbs sliding across the floor as it targets Lilah. I draw an arrow and let it loose, running the bandit clean through the back of its skull, and it drops dead before it can touch my baby sister.

We all take a deep breath as Lilah and my mamman step around the bandit's fresh corpse, and I pause for just a moment to yank the arrow from its body before we move on.

Finally, after what feels like an eternity of wandering through these awful, chaos-filled hallways, we find the passageway my mamman had mentioned. She tells us to stop in front of a large painted map of Maran that hangs on the wall. She reaches over and grabs hold of what looks to be a decorative edge to the map's frame, but it's actually a knob. She turns it, opening a piece of the painting to reveal the passage.

"Quick," I tell her, stifling the childhood wonder that briefly sparks within me as I usher my mamman and my sister into the passage. "Get inside."

When they turn to me expectantly, I shake my head.

"Lane, get in here," my mamman orders, waving her hand frantically for me to enter.

"I can't," I tell her. "Alec wouldn't know where to find us, and I can't leave him out here to fight these things off by himself. I know him. He'll face every last one of them if he has to. I have something I need to take care of at dawn, but I'll try to come back. I know where this is, now, so I'll come to find you when I can, okay? In the meantime, please just stay here."

My mamman's expression appears conflicted, but she clenches her jaw and nods. The firelight from the hallway behind me reflects in the tears that well up in her eyes.

"I'm proud of you, Lane," she tells me, her words painfully striking my heart.

I reach over and pull both of them into a tight hug, and when I release them, I brush at some of the blood I've left on their clothing. I kiss Lilah on the forehead.

"I *will* come back for you," I tell her, hating that we're being separated yet again. I reach into my satchel and pull out the orb, still glowing from when I shook it earlier, and I barely register the look of surprise on both of their dirtied faces as I hand it to them. "So that it's not so dark in here," I tell them. I close the door and leave my mamman and sister yet again.

I don't have even a moment to wallow in the pain and fear I feel leaving them here. Several more bandits crawl through the hallway in my direction. I know just by looking at them that there are too many for me to face at once, at least by myself. So instead, I decide to evade them, if I can.

I crouch down and then lie flat on the floor, slowing my breathing and pretending to be dead as they pass. I'm not sure if they can smell me or hear my heartbeat as they crawl past me – I'm not sure *what* these creatures are able to do if they can move the way they do, but I'm filthy enough that I should blend in with the other deceased bodies around me.

The bandits pass me by without giving me a second glance, and I let out a slow sigh of relief before scrambling back to my feet and hurrying in the direction I last saw Alec.

I wonder how long we have until sunrise.

In all the chaos, it feels as if it's been both minutes and an eternity since we left my chambers in search of the magical water below the Keep.

Surely, we're nearing sunrise by now.

I search the hallways of the main floor for Alec, but I don't see him anywhere. I catch a few bandits that look to be patrolling the winding hallways from a distance, but I don't see anyone else who's still alive, so I make my way up the stairs once again, trying to keep my worries in check.

I know Alec is well trained and can handle himself in a fight... I just hope he hasn't been swarmed. I don't think even Alec could handle more than one or two of these things at once.

I'm certain that if Alec has made it upstairs, he's likely in the area he expected me to be searching for my mamman and Lilah. I hope he hasn't already gone to the fountain, and I curse myself for not checking there first, though there are so many bandits on the ground floor I'm not sure I would have made it outside, anyway.

It's as I reach the second floor that I see something that chills me to my very core.

Not twenty feet in front of me, I watch as two shadowy figures wearing long, tattered black translucent robes drag one of the Council members – Salma, I realize – from a room to my left.

They're headed my way, and I duck into the nearest darkened doorway just in time for them to float slowly past me. I listen as the body thumps down the stairs as the figures drag it down to the main floor. I hear the *thud, thud, thud* of the body as it hits each set, and the sounds send my stomach twisting, but I hear no footsteps to accompany the sickening noise.

Now my body is filled with an electrified feeling as I realize that the mentions we received of "shadow people" were legitimate, and that they are here in the Keep with us right now.

I *need* to find Alec. Where could he be?

Doing my best to stay calm and remain quiet, I sneak through the hallway, pausing briefly to check inside each open doorway before rushing past it.

I'm so focused on scouting for more shades that I crash head first into someone tall and sturdy. My arms flail about me as I work to catch my balance and fend off whomever I've just run into. But when my vision comes into focus again, I allow myself to relax, though my heart still beats a million times a minute.

"Alec," I whisper. "Fates, you scared me."

"I was looking for you," he replies in a harsh whisper. "Where have you been? I've been looking everywhere."

I shake my head as I hear the clinking of metal against stone from down the hallway. Putting my index finger to my lips, I usher Alec into a dark, abandoned room.

We listen as the sound of a bandit with blades tied securely to its hands and feet patrols past us. As it passes, it sounds as if it's sniffing for something, and for me, that sound is so much more terrifying than that of the blades scraping and clinking against the ground.

When the sounds have faded and I can no longer hear them echoing through the hallways, I let out the breath I've been holding.

"My mamman knew of a secret place where they would be safe. I had to get them there. I had to get them away from the chaos," I tell him.

Alec brushes some still drying blood off my cheek.

"You scared the living daylights out of me," he says. "I was certain one of those Fates awful things had you. Have you seen the way they drag the bodies around? Why would they do that? *Who does that?*"

I shake my head, trying to forget the image I just saw of the two shades dragging the Council member down the stairs.

"Yes, I saw it. I'm sorry for scaring you. I feared the same would have happened to you." Through the darkness, Alec gives me a strange look. "What?" I ask. "We're in this together, aren't we? Of course I was worried about you."

Alec smiles, and the white of his teeth seem to brighten the room just a little bit.

"We need to get you back with your mamman," Alec says.

"No way!" I tell him. "I'm sure we're getting close to sunrise. We need to get this ceremony over with. I'm hoping that if we do, the Fates will find some way to help us take back the Keep. I just hope we can do that before they kill everyone else..."

"Well," Alec says, standing up straight and grabbing me by the hand. "Get that bow of yours ready to fire. Let's see if we can make it to that fountain."

36

The two of us head toward the stairs for what I sincerely hope will be the last time tonight. As we do, another bandit – whether the same one who patrolled past the room we were just in or another one, I don't know – comes lunging out of a darkened doorway, catching Alec completely by surprise and knocking him to the ground.

Alec only struggles against the bandit for a moment as I nock an arrow and send it flying right through the side of the bandit's head. It screeches once and then goes limp, dropping onto Alec's chest. Alec shoves the bandit off of him, and I pull my arrow free, wiping it on my already blood-soaked shirt.

Alec raises his eyebrows at me.

"What?" I ask, shoving the arrow back into my quiver.

"You've changed," he replies as the hint of a smile pulls at the corners of his lips.

I scoff. "You bet your ass I've changed. We do what we have to, right?" But I don't wait for an answer. I grab his hand and help him to his feet, and we make our way to that stairwell. We've almost made it to the door that will take us out to the Keep's garden area when Alaya steps into view, blocking our exit.

"Alaya!" I whisper loudly. "I'm so glad you're okay!" It looks to me like she doesn't have a single scratch on her. I always imagined she would be a capable fighter, but even Alec has cuts and bruises all over. "Listen, we're headed for the garden. We need to get out there so that—"

"I know what you're trying to do," Alaya says smoothly. The doors to the garden have also been blown away, and beyond the snow-covered garden outside, I can see that the sky beginning to lighten.

"Great," Alec says, gripping my hand even tighter in his, pulling me in an attempt to maneuver past her. "Then you can help us—"

Alaya cuts Alec off, as well. "No, I'm sorry, I can't help you. Well... I guess I could. I just *won't*," she says.

I'm starting to get antsy. Why must she always play games? We don't have time for this. Every second we waste standing here is another moment the sun has to continue its ascent into the sky.

"Fine, then," I tell her, not caring that my voice clearly reflects my irritation. "This isn't a game. Move out of the way." I'm just about to shove my way past her when two shades turn the corner and stand behind Alaya. They hiss, revealing long, yellow, pointed teeth beneath some sheer black cloth that covers their faces much like the bandits wear.

My stomach jumps all the way to my throat, and I backpedal away from them.

"Alaya, watch out!" Alec shouts, letting go of my hand ready to defend her, but Alaya pulls a dagger from her belt and holds it up, pointing nonchalantly at the creatures behind her.

"Awe, that's so sweet," Alaya says. "You're afraid of my little pets."

She plays with her dagger, turning it around in her hands.

"What is this?" I ask, narrowing my eyes at her.

Alaya shrugs. "I've known the plan all along. Get Lane and Alec together. Get them to make their choices to fulfill the Fates' wishes. Blah, blah, blah. But I can't let you go through with that little plan. I've got plans of my own, see? Oh, but I *really* wish you hadn't chosen her," Alaya says, now addressing Alec. "You and I could have done such wonderfully terrible things together. We're one and the same, aren't we, handsome?"

"Not on your life," Alec replies. I don't know when he redrew his sword, but he now stands, blade ready, reaching over to put his free hand on my shoulder. His touch is warm, steadying despite the shivers that rush up my spine as I keep an eye on the shades.

I'm not sure where this is going, but I nock an arrow, taking aim at one of the shades, who hisses in response.

"Ah, well," Alaya says as two more shades appear behind her, and a handful of bandits come crawling up behind her as well. She holds the black blade of her dagger up straight before pointing it at us.

"Alec?" I ask, voice weary and thick.

"Yeah," he says, removing his hand from my shoulder to get a better grip on his sword.

"Run!" I shout, just as all the creatures charge at us at once. Alec and I take off in different directions. We both know we need to make it to the garden, but at this moment, staying out of the clutches of whatever those things are is our number one priority.

I hear Alaya's malicious laughter from the doorway behind me, but I don't slow down to look at her. Instead, I race forward, leaping over bodies left and right and throwing anything I can get my free hand on – potted plants, paintings, urns – behind me in an attempt to slow them down.

"Lane!" Alec calls out from across the wide room.

I do my best to turn to see him without tripping over anyone or getting caught.

"Kind of busy!" I shout back. I do trip now, and I stumble backward onto a couple of still cooling bodies. Several arrows spill from my quiver, and I scoop up as many as I can, though I miss a few in my rush to back away. "Fates!" I whisper to myself as I struggle to drop all the arrows in my grip into my quiver but one. I draw it back and let it loose just as one of the shades is upon me, and I'm shocked to find that the arrow lodges itself directly into its chest, but the thing just keeps moving as if it didn't even realize it's been hit.

My eyes widen in horror as I crawl backward, trying to find my footing.

"They don't die!" I scream at Alec, who – as I can hear from the sound of his blade swinging through the air and his grunting – is fighting off some creature of his own.

"I tried to tell you!" he yells back at me.

If I wasn't so focused on trying to stay alive, I'd roll my eyes. I shoot another arrow at the thing, and this time, the shade's body separates, turning to a curling smoke for just a moment, and both arrows drop to the ground.

"Calling me from across the room when I'm running for my life in the other direction doesn't help me!"

The shade approaches me slowly, and I'm finally able to get to my feet in time as it reaches out to grab me. I drop my bow, and when I scoop it back up, I also grasp the first thing I can find: a long, curved sword from one of the dead members of the Guard. I swing the sword with one hand as hard as I can. I slice through the shade's arm at the elbow, and the limb drops to the ground with a cold sounding *thunk,* and I wonder how the shade can feel so solid at one moment and completely shift into shadow in the next.

The loss of its limb seems to distract the shade long enough to slow it down, and I take the opportunity to race as fast as my feet will take me toward the open doorway, trying to go wide around Alaya and calling out to Alec as I run.

Two bandit creatures chase after me, but with this sword in my dominant hand and my bow in the other, I steady myself, well enough prepared by the time they approach that I'm able to swing the sword in a wide arc, slicing the neck of one and the torso of the other as it leaps into the air. A lucky shot, and I think for the briefest of moments that the Fates must be watching. Both creatures drop to the ground, and I continue toward the door.

Alaya moves to block me again, but I shove my way past her. Still, it isn't long before she's caught up to me again. She jumps up, reaching out with both hands and grabbing me by the shoulders, yanking me down onto the ground with her. The sword I picked up drops from my grip as we tumble.

"Alaya, stop!" I shout, wrestling with her in the snow, reaching out for the sword. "What are you doing?"

Alec rushes out behind us.

"You have to get their heads," he tells me breathlessly, running his sword through the face of the shade that follows him. "That seems to keep them down."

Alaya wraps her legs around my torso, squeezing my neck in the crook of her elbow. I raise my bow – still in my hand – and smack her in the face with it. This action loosens her grip on me enough that I'm able to start wriggling out of her grasp as Alec sheathes his sword and comes to my aid. He pries Alaya's legs off of me, and the two of us roll away from her.

The sky is much lighter now. We must be just minutes away from sunrise.

"Alec! The fountain. Let's go!" I shout, turning away from Alaya and praying she won't chase after me again. To my surprise, Alaya hangs back, and Alec and I scramble clumsily through the snow to reach the fountain.

We fumble over the fountain's edge in our rush to get inside, splashing ice cold water onto our clothing and into the snow that surrounds the fountain. The shallow puddles of water instantly freeze over, creating a ring of ice around us just outside the fountain.

I reach into my pocket and retrieve the piece of paper I scribbled our instructions on earlier. Working to steady my hands, I read what I can, though the blood and cold water has smeared some of the words.

Alec and I join hands, and I draw in a deep breath as Alaya walks slowly toward us, stopping just outside the ring of ice. I do my best to calm the pounding of my heart as I look into Alec's eyes, trying with everything I have to keep from looking around us as more bandit creatures and shades surround us, following Alaya's lead. She's even joined now by members of her clan, some of whom I recognize from the tunnels in which we first met her.

"Look at me," Alec says, softly, drawing my attention back to him. "Just look at me."

I nod and clear my throat.

"I... I choose you, my Fated other," I tell Alec, who stares deeply, intently into my eyes, running his thumbs along the backs of my hands. "Let the dawn bring us a new day." I let go of one of Alec's hands and reach into my satchel to grasp the perfume bottle I filled with water earlier, handing Alec the paper so he can take his turn reciting the words Raonni instructed us to say.

My eyes open wide and my blood runs cold as I realize I can't find the bottle anywhere.

"What?" Alec whispers, expression growing wary as he watches my panic.

"Looking for this?" Alaya asks, her red lips spreading into a wicked grin as she displays the item in her grasp. In one hand, she still grasps her dagger, and in the other she holds the perfume bottle. The white, glowing liquid sloshes around inside as she dangles it in the air.

I gasp. She must have taken the bottle out of my satchel when she had me pinned in the snow.

Fates.

"Alaya," Alec warns with his voice low.

He reaches slowly for his sword.

I eye the horizon, which is now turning from light pink to yellow, the sky above us changing to a lighter blue with every passing second.

"You know, Lane," Alaya says, ignoring Alec completely. "That was cute. So sweet, so sincere. You really mean that shit, don't you?"

"What are you playing at, Alaya?" I ask, trying to keep my eyes on her as the creatures and bandits around us shift restlessly. It looks like they're awaiting orders.

"Lane," Alec says, jerking his head in the direction of the ever-rising sun.

Alaya shrugs.

"It's all so simple to you guys, isn't it?" Alaya asks. "You join forces, the Fates get what they want, everyone lives happily ever after. Right? But the world's been crumbling for far too long, and the Fates have done nothing to stop it. Do you really think renewing the Fates is going to change anything? No. We've lived long enough in the shadows, eating out of the gutters, looked down upon, shunned, even. And for what? The Fates? The precious Women's Council?"

I grip my bow, bringing my hand up slowly to make it look as though I'm nervously playing with my hair, readying myself to grab an arrow and fire as many of them as I can get at the creatures that surround us.

There are three shades left, two bandit creatures still up and ready to pounce, and four men dressed like those visitors I saw as we raced through the Keep join their ranks. Up close, they resemble the people in the tunnels and alleys in Helna, and shock courses through me. These are Alaya's people, the thugs and misfits she mentioned in her stories. Those who call her "boss". I look to Alec, who I hope is ready to make a run for that bottle.

I mouth the word "bottle" at him just in case, and he gives me a nod so tiny I'm not even certain I really saw it, all while Alaya continues her speech, so caught up in her words that she doesn't seem to have noticed the interaction.

In a second, Alec and I break into action. I yank an arrow from my quiver and nock it, sending it into the shade nearest me. I barely watch long enough to see the shade disintegrate before I've nocked another arrow and shot it straight into the face of yet another shade.

In that moment, the two bandit creatures charge at me, but Alec slices the head clean off one of them as he rushes at Alaya.

I don't see if he's actually got the bottle from Alaya or not, because I'm tackled into the freezing fountain water by the bandit creature that's rushed at me. I reach into my belt, where I still have Alec's dagger strapped to me.

I work to get it free, but the bandit knocks it out of my grip, and it tumbles into the water out of my reach.

The frigid temperature of the water is causing my muscles to seize, but I'm able to free another arrow from my quiver with great effort, and I swing it at the bandit's face. I'm able to scrape its eye with my arrowhead, and it jumps back to recover. I whip around in the water, sending more splashes over the fountain's edge in my efforts to reach the dagger.

Finally, my fingers manage to grab hold of the icy metal of the dagger's hilt, and I swing it around blindly with full force, sliding the blade across the bandit creature's throat.

I shove the bandit over the edge of the fountain, and its lifeless body falls to the ground as dark blood spills steadily from the wound in its neck.

Nearly five feet away from me, Alec has just finished off the last of Alaya's men, and he squares off against Alaya, the two of them just staring each other down.

"You don't have to do this," he tells her, but she shakes her head. Her now filthy, tangled auburn hair whips around her.

"I really do," she replies.

My body, now exposed to the icy water and the frigid winter air, is beginning to lock up, and the sun is almost risen. With every ounce of willpower I can muster, I force myself to slowly get out of the fountain, being extra careful to avoid the layer of ice that has formed around its base.

As Alaya speaks, I do my best to sneak around behind her.

"You don't understand," Alaya says. "I'm doing this for all of us. All those of us who lived in someone else's shadow. All those of us who were kicked down and stepped on. It's time we let the Fates fade away once and for all and allow a new age to roll in. The age of shadows. The age of the underdogs. Let a new leader rise. Don't you agree?"

Alec shakes his head. "And who will that leader be? You?"

Now behind her, I watch Alaya as she stands just a little bit straighter.

"Of course it will be me," she says.

"I don't know why you'd want to rise to power, Alaya," I say once I'm close enough behind her that I could simply reach out and touch her. "It sounds like a dreadful gig."

Alaya whips around, her silver-blue eyes wide, crazed.

She opens her mouth to say something else, but I don't give her the opportunity. Instead, I reach down and snag the perfume bottle out of her hand and bolt back toward the fountain as quickly as my frozen limbs will let me.

As Alaya reaches out to grab hold of me, Alec springs into action. Alaya trips over Alec's boot, and she tumbles into the snow, but she's back on her feet in an instant. That moment is just enough time, however, for us to get a head start. Alec and I clamor back into the fountain and take each other's hands. Using my teeth because my fingers are too frozen to function well enough, I twist the cap off the bottle and dump its contents into the water, which shimmers and obtains a soft luminescence.

"No!" Alaya screams from where she stands, merely feet away from the fountain. She runs at us with her dagger in hand, ready to throw.

"I choose you, my Fated other," I say to Alec once again. "Let the dawn bring us a new day." At my words, the light glows yet again, and I feel the warmth of the Fates all around me. The small glow grows into a bubble-like shield of glimmering light that surrounds the fountain, trapping Alaya on the outside.

Alec repeats the words back to me, and he leans in to kiss me, but Alaya's too close. Despite the shield that surrounds us, I can't take my eyes off her. I watch as she brings her dagger downward, imbedding the blade into the orb of light.

The shield retaliates with a brute force, sending her plummeting backward through the air. She impacts hard with the ice-covered ground and remains there. The moment Alaya is rendered unconscious, the shield dissipates, and the dagger she stuck into the shield drops, sliding against my torso above my belt before dropping with a *plop* into the water.

I gasp and lean over, partly to check the stinging pain in my side and partly expecting Alaya to get back up.

As the sun's rays climb over the trees that surround the Keep's garden, the water at our feet warms and begin to bubble.

Across the garden, Zaid comes into view. He's covered in blood, but the way he's running tells me that if he's injured, it's not critical. He races across the clearing and spots Alaya.

Beside me, Alec tenses, but Zaid barely regards us. He rouses Alaya, helping her to her feet. The spot on her forehead that she must have hit when she landed on the ground is open and bleeding, and she seems a little bit out of sorts.

Wrapping Alaya's arm over his shoulder, Zaid aids Alaya in escaping the garden. She looks back at me and gives me a twisted, if not dazed, smile. I step forward, ready to chase after them or at least see what they're doing, but Alec grabs my hand.

"Lane, the sun," Alec says, his words rushed. "Let them go. We'll catch up."

When I turn back to Alec, he leans forward, and just as the first real rays of sunlight sprinkle down onto the fountain's water, Alec rushes forward, sealing the words we stated with a kiss that it takes me a moment to adjust to.

In that kiss, everything that we've been through – our bond, our friendship, our romantic moments, every up and down on this wild adventure – comes flooding through me, and for just a moment, I allow myself to get carried away. I allow myself to wrap up in his embrace as the world spins and seems to brighten around us.

The new rays of sunlight shine brightly on us, filling the area with the warmest, safest light I've ever felt, and then the light fades, and with it, I feel a sad pull, as if the Fates themselves are saying goodbye.

My body begins to tremble, and I'm not sure if it's the sunlight peeking through the trees or the light from the water below us, but Alec seems to have a slight glow about him, and his amber eyes shine with a bright gold.

"Your eyes," I start, but he interrupts me by pressing his palm against my cheek.

"Your eyes... are glowing," he whispers to me.

As I begin to pull away from Alec, my hand slides across something warm and sticky on his hip. When I pull my hand away to see what's wrong, I realize he's been bleeding. In the *exact* same place that I am.

I look back at my own wound to find that it's now healed.

Alec lifts his shirt to confirm that his wound has already sealed, too.

Our bond... it's back.

37

It may be the cold, or the rush I feel as Alec and I complete our ceremony, fulfilling the Fates' wishes to relieve them of their burden, or the renewal of the bond I've shared with Alec for most of my life; but I feel so whole and so completely overwhelmed that I just start laughing.

Alec looks at me as if I've lost my mind, but he joins in the laughter, and the two of us clash together into a tight embrace that's followed by several short, happy kisses. It's only when the two of us are visibly shivering that Alec offers his hand to help me out of the fountain.

"Let's go get your sister and clean up this mess, shall we?" Alec asks.

He grins at me as if we haven't just witnessed countless deaths and let the leader of the thugs, bandit creatures, and shades we've just been fighting go free... with Zaid of all people at her side. But still, I can't help but smile back at him. As he helps me cross the ice that surrounds the fountain, I look back at the place where this magical moment just occurred, expecting to see the same bright white, bubbling water that had just been there a moment ago.

Instead, there's only the same dark clear sloshing water there was before any of this happened.

I don't need to wonder where the light went, however. I feel it inside of me, and I see it in Alec.

Alec and I slowly make our way back inside the Keep, stepping carefully over the bodies that litter the ground. We'll give them a proper burial, but for now, the two most important things to me are finding my family and getting warm.

The Keep is eerily quiet after such chaos, and although there are now a few people – Council members and staff – emerging from various hiding places now that things seem to have settled, I think everyone is too frightened and deeply rattled to make a sound.

As Alec and I make our way back through the main floor of the Keep on our way to the secret tunnel my mamman and Lilah have been hiding in, we cross paths with the Grand Countess, who is doubled over with her arms around her torso, bright red blood dripping through her fingers.

"Are you alright?" I ask her, rushing to her aid. I'm in a hurry to get back to my family after all the mayhem, but I can't just let our Grand Countess bleed like this. Not now that I know there's something I can do about it. "Alec, give me your hand," I say. As Alec reaches his hand out, I address the Countess again. "This is going to sound mad, but I need you to trust me."

Now that I'm close enough for the Countess to see my face clearly, she barely speaks. Instead, she just stares wide eyed at me, giving me the slightest of nods.

"What are you doing, Lane?" Alec asks me.

"I'm going to heal her," I tell him as the Countess breathes through some painful sounding coughs that contort her facial expression.

"Aren't you going to kiss me?" Alec asks.

Now the Countess looks genuinely confused as her eyes flit from me to Alec.

"I beg your pardon?" she asks.

I shake my head. "I have a feeling..." I squeeze Alec's hand tightly and place my free hand on the Countess's shivering shoulder. I close my eyes, take a deep, calming breath, and imagine how I've felt every time I've shared a special moment with Alec. Every time it's felt like we were truly meant to be together, two halves of a whole. I think healing thoughts, and I allow myself to focus all of those thoughts on the Countess.

The Grand Countess gasps as her body heats beneath my touch, and she stands up straighter. When I open my eyes, she stares at her still blood-soaked hands, and then her hands pat down her torso, which is now wound-free. Her dark eyes grow even wider in surprise.

"Remarkable," she whispers. "How did you do that?"

A small smile spreads across my lips as I squeeze Alec's hand. "Magic," I tell her.

"What do you know?" Alec says incredulously as the Countess offers me her sincere appreciation. "That's new."

I shake off the Countess's thanks as politely as I can, and let her know that I'm in a hurry to get to my mamman and Lilah.

"Of course," she says, waving me away. "Go, go. I've got plenty to do here myself, but I'd love to speak with you later."

Alec and I continue through the Keep until we come to the secret tunnel that hides behind the map of Maran. When we get there, I open the painting the same way I saw my mamman do earlier, and I step inside, but I see neither my mamman nor Lilah.

"They're not here," I tell Alec breathlessly when I peek my head back through the door.

"What do you mean?" Alec asks as my stomach drops and my body is filled with a white-hot panic.

"I mean *they're not here!* I have to go. I have to go look for them," I start, already turning back into the passageway. "I'm not sure how far this goes, but maybe…"

Alec follows me into the tunnel, but two steps in, he calls out, "Lane."

"What?" I say without looking back at him.

"Lane."

"What?" I ask, finally turning back.

"Look," he says. Alec's expression is pained, his jaw clenched. He bends and scoops up a piece of parchment with neat, confident handwriting on it and holds the parchment out to me.

I rush back to him and snatch the parchment greedily from his hands to read the note he already seems to have read.

Your ceremony may have been successful, Lane, but we're not through. The time of the Fates is over, and I will usher in the new era. In fact, you are going to help me.

Would you like me to say anything to your beloved mamman and sister? They're right here with me, and they'll remain my hostages until you give me what I want. Or until I get bored and just kill them anyway, but your dear old friend Zaid recommended I try not to do that.

My entire body begins to tremble uncontrollably as I try to get myself to exit the small passageway, suddenly feeling claustrophobic in the tiny space. Out in the hallway, things aren't much better, and I let out a guttural scream. Every time I get my family back together, something happens, and this time, they're in the hands of someone I know is capable of truly awful things, someone who takes pleasure in toying with and hurting others.

The edges of my vision blur, and I can't seem to catch my breath. I collapse to the ground on my knees, rage filling me to my very core.

Alec crouches down right beside me, placing a hesitant hand on my shoulder. We're soon joined by the Countess and a few other Council members who came to see what the scream was all about. I ignore them all.

Dropping Alaya's note to the ground, I draw an arrow and focus every ounce of anger I feel at the piece of parchment. As I let the arrow fly, its tip fills with light, and the moment it reaches the parchment, it catches fire, setting the whole note ablaze.

Normally, I would be shocked – or at least curious as to how this has happened, but right now, I don't care.

All I want is for Alaya to burn for what she has done.

"What is wrong?" the Countess asks as she rushes to my side. She reaches out to touch me, but Alec stops her.

In what little peripheral vision I have at the moment, I see Alec whisper to the Countess. She gasps, but she regains her composure quickly, already starting to formulate a plan as she turns to a girl who seems about my age.

"Mara," she says to the girl. "Send word to anyone you can find. We need a headcount for Council members and staff here as soon as possible. Once you've located everyone you can, tell them to meet me in the Council room at once. Then, please assemble a team to move all those we lost today outside, where the cool air can comfort their spirits until we can properly lay them to rest."

"Yes, of course," the girl says, bowing her head and immediately getting to work.

"Lane," the Countess says to me. It takes far too much willpower to pull my gaze from the still burning piece of parchment, but I manage to do it. "We are going to get your mamman and sister back. Whatever you need will be at your disposal. Now that I've seen what we are up against, I think it's time I sent for reinforcements, as I should have done much sooner."

"Yes," I respond to the Countess, and my voice quivers in anger. "Send for reinforcements. Alec, we need to make a list of everyone we know that would be willing to help, and we need to work fast."

"Of course," Alec answers me. He steps into view and turns me to face him, placing both hands supportively on my shoulders. "What should I tell them?"

My gaze falls once again to the piece of parchment, which has now broken into several blackened, smoldering pieces.

"Tell them to prepare," I say through gritted teeth, clenching my fists at my sides and blinking past the sting of tears in my eyes. "We're going to war."

Don't miss part one of Lane and Alec's journey!

Enjoy the story?

Lane and Alec's journey will continue in book 3:

Fated

Coming 2026

Turn the page to read the first chapter!

SEVERED

BREYANNA I. L. EVANS

Fated

Chapter 1

My family and I have been separated. Again.

My sister has been kidnapped by someone I thought was becoming my friend, and my mamman has disappeared with her.

On top of all of that, the person I thought would always have my back, my second in command, has sided with the enemy. I've just spent the last several hours fighting with bandits that are more animal than human and shadow creatures I've never seen before while racing the rising sun.

All in all, this has not been a great start to my day.

I'm working hard now to keep control of my temper as the Women's Council gathers around me, arguing about what we should do about the new threats that keep cropping up and what takes precedence – burying our dead and repairing the damages last night's battle has caused the Grand Council Keep, or reaching out for reinforcements in case the enemies that withdrew from the fight early this morning decide to come back.

My eyes burn – not just with the sting of tears, but with the newfound power I have gained by taking the Fates' burden as my own with Alec at my side, and with the rage that boils within me that we're wasting time like this. Every second we waste deliberating is another second Alaya has to get away.

Keep calm, I remind myself, balling my hands into fists so tight that my short fingernails dig into my palms.

"We should send everybody home and tell them to gather reinforcements," says one member of the Council. At this point, I've stopped looking around to see who's speaking. I just keep my gaze intensely focused on one divot in the wood of the large table we all stand around.

"No," argues another. "What we need is to show our dead some respect and take some time to mourn. We lost a lot of good people last night."

Yet another raises her voice to be heard over all the incomprehensible murmurings of those agreeing with the second. "What we *need* to do is set to work fixing the Keep. The longer we stand unguarded and exposed like this, the more likely those creatures are going to be to come back and finish us off. You're exactly right – we did lose a lot of good people last night. Now there are even fewer of us left to defend the place, and I know no one on this Council is trained to fend off enemies like that."

Alec, the person I've shared a magical bond with my entire seventeen years of life, the person I've chosen as my partner in relinquishing the Fates of their burden just this morning, leans over and bumps me with his shoulder. As he does, his shoulder-length blond hair falls in front of his face.

I know he's doing his best to remain positive for me. I appreciate his efforts, but right now, I really want to scream at all of these politicians. This is exactly why I never wanted to join the Women's Council in the first place. They waste too much time fighting amongst themselves instead of actually doing something about the problems they discuss.

Alec models a deep breath and silently prompts me to follow his example.

He's right. I take a deep, shaky breath and hold it for a few seconds before letting it out as slowly as I can manage.

I need to be careful.

I haven't learned yet what taking the Fates' power entails, only that I've already set one thing on fire with my anger this morning. Until I can learn more about what all of this means, it's probably best not to get myself too worked up.

But under the circumstances, not getting worked up seems near impossible.

I take another breath and try to steady myself, focusing instead on the amber of Alec's eyes – which still seem to hold the same glow they obtained earlier this morning, when the first rays of sunlight fell upon the pool of magical water we stood in when we vowed to keep each other in the sight of the Fates.

Like I said, it has been a long, long morning.

All of this sounds crazy.

I tune back into the conversation as Alec reaches over and brushes his hand against mine. I'm just about to take his hand when the woman who speaks now mentions my mamman.

"Aileen is one of us, you know. Just as much a part of this Council as any of us standing here now. We should split up – set the guards we have left to work here, while the rest of us see if we can figure out where Alaya has taken them. It's the only reasonable thing to do. What is the point of being a member of this sacred Council if we aren't here for each other when it matters most?"

Hope rises in my chest. Finally, someone who sees some sense. I lean forward, pressing my hands against the table. My eyes turn to the Grand Countess, who is still covered in blood but has regained much of her color after I healed her barely an hour ago.

She stays quiet as another woman gets her argument in.

"Yes, Aileen is important. I absolutely agree with you. But we cannot just leave everything here to go rescue her. We need to think about the common good first. Aileen would understand that. That is what she would want in this situation – not for us to go galivanting all over Maran looking for her. She and the child will have to wait."

I feel as if my eyes are going to pop right out of my head, and finally I can't contain myself any longer.

"That *child* you're talking about is my little sister, who wouldn't even be in this mess if you hadn't called her here in the first place," I say, struggling to keep my voice level as I look around at all the women that surround me. Some are bruised and battered and filthy like I am, but others look as if they managed to avoid the fight altogether somehow. "Fates, look at all of you. She's not even ten years old yet, and all she's wanted is to work alongside you to make Maran a better place. Now she's off with someone dangerous—"

"Someone dangerous that *you* invited here and *you* vouched for," someone close to me mutters. I think it's the woman who hails from SunSpar. The guilt that her words inspire in me is like a dagger in my chest, but I keep going.

"Right. I did lead her here. I did vouch for her. Had I known her true intentions... trust me when I say I never would have led her here. But I can't change that." I need to be careful, and I need to stay calm. Right now, rage blurs the edges of my vision, and my chest feels tight like any breath I take may be my last. I press my fingers into the steady wooden table in an effort to ground myself as I look to the Countess. "I can't stay in here and listen to you all squabble any longer. I need to find my sister and my mamman, and Alaya needs to pay for what she's done. I will be going after her with or without your help."

"I've heard enough," the Grand Countess says, her voice so cold it sends ice through my veins, but her next words take me by surprise. "Lane, thank you for voicing your concerns. I have heard all of your arguments, and I am ready to make my final decision."

The room quiets as the last murmurings die down, eagerly awaiting what the Countess will decide.

My skin itches with anticipation, and I'm painfully aware that the sun has now inched its way high into the sky. It's already almost noon. Alaya is probably miles away by now. Alec places his hand on my back, and his touch calms me ever so slightly.

Now that she's certain she's got everyone's attention, the Countess continues. "We will split ranks. Each of you write your second in command at home. Tell them the dire nature of our situation, and ask them to gather as many able bodied soldiers as possible and send them our way. Tell them also to be on high alert for Alaya and her creatures.

"Salma, Elise, Amara, and Gaelyn, you four will stay here and guide the rest of the guard. First, give the bodies of our beloved fallen a proper burial. When all this is over, we will celebrate their lives more graciously. For now, they deserve to be put to rest. Once you're finished with that, get right to work reinforcing the Keep. Work with the folks in Nerine and Parth to rebuild our doors with lumber from the forest. Make them sturdy. I will write to Julienne and have her join you. I hate to end her rest period so early, but we need everyone we can get."

At the mention of Alec's mamman, I see him tense in my peripheral vision, and I feel the worry that ties his stomach in knots in my own gut. I hope she will be safer here with the others than in Nerine, where – should they be attacked – I fear she might try to face them herself to protect her city.

Alec meets my gaze and nods his head, blinking slowly as the Countess finishes giving her orders, drawing our attention back to her for the final time.

"Lane, the rest of us will be at your disposal. It is true that you called Alaya here, but this Keep would have fallen if it weren't for you and Alec, and I don't know what you've done, but I sense the Fates in you. We will follow you anywhere, and any members of this Council who contest will take their issues directly to me."

My vision blurs again, but this time, it's thanks to the tears that now sting my eyes. "Thank you," I manage, the words barely loud enough for her to hear. The Countess gives me a solemn nod.

"Where would you have us start?" she asks me.

I straighten my back, pulling my hands away from the table, where they've remained for the rest of this conversation to this point.

"Let's start with the cities and villages nearest to us," I start. "Ask them to lend what support they can, just like you asked the others. It's important to have some join us here to help defend and rebuild the Keep, but I will also accept any who are willing to join me as I find Alaya. Alec, can you write to Rodrick and ask him to keep his eyes on the lookout for Alaya and Zaid?"

Saying Zaid's name aloud fills me with grief. For the longest time, I wanted nothing more than to be with Zaid. In the course of one day I've managed to hurt him deeply by choosing Alec, and he's hurt me right back by joining ranks with Alaya in kidnapping my sister.

"I will," Alec says, bringing me back from my spiraling thoughts. "Anything else you need in the meantime?" he asks.

"Yes, what are your plans right now?" the Countess asks.

I take a long, deep breath and let it out. "I'm going to get packed. The moment I know which direction Alaya headed in,

I'm leaving," I tell her. Then, more quietly I add, "Are you with me?" I ask Alec, my hazel eyes pleading.

He brushes my still-drying dark hair out of my eyes.

"To the ends of the earth," he whispers, a half-smile tugging up the corners of his lips.

Nodding, I step backward, ready to get myself packed and leave this suffocating room behind me. As I move, something on the table catches my eye. Right there where my hands were just moments ago sits ten faint, fingertip shaped burn marks.

I really do need to try and keep my temper under control until I can figure all of this out. I stuff my hands into the pockets of my trousers, worried I just might burn somebody.

What have I gotten us all into?

Acknowledgements

To everyone who read Bound and shared your support, thank you so much. You all are largely responsible for the inspiration I received for finishing and polishing Severed, and I love all the messages you have shared with me!

To all my readers, thank you for reading my books. You bring their stories to life and give them purpose!

To Brandon, thank you for always reading my work and giving suggestions to make it better.

To Elivia, thank you for reading these two books and getting so hyped about them! Your hype wore off on me.

To Gilbert, thank you for working so hard to provide timely feedback even when your schedule didn't want you to.

To everyone who participated in beta reading or ARC reading this book: I appreciate you more than you know! Thank you for all your honest feedback and reviews. You are wonderful!

The Fog
Golden Gateway
Temple of the Fates
The Unruly Sea
Maran
Ladia's Way
Darkwood
Marance River
Siren's Way
Murkwater Lake
Grand Council Keep
Nerine
Parth
Helan
Helnar Grasslands
Shade
Marance Falls
Dunnen
Shandar
SunSpur
Palanora
Shandar Mines

Lithe
Whispering Isles
Bashar Mountains
Bashar Desert
Machantor Swamp
Nodor
N
E
S
W

www.ingramcontent.com/pod-product-compliance
Lightning Source LLC
Chambersburg PA
CBHW011148310726
48973CB00010B/2823